Fascination

Fascination

Leona Blair

BANTAM BOOKS
New York   Toronto   London
Sydney   Auckland

FASCINATION

A Bantam Book / February 1997

All rights reserved.
Copyright © 1997 by Leona Blair.
Book design by Caroline Cunningham

Library of Congress Cataloging-in-Publication Data

Blair, Leona.
Fascination / Leona Blair.
p.   cm.
ISBN 0-553-09310-X (hc)
I. Title.
PS3552.L3463F37   1996
813'.54—dc20   96-31196
CIP

Published simultaneously in the United States and Canada

Bantam Books are published by Bantam Books, a division of Bantam Doubleday Dell Publishing Group, Inc. Its trademark, consisting of the words "Bantam Books" and the portrayal of a rooster, is Registered in U.S. Patent and Trademark Office and in other countries. Marca Registrada. Bantam Books, 1540 Broadway. New York, New York 10036.

PRINTED IN THE UNITED STATES OF AMERICA

BVG   10 9 8 7 6 5 4 3 2 1

$\mathscr{A}$cknowledgments

Beverly Lewis, dream editor, who falters not, neither does she flinch.

The following sources were invaluable: *1900* by Rebecca West, Viking Press, N.Y., 1982; *The Golden Age of Travel* by Alexis Gregory, Rizzoli International Publishers, N.Y., 1990; *Passenger Liners of the World Since 1893* by Nicholast Cairis, Bonanza Books, N.Y., 1979; *Sail, Steam and Splendor* by Byron S. Miller, Times Books, N.Y., 1977; *The Age of Excess* by Ray Ginger, Macmillan Co., N.Y., 1965; *Traveling by Sea in the Nineteenth Century* by Basil Greenhill and Ann Giffard, Hastings House Publishers, N.Y., 1974; *Life in the Gilded Age* by Alexis Gregory, Rizzoli International Publishers, N.Y., 1993; *America's Gilded Age* by Milton Rogoff, Henry Holt & Co., N.Y., 1989; *The Sway of the Grand Saloon* by John Malcolm Brinnin, Delacorte Press/Seymour Lawrence, N.Y., 1971; *The Rape of the Nile* by Brian M. Fagan, Charles Scribner's Sons, N.Y., 1975; *After the Civil War* by John S. Blay, Bonanza Books, N.Y., 1960; *Maverick in Mauve* by Florence Adele Sloane with Commentary by Louis Auchincloss, Doubleday & Company, Garden City, N.Y., 1983; *Katharine Hepburn* by Barbara Leaming, Crown Publishing, N.Y., 1995; *Compton's Interactive Encyclopedia*, Version 2.01VW, Compton's New Media, 1994.

This one's for you.

Shall I love you a little forever,
Or love you superbly a day?

Helen Choate

Book
One

$\mathcal{O}$ne

$\mathcal{H}$e always waited at the window when Miranda was expected. Hidden by the green velvet draperies, he would see the brougham pull up and stop. Then he would watch her emerge, revealing herself bit by bit, as if she were undressing before him.

On this September morning in 1900 he heard the carriage on the cobbled streets of New York's financial district before he saw it, a handsome coach pulled by matched horses. He waited, moistening his lips as the footman reached in to help her down and her gloved hand appeared. Then he saw her head, her glossy dark hair covered by her hat, and finally her long skirts, raised enough for him to see a flash of lace-trimmed taffeta petticoat and a glimpse of stockinged leg that made him gasp.

Then she was there in full view, tall, statuesque, the curves of her body voluptuous. He always admired the way she dressed, and today was no exception. Her dress was of deep red, the silk bodice tucked and piped with satin and puffed out over a bell-shaped skirt tightly belted at the waist. He knew that like all fashionable women, she was laced into an S-curve corset that thrust her bosom forward and her hips back, leaving the magnificent nakedness beneath it to his feverish imagination. The dress was relieved by a fluffy jabot of gossamer white lace.

He fingered his high, starched collar, stiffly uncomfortable in the heat but required dress for gentlemen, as were her garments for ladies. Then he settled and resettled his wide tie inside the vest beneath his frock coat. He smoothed the top of his bald head as if a miraculous growth might suddenly appear where no hair had grown for ten years. His face was handsome despite his baldness. All the Cunningham men were handsome.

Hobart's office was on the first floor of the Cunningham Building on Pine Street, and from that vantage point her face was hidden by a white platter of a hat trimmed with more lace and some object the same deep red as her dress—a stuffed bird, he supposed, as was the fashion. No matter, he knew every feature of her face: the luminous complexion, the tilted dark eyes sparkling with vitality, the straight, aristocratic nose, and the tender, avid mouth he had been aching to kiss for over twenty years.

In his mind he was stripping her naked, pushing her down on a bed somewhere. He was standing over her, erect and omnipotent. He was bending over her and his mouth moved from the white neck he nipped with his teeth to the breasts he sucked, from the belly he licked with his tongue to the tangle of dark hair between those creamy thighs. He pushed them apart. . . .

He stroked his muttonchop whiskers but their springy feel only made his fantasy more painfully real. He resented her fiercely for reducing him to such a state of physical hunger—no other woman ever had—but mere resentment could not smother desire like his. It was more intense than the animal lust he expended on prostitutes, more intense because of one vital fact: Miranda was no whore. She would certainly resist him, and that made possession of her an infinitely more exciting prospect.

He went quickly to sit behind his desk, the better to hide his erection, to control himself and the interview. He pretended to

study some documents while he listened like a hunter tracking game as she was escorted up the stairs by his private secretary.

A discreet knock sounded at his office door.

"Come," he commanded in the baritone voice that was so at odds with his thin body, his hawkish face with its sharp, high-bridged nose, his granite-gray eyes. His mouth had a full lower lip, as unexpected with those eyes as lilacs in the snow.

His secretary opened the door. "Mrs. Paul," he announced, and stepped back to let her pass. The admiration Hobart heard in the man's voice was not there when the wives of Hobart's two other brothers, Mrs. George or Mrs. Roger, were announced. As for Hobart's wife, she never came. He had expressly forbidden it.

Damned impertinence, Hobart steamed silently at the secretary, jealous of his youth, his height, and his crop of wavy hair.

Hobart dismissed the man with a peremptory movement of his head and came around his desk to take Miranda's hand. He leaned forward to kiss her cheek, letting his arm brush her breast. Then he held a chair for her under the two–bladed ceiling fan that did little to cool the humid air and again retreated behind his desk as if it could protect him from the power she exerted over him. Power was a prerogative of males; they had to be virile and aggressive and bold enough to seize it; it was maddening that women were born with it hidden between their legs.

"How are you, Hobart?" she asked in her low, musical voice.

"Very fine," he replied gruffly, studying her. "No need to ask you." She was, as always, even more alluring in the flesh than in his fantasies. In those erotic fancies, she was not married to his youngest brother, Paul, nor the mother of Paul's two grown sons. She was the most tempting sea of sensuality Hobart had ever known. He reminded himself that she was forty, for the love of heaven! Middle-aged, even if she didn't look it. Most of all, she was indifferent to him except as her husband's brother and the head of the family.

He wrestled often with the riddle of her appeal to virtually every man who met her. She never behaved indecorously; she seemed unaware of the sensuality that shimmered around her, a gossamer web to trap the unwary. During Sunday sermons about sin and fornication he always thought of Miranda as the temptress. When he read the Song of Songs he thought of Miranda. When he plunged into the body of his mistress he thought of Miranda.

After all these years she still affected him as she had when he first saw her, at her debut, a girl of seventeen in virginal white.

He cleared his throat, reminded by his musings of the reason he had asked her to come to his office in the first place. Wall Street was a man's preserve. But this was a private conversation.

"I need a favor of you," he said abruptly.

She listened attentively, as if *she* would decide whether to accord the favor after she had heard him out, as if the choice were hers. It irked him.

"It's Cynthia," he said. "It's high time she married."

"I wouldn't worry," Miranda said. "She's only eighteen and she certainly has enough offers."

He shook his head. "Not from the right men. All her proposals are from second-rate families or worthless younger sons. Damn those people! Will they never forget? It was our one transgression!"

He embarked upon the glowing history of the Cunninghams that she had heard so many times. They had been early settlers in the new world, people of means and impeccable reputation even before they became terribly rich. The family had prospered in merchant shipping through the Revolution and the Civil War, but under Hobart Senior, now eighty-three, and his wily oldest son, the modest Cunningham fortune had been tripled in real estate. Managing their properties and land speculation had become an enterprise so large, it had to be directed by the brothers from this square granite building on Pine Street.

Their social status had been all but destroyed a quarter century earlier, when Miss Charlotte Cunningham was shot dead on the eve of her wedding by her father, who then turned the pistol on himself.

It was widely whispered that the authorities had been paid to call the girl's murder a tragic accident and the father's suicide the act of a man maddened by grief. There were other, far more salacious explanations for the incident, things about fathers and daughters that were not discussed in mixed company and mentioned only in euphemisms even when the women left the men to their cigars and cognac and off-color stories behind closed doors.

It had left a stain on the Cunninghams at a time when reputation, ancestry, and appearances mattered more than anything in society, a time when those things mattered more than money. That was understandable in an era when economic boom was followed by bust, each succeeding the other with alarming frequency.

"From shirtsleeves to shirtsleeves in three generations," went the maxim. "Because," Paul Cunningham had told his wife, "fathers rolling in new millions do not want any interference from their sons and condemn them to a life of expensive indolence. I have no intention of doing that to our two boys."

Some hard-pressed families, impoverished but proud, rationed their food in private so they could afford to give the lavish dinners and balls that, with the opera and legitimate theater, were the principal forms of entertainment. Appearances were still everything: the upper floors of great houses were often barely furnished or nearly empty, the contents sold for necessities, in stark contrast to the sumptuous decor and ten-course meals the guests enjoyed below.

After the murder-suicide the Cunninghams' wealth had kept the family in society but on its outer fringes. No amount of philanthropy seemed to help, no service for parish or church, no donations to build schools for immigrant children, no long-time memberships in the right new clubs. The Cunninghams appeared untroubled in public but despaired among themselves. As soon as it was clear that Hobart's girl, Cynthia, would be a great beauty, she had been chosen to reinstate them by making the right marriage.

"Cynthia will change things," Hobart said to his sister-in-law now. "When she marries into the right family she'll sweep her relatives in with her and the past will be forgotten."

"They'll never forget until a juicier scandal comes along to amuse them," Miranda said.

"It had damn well better not come from anyone in *this* family!" he snapped. Then he paused, watching her closely. "I've often wondered why you agreed to marry Paul so soon after that disgraceful business."

She shrugged, recalling the violent opposition of her parents all those years ago when she was so deeply in love with Paul that she would have eloped and created a scandal in her family to add to the one in his.

"It had nothing to do with us," she told Hobart. "And I've never regretted it. We're happy together."

"Come now, Miranda," Hobart scoffed. "You can be honest with me. What do you do with yourself while Paul's off digging up the dead in Egypt?"

"I keep busy."

She leaned back serenely in the chair and rearranged her skirts, crossing her legs, stripping off one of her gloves, abandoning the rigid posture—spine stiff and several inches from the chair back, skirts decorously draped to conceal, hands meekly folded—expected of ladies except *en famille*. She treated him like an elderly uncle, and that infuriated him.

Her movements had stirred the air and it carried her fresh scent across the desk to him. It was light and delicate—only whores and French actresses wore heavy perfume—probably the sachet she used in her linen press that had been released by the warmth of her body. He closed his eyes briefly, breathing her in.

He could not restrain himself. "You don't enjoy charities and lectures by somber missionaries back from the bush. And what about the nights?"

She appeared not to have heard him. "How may I help with Cynthia?" she asked.

His pale face turned bright scarlet at the rebuke. He took a cigar from the humidor on his desk, using the cutting and moistening process to hide his confusion.

"May I?" he asked as a matter of form, gesturing with the cigar.

"I wish you wouldn't," she said. "It lingers in my clothes and my hair." It was she who had the upper hand now, and he cursed his stupidity in revealing that he thought about her nights.

He blew out the match he had already lighted and tossed the unlit cigar onto his desk. Her nonchalance galled him. He wanted so much more from her. He wanted the tension that desire creates between a man and a woman. Now he wanted to do more than have her; he wanted to dominate her, grind into her, rape her.

"You will take Cynthia with you when you go to London to meet Paul," he said curtly. "She needs to cast her net in wider waters."

"I'd be delighted," she said. "Cynthia and I are great friends."

"So I gather," he said sourly. "She talks about you all the time—you and Paul. Prince Charming! He couldn't care less about real estate unless it's four thousand years old and buried under tons of sand. What's he up to now?"

"He writes that they've found a new tomb in the Valley of the Kings."

"Much good may it do him! What kind of man deserts his home and family every year to dig holes in Egypt?"

"An archeologist," she replied lazily. "He's always been fasci-nated by it. He'd have been miserable spending all his time in an office. You know he was never interested in real estate."

"Only the income from it."

"Which, thanks to you, continues to increase without Paul's help." She was not to be goaded.

But she knew as well as Hobart that she and Paul and their sons could not have lived in the style they did on Paul's share of the profits alone. The three active brothers had salaries, bonuses, and frequent gifts of stock in addition to an equal share in the profits.

Paul had a generous annual allowance as well, provided by their father. Hobart Senior doted on Paul. Everyone did.

Since the father had become an invalid, it was Hobart who made up the difference between Paul's income and his lavish expenditures.

At the start of Paul's treks to Egypt, Hobart had hoped to fill the empty place in Miranda's bed, but if she recognized his advances, she had never given a sign. He wondered now if it would help to remind her who held the purse strings.

She glanced up, saw him watching her, and returned his gaze, her expression calm. Any other woman would have blushed to see the naked desire on his face, but he had never been able to rattle her in the smallest degree, not even at the Cunningham weekly board meetings where she used the power her reckless husband had given her to vote as she saw fit. It was highly irregular for a lady to engage in business unless she was a widow, and then she was expected to assign her votes to the head of the family, in this case himself.

But not Miranda! No, Miranda came to board meetings and frequently refused to budge on votes requiring a unanimous decision. She always had very sound reasons for differing with her brothers-in-law. Hobart had suspected she was getting advice from a lover and hired an investigator to look into her private life. The man found nothing more damning than an occasional visit to a tearoom with her cousin, Birkett Price, a stripling of twenty-five who knew nothing about real estate and, Hobart was sure, had never read Benjamin Franklin's essay in praise of older women who "are so grateful" for male attentions. All women were grateful, except for Miranda.

He cleared his throat. "When are you sailing?"

"Next week aboard the *Sylvania*," she said.

"Not alone." It was not a question. Ladies of her class did not travel alone.

"With my maid. I've booked a cabin for her near my stateroom."

He scribbled on a pad atop his desk. "I'll arrange for a suite for you and Cynthia and a cabin for her maid as well."

"It will be a rush to get her ready."

"I'm sure you can manage it."

He wrote again, then stood, signaling an end to their meeting, but she remained where she was.

"Hobart, how does Elsie feel about sending Cynthia abroad with me?"

He moved his arm as if to shake off a gnat. "She doesn't know," he said harshly.

"But you must tell her!"

"Why? You've been more of a mother to Cynthia than Elsie has."

"That isn't true. I'm a friend. And I want Elsie to know."

He glared at her, his temper almost equal to his desire. When Hobart barked at people, they obeyed, afraid of his bite. But Miranda regarded him with her customary composure until he promised to tell his wife.

He promised. Anything to get Miranda out of his office. It was dangerous to be alone with her: the devil knew what he might say or do.

She smiled, stood, and, pulling on the glove she had removed, went to the door. "Thank you for entrusting Cynthia to me. I'll take very good care of her."

"Just get her engaged to the right man." He opened the door.

"A title?" she asked with a faint smile.

"No objection—but it's not necessary if he's top of the tree."

She nodded. "I'm on my way to see her. I'll tell her she's sailing with me."

He bowed stiffly and she went through the door. He closed it behind her and returned to his desk, where he lit the cigar to obliterate her maddening scent. Sucking hungrily on it, he persuaded himself yet again that she was unaware of the depth of his lust and the power she had over him because of it.

TWO

*M*iranda was aware.

His lechery was like a fungus creeping over her whenever she was in his company. His desire was loathsome and frightening, even though she knew Hobart was terrified of impropriety, real or imagined, and would not risk a scandal with any woman, particularly a sister-in-law. But that didn't stop him from imagining.

She was contemptuous of his hypocrisy. A man who demanded decorum of his family asking about her nights! But from her very first introduction to him she had avoided him when no one was within call.

Once the carriage was moving north, Miranda relaxed, pleased, for more than one reason, that she would have Cynthia's company on the crossing.

With Cynthia in her charge, Hobart would pay for the entire voyage—provided it was successful—without lecturing Paul and Miranda about their extravagance. Hobart gave with one hand and took away with the other, exacting subservience for his generosity.

"Better to listen to one of his lectures now and then," Paul had told her after his first trip to Egypt, "than waste my life doing what I hate."

Paul had asked Miranda to accompany him on his subsequent trips to the Middle East, but having experienced the hardships of life on a dig in the desert, he did not insist when she refused. She had not expected his trips to become a regular part of his life or to last longer each year.

Miranda sighed, thinking of her husband. He had left for Egypt soon after the turn of the year—*of the century,* she reminded herself with that sharpened sense of time rushing by that had begun to trouble her recently—and he had not returned in May, as planned, because of a new tomb!

My rivals have been dead for over four thousand years!

Once she would have laughed at that, but after this long separation from Paul, certain things no longer amused her. Hobart's lechery seemed to mock the gallantry she had commanded before middle age began to overtake her. Even her appointment as Cynthia's chaperone/marriage broker made her feel more like a dependent relative than the acclaimed beauty she had been all her life.

She missed Paul, who seemed to think she was still young and bewitching, but she resented his absence too, and the restricted life she led because of it: a married woman with no escort for several months of the season was a problem for New York's hostesses. She relied on her young cousin, Birkett Price, to accompany her to dinners, parties, dances, the opera. But Birkett was a poor substitute for Paul. And lately he appeared to be smitten.

She had never sought the attentions of other men, even if she was as flattered by them as any woman. She had married for love and had never responded to the guarded invitations to have an affair that she received from this one or that—except to feel revulsion for Hobart and real anger with Birkett the last time she saw him.

———— • ————

"Miranda, I'm in love with you," Birkett had said, taking her hand, his young face flushed with intensity. "I can't live without you."

"I'm so sorry," she told him, removing her hand from beneath his. "But it's not uncommon at your age to fancy yourself in love. You'll get over it, I'm sure."

But when they were outside the tearoom and walking toward a small park nearby, he had been shockingly explicit about what delights his lovemaking would provide, using words she had never heard before. It had upset her enough to hail a hansom cab just turning into the street.

"You're wasted on Paul," he told her while they waited for the cab to slow and stop. "He's too much of a gentleman for a woman like you. He probably still treats you like a virgin bride when he takes you to bed."

"I forbid you to say another word. Or to call on me ever again." The hansom stopped and he opened the door for her. She had refused his attempt to help her in and had gone directly home.

But what he said had disturbed her. When her anger cooled she wondered if her life with Paul was as tame and incomplete as Birkett insisted it was.

Did people really shake with passion when they made love? Or touch a woman in the way her cousin had suggested? Did women cry out at the peak of ecstasy?

She shook her head. Virtuous women were not supposed to feel desire or response. Birkett was exaggerating. How savagely sexual young men were! And then came the cruel thought: *young men won't be falling in love with me for too much longer.*

Suddenly Hobart's hands came to mind, the hair-tufted fingers long and blunt. She shuddered with something more than disgust, transfixed by the image as a snake is by a mongoose. He must be obscene with a woman. She wondered what he did in bed and flushed hotly at the things her imagination conjured up. Then she

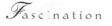

shook her head and turned back to the safer contemplation of her beloved, considerate husband, the only man she had ever known intimately even if dozens had made advances over the years.

Paul, not she, had yielded to seduction—but he was seduced by the desert, by Egypt's history, by her soaring monuments and, most of all, by the secrets and the treasures that lay buried with the great pharaohs and their queens under the stark, eternal sands. She had chosen not to go with him on his first trips, but now with both their sons at Harvard she was too much alone.

The desert was terribly hot by day and cold at night. Living conditions on a dig were rough and comforts few, but she needed her husband too much to let that stop her. She had persuaded him to take her to Cairo after they spent a month in London. And now, on her first visit to Egypt, she would enjoy Cynthia's company as well.

"Cynthia's problem is a godsend," she said, smiling to herself.

Her niece, thank heaven, was no mealy-mouthed debutante. Cynthia was Miranda's favorite among the younger Cunninghams, an exquisite girl, very spirited, who asked startling questions about "life" that showed she resented the ignorance to which she was condemned until she married.

No one but Miranda knew that Cynthia was rebellious, not even Paul. Nor could she tell Paul that his niece had never had the slightest crush on any male except him, and that the girl's feelings for him were growing intense enough to be disturbing.

She and Miranda were the two acknowledged beauties of the family, although Miranda reminded herself, with a pang every time she thought of it, that by now her own claim was purely honorary. She hated that. If a woman didn't feel her age or look it, why must she be forced to dwindle into death?

Miranda stirred against the padded velvet cushions of the brougham, grateful for the slight breeze that flowed into the carriage. Her own feelings were disturbing too.

———— • ————

The carriage stopped in front of Hobart's mansion on Fifth Avenue. Directing the sweating coachman to take the carriage to the shaded mews and then have a cool drink in Hobart's kitchen, Miranda went up the steps and rang the bell. A pretty parlor maid in a black dress with a starched white apron, bib, and cap opened the door.

"Good afternoon, Mrs. Paul," she said with a little bob.

"Hello, Biddy," Miranda replied graciously. "Is Mrs. Hobart at home?"

"Yes, ma'am, but she has the headache and is resting."

It was a charade. Elsie Cunningham was almost always "resting" and they both knew her "headache" was an alcoholic stupor. Miranda was struck by the loyalty of Elsie's servants: no one outside the family knew that Mrs. Hobart drank in secret.

Elsie could still be sobered up and made presentable for the many social functions the couple attended. She never objected when her bottle was temporarily taken away. She was like a puppet with no will of her own, her only objective to insulate herself with alcohol until she was required to do something else. And she was afraid of Hobart.

"The servants won't gossip about her because she's so good-hearted!" Miranda once told Paul. "She wouldn't hurt a fly. And it's no wonder she drinks. What woman wouldn't, married to that man!"

"I've never seen any sign that he's cruel to her," Paul had replied, assessing his brother rather than defending him. "His life is real estate and he's as cold as flint about everything else."

Not so cold, Miranda was certain. Only his anger was frosty. Hobart was licentious. But it was better left unsaid.

"And Miss Cynthia?" she asked the parlor maid now.

"In her room, ma'am. She's expectin' you."

"Thank you, Biddy, I'll go right up." She started up the curved staircase, then turned back to the maid. "Tell Baxter to have Miss

Cynthia's trunks dusted and brought up to her room, Biddy." She smiled. "Our young lady is going on a trip."

Miranda continued up the stairs, glancing into the drawing room when she passed the second floor landing. It was richly furnished in the fashion that had prevailed for the second half of the century just ended: paneled in dark wood and cluttered with all manner of curios, postcards, flowers fresh and dried, mementos of holidays long past, scrapbooks, and stuffed birds. Aspidistras struggled for life in every gloomy corner. Any empty spaces were filled with tables: pie-crust tables, gateleg tables, half-moon tables, tiered tables, eighteenth-century butler's cake servers—all of them crowned with family photographs.

The draperies were looped and tasseled, the lamps trimmed with braid and fringe, the furniture mammoth, somber, the chairs foaming with doilies to protect the upholstery from the macassar oil that men used on their hair. Cushions of every size and shape were strewn about. It was an oppressive atmosphere and Miranda wondered how Cynthia, with her excellent taste, sunny nature, and bright mind, could have flourished in such a dreary place.

Miranda's own home, although paneled, carpeted, and draped, was not cluttered; the furniture was mainly rosewood and fruitwood and the upholstery various hues of a soft dusty rose that flattered women and lifted men's spirits.

On the third floor Miranda paused in the doorway of the bright and airy bedroom she and Cynthia had decorated together. Blue was Cynthia's color and the bed hangings, the draperies, the upholstery, and the specially woven floral carpet were predominantly blue. The walls were ivory, although fashion called for colors like burgundy, sienna, and dark green: light paint usually meant poverty. On the walls, pastels and oils of flowers and landscapes made the room even brighter.

Cynthia had been reading in the window seat. Now the book lay open on her lap and her blue eyes were closed, but the smile that played around her lips showed she was not sleeping.

"What are you dreaming about?" Miranda asked.

"Aunt Miranda!" Cynthia sprang up and came to embrace her. "I didn't expect you so early. Come and sit down. Would you like tea?"

"Not yet. Darling, I've just come from your papa and I have good news for you. When I sail next week to meet Paul, you're coming with me!"

"Next week!" Cynthia repeated after she had hugged her aunt again. She whirled around and opened the doors of two large wardrobes filled with summer dresses in white and pastels and with evening gowns of silk, chiffon, and organdy trimmed with braid, lace, and satin or embroidered with pearls, butterflies, and rosettes. "Will these be enough?"

"If you need more, we'll have them made in London. We'll be there for a month. Baxter is having your trunks brought up."

Cynthia hugged herself and smiled ecstatically. "Just the two of us on the *Sylvania*? And then London with Uncle Paul?"

"And then Cairo," Miranda added.

"Cairo too!" Cynthia spun around, the skirt of her white afternoon dress floating up to show her pale blue kid boots. She was not as tall as Miranda, but her figure was as perfect as her face and the silky pale brown curls that framed it. The dress had leg-o'-mutton sleeves, but the puffs were smaller this season and scaled to suit Cynthia's frame, as were the vertical rows of ruching on the skirt. The wide blue velvet sash set off a small waist made tinier by her corset. She had a small bunch of violets tucked into her bodice, no doubt a token from one of her many admirers.

"This is not supposed to be a pleasure trip," Miranda said dryly, sitting in a blue satin armchair. "This is serious business."

Cynthia returned to the window seat. "I know. We must capture a husband for me," she said.

"Your father phrased it differently, but that's what we must do."

"Someone who knows nothing about Charlotte's curse—at least not until after the wedding!"

Miranda nodded.

Cynthia studied her aunt. "Why do you suppose her father shot her in the first place?"

"Since no one will ever know, why discuss it?"

The girl shrugged, but a moment later she sounded impatient. "Why must I marry now? Why must I belong body and soul to some man I've not even met?"

"You know why."

"Yes, I do. It's because I'm in my second season and there is no third. I'll be put upon the shelf and end up an old maid."

"That's the general rule."

Cynthia shook her head until her curls bounced. "It's a stupid rule! I'm not ready to be married yet, even if I *am* eighteen."

"You haven't met the right man."

The girl's voice was very low. "I haven't met anyone with whom I'd care to spend my whole life." She faced Miranda boldly. "Or agree to have sleeping in my bed."

Miranda shook her head. "You haven't met the right man," she repeated.

"Suppose I never do?"

"Trust me, you will. Cynthia, people were not meant to live alone."

"You live alone."

"Only for a few months of the year when Paul is on a dig. And don't imagine that I like it! I don't object, because he loves it so, and when he's home we're together constantly. Hour for hour, it comes to the same amount of time most couples spend with each other."

That, Cynthia knew, was because Paul rarely went to the Pine Street office. Although Cynthia's father was the director of Cunningham's and head of the family—Hobart only pretending to defer to his elderly father's opinions—there was no love lost between the oldest and youngest sons.

Even so, Hobart had no choice but to keep Paul in adequate funds: what would people say if a Cunningham were to lower his customary standard of living? It could raise questions about the company's solvency, which could affect the company's credit. And land speculation, apparently, required unlimited credit.

Cynthia spoke hesitantly. "Aunt Miranda, what happens between married people when they're alone together?"

"Your mother will tell you at the right time."

Cynthia regarded her aunt skeptically.

"All right," Miranda said. "If she doesn't, your husband will. It's nothing to be alarmed about. Now, let me see if you have anything suitable for trekking over the desert on a camel."

"A camel! How exciting!"

"I understand they're smelly too, so don't get carried away."

They inspected Cynthia's wardrobe and made a list of accessories they could buy in New York, then rang for tea to be brought. Over it they talked about Mr. Henry James's *Washington Square,* the book Cynthia had been reading.

"Why didn't that young man come to take Catherine away?" she demanded. "Even if he didn't love *her,* he loved her money!" It was the kind of cynical, worldly observation Cynthia dared make only to her aunt.

She clasped her hands and closed her eyes. "Can you imagine what it must be like to fall madly in love, as she did, and not care a hoot for the consequences?"

"Consequences tend to last longer than mad love. But she thought he loved her too. That is a powerful persuasion."

"She couldn't have believed he loved *her,* handsome as he was!"

"It's something every woman wants to believe," Miranda said.

Cynthia's expression shifted suddenly to cold fury. "She should have killed her father before he could disinherit her! That's what I'd have done. That's what Charlotte Cunningham should have done before her crazy father killed *her*." She glanced at Miranda. "Do you suppose it runs in the family?"

"Nonsense, Cynthia! You mustn't be so melodramatic! Not everyone knows you don't mean half the things you say." Miranda finished her tea, glanced at the clock on the mantel, and rang for the maid. It was time for her to leave. It was almost six, and Hobart would arrive promptly at half past; one visit with Hobart in a day— or a month or a year for that matter—was more than sufficient. She gathered her things.

"I must go, darling. I'll come for you at ten o'clock tomorrow morning and we'll shop. If Lord & Taylor has nothing light and practical for the desert, I'll write to a London outfitter with your measurements and give them a little head start."

They went downstairs and Cynthia waved good-bye to her aunt from the morning room on the ground floor, then ran up the steps. A transatlantic crossing with Miranda! Then Uncle Paul! And London! And Cairo!

She caught a glimpse of herself in the mirror over her dressing table. She sat down and practiced her debutante smile.

"Sweet enough to gag on," she told her reflection. Then her smile faded. Although she certainly must marry, she would *not* be hustled into it. She dreaded the prospect of having children: she had heard too many whispers about its horrors to believe that the darling baby made up for the agony.

As for how the darling baby got in there in the first place, she was as totally ignorant as her friends, who guessed at everything from kissing a man to something a husband rubbed into his wife's navel whenever he wanted a baby.

Even that idea made the girls shrink; they had been brought up in complete innocence, insulated by the general contempt for "fast" women, barricaded behind layers of clothes, their bodies twisted, padded, bustled, transformed as if their natural shapes were in some way not fit to be seen. Fancy a man rubbing their bare navels! It was horrible!

Sex did not exist in polite circles. Legs were called limbs if they were mentioned at all, and some women covered the limbs of their pianos in ruffled casings that resembled mid-century pantalettes. Books that referred to sex were not allowed in decent homes or were doctored for the innocent. Cynthia had searched the shelves of her father's library in vain for enlightenment on the subject, finding more references to sex in the Bible than anywhere else.

To judge by the expression on women's faces whenever the conversation hovered near the forbidden topic, sex was another burden for females to bear along with childbirth and inferior intelligence and monthly discomfort for having tempted Adam.

"It's God's fault," Cynthia assured her reflection. "He should have made Adam man enough to resist a miserable apple!"

She retrieved her book from the window seat and tried to read, but she was too excited by the upcoming voyage, seeing herself as she would look when she first appeared in evening clothes. She would be the center of attention—she always was. She might even meet the "right" man.

Marriage, she told herself in one of her swift changes of mood, was inevitable. What else could a woman be but a wife, a mother, and a leader of her community? To be a spinster was a terrible fate, and motherhood the one justification for the space a woman occupied on the planet. But another part of Cynthia yearned for more than domesticity. It longed for high romance and something beyond romance for which she had no name.

"Do you really believe," Cynthia had demanded of her friends only yesterday, "that marriage will make up for being owned body and soul?"

"I haven't minded being owned by Papa," one of them said. "And I'll have my own servants and a house to run as I like."

"As *he* likes! Most women can't set foot outside their houses without their husband's permission!"

"It's only to protect us. That's what men are for, to protect women."

"And what are women for?"

"To provide comfort for their husbands and an example for their children."

There was no arguing with that, but Cynthia resented it nonetheless. Being pious and protected was so dull!

She did not want to attend board meetings for excitement as Miranda did with apparent enjoyment. Her aunt seemed content, but Cynthia often wondered if Miranda's equanimity was a sham. She wondered if Miranda had a lover, someone to meet discreetly, to gaze at and murmur with, a man who would kiss her hand and pay her extravagant compliments—for that was what Cynthia believed lovers did. But the only man Miranda ever met for tea or at the museum was her cousin, Birkett Price, and he was young enough to be her son.

Miranda was a striking woman, poised and imposing, who did nothing to attract attention. She had merely to walk into a room to turn heads. Miranda was "different," far more interesting than Cynthia's friends, and she attracted more men than Cynthia did herself, young men as well as older ones.

Cynthia felt a brief flash of jealousy, as for a rival, until she reminded herself that she was young and Miranda was old. Still, Miranda didn't look her age and she was elegant, sophisticated, and knowledgeable about certain things of which Cynthia was ignorant.

"And she has Paul too," Cynthia said, rearranging herself on the window seat. That seemed unfair. She secretly envied Miranda her stunning husband. Paul was one of the patrician Cunninghams, several inches taller than his tall wife, slender and handsome.

He was fair-haired with dreamy hazel eyes and a wide, kind mouth. He was clean shaven, unlike the bewhiskered men of the family and its circle of friends. He was gentle and clever, kind and amusing. He was, in short, the very sort of man Cynthia wanted to marry. Cynthia flirted with him, although she did it more circumspectly than with other men. And she tried to impress him with her intelligence because he admired clever women.

"Like his wife!" Cynthia pouted.

She sprang up and opened the window seat, where a dozen books were neatly stacked. Cynthia made herself study archeology no matter how tedious it was, so that she could discuss Paul's favorite subject with him. She leafed through the books, but the prospect of the sailing made the study of death in ancient Egypt a chore. She decided to bring a few books to read on the voyage.

She hoped fervently that the coming week would fly by. Then she went back to *Washington Square,* wishing that Catherine Sloper would undergo a transformation and become, quite suddenly, beautiful.

*T*hree

The *Sylvania* rode at anchor on New York City's Hudson River. A steady stream of first-class passengers, most of them with friends and families who had come to wish them bon voyage, flowed up the gangway connecting the pier to the promenade deck.

The bon voyage party was a custom held over from the days of sailing ships when Atlantic crossings were as capricious—and as dangerous—as the winds they depended upon. But this vessel had two three-cylinder steam engines, twin screws, twelve watertight bulkheads, and four decks. Most of the visitors were there to drink champagne aboard one of the most luxurious ships afloat.

Two men stood at the railing watching the parade of elegantly dressed travelers. The elder of the two was short and square with broad shoulders over an ample stomach and muscular legs. What could be seen of his hair under his hat was as gray as his beard and bushy sideburns. He had the high color of a drinking man, but from a distance he merely looked rosy with health. His blue eyes were bright with vigor. Short and square as he was, his tailor had done a masterful job of dressing him.

"Haggerty looks like a cherub and dresses like a gentleman," warned the money barons on Wall Street. "He'll make you a fortune, but he's a pirate, so keep a sharp eye on him or he'll steal it back."

"Ah, here's a bevy of beauties for you," Haggerty was saying to his companion, nodding at a group of women coming up the gangway escorted by several of the ship's junior officers. "That's the best medicine for you, Steven," he told the much younger man at his side. "Take your old pa-in-law's word for it!"

"Dammit, Gus!" Steven James smiled. "I'm not sure I want to trade banalities with a lady. They can be remarkably dull."

Steven's was a strong face dominated by brown eyes under dark, unarched brows. He had a straight, high-bridged nose and a mouth women noticed. It was a face more rugged than fair, but the impression he gave was of an exceptionally handsome man.

That he was well above average height and had a powerful body probably strengthened the impression. Or perhaps it was his lazy grace with its promise of passion. He had an attribute that was not even named, much less discussed, among decent people: sexual magnetism.

Gus shook his head impatiently. "Who said anything about conversation? Take 'em to bed, that's what you need to do. They're all made the same, lady or laundress, a kindness to the body and a balm to the soul."

The little man didn't care what anyone thought about what he did or what he said. It was a quality Steven envied but had decided not to adopt. He preferred to observe the protocols of business and society, even if only by a whisker.

"For the moment," Steven said, "I prefer the girls at Mrs. Upshaw's. No complications."

Gus guffawed. "You were always partial to them—before you married my Alicia, of course."

It had continued after his marriage to Haggerty's daughter, but it was a commonly accepted little sin indulged in by most men.

Gus patted Steven's shoulder. "Now she's gone, my little girl, but *you're* here!"

"Yes, I'm here," Steven agreed.

"But for months you haven't really paid attention to what was happening on the Street. You'll be ruined if you don't look sharp."

"It would be a conflict of interest for a state senator to be involved in what happens on Wall Street."

"Not if he's discreet about it—and it's his own portfolio."

"Not at *all*, Gus. We agreed on that when you got me appointed to serve out Townley's term in Albany. That was why I gave you power of attorney on all my holdings."

Haggerty shrugged, conceding the point. This was not the time to tell Steven that no matter what the two had agreed upon, Steven was expected to be Haggerty's man in Albany and eventually his man in Washington. In a way it was all to the good that the boy had become interested in politics—but to an extent Haggerty had not planned.

"Who can tell how much more the Congress will meddle in business?" Haggerty said, voicing his favorite complaint. "If those fools could pass the Antitrust Act, they're capable of anything! What's become of rugged individualism?"

Steven made no reply.

Augustus turned to his difficult son-in-law with a fond smile. "Are you as high-handed in the state senate as you are with me, Steven darlin'?" he asked, hands clasped behind him as he raised himself on his toes. It was his habit when speaking with tall men. "No wonder they gave you a leave of absence so readily."

Steven smiled faintly at his father-in-law. "Let's not argue, Gus. We can do that when I come back."

Haggerty held his tongue. Steven was his son by marriage and Gus wanted to keep *him* even more than he wanted Steven to be his man in the U.S. senate. Like many rogues, Gus had a craving to leave more behind him than his fortune. He wanted to leave a custodian for it.

But aside from that, there was something in the younger man
that called to Gus, called to almost everyone, come to that, male or
female. Steven was no model of propriety: He liked the pleasures of
the flesh. But it was also clear that Steven was decent. He radiated
confidence, making friends among men and inspiring affection—
and more—among women.

"He's irresistible," Alicia had told her father. "He's the most
fascinating man I ever met."

It had embarrassed Augustus, that unconsciously erotic appetite
his delicate daughter had displayed. But the boy *was* irresistible.

———— • ————

It was not how Steven thought of himself. But the impression, once
cast, was not one he took pains to dispel. Having grown up as the
baby of a large and loving family, he had always accepted approba-
tion as natural, not as something he had to earn. As a result, there
was a vast part of Steven James that had never been touched: he had
never loved any woman as much as women had loved him.

As for his family, he was devoted to them and determined to
justify their pride in him. He was convinced that he had made the
right choice when he gave up his share of his family's large and
prosperous farm to study law.

"If you end up the way you're starting out," his sister, Claire,
had told him before he went off to Harvard, "you'll be a fine man."

"Why shouldn't I end up the way I've started out?" he demanded. "What would change me?"

Claire, married by then and already the mother of two, always
considered his questions carefully before she answered them, her
gray eyes looking into her own distance while her ever-busy hands
knitted or sewed for her family.

"Ambition, perhaps," she said finally. "It will tempt you to do
certain things, things you'd never have known about if you stayed
here."

"But you agreed that I should go!" Claire was ten years older and his principal confidant. Steven set great store by her opinion.

"And so you should. But the world isn't Greenhill Farm. From now on you'll have to think before you leap into anything more complicated than a haystack." She had looked at him with those clear eyes that seemed to see everything. "And there's always the possibility that the little man inside you will go away."

"What do you mean? What little man?"

"I've always thought of him as the troll who lives under the bridge. He's the one who guards your feelings."

That had hurt. "I feel as much as the next man," he protested.

"Have you ever been in love?"

He was taken aback. "Love means different things to men and women."

"Oh, of course!" she replied tartly. " 'Love is of man's life a thing apart; 'tis woman's whole existence.' " She tossed her head. "Lord Byron was a good poet but a great fool. And after all I've taught you about women!"

She had taught him a lot and he had listened carefully, but he was still convinced that love was more important to women than to men.

After law school he had gone to work for a firm in New York and in two years had set aside enough money to begin investing in the stock market—judiciously at first but more and more often because it was an exciting gamble.

His sister had been right, as usual. There was enormous profit to be made by skating close to questionable practices. A time or two he had been tempted to cross the line, but the shame his family would feel should he be discovered was enough to stop him. And there was money to be made legally.

"All I have to do," he told a banker, "is figure out in which direction the country will expand and get there first."

"I'd rather deal in paper than in dirt," the banker scoffed.

Steven went ahead without borrowing capital, buying land where towns and factories would logically spring up, and for that he needed more cash than he had. He got it by investing in—"gambling on" might have been a better description—the infant industries fostered by the country's technological explosion.

His success in the market had brought him to the attention of Augustus Haggerty, who was more of a speculator than an investor, and had plenty of capital. That was how Steven had met Alicia Haggerty and married her. . . .

His attention was caught by the girl just boarding the *Sylvaria*. She was graceful and, although far more beautiful than Alicia, she had the same coloring, even to her vividly blue eyes. But the great difference was in her animation.

This girl radiated far more spirit. It was in the way she walked, the way she held her head. She knew she was breathtaking and he was sure she was aware that many pairs of admiring eyes were on her now. But she was so intent upon the impression she was making that she saw nothing and no one outside the magic circle of herself.

"Beautiful women are self-involved," Claire had told him. "It's because beauty is a factor in how well they will marry—unless they have money, in which case they can look like the crones of Endor and no one would care."

"And men?"

"Steven, you know a man has only to be a little better-looking than the devil to be called handsome."

"Do I qualify?"

"Not with that fatuous expression on your face. Otherwise, you'll do."

Steven smiled now, thinking of the clever, forthright sister who had taught him not to assume that all women wanted only domesticity and dependence. Some women, Claire had told him, resented belonging to a man like a bookcase or a barn. Blushing, she had told

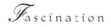

him that their secret frustration was not physical but had to do with their wasted talents.

What would Claire say of the vision on the gangway, clearly raised to attract a man, to make a good marriage?

Gus was clutching his arm. "Do you see her?"

"Yes, and there *is* a slight resemblance."

"Gives me the creeps," Gus said. "As if Alicia was back from the other side."

"Nonsense!" Steven shook his head. "How can an old pirate like you be so superstitious?"

"Who says I'm a pirate?" Gus demanded, his eyes still fixed on the girl.

"Everyone on the Street."

"I'm no worse than Carnegie and the Vanderbilts!"

"But they've learned to keep quiet about it, and you haven't."

"To the devil with the lot of them. Look! Here's another stunner."

Steven looked at the woman—her age was impossible to guess—and nodded agreement. She was tall and she moved as gracefully as the younger beauty who was just ahead of her, but with the commanding assurance of maturity. Richly dressed, she had a figure that would have caught Steven's attention even had her face not been as lovely as it was. Her eyes moved swiftly over the people at the rail, stopped an instant on Steven, and then moved on.

The bald man behind her, almost painfully thin with a sharp nose and an impatient air, helped both ladies to clear the gangway and step down to the deck, then rapped his walking stick imperiously to summon the nearest officer.

"Is that man the girl's husband?" Steven asked as the party was led off to their quarters. "Or the woman's?"

"Neither. That's Hobart Cunningham and the girl's his daughter. I'd heard she was a looker. The woman's Mrs. Paul Cunningham, his sister-in-law, the lady who sits on their board in her husband's absence."

"Ah, the real estate Cunninghams." Steven nodded.

"This one's the big boy," Gus said. "His brothers are nothing much, but Hobart's craftier than his father, and that old man can still smell a deal all the way from his sickbed. This journey is a good opportunity for you to get to know him, maybe find out where Cunningham's is thinking of buying land."

"He doesn't look like someone I'd want to know."

"The woman does. Cultivate *her*. Or the daughter." Gus laughed. "Or both."

Steven smiled. "What a rake you are," he said, shaking his head.

The atmosphere was growing more festive by the moment as the first bell rang to coax visitors ashore and people began to bubble up onto the deck from the staterooms. The crowd on the pier had grown considerably, and a stream of merrymakers was going down the gangway to join them.

Back toward the stern in steerage—the *Sylvania* called it third class—the passengers waved and shouted boisterously to the people on the pier. Second-class passengers, a cut above steerage, were more restrained in an effort to emulate the rich, who never yielded to strong emotion in public.

Gus took out his pocket watch, an ostentatious affair attached to a heavy gold chain that boasted several solid gold fobs. "Just a few minutes now," he said. "I won't wait for the last call ashore. I have an appointment."

He extended his hand and shook Steven's warmly. "Have a good trip, my boy, and above all have a good time. I'm damned if I know why you brought six months' worth of files with you."

"You complain when I'm not interested in my finances and you complain when I am. Make up your mind, Gus."

You'll complain too, boyo, Gus thought ruefully, *when you see what I've done to your portfolio.*

Gus reached up to pat Steven's shoulder. "I'll be writing to you at Brown's and I expect good news about European investment capital for America."

Steven accompanied Gus to the gangway. "If the Europeans had any vision, they'd have bought up half the country already. There's no basis for supposing they'll have a sudden change of heart about the future of mongrels and barbarians like us."

"Mongrels and barbarians we may be, Steven, but we've been busy moving in on Hawaii, the Philippines, Puerto Rico. Makes us a member of the imperialist club and gives us the rank of a world power, not so easily dismissed as we were before the war with Dixie. And then, there's you and your winning ways. You can be mighty persuasive. It's a trump you don't play often enough."

"Now that you've pointed it out to me, I'll be charm itself. Good-bye, Gus."

They shook hands again and Haggerty went quickly down the gangway. He strode across the pier feeling more optimistic about the success of Steven's mission. Gus had a scheme to corner utility companies, a scheme so clever that it would escape the limitations of the Sherman Antitrust Act. To put it into motion he needed capital, but he also needed information.

That was why he had booked Steven's passage himself. The Cunninghams were the reason he had chosen the *Sylvania*. If the girl didn't interest Steven, there was always the woman. She would know about Cunningham's plans to develop future communities that would require utilities. Whoever controlled those utilities would make millions. Once Steven was back in the world of finance, he would be eager to get in on it!

Gus, pleased with himself, crossed the pier without a backward glance.

Steven watched him strut out of sight—like a bantam cock, he thought. He was fond of his father-in-law, although Gus was a rascal who had to be watched. Steven intended to study Gus's new anti-trust dodge thoroughly before letting the man risk it.

Four

Then he forgot about Haggerty. A young woman was crossing the pier in a great hurry. She reached the gangway and started up, bucking the tide of departing guests like a salmon swimming upstream. She was breathing fast after rushing across the pier.

Steven marveled at women. Compressed in corsets as their ribs were, it was a miracle they could breathe, much less play lawn tennis or ride horses. No wonder they fainted so easily.

This one was slim and tall for a woman. She wore the flared, belted black skirt and the high-collared white shirtwaist that were coming into fashion, under a fitted black jacket.

She was panting as she climbed, carrying a vanity case and reticule in one hand and trying to protect her hat from a playful breeze with the other. She seemed to glow with anticipation and what he guessed was relief that she had not missed the sailing. In her hurry, several tendrils of hair had come loose and escaped her boater. It was quite the reddest hair Steven had ever seen, and it glinted in the sunlight like strands of polished copper wire.

"American girls," said a voice at his side, and Steven turned. He

saw a pale, slender man of average height, elegantly attired, with large brown eyes and a kindly air. The gentleman bowed.

"I am Jean-Baptiste Rouel," he said in an unmistakably French accent. "I cannot help admiring your countrywomen. They are so—how shall I say?—intrepid."

"Steven James," Steven said. They shook hands. "And at the same time so charming," Steven added.

They both turned back to the young woman on the gangway. When she reached the top she looked around for a source of information. She was so late that there was no officer waiting to hand her aboard and escort her to her stateroom. Steven stepped forward.

"May I help you?" he asked. He took her hand to steady her while she negotiated the high step onto the deck.

"Thank you. I'm Kitt McAllister."

"Steven James."

"Jean-Baptiste Rouel," the Frenchman said. "Let me take your things."

"Pardon me," Steven said, and, reaching out, he carefully straightened the hat that had been completely knocked askew by her efforts. He did it formally and very gravely until he saw that she was laughing at his solemnity, and he laughed too, a hearty laugh that further scandalized everyone on deck.

"What have I missed?" Rouel asked. "Why are they all watching you?"

"We have seriously flouted the conventions," Steven said. "In the first place, all three of us introduced ourselves. Then, to add insult to impropriety, I dared to adjust the lady's hat."

Rouel chuckled. "I see. How rigid you Americans are."

"Gentlemen, I'm overcome," Kitt said.

She *was* overcome, but she was not about to flutter like a spinster unaccustomed to the attentions of handsome men, which she was also.

"Will you permit us to escort you ourselves?" Rouel asked with a courtly bow that would have been startling coming from an American but was charming coming from him.

Kitt's green eyes danced. "I will," she agreed, glancing at the passengers still watching their little tableau, the women with obvious disapproval. They would consider Kitt "fast." It gave her a heady feeling.

Just then an officer appeared, apologizing for his tardiness. Kitt told him her name and he nodded.

"If you'll just come with me," he said. He snapped his fingers for a steward to take the vanity case from Rouel and thanked both gentlemen before turning back to his charge. "This way, please, madam."

"Now, there," said Rouel when the pair was out of earshot, "is a fascinating young woman."

Steven watched the tall, slender figure as the officer held open the swinging doors to the inner deck. She turned and waved, and each of the two men watching was sure she had waved at him.

———— . ————

Kitt McAllister followed the officer, annoyed with him for having whisked her away from her charming protectors. What an attractive man Steven James was—but was he a passenger? Her smile faded at the possibility that he had come aboard to see someone off and might now be going ashore. She was dismayed at how disappointed she felt, like a child not invited to a party.

Serves you right, she lectured herself. A woman traveling alone had to be more circumspect about accepting assistance from strange men, no matter how good-looking they were. She should have refused his help, as convention required.

"Convention be damned," she muttered, not for the first time in her life. Kitt had been a scamp as a little girl and as a young lady had frequently rebelled against the many restrictions the times imposed upon her behavior.

"This will never do" was a phrase Kitt knew well. She had heard

it initially from her aunt Louisa when that good woman came to help Sam McAllister raise his child after his wife died. Kitt had been four years old at the time.

Her memories of her mother were still sharp enough to hurt, clear enough to remind her that even great beauty was no guarantee of immortality, and terrifying enough to make her use her own appearance—"plain," people said it was—as a bargaining chip in the game with fate. She promised God she would never complain of being plain as pudding if she could live longer than twenty-two, the age at which her mother had died.

Rather than hide her plainness under frills and furbelows, Kitt ignored it. She never noticed when her red hair, green eyes, perfect complexion, and slim elegance changed from plain to pretty. In an age of artifice, whether of manner or dress, Kitt was militantly Kitt.

Her father had always told her she was pretty, but although she pretended to believe him, she never had, not deep inside, where her convictions lived. But she had no doubts about how bright she was and she used her wits as a shield and buckler against a society that judged women solely by appearance.

Early on she had discovered she had a knack for leadership as well. Her knack almost got her expelled from Bryn Mawr.

It happened soon after Kitt was severely censured by the student self-government committee for breaches of behavior that included dressing in men's clothes borrowed from the Drama Society's wardrobe, smoking cigarettes in public, and speaking at a local suffragist meeting.

"I regret to report," a member of the faculty wrote to Sam, "that your daughter, although a brilliant student, has a rebellious streak that seems to be incorrigible. I will refrain from cataloguing her prior escapades, but this latest one is too outrageous."

The details made her father laugh heartily. The upshot of it all was a visit by Sam to the college to have it out with Kitt.

"Bad enough," he said, "to make suffragist speeches in public without permission. But why on earth did you wear men's clothes?"

"To remind people that many men support the vote for women."

"Not nearly enough to make any significant change at this point." He had sighed. "You must live in the world as it is. Kitt."

"I prefer to change it."

"It's far too big for you to do that."

"If I were your son you wouldn't say so."

"That would depend upon what he was after. But you're not my son, you're my daughter."

"You always said I could do anything," she had reproached him.

"Within reason. Inciting women to bar their husbands from their bedrooms is not reasonable." Sam said, barely managing not to chuckle.

"The women did it in *Lysistrata*. They wouldn't have anything to do with their husbands until the men stopped the war."

"*Lysistrata* is a play, a Greek story about pagans. You're a real person living now."

"And I must accept the world as it is," she said mournfully, shaking her head.

He nodded. "Do I have your word?"

"Within reason," she parried. But she loved him and she gave him her word.

It was her love for him that made Kitt keep it. How could she disappoint a man like Sam? Absolutely no one knew her as well as he did. She had kept her promise even when her father refused to let her go on studying to qualify as a teacher.

"I'm lonely, Kitt," he told her. "You've been away at school for years and now I want you home with me."

When his heart gave out, she wondered if he'd known how little time they had left together. And she was grateful that although ignorant of his illness, and with her mind and body imprisoned in the

narrow little world of Branford, Connecticut, she had spent the last years of his life at his side.

When Sam died, her heart went with him. When, soon after, Aunt Louisa died too, Kitt's youth seemed to follow her. Always prepared for the worst, she resigned herself to spinsterhood at a time when an unmarried woman over twenty-two was an old maid.

Kitt was twenty-five, but right now, aboard the *Sylvania,* she felt as young and vulnerable as a rose in bloom and not in the least prepared for the tumult that had started inside her at the sight of Steven James and became overwhelming the moment he took her hand, even though both of them wore gloves.

Breathless, feeling ridiculous because of her uncontrollable reaction to him, she barely managed to thank the officer when they reached her suite. She took her vanity case from the steward and went quickly inside and closed the door. Leaning against it, she realized she was trembling. She crossed the sitting room to the bedroom, sat down at the dressing table, and looked at herself.

"I don't want to love anyone, ever again," she said to her reflection. Everything she loved had been taken from her: her mother, her father, her aunt, her aspiration to a career and a full life as a teacher. She had the freedom and the means to become a teacher, but she seemed to have lost the heart.

She peered at herself more closely. She looked different, but could that be because of a chance meeting that had lasted only moments?

"What utter idiocy," she told herself. But she *did* look different. She looked almost pretty!

She heard the second shore bell ring and shortly afterward the third. They would be sailing in moments, with or without the engaging Mr. James. She removed her hat and tucked in the loose strands of hair before replacing the boater, then took her reticule and the key to her cabin and went back up to the deck as quickly as she could.

The passengers were crowded near the rails, waving to people on the pier as the gangways were taken up and the slow rumble began that meant the engines were turning over.

She searched among the faces at the rail and on the pier, but she could not find him.

That, she decided, was that.

Two pilot boats on either side of the great ship, like ugly ducklings escorting a swan, led the *Sylvania* out of her berth and into the harbor. The breeze quickened on the water, refreshing the passengers after the lingering summer heat of the city. The city's skyline looked like fairyland in the mist as the tugs escorted their charge past the Statue of Liberty on Bedloe's Island and out toward the ocean before loosing the *Sylvania,* securing their lines, and heading back to safe harbor.

Her engines now humming, the ship made for the high Atlantic. That was when Kitt became aware that Mr. James was standing next to her, whether by accident or design she had no way of knowing. His hand went up to touch the brim of his hat, and she nodded. There was a look in his eyes that made her want to comfort him in some way.

"Do you realize," she said softly, speaking without preamble, as if she knew him well, "that until we reach Liverpool the *Sylvania* and all aboard her will have absolutely no link at all to any other humans on the face of the earth?"

"In some ways that's a comforting thought," he said, not surprised that she did not make banal conversation. After his sister, Claire, she was the least flirtatious young lady he had ever met.

"Do you suppose that's why there are always several moments of utter silence when the land disappears over the horizon?" she went on.

"It could be," he replied, thinking how pretty she was in the same way as Claire: both their faces had strength of character. There was no pretense about Miss McAllister either. He wondered why she had boarded alone, and decided she must be with a companion or that she was older than she looked.

"You've crossed before, Miss McAllister?"

"Yes, with my father when I was a schoolgirl. Is this your first crossing?"

"It is. May I ask you to steer me in the right direction from time to time?"

Her eyes inventoried his face before she smiled her assent, and they turned to watch the departure. A silence fell when New York City sank below the horizon and they nodded to each other like soothsayers whose predictions had come true. When the passengers began to move and talk again, he asked if she would like a sherry in the Grand Saloon.

"Thank you, yes."

He offered his arm and she took it. She had never felt as she did walking into the saloon with him. She behaved as if she were accustomed to being escorted by handsome men, and no one could have guessed that in the space of an hour—no, it had happened in a second—Louisa Kittredge McAllister had fallen in love.

Five

Mary Frances Alton took her job seriously, as a stewardess for lady passengers in first class must. These women expected superior service and would tolerate nothing less. Most of them brought their own maids, but those who did not depended upon Alton and other senior stewardesses. To her it was a profession, not just a job.

But much as she loved this ship, she was thinking seriously about leaving it.

"And after I give in my notice," she murmured to herself as she unpacked Miss McAllister's trunk, "I'll tell that miserable swine what I think of him."

The swine was the ship's purser, a vain man who wanted to have his way with Mary Frances. She had told him no a dozen times already, but he was always lurking in corners, darting out at her, trying to kiss her.

"Disgusting!" Mary Frances said, putting a pile of fine lawn petticoats into a drawer.

He was more than disgusting. The pig was threatening to sack her if she didn't give him what he wanted. And she mustn't be

sacked! It would ruin her record, waste all the years she had worked to get this far. Nothing was going to stop her life plan, not even the purser!

Her dream was that someday a famous lady would board—a title if they sailed from Liverpool or a millionaire's wife if they sailed from New York—and the lady's maid would fall ill.

"The maid won't die," Alton always amended, crossing herself. "But she'll be too sick to stir for the entire voyage. I will tend to the lady so well that I'll replace the sickly one as soon as we arrive at Liverpool."

Unfortunately, this McAllister woman did not travel with a maid, sickly or otherwise.

Mary Frances, hanging dresses in the armoire, could tell a lot from a woman's clothes. Miss McAllister was not young. She couldn't be, traveling alone as she was. She was well to do: her dresses and gowns, although simple in design and classic in color, were fashionable, of the best materials and very well made.

She held up a dress and looked at it carefully in the mirror.

"Miss McAllister is slender, maybe too slender for the fashion," Alton murmured to herself. "She's taller than average and probably moves like a bird. She's a plain woman who's never been sure a man was proposing to her or her money, and so she's decided to stay single."

For herself, Alton was too intent upon her career to consider marriage.

She went on putting things away, unpacking all she could without Miss McAllister, of whom there was still no sign except for the vanity case. Alton removed several items from it and arranged them neatly on the dressing table: a brush and a comb of ivory and silver, a bottle of glycerine and rosewater, a nail buffer, and a small box of hairpins. The lady was modern enough to have a box of *papier poudré*, leaves of ground rice-powder papers to take the shine off her nose. Alton found talcum just as good and a sight cheaper.

Alton looked at herself in the full-length mirror before closing the armoire door. In her dark blue dress with a ruffled apron and cap starched to a shine, she looked very smart. Her curly brown hair was piled high on her head with the cap set atop it, her brown eyes were modestly cast down, and her fresh complexion glowed with health. She had apple cheeks and a pretty mouth, but her manner was reserved with the passengers. When she wasn't on duty, she was what her coworkers called good fun.

Alton left the bedroom and surveyed the little parlor. The entire suite was small but handsome, high-ceilinged, and well-ventilated. As in the bedroom, there was a Turkish carpet underfoot and silk curtains at the portholes. The furniture was of satinwood; the lounge chair and ottoman and a small but welcoming settee were plump and upholstered in blue brocade. It might have been a lady's boudoir ashore.

Alton adjusted a bowl of fruit and flicked a speck of dust from a table. She left a light burning and went into the hall. On the other side of the corridor was a much larger suite with two bedrooms separated by a parlor. All of the suites, large or small, had a private water closet and most had a private bath.

Alton knocked, and a woman's voice invited her in. It was the maid, unpacking for her mistress.

"Need a hand?" Alton asked.

"Oh, could you help? Baxter's so frightened of sailing—she's Miss Cunningham's maid—she's made herself sick, and it's a rush taking care of two."

Try supervising ten, Alton snorted to herself. But she had decided long since that she could learn a lot by being friendly with the ladies' maids and she began taking gowns and dresses from the trunk and hanging them in the wardrobe. They were all splendid—and to judge from how they looked on the hangers, their owner was a tall, curvaceous woman with a high sense of style and the money to indulge it.

"Aren't they ever beautiful!" Alton said of the dresses. "Is the lady American?"

"Yes, she's Mrs. Paul Cunningham." The maid jerked her head at the other bedroom. "In there's her niece, Miss Cynthia Cunningham. She's more finicky than Mrs. Paul."

"Why don't I finish unpacking Mrs. Paul and you do Miss Finicky? My name's Alton, by the way. Senior stewardess. Here to help."

"I'm Rooney. Pleased to meet you."

Rooney scuttled off to the other bedroom and Alton soon finished hanging Mrs. Cunningham's gowns and putting her lingerie — all silk and batiste and cambric, lavishly trimmed and handmade, of course — into bureau drawers.

She called good-bye to Rooney when she had finished and went on to complete her inspection of the staterooms assigned to her. Then she went below for a cup of tea before the passengers came back from watching the departure to tidy up for dinner.

She got a cup of sweet, milky tea from the staff galley and took it to her cabin to drink, greeting the only one of her three bunkmates who was there.

"Hullo, Maizy," she said. "What's to do?"

"Lively crowd in second class," Maizy said while she buffed her nails. "I'll lay odds there'll be some serious pairing off, especially among the anarchists."

"Anarchists?" Alton stretched out on her bunk and placed the thick blue saucer and cup on her flat stomach.

"You know what I mean," Maizy said. "Them young ones who's always preachin' free love and the like."

"Oh, them," Alton said. "But they don't have to be anarchists to go on about free love."

Maizy shrugged. "My mum says one begets the other." She glanced at Alton across the narrow space between their bunks. "But then, himself is no anarchist and free love's what he wants. Has he been at you again?"

"Not today. He's too busy on embarkation days to come sniffing after me."

"Filthy sod," Maizy muttered. "Makes me sick just thinkin' about what he'll do if he ever traps you."

"And no wonder," Alton said. The purser was a stick of a man. Son of a naval family, he had a drooping mustache, pomaded, colorless hair, a damp red mouth, and too-prominent eyes of milky blue.

Mary Frances finished her tea, got up, and went to the mirror to make sure every hair was in place. "I'll just take care not to get trapped. And now they'll be comin' back from the sailin'. I must go." She retied her starched apron. "There, how do I look?"

"Like a proper lady's maid."

Alton usually didn't mind when the other girls teased her about her plans. She always knew that someday they'd be laughing out the other side of their faces.

But not if she had to give her notice because of that randy bastard!

She said good-bye to Maizy and made her way up to the promenade deck by the service stairway, which was closed to passengers.

She arrived at Miss McAllister's cabin just as that lady was unlocking the door. Alton introduced herself and followed her in.

In the brightly lighted cabin Alton discovered she had been dead wrong about Miss McAllister. She was not plain at all. She was not a conventional beauty, but she had a glow about her—and the most glorious hair!

"Can I be of service, ma'am?"

The lady—who looked no older than Mary Frances herself—glanced around at the open trunk, the contents of her vanity case arranged on the dressing table, and the silver-framed photographs of Sam and Aunt Louisa placed on her nightstand.

"Did you unpack for me?"

"Yes, ma'am. I hope that was all right."

Miss McAllister smiled. It was a friendly smile and Alton took to her at the sight of it. Americans weren't snobbish like the Brits or rude like the French.

"It was more than all right," the lady said. "Thank you very much."

"You'll not be changing for dinner first night out," Alton said breezily, "but I can do your hair if you like."

"Is it that messy?" Miss McAllister seated herself at the dressing table and looked at herself in the mirror for the second time in a few hours.

"I'll have it done in the blink of an eye." Alton began removing pins and taking down the high-piled hair. She brushed it out, enjoying the feel of it. The two regarded each other in the glass, and this time they both smiled with that unspoken understanding that comes immediately between two women or not at all. Miss McAllister's hair was finished by the time the first dinner gong sounded in the corridors.

———— . ————

It had been a long day, and when Alton had finished turning back the beds she sat down on one of them to ease her aching feet. She must have dozed off, because she was startled awake when the door to the cabin closed. The lamp had been turned off. She knew there was someone in the cabin with her, and in another second, from the smell of his hair pomade, she knew it was the purser.

"You touch me and I'll scream," she said into the darkness.

"Not when you find out how good it feels." He sounded drunk.

She was disoriented and could not tell from what direction his voice was coming. Then he was on her, her wrists clamped in one of his hands while he pushed her skirts up with the other. His mouth, smelling of brandy, was smeared wetly across hers, and he thrust his tongue between her lips, muffling her screams.

She struggled fiercely but could not free her hands. Her legs kicked frantically when he tore her drawers open and touched her skin.

"There's a nice pussy," he mumbled into her mouth. "I know it wants me to pet it."

She would have killed him if she could. Then she remembered what her mum had told her to do if any man tried to force her.

She stopped struggling. It confused him and she was able to roll onto her side and face him, displacing his probing hand. She brought up her knee and drove it with all her strength into his groin.

He howled and clutched himself, freeing her hands, and she slipped away from him and out of the stateroom, ducking into the service stairway. Breathing hard, almost crying, she took the steps two at a time, holding up her torn drawers through her skirt and petticoats, until she was down on A deck.

She used a safety pin to secure her drawers before she ran aft toward the staff dining room, wondering what would happen now.

Six

"This way, please," the chief dining room steward said and strode off, Miranda and Cynthia gliding after him. Under a coffered white and gold ceiling supported by Ionic columns, they swept past a long center table and three shorter ones to a private table, one of several in the room.

"I've asked for one of the small tables for tonight," Miranda told her niece. "We can change to a long one when we decide which has the most interesting people."

"There must be a husband for me somewhere in this collection," Cynthia whispered.

"Hush!" her aunt replied. Cynthia was growing more headstrong by the day and Hobart had been even more emphatic about a suitable marriage before he went ashore that afternoon.

"I hold you responsible," he had warned as he left Miranda.

"That's ridiculous! I can't force her to accept just anyone."

"Well, I can, and I will if I must. If you're as fond of her as she thinks you are, you'll see that she finds someone she likes."

But Miranda's spirits rose as they followed the maître d'. The first-class dining room of the *Sylvania* seated 430 people and stretched from one side of the ship to the other. With its carved mahogany panels, its atmosphere was more like a town house than the interior of a steel-hulled ship.

There were two women already seated at the table. The elder of the two—she must be past sixty but it was difficult to say by how much—had a lovely English complexion and the carriage of an empress. The four-strand "dog collar" of pearls she wore was as white and lustrous as her beautifully dressed hair, both dramatic accents for her black suit and swooping black hat. But, for Miranda, the most striking thing about her was the force of her personality: even at a distance it glittered like her diamond rings and brooches. She was quite clearly accustomed to giving orders.

The younger woman was spartanly elegant in her dress. That didn't matter, Miranda decided. Her flaming hair was all anyone would notice—and the gorgeous green eyes that went with it.

They were engaged in an animated conversation as Miranda and Cynthia approached.

"Lady Burdon, Miss McAllister," said the maître d'. "May I introduce Mrs. Cunningham and Miss Cunningham."

There was an exchange of greetings. The two newcomers were seated and consulted the dinner card in its silver holder. Cynthia looked up and smiled at the carrot top who, she had already decided, was a spinster, probably a poor relation or paid companion to Her Ladyship. Cynthia was delighted to be dining with a title. She had the same admiration for the aristocracy as the rest of America did.

"Have you tried anything yet?" she inquired.

"Not yet," Lady Burdon replied. "But the food on the ship has always been excellent."

"England is not famous for gourmet food," Cynthia said. It was clear to Miranda that the girl was reacting to Lady Burdon's imperious air.

"Neither is America," Lady Burdon said breezily, "so we shall all of us feel quite at home."

Unused to being so easily squelched, Cynthia opened her mouth to reply.

"Cynthia!" Miranda silenced her before she said to Lady Burdon, "My niece is very naughty." Miranda's eyes flashed at Cynthia.

"I'm so sorry, Lady Burdon," Cynthia said with a penitent air. "Please forgive me."

The lady nodded and smiled faintly, apparently more interested in the menu. Cynthia winked at the redhead, who winked back. They smiled tentatively at each other.

Cynthia was suddenly grateful that she had no need to earn her keep with such an old dragon as this young woman did. She had never even thought of such a thing before, but it quite horrified her.

Then she noticed the two rings on Miss McAllister's hands: One was a star sapphire set in diamonds, the other a single diamond surrounded by seed pearls and tiny amethysts. They were definitely not the sort of thing worn by impoverished spinsters.

Nor, Cynthia decided, were her smart travel suit and her independent manner. Even seated, it was apparent that Miss McAllister was tall, slender, and had an excellent carriage, as straight as that of the awesome Lady B. Cynthia didn't know whether to envy or pity Miss McAllister for her red hair. Of all Cynthia's own attributes, her soft, baby-fine hair pleased her least, although men were impatient to touch it. Of course, women kept their hair hidden under hats—even while dining—except when evening dress was worn. And no woman wore her hair loose once she had been presented to society, except in the privacy of her bedroom. Long, flowing hair, it was believed, was erotic and tended to arouse the beast in men—whatever that was.

Their waiter came to take their orders. All four chose clear soup, grilled Dover sole, leg of lamb with green peas and parsleyed potatoes and sorbet to clear the palate, with cheese and fruit and pudding or pastry to follow.

"Are you two ladies traveling together?" Miranda asked just as Cynthia was about to.

"No, we met here this evening," Miss McAllister said.

"And immediately discovered that we are kindred spirits." Lady Burdon beamed at Miss McAllister.

They made idle conversation for a while, then turned their attention to the soup when it arrived.

——— • ———

So they are not mother and daughter, but aunt and niece!

Kitt had never seen a girl quite as exquisite as Cynthia. She had all the airs of a beauty too, but they were hers by right of perfect features, a small but splendid figure, and the tender curls and tendrils of her silky, little-girl's hair. Kitt had known one or two like her at Bryn Mawr. They occupied a different stratum, breathed air different from that of ordinary or merely comely females.

But it was Mrs. Cunningham who was really intriguing. She had no need of airs; all she had to do was be. She was one of those women who is most beautiful in her middle years, just before a spiteful Mother Nature assaults her with the wrinkles and blotches of age.

As the lamb was served, Kitt saw that the charming Mr. James was just taking his seat at one of the long tables and in her direct line of vision. He saw her a second later and inclined his head with a smile.

"Who is that stunning man?" Cynthia asked, astonished that Miss McAllister should know him. Cynthia had to acknowledge that she had been totally mistaken about this woman, and that was troublesome. Cynthia depended greatly on her ability to label people and file them neatly away.

"His name is Steven James," Miss McAllister said. "I met him this afternoon when I boarded."

"So I observed," Lady Burdon said without malice. "As did everyone else. I simply had to meet the young woman who had captured the two most attractive men on the ship." She glanced at Cynthia, who was picking at her food.

"Is Mr. James the state senator?" Miranda inquired. Good manners forbade her turning around to see for herself, but his face had been familiar enough when she boarded to make her think she knew him.

"Is he?" Kitt said, surprised. "He didn't say."

"You are not from New York State, then, Miss McAllister?" Mrs. Cunningham said.

"No, from Branford in Connecticut."

"That explains it. We heard a great deal about him when he was appointed to fill a vacant seat in the state senate."

"I knew nothing about him," Cynthia said, admiring him from under her long lashes, "until Papa carried on about his appointment."

"You're not interested in politics, darling," her aunt said.

"I am now," Cynthia said.

"So would all of us be if more politicians looked like that," Lady Burdon said.

Why didn't he tell me? Kitt wondered, and decided he was not the sort to trade upon his position. It made her like him all the more.

"It's a sad story," Miranda said. "He married a young girl— Augustus Haggerty's daughter—after a whirlwind courtship." Miranda put a few peas into her mouth and chewed them daintily; both the younger women sat motionless until she went on.

"But the poor little thing died a year later and her newborn son with her."

"He doesn't seem heartbroken to me," Lady Burdon remarked.

"I've concluded that heartbreak in the male does not last overlong," Cynthia said.

"True, young lady, but they are not *all* Neanderthals," Her Ladyship observed. "Some are even quite docile."

"Thank heaven for small mercies," Cynthia sighed, "since we are obliged to marry them."

The sorbet was served and eaten, but anything more was declined by all four women and a decision made to move to the Grand Saloon for coffee. Stewards rushed forward to help them out of their chairs, and Lady Burdon started off with Kitt behind her, followed by Miranda and Cynthia.

"Look, Aunt Miranda," Cynthia whispered. "He's at that table just to your right, six places from the end."

Miranda glanced at him; he was, indeed, the state senator foisted upon them by that brigand, Haggerty, although the senator was said to have been doing an honest job before death had claimed his wife and child. He looked older now than he had when his grainy picture appeared in the newspapers, but she knew he was no more than thirty.

He was a marvelous-looking man, attractive in a different way from her husband. Paul was strikingly handsome, but this man was— she searched for a word but couldn't find one. She wanted to smile at him, but that was out of the question. She didn't know him and there was no one to introduce him. Still, this was a ship, not Fifth Avenue, and they had days ahead of them. . . .

"Is that the senator?" Cynthia whispered.

"Yes," Miranda said, her eyes held by his as she passed.

Kitt, having exchanged a nod and a smile with him before she walked by, never saw that they had noticed each other, nor did Cynthia, following behind her aunt and waiting until she caught his eye boldly for a moment before she looked away and walked on.

———— · ————

The four women were seated and ordered coffee in the elegant room with a coal fire burning in a grate at one end. Its hearth tiles were Persian, as were the rugs. The settees, chairs, and ottomans were upholstered in velvets and brocades. A grand piano and an American organ stood at the far end of the room, which was abuzz with laughter and conversation.

"What fun," Cynthia said. "We can sit here and talk about ev-

eryone who is talking about us." But she was watching the door, waiting for the senator.

"A little gossip before bedtime settles the nerves," Lady Burdon agreed.

"He never told me he was a senator," Miss McAllister said, still surprised by that.

"Put there by a man with political influence," Miranda reminded them.

"I'm sure Senator James is honest," Kitt protested.

"That's the consensus," Miranda agreed.

"Who cares when he's so handsome!"

"Please, Cynthia," her aunt admonished mildly. "Someone will hear you."

"I hope he's the someone who does," Cynthia said, tossing her curls. Her aunt smiled and shook her head.

"How did you find the Count d'Yveine?" Lady Burdon asked Kitt.

"I don't know him," Kitt replied.

"Of course you do. He was your other smitten cavalier."

"He told me his name was Jean-Baptiste Rouel!" Kitt exclaimed.

"That is his family name. Count d'Yveine is his title."

"I had no idea about either of them," Kitt said, newly astonished.

"Obviously your instincts are sound," Cynthia said.

Kitt shook her head. "The onlookers thought otherwise."

"Jealousy, plain and simple," Lady Burdon said, waving it aside.

A half hour later, with no sign of Senator James, the four left the drawing room for their staterooms and discovered they were near neighbors.

"How perfectly charming," Cynthia said. "Miss McAllister, let's meet tomorrow morning in the Garden Room and have a chat."

"I'd like that very much," Kitt said. "At ten?"

"Make it eleven," Cynthia suggested. "I am not an early riser."

Kitt nodded and turned to Miranda and Lady Burdon. "Will you join us?"

"Thank you, but I never make appointments when I'm at sea." Lady Burdon smiled and wished them a restful night.

"Neither do I," Miranda said. "But you two go ahead. I'll come to the Garden Room to collect you before luncheon."

When the two Cunninghams were alone, Cynthia turned to her aunt, her eyes shining. "Aunt Miranda, I just know this trip is going to be absolutely the best time I've ever had."

"I'm sure it will be, especially now that you have a friend." Miranda didn't add that Cynthia, true to form, had chosen someone she could comfortably outshine. "Odd, though, that such a young woman is traveling alone."

"I'll find out everything tomorrow, but we must change to one of the long tables," Cynthia said pointedly. "We'll never meet anyone hidden away as we were this evening. And I think we should meet the senator as soon as possible."

"I'll have a talk with the dining room steward before luncheon and see who else is at his table."

Cynthia kissed her aunt's cheek and gave her a hug. "Good night, dear Aunt Miranda. Sleep well."

"Good night, darling. It's lovely to see you so happy."

Miranda, after Rooney had helped her undress, got into bed thinking of Senator James and what a good match he would be for Cynthia. For any woman.

———— · ————

Cynthia was thinking about him too. He was absolutely divine to look at and he was a senator and—best of all—a widower. He was successful; he must be if he had the political backing of an influential man, even one like this Haggerty her father so detested. In any event, she knew that she was wealthy enough to marry anyone she chose.

She wasn't wild about the senator's farm-boy upbringing. Ho-

bart had been most explicit on the subject when "that hayseed" was appointed.

"After all, Papa, you say it's a very large farm and people have to eat," she'd told him saucily. "Who could possibly object to cows?"

"Never you mind, missy," her father had replied, but he hadn't been angry. Cynthia was his only daughter and he was easier with her than with the two sons who had survived out of the eight his fragile wife had borne him.

Cynthia put out the light, having already decided to befriend Miss McAllister in order to get an introduction to the senator. The spinster was no match for her.

———— • ————

Kitt was once more at her dressing table, examining herself in the mirror.

"I thought you'd given over hoping for the impossible," she told herself angrily, pulling the hairpins out of her hair and watching it tumble down around her shoulders.

The old longings and the nagging awareness of her imperfections were putting a blight on the sailing for her. She had truly believed she was beyond that sort of thing, that to be seated between a belle like Cynthia and a goddess like Mrs. Cunningham would not make her feel drab and dry and old-maidish. But that was exactly how she felt. At least she was sure that no one had suspected it from her comportment during the evening, and that was how it would stay.

"I know you wouldn't approve of this trip," she said to the memories of her father and Aunt Louisa. "But I'm doing it and I'm going to enjoy it or die trying!"

Thank heaven for Lady Burdon! Cynthia had never come up against anyone like *her*! Kitt had taken to the wry, outspoken baroness immediately. The woman had no patience with artifice or pretense, both of which Kitt detested too.

Lady Burdon was an aristocrat to the marrow of her bones. Her rank and its privileges were, to her, the natural order of things. As an earl's daughter she was a peeress in her own right with the title of Lady Burdon; the title Baroness came from one of her husbands.

"And she'd see rank as her God-given right," Kitt reminded herself in defense of democracy while braiding her hair, "even if she were Lucrezia Borgia."

No, it was not Lady Burdon's view of class that so charmed Kitt but rather her keen perception of people. Especially of Cynthia.

Kitt got into bed, turned out the light, and pulled up the covers. She thought of Steven James and wondered how long it would take Cynthia, whose interest in him was obvious, to engineer an introduction and start beguiling him.

"Fool!" she berated herself, and turned over to go to sleep.

Seven

iranda had breakfast in bed. There was, of course, no
morning paper, and no way to know what was going on
in the world: long distance wireless communication would not be
the norm on oceangoing vessels for at least another year.

Still, she welcomed a ship's temporary insulation from real life,
its limitations, and its responsibilities. It was foolish, she knew, but
for the next week she wanted to feel as carefree as Cynthia.

The Cunninghams would have been amazed by that. They considered Miranda a cross between a bluestocking and a supporter of
dubious causes.

"I'm glad," she had remarked recently at a family dinner, "that
this country has an open door for the world's inventors. They say
Marconi's own country saw no commercial future in the wireless,
but we did. I hope the door stays open for other immigrants as
well."

"Drivel," Hobart had snapped from the head of the table. "If
things go on as they are, we'll soon be drowning in immigrants."

"Mother's just being sentimental," her elder son, Paul Price
Cunningham—he was called Price to avoid confusion—said

quickly, defending Miranda as always. Price didn't like Hobart any more than she did.

"Not at all, Price," Miranda told her son. "Unless our big corporations are sentimental too." She looked at the others. "They're the ones who go to Europe to recruit immigrant labor. The corporations lure them by paying for their steerage passage."

"No one forces them to come," Hobart said.

"They're seduced by fairy tales about riches in America, streets paved with gold. When they get here, they're forced to live in wretched company shacks and to pay outrageous prices at company stores while earning pitiful company wages. They never get out of debt. It's another form of slavery—and we fought a war over slavery not forty years ago."

"That's no kind of talk for the dinner table," Hobart barked.

"Mother, please!" said her embarrassed younger son, Miles, dark-haired like his mother. "I don't know where you find all that rubbish about immigrants and slavery."

"In those newspapers her husband allows her to read," one of the sisters-in-law explained in a tone that dripped acid.

"I prefer to be well informed about more than ruffles and hats," Miranda shot back.

"It's unwomanly," the other woman persisted. "It's men's business to run the world, not ours. A woman's place is in the home."

Miranda shook her head. "The only difference between politics and housekeeping is hypocrisy. You should read more, Rosemary. Then you'd also know that the great majority of immigrants who come on their own succeed on their own, just as the Prices and the Cunninghams did."

There had been a cold glare from the in-laws—the idea of calling Cunninghams immigrants!—and then a thick silence had prevailed until Miranda said, "I'm sure you know nothing about the new law in New York State permitting women to own property and giving them the right to their children."

Rosemary sniffed. "I don't know how you were raised, but that has never been a problem in the best circles of society."

"Doesn't it trouble you that in other states a woman's children, like her person and her dowry, are her husband's property to do with as he likes? That includes beating her with belts, straps, and buggy whips! Don't you find it strange that a wife's adultery can be a mitigating circumstance for murder, while a man's adultery is expected and tolerated?"

"Miranda, that will *do*!" Hobart growled. "I will not have my daughter exposed to indecent talk."

Satisfied that she had thoroughly annoyed him, Miranda had returned to her dinner.

"Things were even worse when I was a girl," Miranda told Cynthia the next day as they drove along Ladies' Mile, that unique collection of shops that extended from Madison Square to Union Square.

"How much worse could it have been?" Cynthia had asked.

"Behavior and deportment were even stricter than they are now. For example, a woman couldn't take the arm of a man who was not a family member. Even to speak to one was cause for gossip."

The memory had made Miranda shake her head in dismay. "It's ironic that Victorian rules of behavior are slower to change in America than in England, where they originated."

"Men pretend all those rules are to protect us," Cynthia had remarked. "But I'll bet they made them up to protect themselves."

"From what?"

"From wives as clever as you are. How many other women sit on boards and drive their in-laws mad by refusing to vote as they're told?"

"You exaggerate, Cynthia."

"I do not! You should hear Papa rant about you after a board meeting! He always says you should stay at home, where you belong. That's because men have to outsmart other men to be successful.

Having to outsmart us as well would be too much. They couldn't cope!"

"What a cynic you are!"

"I know, I know." And Cynthia had assumed the accent and manner of her French governess: "Cynicism ees unbecoming een a lah-dee of any ahge, but in a *jeune fille* eet ees decidedly offpooting."

They had both laughed and talked of something else, but with respect to most men Miranda felt there was truth in what Cynthia said.

Paul was different. He had never treated her like someone of inferior status and intelligence. It was why they were so well suited, part of why she loved him.

"He's an eccentric," his family said of him, and they had not been overly surprised when he became absorbed in archeology and sent his wife to board meetings while he was away.

"Heaven help us," one of the sisters-in-law told the others, "if she starts cycling about the countryside wearing bloomers."

"The real danger," said another, "is that Miranda will become one of those creatures who demand the vote."

But Miranda was not that radical. "The only vote I want," she assured her husband, "is the one I cast on Cunningham's board. It makes them all so angry." But she tried to move things along by joining several of the more conservative women's organizations. Sometimes she felt tethered to the pattern of her life, which seemed one day tranquil and the next day monotonous. There was something deep inside her that prowled like a tiger in a cage, longing to break free.

Fortunately, her life was not as stultifying as most women's. How many times had she and Paul laughed together at his sanctimonious brothers and their preachy wives. The two of them were good friends as well as husband and wife. She realized, though, that her impatience for this reunion was not confined to friendship.

A ripple of excitement went through her, and she stretched lan-

guorously, eager to be in his arms, to feel the weight of his body on hers, the joining.

She sighed, then shook her head impatiently and rang for Rooney to run her bath and lay out her clothes.

Rooney sprinkled some perfumed salts in the bath and Miranda luxuriated for a while in the warm water and the lather of French milled soap with the same crisp, light scent as the bath salts.

She patted herself dry and slipped into her chemise, then called Rooney to lace her into her whalebone corset and corset cover and help her attach black silk stockings to the garters. Next came white cotton drawers, a flannel petticoat, several sheer cotton petticoats, and then a silk taffeta underskirt that rustled when she walked.

"I've heard tell there's Englishwomen wants to do away with our underpinnings," Rooney said, hooking the taffeta petticoat.

"Not entirely. I think you must mean the Rational Dress Society. They were against trailing skirts, high heels, and tight lacing. They also believed that underclothing should not weigh more than seven pounds."

Rooney clucked and helped Miranda to dress in the latest daytime fashion from Europe. Called a "tailor made," it was a simple two-piece ensemble with a flared skirt and a fitted hip-length jacket made in any fabric that suited the season. It was worn with a boater, a shirtwaist, and a tie. A light cape completed Miranda's outfit.

"You look lovely, Mrs. Paul," Rooney told her. "Who'd have thought that such mannish things could look so womanish."

"Thank you, Rooney. I won't need you today until it's time to dress for dinner, so go exploring and amuse yourself." Miranda pulled on her gloves as she made for the door.

"Thank you, ma'am," Rooney said, her round face shining. She gathered yesterday's lingerie into a satin bag for hand laundering and left the suite to the attentions of the ship's maids. Rooney was a lady's maid, not a cleaning woman.

Miranda walked to the rail and watched the horizon for a while as the vessel glided northeastward. She had ample time for a walk before she went in to make better table arrangements, more to broaden Cynthia's acquaintances aboard ship than to please herself.

Cynthia obviously wanted to be seated at Senator James's table, and that was an inviting prospect, but after thinking it over, Miranda decided it would be too obvious a ploy. And it was premature for Cynthia to set her cap for the attractive senator. First Miranda must find out if he was suitable.

Miranda took a few deep breaths of ocean air and started walking. The immensity of the sea was as much a tonic to her as the air. She had been brought up on a large estate on the Hudson and living in the city, so close to so many people, was sometimes oppressive.

She spotted Senator James standing at the railing. He smiled as she passed and raised his hat. Shipboard courtesy permitted her to nod to a man who had not been formally introduced, but she still continued on her way. She passed him twice more, and the next time she had to smile as they exchanged the same stilted, silent greeting. Sometimes the rules were ridiculous!

"I wondered how many times you had to pass until we became old acquaintances and could speak," he said.

"I'm Mrs. Paul Cunningham," she said, extending her hand. "I know who you are."

He took her hand. "I know you too. I saw you boarding yesterday with Hobart Cunningham and his daughter."

"And I recognized you from the newspaper photographs when you were appointed to the senate."

"Would you like to take a chair, or do you prefer to walk?"

"I'd like a few more turns," she said.

"I'd like that too."

She took the arm he offered without a second thought.

"I haven't seen Mr. Cunningham since we sailed," he said.

"He only came to see us off. I now have sole charge of my niece until my husband meets us in Liverpool."

"I saw your niece earlier this morning. She was with Miss McAllister, both of them very intent upon their conversation."

"A firm, new friendship—at least until we reach Liverpool."

He nodded. "I'm told that friendships made on a voyage rarely last beyond the ship's destination. I hope that isn't true."

He was an engaging man. She felt a wave of sympathy for his bereavement and realized how fortunate she had been to bear two sons, be up and about very soon after each confinement, and watch Price and Miles grow to young manhood with nothing more serious than the usual childhood illnesses and a few sprains.

How would she have survived the loss of a baby son and her husband at the same time? But, of course, men were not so vulnerable, so invested in marriage and children. Most men, at any rate. Paul was different.

She glanced at the young man as they walked, and decided he might be different too. He was more than attractive, he was captivating.

From out of her very depths came a wave of overpowering anguish that the best years of her life were behind her, had scudded past while she was attending to the small details of living, that soon she would look her age, soon be beyond the delicious turmoil of romance, even of idle flirtation.

She would have given anything to be young again, just for a little while. She longed for the dreams and the expectations of youth, the extremes of mood, the high emotions evoked by a tree, a waterfall, a sunset, a kiss.

Life was cruelly short. The average person's life expectancy was fifty-one years. Miranda, who was not average and could expect at least a decade more, still felt that too many of her precious hours were a waste.

"What about the nights?" Hobart had asked.

What about the dwindling days?

She looked at Steven James again. Amazing, that this young man should ignite such a longing in her for the days when everything mattered so intensely, when time moved at an achingly slow pace and a month was forever, a year an eternity. What would the senator say if he knew? Would he be amused by the emotions he aroused in a woman ten years older than himself?

When the charged silence between them became embarrassing, she searched for something to say.

"Will you run for office when you've served out Mr. Townley's term?"

Imagine! A woman sought after by men, admired for her beauty and poise, who had to take refuge in politics to hide the effect this man had on her!

"I must first decide if I prefer politics to stocks or real estate," he said.

"Is politics as lucrative?"

He shrugged. "I used to think wealth was far ahead of whatever's in second place. I can't believe I was ever such a fool. It's life itself that matters."

Her dark eyes studied his face sympathetically. "Tragedy is a cruelly effective teacher of what matters," she said.

They stood in silence again, looking at each other. His usually affable manner had faded. He seemed stricken with what she assumed was grief. It stirred what was an unthinkable impulse: that she should put her arms around him and comfort him for his crushing loss.

———— • ————

Steven's first reaction to her was reinforced. She was much more than a society beauty. There was sympathy and genuine warmth behind her dignity.

He would have sworn there was something more. The effect she

had on him was as mystifying as it was compelling. He had to turn his eyes away from her.

They were at the stern, silently watching the creamy foam of the ship's wake. It was a calm, blue day. The breeze was light and balmy and the few clouds in the cerulean bowl that covered them were soft, pure white and as inviting as feather beds. There was no one on the deck they overlooked, only equipment secured under tarpaulins.

Battened down and rigid, Steven thought. *Just as we are.* Otherwise he could have thanked her for so tactfully acknowledging his loss and her compassion. He could have told her how much he admired her, how sympathetic she was and how kind.

"Would you like to sit for a while?" he asked, turning to look at her. Their eyes met again. He had not anticipated the force of raw desire that swept over him. It grew stronger as the seconds passed. The nature of the tension between them was unmistakable: there *was* heat behind her warmth.

She shook her head—so slightly he might have imagined the movement—and he knew it was a warning for herself as well as for him. Whatever this was, it had happened to them both.

After another long moment Miranda turned away and glanced at the fob watch pinned to her cape. "I must go. I have an errand to do before I collect the girls," she said.

He understood that she must resist what threatened to sweep them away and he retreated. "Then I mustn't keep you. Another time, perhaps?" He raised his hat and watched her until she was out of sight.

———— • ————

Cynthia and Kitt, having quickly agreed to defy etiquette and call each other by their given names, were talking in the Garden Room over a cup of midmorning bouillon. Cynthia was expressing admiration—to hide her secret shock and a superior kind of pity—for Kitt's state of single blessedness.

"How I envy you your independence," Cynthia said. "I'm going to live as you do as soon as I come of age." It was the last thing she wanted. Cynthia could not imagine herself without a man—in particular Senator James—at her side to protect and adore her. Spinsterhood was a fate worse than death or childbirth.

"I'm sure that is not what your family has planned for you," Kitt said.

"Of course not! They've sent me off with Aunt Miranda to find a husband abroad, since the local crop doesn't appeal to me. I couldn't be happier. You've met my divine aunt, but just wait until you meet my heavenly uncle! He's my favorite gentleman, not stuffy and dull like Papa and my other uncles."

"He must be extraordinary," Kitt said, privately doubting it. Belles like Cynthia were inclined to burble over men.

Cynthia told her about Paul. "When he knew he couldn't face Wall Street for the rest of his days," she finished, "he went off to the Middle East and was immediately enchanted by all those mummies. Now he goes regularly."

"Without your aunt?"

"She doesn't fancy living in a tent with only native women for company while she watches him sift sand. In New York she has tons of things to do and she attends Cunningham's board meetings and votes for Uncle Paul in his absence. I know that's most unusual, but she's something of a rebel."

"I thought so," Kitt murmured.

Cynthia nodded. "As he is in his way. They're a fabulous couple! The three of us will spend a month in London until the heat breaks in Egypt and then go to Cairo before we visit his latest find—someone who reigned ages ago."

"How very exciting," Kitt said, although a necropolis appealed to her far less than London and Paris, Rome, Florence, and Venice.

"Kitt! I've just had a brilliant idea!" Cynthia said, eyes sparkling, hands clasped. "You must come to Cairo with us!"

"Thank you, but I really can't," Kitt said, and searched for a reason more tactful than her reluctance to join a family she barely knew, bound for a place she did not care to see right now.

She had met other girls like Cynthia: they expected the Kitts of this world to play whatever role they chose for them, in this case handmaiden to a debutante. But Kitt's reaction to commands, no matter what their source, had always been negative.

"I have business in London about my father's estate and it's bound to take a long time," she lied firmly.

"Maybe it won't take as long as you expect," Cynthia said.

"The law moves very slowly," Kitt said. "Ah, here's Mrs. Cunningham now."

Miranda had entered the room at the other end and was approaching them.

"What a stunning woman she is," Kitt said.

Cynthia nodded. "I always wonder how she manages to improve with age. Today she looks positively dewy!"

They both stood until Miranda had taken a seat next to them. "I've moved us to a long table," she said.

"And Lady Burdon?" Cynthia asked. The blunt and self-assured baroness put a decided crimp in Cynthia's style.

"She chose the same one."

Cynthia tried not to scowl. "And Kitt?"

"Mrs. Cunningham," Kitt said quickly, "you mustn't trouble yourself about me."

"It was no trouble." Miranda smiled. "And of course you're free to come with us or not, as you like."

"Of course she'll come."

"The final decision is Miss McAllister's, Cynthia."

"I'll be happy to join you and I thank you for arranging it," Kitt said. She wanted to continue her acquaintance with Mrs. Cunningham regardless of her bossy niece, and she thoroughly enjoyed Lady Burdon's company.

A steward appeared and with some ceremony struck the round brass gong he held suspended in one hand with the baton he held in the other. A small stir rippled through the room as women got to their feet, smoothing their skirts, patting their hair to be sure it was in place, settling their hats.

"Good," Miranda said. "I'm starving. I've been walking on deck for an hour."

"I detest physical exercise," Cynthia said, turning up her nose.

"It sounds exhilarating to me," Kitt said.

"It was," Miranda replied, and led the way to the dining room.

All three were disappointed that they were not seated at the senator's table, but none of them mentioned it.

Eight

A string orchestra was playing English airs behind some potted palms in the Grand Saloon, where the four women adjourned after dinner the second evening, along with several of their new dining companions.

They chose a group of comfortable chairs not too far from the fireplace and settled themselves. Alastair, Lord Walford, an English viscount in his middle twenties, leaned over the back of Cynthia's chair, *the better to ogle Miranda,* Kitt soon decided.

In that activity Walford was joined by Gerold Eberhardt of Eberhardt Chemie in Munich, whose square head, beard, and unwavering stare made him look more like a Prussian general planning a siege than a gentleman admiring a lady.

"Will there be dancing?" he wondered in his heavy German accent.

"I shall insist upon it," Lady Burdon said.

"If country dances are all they can play," Kitt said, "we'll need a maypole."

There were chuckles from Walford and one of the American couples in their party: Sylvester Seeley, an American railroad tycoon whose heavy investment in the fledgling automobile industry was his one topic of conversation; and his wife, Bertha, who already knew the names of everyone who was anyone on board.

The other Americans were Mr. Adam Wendall of the Plymouth Rock Wendalls, his gaunt, patrician wife, Ellen, and their son, Lewis, who was worshipping Cynthia from afar.

"Has anyone seen Senator James?" Bertha Seeley asked. "He seems to have disappeared."

"He wasn't at luncheon," Lewis reported.

"Nor was the Count d'Yveine," Bertha remarked.

"Perhaps they are not comfortable at sea," Lord Walford said with an Englishman's disdain for those who are not born sailors.

Mr. Seeley harrumphed. "He's not going to be comfortable in the senate for too much longer if he keeps fighting against high tariffs."

"If America has high tariffs," Eberhardt said ominously, "trade will suffer."

"I think not," Mr. Wendall said pontifically. "Ours is a large and growing country. We have our own markets for all we can produce."

"But what happens to the markets when your expansion is complete?" Lord Walford put in, attracting Miranda's attention. He had not struck her as a young man who thought of anything but high life.

"*Ja!*" Eberhardt urged. "What happens then?"

"It's all very well," Walford went on, "for an emerging industrial giant to put up prohibitive tariffs now, but you can't live in a vacuum forever. You'll soon need foreign markets to buy the flood of goods America will produce."

"And that will be sooner rather than later with all the new technology," Miranda said, surprising everyone. Trade and technology were not subjects she was expected to understand, much less discuss.

Mrs. Wendall, as stiff as her high bandeau collar, wore a pained

expression. She considered Mrs. Seeley's preoccupation with people's whereabouts vulgar and Miranda's contribution to talk of trade shocking.

"Ah, there is Senator James now!" Mrs. Seeley said in the little pause that followed. "Deep in conversation with the count."

Everyone turned to look.

———— . ————

A pianist and two more violinists joined the musicians and began to play a waltz, and Lord Walford immediately asked Cynthia to dance. Lewis Wendall, ignoring his mother's disapproving expression—*or maybe that's just how her face is put together,* Kitt reflected—invited Kitt although she was a single woman traveling alone and therefore socially suspect.

Herr Eberhardt swooped down on Miranda and the Seeleys followed them onto the dance floor, leaving only the Wendalls to sit like carvings and watch the the rainbow-colored gowns of the other women, dresses beautifully made, lavishly embroidered, and cut to show a lot of white shoulder but no cleavage. Cleavage was vulgar.

Kitt loved dancing and gave herself up to the music, trying to forget that her partner was the juvenile Lewis Wendall instead of Senator James.

Over Lewis's shoulder she watched Walford and Cynthia. They made a glorious couple, quite comfortable with their gorgeousness. He was blond with light, changeable eyes and lashes any girl but Cynthia would envy. He had a sculptured face with high cheekbones and a decidedly aristocratic nose.

Like Cynthia, he seemed wrapped and insulated in status, accustomed to privilege and instant veneration simply for how he looked and who he was. *What* he was did not signify.

Kitt was familiar with that attitude of superiority; she had seen it on some of the girls at school. But Kitt had been prepared for it. Her father had explained it to her before she left for boarding school.

Kitt, Sam said, was a hybrid.

"On your mother's side, God rest her sweet soul, you're a *Mayflower* Kittredge. But I still dirty my hands tinkering with my looms and my money's not old enough to qualify, not even for Mrs. Astor's Four Hundred. Don't be surprised if some of the girls at school are snippy."

"I couldn't care less how those girls are," Kitt had replied serenely.

But without intending to, Kitt had become popular at school. She made no attempt to enter into rivalries she could not win—over curls or beaus—but relied instead on her strengths. She was quick and clever, with a wry sense of humor, and she was exceptionally bright at her studies, someone the beauties could call upon for help with their lessons.

She had discovered many things about reproduction by learning to read Latin, Greek, and German, and she told the girls some of what she knew. She was much sought after for that, although the younger ones covered their ears and fled at the mere mention of genitalia, even in Latin.

But now she was no longer at school, no longer the apple of her father's eye or her aunt Louisa's cherished namesake. Here in the Grand Saloon of the *Sylvania,* surrounded by music, laughter, and people intent upon enjoyment, she wondered if she had made a great mistake in taking this journey. Then she remembered Senator James and knew she had not.

——— · ———

"I think His Lordship is ga-ga over Miss Cunningham," Lewis Wendall said.

"Nothing odd about that," Kitt said.

"Except for her American pedigree."

Kitt shrugged. "We may be years behind Europe in culture, history, and tradition, but we're far ahead in making money. The

European aristocracy is hard pressed these days and it's no secret they've been marrying Yankee fortunes."

"Despite contempt for Yankees in general and tycoons in particular," Lewis commented.

The little twit is furious because he's been outsnobbed and upstaged by Lord Walford, Kitt fumed silently. *Lewis is ga-ga over Cynthia too.*

"To marry the daughters, they must be civil to the tycoons," she said.

"Some people don't know when they're being patronized."

"Some people are not very bright," Kitt said, and danced on. At least he didn't trip over her feet.

Then she saw the senator standing just across the room. He acknowledged Kitt with a nod, as did the French count. But the senator's eyes seemed to follow Cynthia with particular attention, and Kitt's heart sank.

The music stopped and the ladies were escorted back to their places. Senator James and the count came toward them. Kitt watched the younger man, breathless with anticipation. He was even more attractive in evening clothes.

He greeted Kitt by name and she introduced both men to Miranda, Cynthia, and the others. Even the icy Mrs. Wendall melted a little, while Mrs. Seeley was effusive. Kitt waited for the senator's invitation to dance, but when the musicians struck up, he asked Miranda.

Lord Walford had captured Cynthia again, and Kitt found herself dancing with "Monsieur Rouel."

"I had no idea you were a count," Kitt said, wondering why he hadn't simply told her.

"It's not a thing one announces!" he said. "Probably because I'd have been guillotined for it in France little over one hundred years ago."

Kitt laughed. "You could have fled to the United States—although a little over one hundred years ago we were just a colony. To most Europeans, we still are."

"A totally mistaken impression," he said, his deep brown eyes laughing with her.

He was a marvelous dancer and, unlike Lewis, did not need to concentrate in order to lead her smoothly and expertly. They talked on, about her travel plans and Molière's plays, about the Loire and the Nile and the Mississippi. She felt absolutely comfortable with him, and so diverted that she didn't watch the senator and Miranda once.

————— · —————

Steven and Miranda moved in silence, the tempest between them almost palpable. The waltz was danced at arm's length, but he wanted to draw her close and feel her warm against him. His hand, resting on her waist, felt the stiff corset under her butter-yellow satin gown, and he imagined the naked, pliant flesh beneath the harness. He had an overwhelming impulse to kiss her voluptuous mouth and—slowly, very slowly—to make passionate love to her.

He had not wanted a woman so totally and so fiercely in a long time. When his wife and son died, they left him a legacy of guilt that had shut down all his drives, barring an occasional adolescent surge of simple lust. The sensuality that was so much a part of his nature had been smothered by remorse, as had his other enthusiasms. He had virtually ignored money, politics, and the boisterous sex he had once enjoyed regularly with merry widows or ladies of the demi-monde.

They were courtesans, not harlots, upon whose willing bodies he could satisfy his "baser" instincts. Most gentlemen went to bordellos to spare their wives, although lesser men forced their spouses to perform acts abhorrent to decent women.

But it was not only the constraint of the past year that made him

so avid for this woman. It was the warmth she projected. He wanted to be surrounded by that warmth, engulfed by it. He knew he would feel alive again inside her.

Her head was tilted back, her eyes half closed, and there was a look of secret pleasure on her face. *This is how she must look in passion,* he thought. He would have sworn she felt the same excitement that flooded him.

But I can't know that! he reprimanded himself. She was a lady traveling to meet her husband. She had given him no indication that she was open to an adventure or even a flirtation! He told himself to stop behaving like a sophomoric ass, to stop reading in her what he felt in himself.

Miranda felt separated from herself; she was a part of him. They anticipated each other's movements, responding to the rhythm of the music and the dips and turns and hesitations of the waltz. They were moving together through a cloud of exquisite colors as the women's dresses whirled around them; the blues, plums, apricots, and berry pinks glowed under sparkling crystal chandeliers.

The music, romantic and soaring, was a magic carpet. The two of them seemed completely removed from everyone else.

She tried not to look at him, but when she did she was convinced he felt the same way: aroused and intoxicated by color and melody and movement, by his desire for her and—she could no longer deny it—hers for him.

His hair was dark and thick and wavy, like hers. She wanted to touch it. She wanted to touch him. She wanted to take his face between her hands and kiss him deeply. She wanted to feel his head between her breasts.

She longed to lie down beside him and comfort him, and she wanted him to comfort her, although for what loss or lack, she had no idea. Until that morning she had not consciously wanted for anything she could identify. Now she wanted more time, more youth, more passion, more life. She wanted him. She wanted to soar like a bird, as she had in girlhood dreams, and she knew instinctively that this man would make her fly.

When the music stopped, it seemed they had been together for mere seconds. She craved more and was ashamed of herself for craving it, but when he released her, she felt bereft of his touch, of the clasp of their two gloved hands. They stayed where they were, applauding the musicians.

"Was that a dream?" he asked.

"It should have been." She smiled just enough to make any observers think they were talking casually, but her eyes were serious, virtually acknowledging that there had been another dimension to this dance.

"Do you suppose we might dream it again?"

"That would be indiscreet." She was very grave. A married woman did not dance more than once except with her husband or with family members and old friends. The rules were somewhat relaxed aboard a ship, but they were still there.

He spoke urgently. They were running out of time. "If we can't dance, can we walk again tomorrow?"

"Weather permitting, at about three o'clock."

"On deck," he said, as delighted as one of her sons would have been over an unexpected gift. But then, he was not much older than her sons, and she was ten years older than he! And what she wanted of him was in no way maternal. She was alarmed and aroused by the nature and depth of her response.

She made herself turn away from him and walk back to her chair. She could feel the ties that bound them stretching taut but not breaking, and she spent the evening talking with Lady Burdon, declining to dance with Lord Walford or Herr Eberhardt.

——— • ———

"My dear," Lady Burdon said brightly, "you're far too young to sit quietly with the older generation."

"How I wish that were true."

Lady Burdon looked at her closely and nodded. "Yours is a difficult time of life for a woman. No longer young but not nearly as old as people think."

"Does it get better?" Miranda asked wistfully.

The baroness shook her head. "It gets worse. Then one begins to live more in the past than in the present. Not all forgetful old people are dotty, you know. Some merely have retreated to another place, another time."

"But you prefer *this* time?"

Lady Burdon nodded. "It is an exciting time. Everything is changing and most of the changes will come from your country. With a little luck, women may even get the vote. Are you a suffragist?"

"Only marginally."

"Husband object?"

"In-laws."

Lady Burdon was sympathetic. "One of the banes of a woman's existence."

Miranda smiled. "I'm sure you're not nearly as wicked as you sound."

"I am considerably more so. I've had three husbands."

"Good heavens!"

"Ah, but each was superior in one way or another, within the limitations of their sex. And I was much more patient with men at the time. I've grown peevish and crotchety. That is one of the few good things about advancing years. One can vent one's wrath."

Lady Burdon shook out a white lace shawl and pulled it around her handsome shoulders as she rose. "Would you care to join me out on deck for a few minutes? I shall tell you all about my husbands."

———— · ————

Later, after she was in bed, Miranda clasped her hands as if in prayer. "No," she declared firmly. "I cannot meet him tomorrow or any other day. It wouldn't be fair to Paul."

But it had nothing to do with her love for her husband, only with herself and this stranger who aroused her as no man ever had. The wildness inside her threatened to escape from its bonds, to climb heights she had never reached. And she must do that now, before time gobbled up her youth completely and it was too late. On this magic ship it seemed the only thing to do. Here they seemed suspended between sea and sky, in another dimension.

But no, she said again. She dared not meet him.

On the other hand, if she failed to appear, he would guess why. Better to make a walk on deck seem as casual as it would appear to everyone else. What harm, after all, was there in a public stroll with another passenger? She thought of the pressure of his arm against her breast, and a thrill shot through her.

"I'll let the weather decide," she said to the dark cabin, but only the rational side of her prayed for rain.

Nine

Cynthia was awakened early the next morning by the decided roll the *Sylvania* had picked up during the night. She lay in her bed, going through the events of the previous evening as if she were looking at a photo album.

First she considered Lord Walford, ticking off his good points on her fingers.

"Alastair is engaging, almost as engaging as his title. One day he'll be an earl and his wife a countess, but his bride will be Lady Walford as soon as she takes her vows."

Now, *that* was something to think about. The viscount was the product of Harrow, Oxford, and an aristocratic family tree to which he owed his Anglo-Saxon good looks and his faith in his utter superiority.

"But I have the stronger character, so I shall be able to control him," Cynthia reminded herself.

She was adept at controlling men. It was a talent she had perfected when she realized how easily she could cajole her father with flattery or injured innocence. She had discovered that it worked on most men and was a woman's main insurance in life after wealth and beauty.

Alastair danced like a prince and dressed like one too, although she preferred men who were at least six feet tall and Alastair fell short by an inch. Still, Cynthia could consider being kissed by his neat, dry, wide-bowed mouth without cringing. The envy such a marriage would inspire in all her friends would make up for *that*.

Then she considered Senator James, to whom she responded in a quite different way.

"He's a man, not a youth. He's overpowering, not to be ordered about."

She imagined kissing him, and the thrills that went through her body merged at the place she had been scolded for touching when she was little.

———— · ————

"You will go mad," her governess had predicted. "Your teeth will fall out and your hair as well." Too young to question such a theory, Cynthia had been put to bed wearing mittens taped securely to her wrists so that she could not take them off.

The governess had been even more explicit when, at twelve, Cynthia was caught at it again.

"It is a disgusting habit, to be avoided at all costs. You will fall ill of tuberculosis and epilepsy. You will be pale and pasty with terrible boils on your face. Everyone will know just by looking at you! You will have to be taken to the doctor and that part will be burned away with carbolic acid."

"Then why did God put it there?" a sobbing Cynthia had demanded.

"To teach us self-discipline. If we do not learn it, we will be terribly punished. We are not beasts of the jungle. We are the crown of God's creation and we must behave in such a way as to honor Him."

Cynthia, frightened out of her wits, had stopped the practice and, in her total ignorance of sex, had no idea why Senator James had just resurrected the inclination. Now she resisted the impulse with difficulty and turned her head to look at the unrumpled pillow beside hers. She decided she would not mind sleeping next to him either.

He did not seem as besotted by her as Lord Walford was, but older men didn't betray themselves as young ones did. Perhaps that was why he had danced only once with Cynthia—but he had danced only once with Miranda and Kitt, as well, neither of whom was a potential rival.

Cynthia got out of bed and, reluctant to explain to her maid where she was going so early, got into her corset and attached her black stockings with some difficulty. She dressed in a royal blue skirt and jacket, brushed her shining hair back and tied it with a black velvet ribbon before putting on a floppy black velvet beret at a rakish angle and wrapping herself in a velvet shawl lined in soft wool.

"You're adorable," she told her reflection when she had finished.

She left the suite by her bedroom door rather than go through the parlor between the two cabins and risk having Miranda hear her. Holding on to the side railings, she made her way to the promenade deck. The gabby Seeley woman had reminded them that Senator James was brought up on a dairy farm and Cynthia gambled that he was an early riser.

To her great satisfaction, she saw him disappearing around the bow end as she stepped on to the deck. There was a stiff breeze blowing and the ship's roll from port to starboard was more evident here, the horizon rising and falling alarmingly, the sky a leaden gray swollen with rain. She decided not to chance walking alone— although a graceful fall would have brought him running. Instead, she signaled to the deck steward to help her to a chair. When he had tucked a blanket about her and gone away, she relaxed and lay back to wait for Senator James.

He soon reappeared at the stern end of the promenade deck, but she made no sign and he went right past her, his head down into the wind, his hands in the pockets of his topcoat. He seemed to be deep in thought, and she decided not to speak until his next turn. When she did, he stopped and came across to her, balancing himself on the moving deck.

"Good morning, Senator," she said with her most radiant smile. "Isn't it too rough for walking?"

"Good morning, Miss Cunningham. Yes, now it is. The wind is rising by the minute." He waited while the steward opened the next chair for him but waved away the offered blanket. "You're up early."

"I'm an early bird," she said blithely, although she rarely rose before ten o'clock. Her sports were archery and croquet, both played in the shade on summer afternoons at Bar Harbor or Newport, but she said, "I like to exercise before breakfast."

They slipped into an easy conversation.

She's like a beautiful painting, Steven thought. *She may even have more depth than a painting.*

He enjoyed looking at her although he barely heard what she was saying. Most of it was chat, although she was better read than the women he knew.

He was interested in her because Mrs. Cunningham was her aunt.

"And Mrs. Cunningham?" he asked. "I hope she's not feeling the ship's movement."

"I doubt it, she's a good sailor. She was still asleep when I left."

"You two seem to be close friends," he said.

"My aunt is a second mother to me," she replied, defenseless again. "My own dear mother is an invalid."

"I'm so sorry," he said.

"One grows accustomed to things like that," Cynthia said with saintly resignation. "But I'm very grateful to have my aunt."

"And after London you're off to Egypt," he prompted when she showed no inclination to tell him more.

Cynthia glanced at him. "How did you know that?"

"I met Mrs. Cunningham here on deck yesterday and she told me a little about your travel plans."

"She didn't mention the meeting to me," Cynthia said, her face composed but her ever-present suspicions flaring. If he had met Miranda, why the charade of letting Kitt McAllister introduce them in the Grand Saloon last evening?

"It was a very brief meeting," he was saying. "She probably doesn't recall it."

But you do! Cynthia thought.

"Have you had breakfast?" he asked.

"No, I came right out here."

"Shall we go to the dining room? I'm told they open very early and will serve a light breakfast to mad passengers who rise at dawn."

He helped her up and held her steady as they made their way through the swinging doors and down to the dining room. A delicious warmth suffused her at his touch. She wished they had a longer way to go. She wished that the ship would continue rolling like this for the entire voyage because it gave her an excuse to cling to him and him an excuse to put his hands on her.

Seated opposite him at one of the smaller tables, Cynthia followed the rules and tried to make him talk about himself. Theoretically, all she would need to do then was to nod and smile at the appropriate times and he would go away with the impression that she was a very interesting girl indeed.

She might have succeeded if Miss McAllister hadn't appeared in a walking suit of plum-colored cashmere that went well with her astonishing hair. The senator stood and asked her to join them, and Cynthia put on her social smile and added her invitation to his.

Why must she barge in? Cynthia roiled behind her smile. *I want to be alone with him!*

———— · ————

Kitt was ill at ease. She had no wish to be a third party, nor could she compete with Cynthia for the senator's attentions. At least he had danced with Kitt last evening, right after his turn with Mrs. Cunningham. He had seemed to enjoy dancing with Kitt and she had hoped for more, but he had left the saloon after doing the cakewalk with Cynthia, and Kitt had spent the rest of the evening with the count, who was certainly diverting company.

Kitt was now served coffee and triangles of toast. She devoted herself to the cream-and-sugaring of the first and the butter-and-marmalading of the second while the other two talked on about things to see in London. It was when the conversation turned to London hotels that Kitt joined in.

"We'll be staying at the Bristol," Cynthia was telling Senator James. "And you?"

"At Brown's."

"But I'm booked at Brown's too," Kitt said, and waited for a thunderbolt to strike her dead for such an outrageous lie.

"A happy coincidence." Steven smiled. "I hope you'll let me escort you there from the train station."

"I'd be delighted," Kitt said, totally unconcerned by her disloyalty to the attentive agent at Thomas Cook who had specifically recommended the Bristol.

Steven glanced at his watch. "And now, if you'll excuse me, I have an appointment in the smoking room. I wish you both a good morning."

They watched him walk the length of the enormous dining room and disappear from sight before they glanced at each other.

"I thought you were never up and about before eleven," Kitt

said, absorbed in preparing a second portion of toast which would no doubt stick in her throat as the first was doing.

"The early bird catches the worm," Cynthia replied frostily.

"So they say," Kitt returned, "and here's a worm eager to be caught!"

Lord Walford had just come through the swinging doors and was approaching Kitt and Cynthia, gracefully keeping his balance as the ship danced to a rhythm of its own.

"Jolly rough going," he said when he reached them and almost fell into a chair. "I hope you don't mind my joining you so precipitately."

"Not at all," Cynthia said with a smile that melted her chilly expression of a moment before. "Good morning."

"Good morning," Kitt echoed. The world seemed full of handsome men who were all Cynthia's swains.

"I'd definitely planned to sleep in," he said as if confiding news of great importance before he gave his order to the hovering waiter. Then he turned back to the two young women, *absolutely convinced,* Kitt reflected, *that we'll be enthralled by every wearisome detail of his morning.*

"But that proved to be a bore," Walford went on, "so I did my calisthenics and here I am. Too windy on deck to play any sports. Anything exciting going on inside?"

"I plan to see what the library has to offer," Kitt said. "How's that for excitement?"

Walford laughed and turned to Cynthia. "And you, Miss Cunningham?"

"I'm open to suggestion," Cynthia said.

Now, why didn't I say something like that? Kitt asked herself.

"There's a small parlor, just aft of this place, stocked with games and cards and the like. Why don't we wander down there and I'll challenge you to a game of chess."

"With pleasure. But first I must ring my aunt and tell her where I shall be," Cynthia said.

As proper as an English primrose, Kitt thought. *Maybe she wouldn't be so proper if it was the senator who asked to play games with her.*

Kitt left them shortly afterward. She hung on to the brass side railings in the corridors to keep her balance until she reached the paneled library, where a fire blazed in the grate and books filled the shelves. The library smelled pleasantly of furniture polish and leather bindings. There was no one there at this hour and, ignoring the books, she curled up in a large armchair near the fire and tried to reason herself out of her fixation on Steven James.

———— • ————

The rich aroma of expensive cigars and pipe tobacco hung in the air of the smoking room. Steven found the man he was looking for, a distinguished type who looked like a doctor or a banker. He was neither. He was Raymond Steele, one of Haggerty's inside men, and he was going to London to keep an eye on Steven.

Neither Haggerty nor Steele wanted that known.

"If Steven finds out I've set a nanny to watch him, there'd be hell to pay!" Haggerty had warned Steele when he gave the man his instructions. There'd be hell to pay as it was when Steven saw how his portfolio had been reduced by his father-in-law, in part to keep Steven short of funds and thus dependent, but also to teach him how dangerous it was for a man to ignore his money.

"And why?" Gus had shaken his head mournfully at Steele. "Because he caught himself an itch for politics."

"Let him scratch it for a while," Steele suggested. "And a vacation might make all the difference."

Gus had to be content with that. He had no choice.

Steele had introduced himself to Steven as an investment broker. He seemed very knowledgeable about capital markets in London. Investigating the possibilities was the least Steven could do for Gus, and he had made this appointment before leaving Steele the night before.

Now they shook hands and Steven took off his overcoat and sank into a wing chair in the remote corner Steele had chosen.

"Cigar?" Steele said, offering one from his breast pocket.

"Thank you, I prefer a pipe," Steven said, taking out his pipe and tobacco pouch. "Now, where were we last night?" he asked when the pipe was drawing well. He relaxed, his long legs stretched out in front of him.

"We were discussing British investments in America," Steele said.

Steven nodded. "As I recall, you think it better to raise capital among private investors than from the banks." Steven turned his head to look at Steele. "What would you say about setting up a corporation and taking it public, raising the money by selling shares?"

Steele shook his impressive head. "Land speculation isn't the kind of thing you can sell to the public."

"Why not, if it's bona fide?"

"Because you don't want the other fellow to know in which direction you're planning to expand. Drives land prices up long before you want that to happen. But stockholders must be told such things, and the other fellow would soon find out."

"Not if the company's set up as an investment trust with a guaranteed minimum return. Investment would be at the sole discretion of the trustees."

Steele studied Steven sharply for a moment, then smiled. "Very canny. Your reputation for finding ways around obstacles is well founded. Still, I think it's wiser to see what private capital you can organize before getting into anything as complicated as a guaranteed-return investment trust. Too many cooks can spoil a speculative broth. I'd be happy to introduce you."

At eleven the steward came to offer them hot bouillon, which they both declined. "The wind seems to have calmed," Steven said hopefully to the steward.

"Yes, sir. We should be out of this bad patch in an hour or so."

"Care to go up and have a look?" Steven asked Steele.

"Thank you, but I'm a lazy fellow."

Steele liked the younger man. He wondered what in the world Steven was doing with a jackal like Gus Haggerty now that the woman who had linked the two men was in her grave.

Steven went out on deck, eager to check the weather. The sky was somewhat improved from the dismal gray of early morning, but there were still very few people about and he went back to the stern and watched the wake, glad of his virtual solitude. He could concentrate on Mrs. Cunningham.

Would she keep the appointment if the weather was bad? But it seemed now that the sun would smile upon their meeting.

He felt a flood of erotic anticipation when he thought of her—and he was thinking about her a great deal. Augustus was right: Steven hadn't been himself for months. This enigmatic woman had brought him to life.

Miranda did not see him in the dining room at luncheon.

"Where could he be?" Cynthia wondered when they came back to their suite afterward to freshen up.

Miranda asked whom Cynthia meant.

"The senator!"

Miranda frowned. "I thought you were busy with Lord Walford."

"The senator is more compelling."

"Compelling?"

Cynthia tossed her head. "It's the best word I can find for how he makes me feel."

Miranda waited.

"I feel breathless," Cynthia said. "Light-headed. I'd do anything he asked of me. I used to feel that way about Uncle Paul when I was little and pretended he was my knight." She smiled. "That was before I understood that he was yours."

"And how does Walford make you feel?"

"I usually know what he's going to say and it would be easy to refuse him anything. He's not nearly as interesting." She started for her bedroom. "Will you be coming to the Garden Room this afternoon?"

"I have a headache," Miranda said on impulse. "I'll stay here. Rooney will bring me a headache powder and then I'll read."

Cynthia had turned back, sincere concern on her lovely face. "Aunt, you're not ill, are you? You hardly ate anything at luncheon."

"No, I'm just being lazy. I usually am on a ship. And you won't be alone."

"No. If the senator isn't around, Walford will be. And in a pinch there's always Kitt. Enjoy your lazy afternoon."

Miranda went into her bedroom and locked the door behind her. She was grateful that the conversation with Cynthia had been short.

Compelling was a good word for Steven James. Apparently he had that effect on females of all ages, but it was disturbing that both she and her niece were among his admirers.

She returned to the sitting room and sent for Rooney to bring her a headache powder.

"Will I help you undress?" the maid asked, concern for her mistress wrinkling her brow.

"No, I'll just have a compress until the powder works. I may even feel well enough to go up on deck." Miranda picked up Mary Johnston's popular historical novel, *To Have and to Hold*. "Don't disturb me until I ring," she told her maid.

"No, ma'am, I surely won't." Rooney left by the corridor.

Alone, Miranda opened the book but she did not read. Pictures whisked through her head like photos from the new Brownie camera—pictures that no ordinary Brownie would ever take. She was naked in Steven James's arms and his strong hands were warm on her skin.

"I must be mad," she whispered, "to even imagine betraying Paul with a man I hardly know. Am I the kind of woman Birkett thinks I am, burning with unsatisfied animal passions?"

No, she was still in command of herself. Regardless of the improved weather, she was not going to meet Senator James. She was going to remember who she was and not yield to a sordid attraction.

She sat back in the chair, eyes closed, and imagined him next to her, kissing her, touching her, taking her. The warm, soft cradle of the ship rocked her, and she gave herself up to fantasy.

Cynthia looked in vain for Senator James. Had she thought a moment, she would have remembered something he'd said about having some papers to go over in his cabin.

Walford had mentioned no plans, but she did not see him anywhere, and not in a million years could she have imagined what Walford was doing.

———— · ————

Walford was naked on the bed in his cabin, pumping his hips and thrusting his penis deeply into the body that lay facedown beneath him. He heard the grunts of pain and pleasure under him and increased his pace until climax. Seconds afterward he pulled himself out of Lewis Wendall and rolled over onto his back, reaching for the towel on the bedside table.

"You play rough," Lewis said, not moving, his voice muffled by the pillow.

"You seemed to enjoy it," Walford replied. He flung away the towel, reached for a humidor on the bedside table, extracted a cigar,

and rolled it between his thumb and four fingers. "Care for a smoke?" he asked his bedmate.

Lewis, turning over to lie on his back, accepted, and the two young men lit up and lay there, smoking silently.

"It's amazing," Lewis said at length, "but I'm never wrong. I spotted you the moment I saw you."

"Spotted me for what?"

"For preferring men in bed."

The other shook his head. "Not true. I rarely have it off with men. I fancy women, the way they're made and the way they smell. Sometimes I think I'd prefer to have no sex at all."

Lewis was thoroughly surprised. Sex went with manhood, no matter what the gender of a man's partner. "Why the hell not?"

"It complicates things."

Lewis laughed bleakly. "You don't show any signs of incipient celibacy. You must have tried everything there is."

Walford went on puffing and staring up at the bed's canopy. "God, I hope not. It's still early days for me. And first I have to marry Miss Cunningham and get a few heirs on her."

Lewis turned his head. "You barely know her, so it must be money."

Walford looked back steadily. "My reasons do not concern you."

"Get off your high horse!" Lewis protested. "After what just happened between us, do you think I'd gossip about you behind your back?"

Alastair puffed on his cigar. "Probably not, if you value your nose, because I'll punch it in if you ever imply that I don't worship the angelic Miss Cunningham—or that I'd far rather take her aunt to bed than I would her. But as it happens, the girl's a tearing beauty and I wouldn't mind having her for a wife."

Lewis scowled. "You could probably have her without marrying her."

"Now, that shows your total ignorance about these matters.

There are females I want and females I want to marry. Cynthia is the sort I want to marry."

"And whom does Cynthia want to marry?"

"It's *what* she wants to marry that counts."

"Your title."

His companion nodded.

"Wouldn't you rather be loved for yourself?" Lewis asked almost wistfully.

Walford laughed. For all his perfect looks, he had a nasty laugh. "You Yankees have such naive notions of love," he said. "You think it's a state of heart. It isn't. It's a state of mind." He paused. "And cock. One can talk oneself into hardening either of those."

Lewis, stricken but damned if he would show it, said nothing. He was falling in love with Walford, and for him it was definitely a state of heart.

They smoked the cheroots down and Lewis put a tentative hand on Walford's groin, but the viscount pushed it away.

"Sorry, old boy, but I must be off and find my bride. She thrives on my slavish devotion."

"That won't last long after the ceremony!"

"After the ceremony it won't matter."

"She might not like that side of marriage."

"Once she's my wife, what she likes won't signify."

He went into the bathroom and left Lewis lying alone on the rumpled bed with a familiar feeling of rejection and a rare flicker of compassion for what would befall Cynthia if she married Walford.

Ten

Steven sat in his cabin, his briefcase lying unopened on the table before him. He was trying not to watch the hands of his pocket watch as they labored toward three o'clock. At five minutes before the hour he snapped the watch shut and put it into his waistcoat pocket. He left the cabin, shrugging into his coat as he strode along the passageways, through the storm doors, and cut onto the deck. It was sunny, but the wind still blustered.

She was not there nor did she appear, although three quarters of an hour went by while he faced the wind, not thinking, just anticipating the sight of her. A gust of wind buffeted him hard enough to convince him that the weather must have kept her from coming out on deck. But where had she gone?

He went from one public room to another, taking care to avoid Cynthia and the viscount. He went unnoticed by Miss McAllister, who was playing chess with the count in the library, and he managed to escape with brief greetings to people he had not set eyes on until two days before but whose faces had quickly become familiar. The first-class passengers already formed a small community, and he knew how damaging gossip could be.

Mrs. Cunningham was nowhere in sight.

Maybe she *was* feeling the motion of the ship. He decided to telephone her cabin. That was certainly permissible, and if he could not see her, he had to have some contact with her, the attraction was that strong.

He wondered again why they were drawn to each other. There could be no rational explanation for such powerful magnetism between two strangers, one of them a lady. There was something about her that seduced him, a rich, sweet radiance that he needed—and had been unaware of needing before he met her.

A man couldn't miss what he never knew existed.

He went to his stateroom and asked the telephonist to ring Mrs. Cunningham. She answered almost immediately but her voice did not calm him. It only sharpened his craving to possess her, at the very least to be near her.

"When you didn't come up on deck I thought you must be ill," he said.

"I'm very well, thank you."

"I'm glad of that." He hesitated. "Then why didn't you come?"

"I thought it wiser not to," she said after a moment's pause.

"Why not?"

"You know the answer to that."

Her honesty made him lose command of himself. "I *must* see you."

"There's no point," she said, losing her composure too. "It's an impossible situation."

"I know that, but we have so little time," he pleaded, heedless of what she said, hearing only how she had said it, with the same desperation he felt. "Let me talk to you!"

"Please," she said, responding to the urgency in his voice. "Not on the telephone!"

"Where, then?" He waited. When she said nothing more, he hung up and left his cabin again. The ship's passageways were silent and empty as he went swiftly to her, not thinking, not considering the consequences, all caution blotted out.

———— • ————

She knew he was coming to her as soon as the telephone connection was broken. She should have said something, anything. She could have said "tomorrow." Or "this evening." Her silence had been an invitation.

She waited for him in the parlor, aware that she was playing with fire, determined to retreat before she was burned.

When he arrived, they stood without speaking, just inside the door of the little sitting room. It was not the awkward silence of strangers, but rather the difficulty of making mere conversation. Their eyes met and held as if they were locked together. He wanted to put his arms around her, but her demeanor placed a barrier between them and forbade him to cross it. And so he stood and waited in the soft lamplight of the parlor.

"I don't understand this," she said explosively, clasping her hands. "I don't understand myself. This has never happened to me before."

"Nor to me. Not like this."

"But you must listen!" she said with anguish. "It isn't just a game for me."

"I know that! And the last thing I want is to distress you. I'll go if you tell me to."

She turned and took a few steps away from him. "I want you to go, but I couldn't bear it if you did."

He reached her in one stride and put his hands on her waist. His lips brushed the nape of her neck. She literally trembled at his touch. She wanted to tell him to forget the last few seconds and leave her at peace with her world, her home, her husband. Whatever she did, she knew she would regret it for the rest of her life.

The pressure of his hands at her waist was intoxicating. With a little cry she turned and put her arms around his neck. His eyes searched her face and saw something there that made him kiss her ardently. Before that kiss she might have stopped him, but now she was lost.

He kissed her again and her senses clamored for him. She gestured toward the bedroom door and let him lead her in, feeling as if she were someone else, some other woman who watched from a distance with shock and envy.

It was so simple: she wanted him in the deepest part of her. She wanted to feel him there. She wanted to be possessed by him, possessed wildly, taken without restraint of any kind.

It was adultery, a mortal sin. She moved one last time as if to stop him, but instead she melted into the curve of his body and let him go on. Her mind, convention bound, said no, but her body shouted yes, and she felt herself slipping into the hot cradle of sex, savage and sweet, tender and relentless. She was a strong-minded woman, but this was stronger than she, resonating with a primal force.

He was kissing her when he undid the buttons at the back of her dress. She dropped her arms and let it slide to the floor. He unfastened the petticoats and they spilled down her body one by one. He undid the corset strings and parted the lacings until the restraint slid downward with all the other underthings, and she stepped out of the pool of silk and lawn, wearing only her shift.

His mouth clung to hers while he pulled off his jacket and opened his shirt. Then his hands rolled her shift down the length of her body and he followed its path, kneeling with his head against her, his lips tracing the creases where her thighs met her body, his tongue flickering against her skin.

When he stood again she could feel his bare chest with the soft tips of her breasts. She gasped at the sensation and breathed deeply when he bent his head to kiss her nipples. She had neither the will nor the wish to stop him when he lay down beside her on the bed and took her into his arms.

His hand moved down her body, his fingers lacing through the hair between her legs before moving to slide inside her. She opened her thighs and he stroked her slowly, both of them excited by her pearling wetness and the way her breathing quickened and changed.

He knew when she was at the brink of rapture and her sobbing cry told him when she reached it. He went quickly inside her, prolonging her shudders of release, summoning them from another place as she pulled him deep within her. Her arms and legs came up to encircle him. Her hips rose and fell to his rhythm, and then there was only an uproar of the blood that gathered both of them up in a moment of searing bliss so acute that it was almost painful.

He held her close while the echoes of delight grew fainter and became an indelible memory. She curled up in his arms, astonished by what had been coiled inside her for so long. It had survived because it was occasionally stirred, but it had never been brought to full life.

Now she was brimming over with it and with an ecstatic languor that lulled the darker implications of this day. They drifted.

She was startled out of her doze by the sound of people in the corridor. She shook him.

"You must go!"

"I can't leave you like this!"

"You *must*! My niece could return at any moment. *Please!*"

"Yes, all right." He got out of bed, finding his clothes and putting them on in the deepening dark of late afternoon.

"There's a comb and brush on the vanity," she said. She reached for her robe and watched while he found the comb and brush and used them.

He turned to go. "When shall I see you?"

"In the dining room. In the saloon. Dance with me."

"But when shall I see you alone?"

"I don't know yet. Soon. Only go, before it's too late."

She walked to the corridor door with him and listened intently. Then she opened it an inch and listened again. When she nodded and opened it wider, he went through it, striding along the corridor as if he had been coming from its other end, should someone suddenly appear.

She closed the door softly and stood there, aghast at what she had done, at the mingled wetness inside her body and out that was hers and another man's. The feel of it made her throb where he had touched her.

"What kind of woman am I?" she whispered. She had always believed she knew. Now she was at a loss.

But to ponder it would interfere with what she wanted to hold on to just a little longer. She wrapped her arms around herself, remembering. "Steven," she said exultantly, and closed her eyes. "Steven."

A memory is not enough, she admitted to herself. *I want more of him.*

She heard voices in the corridor and hurriedly gathered her clothes and threw them over a chair. Then she turned on the taps in the tub. She had a quick bath, dried herself, and put on her robe before she unlocked both doors and got into bed.

When Cynthia knocked and came in soon afterward, Miranda was reading. Her luxuriant dark hair was loose. It framed a face that looked even younger and fresher than it had that morning.

"How are you feeling?" Cynthia asked.

"Much better, thank you, dear, since I gave in to it and had a little sleep. It must have been mal de mer."

"But you're never seasick."

"I suppose there's a first time for everything."

"Will you come to dinner? They say it's worse if your tummy's empty. You can order something light."

"Yes, I'll come. Did you have a pleasant afternoon?"

Cynthia shrugged indifferently. "I watched Kitt play chess with the count. Walford didn't appear until teatime and Senator James never showed himself at all."

"Walford," Miranda said. "He's such an attractive young man."

"Very conscious of his looks and his position in life."

"Most attractive people are," Miranda said.

"Meaning that I am," Cynthia said.

"I mean most attractive people are." Miranda smiled winningly.

"You like holding up a mirror to my follies, don't you, Aunt Miranda," Cynthia said, smiling back despite the sharp resentment she felt.

"Folly can be amusing and I want you to enjoy yourself."

Cynthia, somewhat mollified by that, sat on the small armchair near the bed. "How could I enjoy myself when the senator was nowhere to be seen all afternoon? Where can he have been?"

"I hope you weren't actively searching for him," Miranda said after a second's panic, as much alarmed for Cynthia's reputation as for her own. Miranda, after all, was answerable to Hobart for both.

"Of course not. I don't fancy making a fool of myself." Cynthia paused. "But if I did, it would be over him. You've told me often enough that I hadn't met the right man. Now I have." She leaned forward. "Aunt Miranda, I'm in love. I never believed I could feel like this!"

"Cynthia, you can't be sure of that! You hardly know him!"

"I know him well enough to think about him all the time and dream about him too. We have six days and nights still ahead of us, and he can't stay sequestered for all that time. I intend to know him better."

"Remember that he's a recent widower."

"I'm willing to wait. He's had a year, and it will take at least six months more to make wedding arrangements and prepare my trousseau. Almost two years is a decent interval, isn't it, Aunt Miranda?"

Miranda made herself speak calmly. "The engagement alone

should last for two years—but, Cynthia, your father will not approve. Mr. James is not only a politician, he's one of Augustus Haggerty's men, and your father dislikes both species."

"I don't care! If Papa wants me to marry, he'll have to let me choose my husband. The senator's certainly eligible—and I know Papa. He'd die of shame if he had a spinster daughter on his hands as well as a drunken wife."

"Please don't speak of your mother like that!"

"It's the truth, isn't it?"

"The truth is often shortsighted. It's unfair to judge any woman unless you've lived her life."

Cynthia tossed her head. "I'm sure in Mama's case it has something to do with being married to Papa. For some reason she's frightened to death of him." She studied her aunt, her blue eyes piercing. "Why didn't you tell me you two had met before Kitt introduced you in the saloon last evening?"

"Met?"

"Steven James. I've been waiting for you to tell me."

"Didn't I tell you? Then how did you know?"

"I met him on deck early this morning. He knew we were going to Cairo with Uncle Paul."

"Ah, now I remember mentioning that. It was a very brief conversation with other passengers and we were not formally introduced at the time."

Cynthia sat back in the chair. "I'm not the only one who thinks he's wonderful," she said, irritated. "Kitt almost swoons whenever she sees him, not that it'll do her any good." She paused and tilted her head, watching her aunt. "I'm sure you think Walford is more suitable."

"Not necessarily," Miranda said honestly. "You don't know *him* that well either. You can't make the decision of a lifetime based on a few days acquaintance! I know it seems very romantic to do that, but we've only just begun this trip. There are so many new places and people ahead of us. Try to enjoy each moment as it comes."

Cynthia stood and moved toward the connecting door to the parlor. "That's precisely what I plan to do," she said over her shoulder. "I'm going to marry him, Aunt, I promise you that."

When she was gone, Miranda covered her face with her hands. "Oh, my God," she murmured. "I can't let that happen."

She would have to convince Hobart that it was an impossible match. But what reason could Miranda give? Why shouldn't Cynthia marry a young, handsome, successful man with a brilliant future and a talent for real estate speculation?

And why shouldn't Steven marry *her*? Why shouldn't Cynthia's fresh youth and beauty win him? Cynthia was irresistible to men when she wanted to be. She would charm him. She was *free* to charm him, to marry him, to sleep with him, and to bear his children.

Miranda shuddered. The very thought was unendurable.

Eleven

Kitt sat at her dressing table letting Alton's nimble fingers pile her hair on top of her head in sleek rolls, securing them with small combs and hairpins. One of the ship's large linen hand towels was draped across her shoulders and bosom to protect her green taffeta gown.

She had spent half the afternoon playing chess with the count and the second half listening to Cynthia go on about the senator and Lord Walford. She was depressed and jealous of young lovers, all of them, real and fictional. And she was amazed that love could be both a torment and a delight.

The two young women now searched through Kitt's jewelry, trying and discarding earrings and necklaces until they agreed on plain gold.

"There," Alton said when the jewelry was in place. "Now the gloves." She sprinkled a little talcum into Kitt's elbow-length gloves and helped her to draw them on. Then she snapped a heavy gold bracelet over the white kidskin on each wrist and stood back to admire the effect.

"How fine you look!"

"Thank you, Alton."

Kitt was growing fonder of this young woman by the hour. She had found her a little stiff at first but soon realized that it was Alton's idea of gentility to be frosty and aloof.

In Kitt's opinion, Alton was a more interesting companion than Cynthia, who thought of nothing but herself, the man she had snared so easily—Walford—and the one she really wanted.

Well, why shouldn't she want him? Kitt upbraided herself. *I do!*

"Miss?" Alton said with a tentative manner that was unlike her. "Could I ask your advice about something?"

"Of course, Alton. What is it?"

"It's about a friend of mine as works aboard another ship. There's an officer wants her . . . I mean he wants her to . . ." Alton's voice trailed off.

"I understand. She must report him to his superiors."

"She can't," Alton said sadly. "He's threatened to have her sacked without a character if she does. He says they'll not take her word over his. And it's true, they won't. He's from the gentry and she's—well, she's nobody."

"She might find work on another ship," Kitt suggested, aware that the girl was talking about herself.

"The officer says he'll have her blacklisted."

"That's outrageous!" Kitt said, her cheeks flushing with anger. "We must find a way to stop him."

"Yes, miss, but how? How does a girl get rid of a man who can ruin her reputation and her future?"

Kitt shook her head. "I don't know." She glanced at Alton in the mirror. "Can't your friend work anywhere but at sea?" she asked gently.

"It's the fastest way to a better life," Alton said, and found herself telling Miss McAllister what hard work it had taken to get where she was so soon.

"Otherwise," she finished, "it might take years to be personal maid to the mistress of a grand house. That's my dream."

Kitt nodded, frustrated by her impotence. Her father would have gone to the captain and had the man disciplined, but Kitt wasn't supposed to know about such things, much less talk about them. She wished she were as old as she often felt.

"I'll find some way to help," Kitt said firmly, as much to bolster her own courage as Alton's. "And tell your friend I'll be discreet."

Alton turned away. "You know it's me. I can't lie to you, miss."

"It doesn't matter who it is. It's intolerable and must stop. Who's the officer?" At the look of terror on Alton's face, Kitt quickly added, "Never mind, it isn't important."

She picked up a small beaded purse and patted Alton's hand before she left the cabin and walked toward the dining room. She had absolutely no idea how she could help, but help she would! She set her jaw, lifted her chin, and swept into the dining room like a cruiser in full rig.

——— · ———

After dinner the same group of table mates adjourned again to the Grand Saloon and took up their customary places with Lady Burdon next to Miranda on the settee. *How quickly people fall into habit,* Miranda reflected, noticing the way Alastair stood guard at Cynthia's side while Lewis Wendall gazed at the girl.

But no! Miranda suddenly realized: Lewis's gaze was not fixed on Cynthia's face, but on Alastair's! She gave herself a mental shake, certain that she was misreading the crosscurrents between the two young men, then equally certain that she was not.

She glanced to her left to find Lady Burdon watching her.

"Do forgive me," Lady Burdon said in a low voice. "I have made an avocation of studying people. In my advanced state of decrepitude there is little else to do."

She glanced briefly at the others. "For example, the Comte d'Yveine is bewitched by the McAllister girl, who is in love with Senator James, as is your niece. The flawless Miss Cynthia hasn't the slightest interest in the angelic Lord Walford except for his title and he, in turn, hasn't much interest in her at the moment except for her fortune. His romantic interest is elsewhere."

"Lewis Wendall," Miranda said.

Lady Burdon turned to Miranda. "Yes, I was right. You know about *les boys*. Still, it doesn't keep Walford from the pursuit of women. He is democratically dissolute. But I fear I shock you."

"You do," Miranda agreed. "Not in what you say but because you dare to say it."

Lady Burdon nodded. "That's another privilege that comes with age. People can pretend I'm losing my wits if my remarks embarrass them. The truth is very often embarrassing."

Miranda nodded. "I know next to nothing about that sort of thing. I always thought it flowered only during adolescence."

"Yes, when there are few females available to satisfy the unruly needs of the young male."

"But I assumed they outgrew those impulses."

"In the case of these two," Lady Burdon said, "the evil inclination lingers on."

They said no more when Kitt approached to chat with them.

But, Miranda wondered to herself, if Lord Walford had not outgrown the evil inclination, why would he be so attentive to Cynthia? Miranda knew the answer the moment her mind formed the question: Walford was after Cynthia's money! She must warn Cynthia. She must find the words to explain aberrant sexuality to a young girl who was completely ignorant of normal sex.

She was distracted from the problem when they were joined by Senator James, Raymond Steele, and the Count d'Yveine. The Frenchman always gravitated to Kitt's side.

Kitt seemed to like him—he was witty, extremely well read, and very articulate—but in the way she would have liked a favorite uncle.

"I think he's fond of you," Miranda whispered to her while the count was talking to Lady Burdon.

"I hope not!" Kitt returned, her eyes straying to Senator James.

"You can't ignore him all evening," Miranda murmured. "Not after playing chess with him all afternoon."

"Why not?"

"It would hurt his feelings."

"What about mine?"

Miranda laughed. "Miss McAllister, you're a caution."

"What are you two on about?" Cynthia demanded.

"Franco-American friendship," Miranda whispered, glancing in the count's direction.

Cynthia, comprehending, nodded, and turned back to Walford, still draped over Cynthia's chair like a guardian angel. *A fallen angel,* Miranda decided. She looked at Lewis. *Two of them.*

Then Steven sat beside her and nothing mattered but her keen awareness of him, his hip just inches away from hers on the settee. Her skin felt electric and her thighs hot. She knew she must not pay him either too much attention or too little.

The key to her bedroom was burning a hole in the small silk pouch that hung from her wrist. She thought of her naked body close to his, of the rapture they would share. . . .

She was startled from her thoughts when the music began and Steven asked her to dance. She slipped the key out of her purse as they walked to the floor.

"You delight me," Steven said. "Looking at you delights me. And walking with you. And listening to you. And thinking about you. And dancing with you."

How disarming he was! And he was not in the least vulgar. He made no allusion to the fact that they had been so passionately entangled only a few hours earlier. She knew he was recalling it too, and a blush suffused her face and shoulders.

"You mustn't look at me like that," she said, hoping he would never stop. "People will notice."

"I'll try not to." They danced in silence for several moments before he spoke again. "I wish we could be alone." His eyes caressed her face.

"We can."

"When?"

"Later tonight when everyone's asleep."

"Where?"

"My cabin. I have the corridor key in my purse. Be ready to take it when the music stops."

I don't care, I don't care! Miranda exulted after the key had changed hands smoothly. Making love with him might be evil, but it was sublime as well. It would soon be over, this interlude, this riot of her senses that made her young once more. Soon she would be Mrs. Paul Cunningham again, the virtuous wife of a man she treasured and loved and admired but who kept a wall of decorum between them even in the most intimate moments of their marriage. It was that wall that made her so much less Paul's than she was Steven's.

For once in her life she did not choose to be decorous. She wanted to be herself, naked and wanton and wild, and when Steven came to her in the early hours of the morning, she was.

———— . ————

She held his face between her hands and kissed him with all the heat and ardor in her, all the pride and passion of her nature. There was an intensity between them that she had never felt before. She wanted more of it, and the way she kissed him told him so.

"Touch me," he said.

She was not certain how; Paul had never invited it and she had never dared. She followed her instincts and marveled at the feel of him: that velvety quiescence at first and then, under the pressure of her fingers, the rigidity that made it possible for him to reach to the core of her and send her spiraling into their private inner space.

He moved her to lie on top of him. He pressed her knees apart and she understood what he wanted and straddled him. She guided him inside her and sank down onto him. She put her head back and laughed softly out of pure physical joy. She bent to kiss him deeply, her hips beginning to rise and fall along the length of him.

His hands reached up to cup her breasts, then moved down between her legs to stroke her again. She began the erotic climb with him inside her and this time the climb was longer, slower, and the climax more explosive. This time she heard his voice and hers mingle in the shadowy cabin, and felt her body shudder when his did. Exhausted and replete, she stretched out and stayed on top of him. He reached down and pulled a sheet over them and rocked her in his arms until they slept.

———— · ————

Not long before, in those same wee hours of the morning, Alton had left a very seasick passenger in the doctor's care and was coming along the corridor on her way to her quarters; she would snatch a few hours' sleep before she had to rise again at six. She froze when she saw Senator James going into Mrs. Cunningham's cabin.

She was incredulous. Mrs. Cunningham was a real lady, not like the grand women who behaved so properly but secretly bedded the officers, not at all like the more obviously willing female passengers in second class. Miss McAllister shared Alton's high opinion of Mrs. Cunningham and Miss McAllister was the best who ever drew breath. And she, too, had been taken in by Mr. James!

It was so quiet that Alton could hear the latch slide into place inside Mrs. Cunningham's door, but she waited another few moments before continuing along the passageway to that door to make certain her weary eyes had not deceived her. They had not. She could hear them inside talking softly and then she heard sounds and silences that left her in no doubt about what they were doing.

She remembered the purser's hand on her secret flesh and shivered with disgust. A wife had to submit but a woman who committed adultery was worse than a prostitute. Alton went on her way, shaking her head, completely disillusioned. Most people were not what they seemed. She should have learned that by now.

Twelve

Kitt waited all day for the few minutes after dinner when Steven danced with her. The pressure of his arm around her waist was intoxicating. By the time he returned her to her place on the settee, she felt incandescent. She always hoped he would suggest a walk before they retired, but when the women left—and of course Kitt had to leave with them!—he went to the smoking room with the men for brandy and a pipe.

Once in bed, she had erotic longings that made her uncomfortable and she awoke from dreams, her arms and legs hugging a pillow as if it were Steven. If he knew! Good Lord, if he knew!

Her imagination was far more specific than Cynthia's. Cynthia's fantasies began with Tennyson and Sir Walter Scott and ended just outside the bedroom door; Kitt's crossed the threshold and got into the bed, where her inventiveness drew on an enormous anthology of literary lovemaking, some of it veiled in euphemism and some of it very explicit.

She told herself that Steven James's appeal was only to the carnal side of her nature. She knew almost nothing about *him,* what he thought, how he felt, what sort of man he really was.

He did not seem smitten by Cynthia Cunningham no matter how the girl tried to charm him. He seemed to prefer talking business with Mr. Steele or Mrs. Cunningham, and he spent most afternoons locked away in his cabin working on documents that were, he said in passing, vital to his business in London.

"A waste," Bertha Seeley clucked one day in the Garden Room. "It's foolish to carry mourning to such an extreme."

"Surely that's a personal choice!" Kitt said, flying to his defense.

"Young men do not choose to live with memories," Mrs. Seeley insisted. "Particularly when there are such lovely young creatures about."

"The gentleman in question," Lady Burdon declared, "is not a callow youth. I m sure his head is not turned by lovely young creatures, not when ladies of the evening are two a penny."

Kitt glanced at Lady Burdon, who smiled benignly. Kitt liked the woman more each day. If she seemed eccentric, Kitt had decided, she was quite aware of it and enjoyed the effect it had. This time the effect was to stop Mrs. Seeley's chatter.

In the afternoon Kitt decided to visit the bridge. She was the only woman in the group who gathered in response to the captain's invitation. Steven James was among the men.

He escorted her during the tour and she happily agreed to a walk on deck afterward, followed by tea served while they sat side by side in deck chairs, just as she had imagined.

"I'm told you've been frightening young Lewis with tales of piracy at sea," he said with the smile that made her feel weak.

She did not show it.

"I read it somewhere. I read a lot."

"So I've noticed."

"My father encouraged it," she said, annoyed with herself for excusing something as exemplary as reading.

"You were fortunate to have such a father," he said quickly. "He sounds very like mine."

She nodded, reminding herself not to hear reproach where none was intended. She cast about for another topic of conversation.

It suddenly occurred to her that Senator James would know what to do for Alton, but how could she discuss such an embarrassing subject with a virtual stranger, and that stranger the man of her fantasies? But they were not strangers! Time was so telescoped aboard a ship that she seemed to have known him always. Besides, he had no idea what her dreams were like or that she was entranced by his mouth and obsessed with wondering how it would feel if he kissed her.

You call yourself a woman of the world, she told herself. *Behave like one!*

"May I have your advice on a difficult matter?" she asked before she lost her courage.

"If I can help in any way, I will," he said.

Kitt took a deep breath. "There's a young stewardess aboard who's being . . . pursued by one of the officers. He's threatened to have her dismissed and blacklisted unless she . . ." Kitt could not control an infuriating blush. "She asked me to help her and I don't know what to do except to go to the captain."

"Let me do that for you," he said. "Do you know the officer's name?"

"No, and the poor girl's too terrified to tell me." She looked at him anxiously. "I've promised not to reveal hers either."

He rubbed his chin. "That complicates matters, doesn't it?"

She watched him closely, feeling foolish. "If I had more time I might be able to persuade her."

"No, don't. There's a way to get around it." He nodded. "I'll see the captain and after this evening you can consider the matter closed."

She sighed deeply and relaxed in her chair. "I don't know how to thank you, Senator."

She was grateful when he changed the subject to her travel

plans. She had decided to revisit Naples and the ruins of Pompeii. She told him tales of the great volcanic eruption that buried it in ash and lava for centuries.

"The shapes of bodies were preserved like castings," she said, her green eyes aglow with enthusiasm for the subject, "under that blanket of ash. When Pompeii was excavated, they poured paraffin and made molds of the casts, of people going about their everyday tasks: having a meal, shopping at the marketplace, in the baths."

She did not tell him that among those macabre castings was a couple in the throes of passion, the man's body covering the woman's. She did not tell him of the huge sculptures of erect phal-luses placed outside Pompeiian brothels to advertise their wares. Women were not permitted to visit the more shocking exhibits and Kitt had learned about them as she learned about most things: from books.

"There was even the shape of a dog still tied to a post in the front garden of a stone house," she finished.

"You're far more entertaining than a travel guide," he said, looking at her with admiration.

"I don't think I'm any threat to Thomas Cook," she said, smil-ing, "but I've often thought I'd like to open a travel agency. It's an excuse to travel all over the world sampling hotels and restaurants and looking at ruins to recommend to clients."

"Do you need an excuse?"

She shook her head and they talked on about the places they wanted to go. She knew it would not happen, but the romantic side of Kitt, not to be denied, saw them visiting those places together.

They talked until it was time to dress for dinner.

If Kitt had been dazzled by Steven James before, she was faint with love for him now. He had understood Alton's problem immediately and had protected Kitt from further embarrassment by offering to deal with it himself. Talking about such a thing had given them a certain type of intimacy and a shared secret.

Returning to her cabin, she rang for Alton and told her that the problem of the purser would be solved by morning.

"Oh, miss," Alton breathed. "I can't hardly believe it. How?" Her expression altered as Kitt explained.

"Senator James said he would take care of it. He didn't tell me how, but I know he's a man of his word and you needn't worry because he'll be completely discreet. He's an admirable person."

Alton had a very different opinion of the man who had seduced Mrs. Cunningham. Did he mean to seduce Miss McAllister as well?

"And he didn't want anything of you?" she said in alarm.

"What would he want?" Kitt asked, frowning.

Alton could not say what she was thinking. She said, "I mean, to know who I am or who the man is."

"Of course not! I told you, he's a perfect gentleman."

He's a nasty bit of work, Alton thought, but she said, "I can't thank you enough, miss," with heartfelt sincerity.

"There's no need. Everything's all right and I'm very much relieved," Kitt said. "You know, I've been thinking," she went on. "Why not get your curling papers and let's see how I'd look with a few ringlets."

Alton, torn between anxiety about the senator's intentions and relief about the purser, went out to the stewardess's station in the corridor to fetch the papers. She knew exactly why Miss McAllister wanted to make herself more attractive: She was under the senator's spell. A lady like Miss McAllister could have no idea what kind of man he really was. Miss Kitt was very, very smart, but she was not worldly.

Alton decided to keep her own counsel for the present. Maybe the affair would fade as they neared Liverpool and end when the passengers were back on dry land, where they belonged.

"People have to behave themselves in the real world!" Mary Frances muttered to herself.

———— · ————

Cynthia could not sleep that night. It was not the movement of the ship that kept her awake: The rolling had virtually subsided. It was the exhilaration of first love.

She was anticipating the most important day of her life. A debut was significant but not nearly as lavish as a church wedding followed by a reception and a formal luncheon or dinner. Fortunes were spent on society weddings; they were the peak experience of a woman's public existence.

Lying in the darkness, Cynthia imagined the announcement of her engagement, the parties that would be given in her honor while she collected her trousseau and had her bridal gown fitted. With any luck she could order it on a side trip to Paris before she sailed back to New York with Miranda. Or she could choose it in one of the shops on Ladies' Mile that carried imports.

She saw herself at her wedding, a radiantly beautiful bride. She saw her happily-ever-after life unfolding in turn-of-the-century New York City.

Cynthia frowned suddenly. No matter what Miranda said, Papa would surely find the senator acceptable. She ticked off his qualities on her fingers once more. Steven was widowed, not divorced. His family was respectable and prosperous. He was a self-made millionaire—not exactly what Papa had in mind—but he was a state senator and would one day sit in the U.S. senate. She had wheedled that out of Mr. Steele.

Unfortunately, Papa had a low opinion of politicians.

After another half hour of tossing and turning, Cynthia put on the light and looked for her book on Egyptology; she was no longer in love with Uncle Paul, but she still wanted his admiration and his support for her marriage. She remembered then that she had left the book in the parlor and, pulling a robe over her nightdress, she went to get it.

An oil lamp was always left burning should the electricity fail, and Cynthia quickly found her book and was returning to her bedroom, when she heard her aunt moan as if in pain.

She went to the door of Miranda's bedroom and listened. It was not pain, but she had no name for what it was. Perhaps Miranda was having a dream. Cynthia's hand was on the doorknob, ready to go to Miranda's aid, when she heard a second voice, a man's voice, making the same primitive sounds while something—it was the bed!—creaked with a steady rhythm.

She felt hot all over. That her aunt was entertaining a man at three in the morning was shocking but not surprising in view of Cynthia's recently aroused suspicions about Miranda. But in bed?! Cynthia sensed the intimate, shameful nature of what they were doing even if the mechanics of the act were unknown to her, and she was shaken to hear such sounds torn from the depths of civilized people.

She leaned against the door, her old suspicions vindicated and some new facts added. *This* was what had been going on when Miranda "napped" in the afternoons. Miranda was scarcely the model wife everyone supposed her to be!

Cynthia felt momentary outrage for Paul—until she realized that this revolting discovery could be useful. It would stop Miranda from objecting to her choice of Steven James as a husband—and make her persuade Uncle Paul not to object as well. Together, Miranda, Paul, and Cynthia would prevail over Papa's objections.

"I'll tell her I know what she's done and that if she gets in the way of my marriage, Uncle Paul will know too!" she murmured softly while those unspeakable noises went on and on. "I'll threaten to tell Papa, too, unless she helps me to convince him."

She had turned to steal back to her bedroom, when she heard

Miranda cry out. This time it was not a shapeless sound. The words included a name.

"I love you, Steven, I love you!"

It seemed wrung from Miranda's vitals, and at the sound of his name Cynthia, without thinking, let the book drop, reached for the door handle, and turned it.

The door was locked. It brought Cynthia back to herself.

The two in the other room, panting and crying out, could not have heard the book drop or seen the movement of the doorknob. But they had stopped what they were doing and the bed had stopped its creaking, as well, while Cynthia clapped both her hands over her mouth to keep from screaming.

How she hated Miranda! Her aunt had not only married the idol of Cynthia's girlhood but had gone on to seduce the first man Cynthia had ever wanted to marry, the one man Cynthia had ever loved.

"Whore!" she screamed inaudibly, the sound muffled by her hands. "Filthy whore! No wonder you objected to my choosing Steven! You want him for your fancy man!" Afraid she would lose control and pound on that infamous door, Cynthia darted back to her bedroom and locked herself inside.

"Well, you can't have him!" she said softly, malevolently. "After tonight you'll never have him again."

She threw herself on the bed and burst into tears.

———— · ————

I can't believe this has happened to me, Miranda thought.

His head lay between her breasts and she ran her fingers through his crisp, dark hair. She could not get enough of him, the smell of him, the taste of him, the amazing things they did together.

She was in love with him. She would remember him with passionate intensity all the days of her life. The mere sight of him aroused her as Paul never had, and she had become instantly addicted to the total freedom of mind and body that she enjoyed with Steven. How would she get through life as she had always lived it, constrained in public and suppressed in private?

She almost said as much to Steven. There was very little they did not talk about. But she wanted first to understand the darkness she still sensed in him and to soothe him as he had soothed her.

"Tell me about your wife," she said.

For a while he did not reply. Then he took a deep breath. "I should never have married her," he said. "I didn't love her."

"Most people don't marry for love."

"You did," he said.

"How do you know that?"

"It's in your face and your voice when you talk about your husband."

"Yes. He's the kindest man I ever knew. And he loves me too."

"How would it have been if he didn't?"

"It would have been like most other marriages."

"I don't care about most other marriages. How would it have been for *you*?"

"Demeaning," she answered. "If I had known."

"It must have been that way for Alicia."

"Surely not! You never let her know."

"But I married her for expedience, not love."

"But she didn't know that! You didn't either, not then. And when you realized the truth, you did everything in your power to hide it from her." She spoke with absolute conviction.

"How can you be so sure?" he asked, at once eager and reluctant to be convinced. "You hardly know me."

"Oh, but I do. A woman gets to know a man very quickly in bed. If he's kind and generous there, he'll be generous elsewhere. And considerate. And attentive. I know you well enough to know you were all of that to her." She paused. "It's true, isn't it?"

"It's true."

"What was she like?"

"She was what women are expected to be. She was sweet and pretty, modest and delicate. She should never have had children." He took a deep breath. "In addition to cheating her out of the real love she richly deserved, I killed her."

"That is *not* what happened!" Miranda insisted.

"Miranda, I married a woman for whom I felt no passion, only mild affection. I made love to her. I got her pregnant and she died giving birth to my son. That's exactly what happened."

"But not by design! Must you spend the rest of your life atoning for an act that is committed knowingly every day by so many, women as well as men? And which on your part was unintentional? You hid your deceit from yourself as much as from her."

He stirred as if to avoid the issue, but in the end he answered her. "Yes, I hid it until she died, but I'll never hurt a woman again."

They were silent in the darkness for a while, listening to the sounds of the ship cutting through endless water, different sounds from those ashore. No dog barked in the distance, no carriages went past with a clash of wheels and hooves, no trees stirred in the wind. They were alone in another element, complete in each other.

Except that she heard echoes of her own voice telling him she loved him not half an hour before. She wondered if he had heard, if he loved her even a little.

"I still don't understand how this could have happened to me," she said.

"To us. It isn't rational, so how can it be understood?"

"Is it just to be enjoyed, then? And forgotten?" There was a break in her voice when she said that.

He stroked her hair. "Miranda, my darling, we have no choice, do we?"

"No," she sighed. "We have no choice."

That was true, but it was not what she wanted to hear. She wanted him to express the same dread she felt at their looming separation. She wanted him to wish desperately that it could be otherwise. She wanted to hear him say he loved her.

———— • ————

Steven walked quickly and quietly back to his cabin. He would not say he loved her, although he did. It would have raised false expectations in her and he could not do that. What Miranda called love he would call fascination. It made it easier to protect himself as he always had done.

He had simply stood apart and let life happen around him while he guarded his deepest feelings from risk. His "little man," Claire had called his guardian. "The troll who lives under the bridge."

Miranda had got past the troll. With the force of her nature she had reached inside Steven to where he lived. He had never felt about a woman as he did about her, but there was no way for them to go on seeing each other once this voyage was over, not in London and above all not in New York, which was a village when it came to gossip.

No, he would never be able to live with himself if he ruined Miranda's life.

He hated the idea of parting from her, but he would not tell her so. He had told her he was enchanted by her, he would always remember her, but a secret affair was not the kind of love she deserved, not the kind she had with her husband. That was built on a lifetime of shared memories and around their children.

Steven was still arguing with himself an hour later.

Thirteen

The two women sat in the parlor of their suite and spoke in whispers, even though the doors were closed and the maids had been dismissed.

"How could you betray Uncle Paul?" Cynthia hissed after she had made her threats clear.

"You could not possibly understand it," Miranda said, pale but controlled.

"It's *you* who do not understand," Cynthia returned. "And I *will* tell Uncle Paul unless this disgusting business stops immediately. The only reason I don't tell him anyway is that it would hurt him so much."

"That is not why. It's because it would be awkward for you to pursue a man who's having an affair with your aunt."

Cynthia's delicate skin reddened, but she said nothing.

"So spare me your moral indignation," Miranda went on. "You haven't the least idea of what this means or why it happened. What's more, you're jealous."

Cynthia shrugged. The slight lift of her shoulders clearly said that jealousy was irrelevant. "Just don't dare raise objections to Steven when I tell Papa about him," she warned. "Papa sent you along to help me find a husband, and I've found one! I told you that days ago."

"Before you knew we were lovers!"

"*Were*, Miranda. It no longer applies."

Because, Miranda realized with a sinking heart, *you're ignorant of what lovers do beyond holding hands and exchanging chaste kisses, of how powerful a bond sex really is.*

The two women regarded each other warily. They were no longer friends. The rivalry, once easily ignored in their relationship, had now become the dominant feature of it. Miranda was furious and not a little uneasy; a scandalized girl was one thing, a jealous woman quite another.

"What makes you so sure he'll want to marry you?" Miranda asked.

"I'll convince him if you stay away from him," Cynthia returned, still whispering. "Just leave him alone."

"I can't suddenly ignore him! Everyone's bound to notice."

"Talk to him, then. Tell him that it's over between you. But you are *not* to tell him that I know. Now, swear it on your life." Cynthia gave an anemic smile. "Better still, swear it on *his* life."

Miranda shook her head. "You can't *make* a man love you enough to marry you, Cynthia. That isn't how it happens."

"I'm waiting for your solemn oath," Cynthia said.

After a long while, Miranda nodded.

"Say it," Cynthia insisted.

"I'll tell him it's over."

"But not why!"

"But not why."

"When will you tell him?"

"Tonight."

"While you're dancing?"

"It's the only opportunity I'll have—unless he comes here later."

Cynthia shook her head emphatically, her face as set as marble.

"Is that all?" Miranda rose.

"That's all, Aunt Miranda."

Miranda went into her cabin. Her legs trembled and she sat down on the bed. She would do as instructed. Cynthia wanted Steven and she was accustomed to getting what she wanted. She would mortify her uncle and make a pariah of her aunt if she had to. And if she told her father, Hobart's wrath could take many forms: financial deprivation for Paul and the boys, and heaven knew what for Miranda herself.

It would certainly destroy Miranda's marriage, that serene and solid partnership of love and trust and honor. Perhaps it had been destroyed from the moment she turned to another man.

She lay back on the bed, cradled by memories of her lover's touch, the excitement of it, the discovery of passion with a man she loved just as much—however differently—as she loved Paul. It was like starting life all over again long after life had anything new to offer her.

She was famished for Steven even though they had parted only hours before. She longed to hear his voice, feel his touch, trail her fingers over his body, give him pleasure, talk to him.

They talked about things she would never discuss with another woman, much less with a man, and certainly not with her husband! It would have destroyed Paul's image of her and of their relationship to talk so openly. Paul needed to idolize her. He did not want to know that she was an ardent woman as well as his wife and the mother of his sons. It would shame him because, to him, erotic desire in a well-bred woman *was* shameful.

———— • ————

"What did you think when you first saw me?" she had asked Steven, captivated as all lovers are by the mysterious genesis of love.

"I couldn't think. I could only want you."

"But you hardly knew me."

"I knew all I had to know the moment I looked at you."

"So did I," she confessed. "Does that shock you?"

He kissed her. "Should it?"

"Women are taught that a display of passion will disgust a husband. Your sister must have been taught the same thing."

He thought that over. "Probably, but Claire always questions what she's taught. She has her own ideas about how men and women differ."

"For example," she urged him.

"She once told me that a man's desire is virtually continuous, while a woman's is intermittent and selective but equally intense."

"Thank heaven for Claire!"

"I do. And for you. You're more to me than pleasure. You're renewal."

"As you are for me."

He kissed her forehead. "I had lost my joy in life until I saw you on that gangway."

Then, she had wanted to ask him, *how can we possibly say good-bye at Liverpool and separate forever?*

But they had no choice.

"I simply cannot give him up," she whispered into the empty cabin. "I love him too much."

Cynthia had made it too risky for them to see each other on the ship, but Miranda was determined to find a way in London.

She sat up suddenly. "Why don't we just run away together?"

Miranda did not share that thought with him. She was too upset as she danced with him that evening, conscious only of fleeting time and the pain of a brutal break with a man she would love until she died.

"If I ask you to do something for me, will you?" she said.

"If it's in my power, you know I will."

"You mustn't come to me again."

For a second he stopped dancing, then remembered where they were and went on. "You mean not tonight."

"I mean not while we're on this ship."

"Miranda! This is all we'll ever have."

"I'll find a way in London," she said.

"No. That would be too dangerous."

"I'll find a way," she insisted.

"What happened?" he asked.

"There's not enough time to tell you."

His dark eyes searched hers. "Does someone suspect?"

"I think so."

"Who?"

Her lips went white. "It doesn't matter who." She looked at him, misery in her eyes. "It will be easier in London."

"It won't be. It'll be more difficult. You're not deceitful by nature."

"Neither are you."

"That's why we mustn't see each other in London. We're bound to give ourselves away. My darling, don't look at me like that. It breaks my heart."

"Mine too. I simply cannot give you up."

He could not help himself. "Until London, then."

She nodded as the music ended. It was incredible that their idyll could end amid music and dancing. They applauded politely and made their way back to their places. To Miranda the evening would have seemed interminable, the people dull, and the conversation witless had it not been for Lady Burdon.

"How are you this evening?" she asked Miranda with unfeigned interest, sitting down beside her.

"Very well, thank you, Lady Burdon."

The older woman raised one eyebrow and spoke quietly. "I'd have said you weren't feeling quite the thing."

Miranda was openly surprised. It was considered even more im-
polite in Britain than it was in America to make personal comments.

"My dear," Lady Burdon said, reading her reaction and tapping
Miranda's hand with her fan. "You must forgive my meddling. I do
it only with people I like."

She paused, watching Miranda with a kindly but quizzical expression. "A keen observer, you know, can sense physical attraction
between two people no matter how they try to hide it. If the attraction is consummated, it becomes even more difficult to hide."

Miranda examined her gloves as if she had never seen them
before. "Words fail me," she said.

"As long as your common sense doesn't," said Lady Burdon.

"That may fail me too," Miranda said, looking at the older
woman as if imploring salvation, her dark eyes filled with tears she
must not shed.

Lady Burdon rose with a swift movement that belied her years.
"I feel in need of some air," she announced to those nearest her.
"Mrs. Cunningham will accompany me. Come along, my dear."
And she put her arm through Miranda's and moved her across the
Persian carpets and out of the Grand Saloon to a small enclosed
promenade just beyond it.

"Get hold of yourself," she said sharply.

"I'm such a fool," Miranda said, and then compressed her lips
firmly.

"You're obviously new at the game," Lady Burdon said.

Miranda nodded.

"Are you aware that society's punishment for adultery is drastic
and unrelenting? If you are discovered—and you will be—your husband will divorce you and you will be banished from society and cut
off from your sons, whose future prospects you will have severely
blighted. You will be given a small allowance and packed off to live
cheaply in Paris or some other foreign city. And heaven alone knows
what punishment your family will mete out for the ruin of Cynthia's
chances."

Again Miranda nodded.

"And why have you risked all this? For a powerful attraction any shopgirl might feel, for physical ecstasy that is as brief as it is intense."

"Not only that," Miranda said. "For a communion with someone who reached me more deeply in a few hours than Paul has done in twenty years! I know my lover in a way I have never known my husband. Even more important, my lover knows me." Miranda took a deep breath. "I know it's impossible."

"Then for mercy's sake have done with it! I can read both your faces as easily as a primer."

"Thank heaven not everyone has your perception." Miranda drew another breath. "I still can't believe it happened."

"It's what the French call a *coup de foudre*." The older woman sighed. "I can still remember how that feels. 'How sad and bad and mad it was, but, then, how it was sweet!' "

"Oh, yes," Miranda whispered. "It is. All of that. I never expected to feel this way, not ever in my life."

"Yes, well. now you have and it must suffice."

"I don't want to accept that."

Lady Burdon stopped strolling and studied Miranda intently. "You can't go skulking about to assignations! For women like you, secret lust is never enough. You'll be discovered because you want things out in the open—and discovery means disaster."

"Tell me you believe it's more than lust," Miranda said.

"Of course I believe it! Do you suppose I was born in my dotage? Just remember what you've had rather than what you've missed, and be content." She took Miranda's arm again. "We must go back."

They returned to their places and Lady Burdon chatted about the World Exhibition in Paris while Miranda pretended to listen.

Cynthia left the saloon when Miranda did, following her back to their private sitting room like a jailer.

"Well?" she asked her aunt when they were inside. "Did you do it?"

"It's done," Miranda said, and turned away. "I'm very tired. I'm going to bed."

"I'm not in the least tired," Cynthia said. "When Baxter leaves, I'll curl up here and read."

"There's no need for you to stand guard at my door."

"What *can* you mean? Good night, Aunt Miranda. Sleep well."

Miranda, closing the door to her bedroom, felt as if she were entering a cell. It was a luxurious cell, but she was a captive in it nevertheless, and when she got into bed and drew up the covers, it was as if she were being smothered by the emotions that consumed her. Remorse was one of them, but it did nothing to blunt her fierce hunger for Steven James.

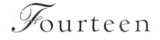

Fourteen

*S*teven lay on his bed, staring at the ceiling. His hands were clasped behind his head and his long legs crossed. It amazed him that he had reached the age of thirty before discovering that a woman could be lover/mother/sister/friend all in one. Miranda was. And she had helped him to put his guilt into perspective.

Up to now he had believed that love was an illusion nurtured by women—and what better place for an illusion to thrive than on a ship suspended between sea and sky! But his feelings for Miranda were real. He was haunted by the idea of never holding her again, never basking in the glow of her smile, the sound of her voice.

His experience with women had taught him one of the most significant differences between the sexes: For men, genuinely erotic sex could remain separate from emotional entanglement. But for women like Miranda, the former inevitably led to the latter.

And for him as well! After all these years of insulation, for him as well!

"Dammit!" he said, rising from the bed and striding around the cabin. "We should have met twenty years ago!"

But the difference in their ages—irrelevant now—would have

mattered then: He had been nine years old on the day she was married! Otherwise they would have been perfect together. Destiny had contrived to have them born out of step with each other, as some people seem to be born ahead of their times or behind them.

He looked at the bed again, but he was too agitated to sleep. For most of his adult life, work had been an infallible distraction, and he hadn't even looked at the papers in his briefcase since the sailing. Most of his waking hours had been spent making love to Miranda or talking with her or thinking about her.

Before he sat down at his desk, he poured some cognac into a snifter and filled his pipe. He reached for the briefcase and, taking a half dozen folders out of it, began riffling through the first one. He frowned as he studied the figures, and then his face darkened. He put down his pipe and turned the pages more slowly before he put the first folder aside and took up the second. By the time he had read through all of them, his face was flushed with anger.

His bank account had been severely depleted by the investments Gus Haggerty had made for him over the past six months! That in itself was astonishing: Gus rarely lost on the market and never as consistently as this.

Therefore the losses had to be intentional.

"You thieving bastard," Steven swore softly at his father-in-law. "Did you really think you'd get away with it?" Steven slammed the folders down on the desktop.

But of course Gus knew he wouldn't get away with it! He had handed Steven proof of his larceny!

"Then, why?" Steven asked. "Why did you do it?"

Unable to sit still, he pushed himself out of the chair, grabbed his topcoat, and went up to the Promenade Deck. The sea was gentle and the ship rode smoothly, now a little over a day out of Liverpool. Steven strode along briskly, thinking hard. It took him the better part of an hour before he had an answer.

At the start of their association Steven had learned a great deal from Gus, but as he got to know this Wall Street legend better, he was dismayed by the man's methods, eventually dismayed enough to challenge Gus about them.

He had taken Gus to a dinner of oysters and beef Wellington in a private room at Delmonico's. By the time they got to the port wine, Steven was telling the little man that unless Augustus mended his ways, Steven was out.

"I'll not be taking that serious!" was Haggerty's first reaction, eyes widening over the rim of his glass.

"You can take it any way you like, but either you stay inside the law or our collaboration is at an end."

Haggerty's surprise had been genuine. He saw nothing wrong in flouting the law. That was *his* way of life.

"I promise you it'll land you in prison," Steven warned. "And I'm not about to go there with you or even to be tarred with the same brush."

Another expression had overspread Gus's round pink face, the look of a man about to be robbed of the one thing he could not bear to lose. He became meek and apologetic, and after discussing each of Steven's objections, he promised on the head of his only child that he would stop venturing so close to the line between clever dealing and felony.

Steven had told it all to Claire on his next visit to his family.

——— · ———

Claire's husband, Tom Harden, had inherited a large farm and orchards a few miles away from Greenhill. The main house was a rambling white clapboard with screened-in verandas and green shutters. Lofty old trees provided shade in the summer and a windbreak in winter.

Claire had coffee ready and they sat together near one of the three stone fireplaces in the large main room.

When Steven had finished talking about his dinner with Gus, he smiled at his sister. "So you see, I resisted temptation. I didn't turn out so badly after all."

"I'd say you've turned out rather well. But you have an advantage over Haggerty."

"In what way?"

"From what you've told me, the man regards you as his son, not only because you're as clever as he is but because he cares for you on a personal level. So he gave in—this time. But he sounds like the sort of man who'll take over your life if you let him."

Steven considered that for a moment. "No, I won't let him. You're right, he treats me more like a son than a business associate. I'm sure of that because he wants to make it official. He wants me to marry his daughter, Alicia."

Claire stopped knitting and looked up at him. "Do you want to marry her?"

"Yes. I came up here to tell you that as well."

"But do you love the girl?" Claire asked him.

"Of course I love her!" He had spoken with unexpected heat. "She's a sweet, gentle, pretty little thing."

"You make her sound more like a trinket than a person."

"Dammit, Claire! That's not true. Look, I came up here to tell you about my engagement. It's a happy event. Don't act as if it were a tragedy!"

She had apologized, hugged him, and wished him happiness, but her observations had come back to haunt Steven very soon after his wedding.

"There's a seat going in the state senate," his father-in-law had told him after Alicia's shy announcement that she was expecting. "Old Townley's croaked and his pew is up for grabs."

Steven looked at the little man quizzically.

Gus smiled. "I can get you appointed to fill it."

"Why would I want to do that?"

"Because you're a lawyer and in the senate you'll have some-

thing to say about legislation. And because you'll meet a lot of moneymen. Now, aren't those reason enough for a beamish boy who wants to get ahead?"

Once Steven was in office, Gus introduced his son-in-law to the men who controlled politics from behind the scenes, all of them supporters of high tariffs, open immigration laws to admit the workers the industrial revolution demanded, and the reluctance by what was now called "big business" to accept any restrictions imposed by the federal government.

It was while Steven was in Albany voting on a transportation bill that Alicia gave birth prematurely to a stillborn son and died herself of a hemorrhage.

———— • ————

"She looks no more than a child herself," Steven had whispered to Gus, who wept openly beside the casket. Alicia lay in her satin-lined coffin with her tiny son nestled between her slender body and the curve of her arm. Steven had been overcome with remorse at the sight of them.

I'm sorry, he thought, hoping she could hear him, knowing that she would forgive him. She had deserved better of life than what he had given her. Tears of self-loathing filled his eyes and rolled down his cheeks.

"I know, son," Haggerty had said, his voice muffled in his handkerchief. "She was a dear little thing." His grief was sincere and he took Steven's remorse for grief, as did everyone else.

Before that day Steven had never questioned his phenomenal success: If a man worked hard and paid attention, there was little he could not accomplish in America. But since Alicia's death he had begun to think that fate had killed his wife and son as a warning.

And now his future was endangered because he didn't want to let go of a woman and because a man—Gus Haggerty—didn't want to let go of him.

——— • ———

"That snake in the grass," Steven muttered, turning away from the rail where he stood shivering in the night air. "He knew I'd find out as soon as I looked at this stuff, but he let me go off with no explanation, no apologies. I'll bet he counted on the ocean breezes to cool me off. The gall of it, stealing from me and then entrusting me with his damned mission!"

Steven was to set up a foreign company. It would be the foundation of a new financial instrument that as yet had no label. Its purpose was to control multiple subsidiaries by means of interlocking directorates—the same men sitting on many boards of directors.

The companies, one piled upon another, would spread upward and outward in a structure that resembled an inverted pyramid. The real control, if anyone ever found the point of the pyramid, would seem to be Haggerty but would actually vest in the original foreign company, difficult for the Sherman Antitrust Act to find, much less to prosecute.

It was a brilliant scheme for getting around those laws and it required both vast capital and the formation of the pivotal foreign-based company to start off the inverted pyramid. There was money enough in America, but the big problem with using American money would be the loss of secrecy.

"It was your idea," Gus had told Steven. "If we can figure out in which direction American towns will grow and buy up that land cheap, we'll make a fortune on its resale or development. And with this company we can sell the land and still keep control of it through the puppets we'll have sitting on all the boards of our subsidiaries."

They would make a further killing, Steven knew, because they would decide which utility companies should service the new townships—in return for healthy stock and cash considerations.

"The trick is to figure the direction of growth before anyone else does," Gus continued, beaming at Steven. "One way would be to know what land the Cunninghams are planning to develop before we sell contracts to the utilities companies."

"Why not influence the direction of growth by developing a town or two on our own?" Steven suggested.

He remembered Gus's delight when he made that suggestion and his own eagerness to see the strategy take form and flower. But after only a few months in the state senate, his interest in land development was lost to politics. And when Alicia went he had lost interest in everything.

Until Miranda.

———— • ————

He left the deck and returned to his cabin. He replaced the folders in his briefcase, undressed, and got into bed, pondering the choices before him, knowing he had to discipline himself in more ways than one.

Either he told Gus to go to the devil and immediately parted company with him, or he played Gus along, showing only part of the fury he felt until he'd rebuilt his financial position. Then he could dump Gus with impunity, maybe even find a few ways to even the score.

Playing Gus along was the wiser choice, he decided. His own father had taught him that a clever man never made decisions in heat or in haste, not about money and not about anything as inflammatory as a woman.

The little man who guarded Steven's heart was back at his post.

Book

Two

Fifteen

Paul Cunningham waited on the Liverpool pier for the *Sylvania*'s gangway to be lowered and secured. The sparkling weather reflected his mood, and his general contentment deepened each time he turned to the young man standing beside him.

"Like two peas in a pod," Paul's aged father always said when he saw his favorite son and grandson together. The patriarch indulged both of them shamelessly—Paul had to admit that—to the barely concealed rancor of Paul's three older brothers, Hobart in particular.

"Never you mind," Cunningham Senior counseled Paul whenever the animosity between his oldest and youngest sons became too heated to ignore. "Hobart controls Cunningham's and that's all he really wants."

"That's why my avocation pleases him," Paul had remarked on one occasion.

"Damn right!" his father guffawed. "You're no threat to him, making mud pies in Egypt."

"I hope my mud pies aren't a disappointment to you, Father."

"Not a bit of it! A man with four sons safely grown to manhood—and one of them a Croesus—can indulge his youngest, no matter how foolish his pleasure might be."

"Archeology is a science, Father, not an indulgence."

"Yes, yes, so it is. And if it sticks in Hobart's craw, so much the better." The old man had cackled. "Apart from his alchemy with money, he's a hard man to like. Always was, even if he's as much my son as you are."

But Paul had observed that in many families there was one child who had the larger claim on one or both parents' affections, if not on their care. For his father, Paul had always been that child—and still was, even at forty-two. For Paul himself that child was Price, the lovable, devoted boy at his side who had rearranged his grand tour of Europe so that he might spend several days in London with both his parents. Quite simply, he enjoyed their company as much as they enjoyed his.

As for why Paul and Miranda preferred Price, neither of them knew. Maybe it was because the boy was almost a mirror image of Paul himself and stirred happy memories for both parents each time they looked at him. Father and son had the same fair hair with a glint of red in it, the same deep-set hazel eyes under arched brows, the same wide, sensitive mouth, the same physique—tall and slender—and the same handsome profile.

"He has your temperament," Miranda often said. "I love Miles with all my heart, but his nature is more Cunningham than yours and Price's."

Paul never upbraided her for her negative opinions of his family. He had very little in common with them himself. Oddly enough, among all the nieces and nephews, Hobart's Cynthia was the only one of whom they were fond, probably because she was quick and bright, like Miranda.

"Look, Father," his son said excitedly, rousing Paul from his reflections. "The gangway's in place."

They waited eagerly for Miranda to appear.

Miranda was reluctant to disembark. She had no idea how to greet Paul, speak to him, touch him, not with her secret between them. She had changed too much. He would almost certainly want to make love to her tonight; the prospect itself was not repellent, but the idea of having sex with two men in the space of a week was.

"And yet," she sighed softly, glancing at the bed, "I'd do it all again."

She was dressed and ready, but she sat in her cabin gathering her forces. If it were in her power, she would have stayed aboard for the return trip to New York. She would have remained sequestered in her cabin until she could sort herself out and arrive home the same woman she had been when she left: a matron who dearly loved her husband, led a far more interesting life than most of her sex, and had no idea how consuming the love between a man and a woman could be, only that she had missed something, wanted a deeper fusion and a more complete release than the controlled and cordial intimacy she had with Paul.

"But I never thought it would be like this," she sighed again.

Rooney put her head in at the door. "Is there anything more, Mrs. Paul? I'm ready to close the trunk."

Miranda, startled, dropped her gloves and Rooney came to retrieve them. "Are you all right, ma'am?" she inquired anxiously, noticing Miranda's trembling hands.

Cynthia spoke from the doorway. "Why, Aunt Miranda, I do believe you're nervous about seeing Uncle Paul after so many months apart." The girl leaned against the jamb wearing a deep blue serge travel costume with a matching hat that framed her exquisite face and darkened her eyes to sapphire. "I think it's hilaricus, an old married woman in love."

Miranda stood. "I can still feel the ship moving."

"You'll have to get your land legs back," Cynthia said pointedly.

Miranda took a last look around the cabin, ostensibly checking for belongings but desperately trying to find any remnants of passion that still lingered, as if she might gather them up and take them with her. "There's nothing," she said at last. "Shall we go?"

Leaving the baggage for the stewards and the baggage master to remove and have placed aboard the boat train to London, the two ladies and their maids stepped into the corridor. The atmosphere of the ship had changed, as if the *Sylvania* took exception to being tethered to land and wanted to be back on the high seas for which she had been created.

The sounds—people talking, stewards shifting trunks, stewardesses beginning to turn out deserted suites—were strangely hollow with all the cabin doors and exits open. The passengers moved hesitantly back to land, leaving the romance and magic of the ship behind, exchanging promises to contact people they would never see again.

The Cunningham group stopped at Kitt's cabin. "Ready?" Cynthia called.

"Not quite," Kitt called back. "I'll be a few more minutes."

"We'll look for you on the pier, then," Cynthia said. "We mustn't keep Uncle Paul waiting."

The Cunninghams and their maids continued on their way.

"I don't know why she doesn't have a maid," Cynthia said. "I know she can afford one."

Aware of the two maids just behind them, Miranda made herself reply normally even as she marveled at Cynthia's talent for dissembling—and her own. For two days they had not exchanged a friendly word in private but had contrived to behave with their former affection in public.

"Some women abhor any kind of dependence," Miranda said. "Even on another woman."

"I'm sure Kitt is not as independent as she pretends," Cynthia said.

"I suspect that *you* are more independent than she."

"Hardly!"

"You can have no idea just how free you want to be until you marry," Miranda replied, thinking, *especially if you were to marry Walford, the little beast.* She knew she must find a way to prevent such a marriage, but right now she had more immediate problems. Walford danced attendance but did not hint at marriage. Perhaps he never would.

Cynthia decided to ignore her aunt's cryptic remark and now they were on the deck where a queue of passengers waited to trickle down the gangway. Miranda and Cynthia went to the rail to wait, searching for one familiar countenance in a mass of upturned faces that from their vantage point resembled a collection of multicolored buttons. Both of them were aware that Steven James was on the deck somewhere, but neither of them looked for him.

After a few moments Cynthia waved excitedly. "There's Uncle Paul!"

Miranda, following her niece's direction, found Paul's dear, familiar face and felt queasy with remorse. It deepened into mortification when she saw her son standing beside him.

———— · ————

"I'm so sorry to be late," Alton said, hurrying into Kitt's cabin. "There was a gentleman took sick sudden like and I had to fetch the doctor." She looked around and smiled self-consciously. "But you've done all the packing yourself."

"I guessed you were busy," Kitt said. "I'm just doing my hair, but I'm very much out of practice, thanks to you."

"Not to worry, I'll have you ready in a wink." She followed Kitt to the dressing table and pressed her gently down onto the bench with the almost maternal air she had developed toward Kitt. She took a brush from the open vanity case and began to wield it expertly.

"I can't believe it's over," Kitt said. "I never saw a week go by so quickly, and yet it seems longer than that since I came aboard.''

Alton nodded. ''For me as well.'' She rolled a section of hair and pinned it securely in place, then started on the next. ''I'll miss you, ma'am.'' She tried to say it mechanically, but it conveyed everything she felt.

Kitt reached up to pat her hand. ''We've promised to write regularly and I'll let you know where I'm going when I leave London.''

She had grown very fond of this girl. Mary Frances Alton was straight as an arrow, as Sam McAllister had been. Alton knew what she wanted and she went about getting it in the most expeditious way she could find. Kitt admired those qualities without realizing they were hers as well.

''Ah, Miss Kitt, you'll never have time for writing to the likes of me. Will you?'' the girl asked wistfully, brushing and pinning.

It was her way of preparing for disappointment, and it touched Kitt profoundly. It was the same ploy Kitt had used since she became aware that she did not conform to contemporary standards of feminine beauty and behavior and must resign herself to a solitary life. If she had no expectations, she would not be disappointed. But Steven James had weakened her resignation and her defenses considerably.

''You'll see,'' she reassured Alton. ''You'll have a letter when you return from your next crossing.'' Kitt turned her head to admire her hair. ''Thank you. That's perfect.'' She reached for her hat, so overcome with anticipation of the cab ride to the hotel that she suddenly confided, ''Senator James will escort me to Brown's when we arrive in London.''

Alton, who had been packing the brush, stopped abruptly. ''You don't mean he's staying at your hotel, miss!''

''Why, yes.'' Kitt smiled, thinking how cleverly she had managed that.

''Mother of God!''

Kitt turned at the sound of Alton's voice. "It was purely coincidence," she said, but her cheeks felt hot because that was untrue.
The stewardess, pale and shaken, looked ill. "What's wrong?" Kitt
asked.

Alton covered her face with her hands. "Nothing," she said. "I
had a bad turn is all."

Kitt turned back to the mirror, the shaken Alton still visible by
reflection. "I want you to tell me why this matter of the hotel upsets
you," Kitt said firmly.

"You'll never believe me. You'll say it's not true."

"I know you'll be telling me what you believe is the truth." Kitt
waited for a few seconds. "Mary Frances," she said gently. "I must
leave. If you have anything to tell me, tell me now." She began to
draw on her gloves.

Mary Frances nodded, turning her head away. "I've seen that
man going into Mrs. Cunningham's bedroom late at night."

Kitt gasped. She clasped her hands together firmly but she could
not control the trembling of her body or the knot in her stomach.

"It must have been someone else!" she said finally. But something in her knew it had not been someone else.

"It was himself," Mary Frances asserted. "I'm certain sure! I saw
him once by accident, coming late off my shift. Then I watched for
him and I saw him twice more. He had a key to her bedroom
door." Mary Frances looked angry. "I'd know him anywhere! But
I'm in his debt so I didn't let on, not even to you. And I liked *her* so
much! I couldn't believe it until I heard them . . ." Her voice
trailed off. "But I can't let you . . . admire him when he'll probably be coming after you next!"

Kitt was silent, choked as much by humiliation as by heartache.
He had been so attentive on the last days of the voyage! They had
never been alone again as they had on those two unforgettable occasions—the day they sailed and the afternoon they spent talking together—because Cynthia had stuck to Kitt like a barnacle and Lord
Walford to Cynthia and, during the last two days, Lady Burdon and

the count had joined them. But during the hours that Steven—it was how she thought of him—had spent with them, he had seemed to prefer Kitt's company to Cynthia's.

But of course! Kitt realized suddenly. He couldn't pay court to Cynthia when he was her aunt's lover! He would probably get around to Cynthia now that he was finishing with Miranda. This man whom Kitt so loved and respected thought nothing of seducing married women; why would he stop at innocent girls?

Unless it was Miranda who had seduced *him!*

Miranda was not the kind, admirable lady that she seemed! She could have used his loss and loneliness to prey upon him. Miranda could speak affectionately of her husband while she seduced another man! Was that possible?

But Kitt remembered how the two of them had talked and laughed and danced together and knew that it was not only possible but true.

And Miranda was so much older than he was! The whole thing was intolerably sordid.

How could Kitt possibly face either of them, knowing what she knew? The hansom cab ride to Brown's, so eagerly anticipated, was a horrifying prospect now. But Kitt swore he would never suspect what she knew or how she felt about it. It was the consensus, after all, that it was the nature of men to be tempted, that it was a virtuous woman's duty to avoid tempting them.

Kitt shivered.

"Please don't cry, Miss Kitt," Alton begged, dabbing at her own wet cheeks with a handkerchief.

"I'm not crying."

"I'm sorry I told you."

"Don't be!" Kitt said. "You did the right thing. You're a good friend, Mary Frances Alton."

"He mustn't know you know. Least said, soonest mended."

Kitt nodded, quaking inwardly. She would have given a great deal to stay in this cabin forever and sail the seas without hope—in

her case, fear—of ever going ashore, like the blasphemous captain of
the *Flying Dutchman*.

Kitt was not guilty of blasphemy, but she had done something
just as dangerous. She had dared to believe that she, an unremarkable
woman with the wrong kind of hair, not enough bosom, and an
intellectual bent, had the same chance at happiness as girls who were
born beautiful enough to beguile men, whose ignorance of so
much—history, science, art, and the facts of life—made them so
attractive to the opposite sex.

Their ignorance was meant to inflate the male ego, but it required an air of helplessness and a stifling of self. Kitt could not
pretend to be helpless and would have choked trying to swallow her
intelligence.

And yet she would have done all of that for Steven James.

Fool! she told herself. Intelligent as she was supposed to be, she
hadn't remembered that even the Constitution of the United States
did not guarantee happiness, only the pursuit of it. And she had
gone in headlong pursuit of what looked like sheer ecstasy.

For seven days she had longed for Steven James, dreamed of him,
indulged in wild fantasies of making love with him. And all the
while he had been in bed with a married woman who drew men
effortlessly, a woman who appeared to be the essence of respectabil-
ity while she was cuckolding her husband on those long afternoons
when she said she was napping and her lover said he was attending to
business in his cabin!

It's your own fault, Kitt told herself. She had wanted to believe
that if a woman loved a man as much as she loved Steven James, he
would eventually love her back. But loving was no guarantee of
being loved. Only charmed people like Cynthia and Alastair could
take it for granted.

She rose and took Alton's hand. "It's time," she said, her voice
unsteady. She took an envelope out of her reticule and handed it to
the girl. "This can't begin to thank you for everything. Write to
me."

It was all she could manage to say. She snatched up her vanity case and fled.

———— . ————

"I see her!" Price said. "And she saw us, I know she did." He wondered why his mother hadn't waved back. Then he saw that she was moving to the gangway in her hurry to reach him.

"She's so beautiful," he murmured to his father.

Paul agreed, watching while her tall figure descended the gangway. His love for her and his pride in her were swiftly followed by a stirring of desire so strong, it unsettled him. Months of celibacy in the desert had left him embarrassingly needy, but he thought he had taken care of that during several visits to one of London's best brothels just before Price arrived.

He hadn't been sure he could control his lust with Miranda, and he hadn't wanted to offend or frighten her; he was responsible for her welfare and her happiness. His restraint throughout twenty years of marriage was part of that responsibility. His regular visits to brothels insured his restraint.

He strode to the bottom of the gangway to meet her. "Miranda!" he said, taking her hands. He would have kissed her, but such displays in public were unseemly and he was somewhat surprised when she threw her arms around him and pressed her cheek to his. He could not see her face, but her perfume and her own warm scent only increased his desire.

"Paul," she whispered. "Oh, Paul!" She sounded sad rather than happy, but she was hugging Price before he could read the expression in her eyes.

Paul turned to Cynthia. "Hello, my beauty," he said, touching her cheek. "Was it a smooth crossing?"

Conversation soon became difficult in the confusion on the pier. Cynthia had to shout to make herself heard when Kitt stepped off the gangway and seemed about to pass them by. Cynthia swooped down on her, brought her into the family circle, and introduced her to Paul and Price.

Is everyone in this family beautiful? Kitt wondered as she met the father and son. Miranda had always spoken very highly of her husband. Why on earth wouldn't she be content with such a man? Why had she cuckolded him with a casual acquaintance?

Paul Cunningham was insisting that having crossed the Atlantic with Miranda and Cynthia, Kitt must travel up to London with them. She could find no reason to refuse him, until the appearance of the elegant Count d'Yveine with Lady Burdon on his arm. Kitt liked Lady Burdon's somewhat jaundiced view of the world, but the count's admiration was beginning to make her uncomfortable. Still, his attentions to her, an embarrassment just yesterday, seemed like a gift from the gods today.

"I promised the count I'd keep him company en route to London," Kitt told Cynthia.

"And so you shall," Cynthia cooed. "Lady Burdon and Monsieur le Comte will join us. And there is Lord Walford." She fluttered her handkerchief, beckoning the young man whom she presented to her uncle and her cousin before turning to him.

"Walford, I'm sure you don't want to travel up to London in the solitary splendor of your private railway car," she said, her lovely face wreathed in smiles. "You must come with us."

"Nonsense," Alastair replied. "We'd have to visit back and forth between compartments. You shall all come with me."

With the innocent enthusiasm of youth, Cynthia accepted for all of them and went on to gather up the three Wendalls, pointedly ignoring Eberhardt and the Seeleys, while Kitt marveled at how this apparently docile girl organized everyone to suit herself. She glanced at the count and Lady Burdon standing beside her and saw that they were watching Cynthia too.

The count smiled. "Remarkable, isn't she?"

"An example to us all," Lady Burdon said in her cryptic fashion that could mean sincerity or sarcasm. "She's swept us into Walford's basket like posies from the garden path."

Kitt was surprised that they had noticed Cynthia's manipulative talents. Most people, rendered breathless by Miss Cunningham's face, figure, fortune, and flair, did not. For some reason their inadvertent support was comforting.

But Kitt's comfort was short-lived. Cynthia had now thrown her gossamer net over Steven James and was hauling him in like a prize catch to meet her uncle. Kitt was not close enough to hear them, but she could see Steven trying not to join them—and failing. He did not look at Miranda beyond a brief greeting, after which Miranda resumed talking to her son.

I'll never get through this, Kitt thought in a panic.

But she knew she must and, once she had, find some clever way to avoid Steven's escort from the station to Brown's Hotel as well. She managed to sit between the count and Lady Burdon in Lord Walford's luxurious railway car, almost Byzantine in its gold leaf and red damask and cut-velvet decor, but she found it difficult to speak. It was one of the few occasions in her life that this had happened to her.

Fortunately, both her titled companions had an inexhaustible fund of gossip to exchange, and she pretended to listen quietly as befitted her age and station—whatever that last was. She had been so sure of it before boarding the *Sylvania.*

Why should love rob a woman of her wits as well as her poise?

As the journey continued, Kitt was aware that Paul Cunningham was sitting with Steven while Cynthia beamed contentedly upon them from where she was, flanked by Alastair and Lewis Wendall and across from the senior Wendalls. Miranda remained engrossed in her son. Kitt thought it was a way to avoid joining her husband while he was with Senator James.

How can she bear to watch them talking together? Kitt wondered. *How can she?*

"This is so very cozy," Lady Burdon announced to everyone as they were nearing London, "that I shall invite you all to dinner in St. John's Wood."

"Formidable," the count said. "You have the best cook in London."

"I'll order the cards tomorrow morning to be sure we meet before some of us drift away upon our travels." Lady Burdon turned to Kitt and spoke more quietly. "How long will you be in London, my dear?"

"I have no definite departure date as yet, Milady," Kitt said, and repeated the tale she had told Cynthia about legalities regarding her father's estate.

"You must feel free to come to me on my Thursday evenings," Lady Burdon said. "And to ring me as often as you like if you want to come round at another time. St. John's Wood is not so very far from Brown's." She smiled at Kitt affectionately. "Allow me the pleasure of taking you there in my carriage today. It's right on my way."

Kitt felt weak with relief. "That would be so very kind," she said. Then she frowned. "The senator did speak of accompanying me, but that was during our first day at sea and I expect he's forgotten."

"Never mind, I shall insist upon taking you—unless, of course, you prefer the senator's company."

"I would prefer to go with you, Lady Burdon."

Lady Burdon exchanged a swift look with the count that Kitt did not see, and her lips silently formed the words *"she knows!"* The count nodded.

"Then it is all arranged," Lady Burdon said. "When we arrive I shall tell the senator I require your assistance."

Kitt nodded, leaned back and closed her eyes. "I don't know

why I'm so tired," she murmured. The other two glanced at each other again and went on talking.

Steven could not remember when he had felt so uncomfortable. It was difficult for him to make polite conversation with Miranda's husband.

To complicate matters, he realized as the moments lengthened that Paul Cunningham was a likable man. To sit there and chat idly with him made Steven feel like a fraud. But the thought of Paul with Miranda made him insanely jealous and conscience was no match for jealousy.

He wanted to turn to Paul and say, "I'm in love with your wife and she's in love with me. We belong together. Let her go. Let me take care of her."

The two men never should have met—and if that could not be avoided, they should have been talking honestly about the cruel and clever traps destiny scatters in our paths to make us regret equally the things we do and those we do not.

Had Steven met this man first, his affair with Miranda might never have taken place. He really liked Paul Cunningham! Steven's association with Haggerty had not entirely stripped him of scruples. Sitting with Cunningham on the train to London, he could almost wish that the interlude aboard ship had never taken place—and if he felt that, so must Miranda. But it hurt to think she might have any regrets.

Don't blame her, Steven wanted to say to Paul. *Don't blame either of us. We didn't mean it to happen. It has nothing to do with you.*

As it was, the two men were talking about the state senate, and the impersonal subject helped to mask the tension Steven felt. He ardently hoped that Cunningham would not sense it.

"It makes it more of a challenge that I'm not in the good graces of my colleagues," Steven said. "I got in through appointment while they had to win at the ballot box."

"Is the wrangle over tariffs still going on?" Paul asked.

Steven nodded. "We don't make such policy in the state senate, but we help to influence it. I'm against high tariffs."

Paul considered that before he replied. "But aren't we far safer with protective tariffs?"

Steven disagreed. "A nation that doesn't trade with other nations will never be a world power. Nor will a nation struggling to invent itself succeed if it's hidden behind the protective walls of the Monroe Doctrine *and* prohibitive trade barriers."

"You have me there," Paul said. "Frankly, I don't know very much about finance or politics. I can't imagine devoting my life to finance, although I can see where politics might be a tremendous force for change." He glanced at Steven. "It's disturbing that sometimes the country's future can hang upon the integrity of a few politicians who are, after all, only human."

"Integrity is a great variable, I agree." Steven was flustered to be discussing integrity with a man who personified it. "But I'm encouraged that you don't believe we're *all* hopelessly corrupt!"

"Hardly!" Paul smiled back, and his sculptured good looks took on added warmth. "Generalities are generally dangerous."

"So you'd rather devote yourself to ancient history."

Cunningham nodded. "I often think I would have been far more comfortable in some other era long past, that because of an error in nature's calendar I was born out of my time."

It was the same error that would have kept Steven and Miranda from marrying even had they met earlier! It was unsettling to discover that he shared something else with her husband, the sense of being out of his time.

"I don't know the least thing about ancient Egypt," Steven said, trying to make Cunningham talk about his chosen field. "Isn't it macabre to unwrap a mummy?" he asked, shaking his head. "I confess the idea turns my stomach."

"The ancient Egyptians knew how to prepare a body for the afterlife."

"The afterlife?"

"They believed that life went on, even if in a different way or on a different plane, that death was merely a passage to another life. That's why they preserved the dead and provided them with grain and oil and their favorite possessions for the journey."

"It's a comforting belief. Still, digging up the dead cannot be a pleasant experience."

"They're like aged parchment, nothing worse. As a matter of interest, there was a booming market in mummy flesh as early as the thirteenth century. Europeans paid fortunes for bits of it."

"What in heaven's name did they want it for?"

"Longevity, I'd say. They reasoned that whatever had preserved those bodies in death would keep their own bodies longer in life— even cure disease. It resembled a substance called pissasphalt which had long been used as a curative."

"What did they do with the mummy flesh?"

"They ate it."

"Good God!" Steven said with an involuntary shudder. "That's revolting."

Paul shrugged. "It's a concept as old as humanity. Savages eat the hearts of lions to partake of the lions' courage and strength. In Spain men still eat the sex glands of brave bulls to share their virility. And all over the world Catholics partake of Christ's body in the sacrament of the Eucharist in order to be one with God." He smiled briefly. "A noble aspiration, but as far-fetched as eating bull testicles."

"I gather that you are not conventionally religious," Steven said.

"The study of antiquity has made me unconventional—but perhaps more religious. Like the French, I believe but do not practice."

"On balance," Steven said after a moment's silence, "I prefer politics and finance."

"I've already confessed to a great ignorance of both subjects."

"And you a Cunningham!" Steven grinned.

"My brothers think I'm some kind of changeling," Paul said.

"So do mine. They're farmers born and bred. They revere nature. I suppose you could say that's *their* religion. I'm the only rene-
gade in the lot."

He refused Cunningham's offer of a cigar but took out his pipe
as the two men walked to the platform at the end of the carriage and
went outside to smoke. The only people in the car who did not
notice their departure were Mr. and Mrs. Wendall.

Sixteen

A uniformed official from the Bristol waited at the railway station to collect the Cunninghams and escort them to their carriage. Thanks to Price, the atmosphere in the carriage was not as tense as Miranda had anticipated, but she was infuriated when Cynthia began to maneuver Paul as cleverly as any concubine would have done.

First she sat leaning against him like a wilted violet until he noticed her distress. It was amazing how easily the brightest of men—and Paul was certainly that—were blind to the wiles of a beautiful girl.

"Why so sad, my pet?" he asked Cynthia right on cue. She raised her huge cornflower-blue eyes with their fringe of luxuriant lashes to his.

"I'm in love, Uncle Paul," Cynthia began with a tremulous smile for her uncle and a quick sidelong glance at her aunt.

"Again?" Price teased. "It must be His Lordship."

"I've never been in love before, not like this," Cynthia told her cousin with dignity, her blue eyes beginning to mist. "And it isn't Walford. Aunt Miranda accomplished her mission. I've met the man

I'm going to marry and I'll accept him the minute he proposes to me."

"Then what's there to moan about?" Price asked impatiently.

"Who is this man?" Paul was very attentive now.

"Senator Steven James," Cynthia said.

As if she were announcing the Second Coming, Miranda thought.

Paul's expression changed. "Come now, my dear," he chided his niece, "you can't agree to marry a man you've known for only a week."

"What has time to do with love?" Cynthia put her head on Paul's shoulder and began to sob quietly.

"A great deal when you're choosing for a lifetime," Paul said. "Senator James is very attractive, I grant you that, and I enjoyed his company, but charm is not a solid basis for marriage."

Price shook his head. "Girls," he said.

Paul looked at his wife as if waiting for an explanation.

Miranda shrugged. "I couldn't keep her locked in her stateroom. These things happen, especially to girls her age."

"They happen to people of all ages," Cynthia wailed, warning Miranda again.

Paul hushed his niece. "I cannot allow you to make a fool of yourself, Cynthia. Let me find out more about this man, what qualities he has other than his natural appeal, before this goes any further." Paul took out his handkerchief and patted her cheeks. "Now, stop crying, there's a good girl, and have a look at London."

They arrived at the Bristol with barely enough time to bathe and change for dinner in the hotel's formal dining room. They were a striking quartet: the man and the boy so handsome, the woman exotic and elegant, and the girl with her dazzling, fresh beauty.

Miranda made them all laugh with her descriptions of some of the people they had met aboard ship and Cynthia soon stopped sighing and joined in. After coffee in the lounge, Price took his cousin out for a stroll and Miranda and Paul smiled at each other.

"Sometimes I forget how very beautiful you are," Paul said, caressing her with his eyes.

"I missed you too," Miranda said. She was completely sincere—he was a lovable man and she enjoyed his company. But now she felt as if the deepest reaches of herself belonged to someone else. She looked for a more manageable subject than the one that preoccupied her.

"What shall we do about Cynthia?" she asked.

"Keep her close until I know more about the senator. Coincidentally I had a letter from Hobart by the mail packet. He knew Senator James was aboard the *Sylvania* and wanted me to contact him here in London because he's knowledgeable about utilities and—which is perhaps more important—he's Augustus Haggerty's son-in-law and therefore knowledgeable about many other things. It's a fluke that Cynthia should think she's in love with him."

"A farmer's son in league with Haggerty is not the kind of connection Hobart wants for Cynthia," Miranda reminded him. "Otherwise he could have married her off long since to any number of wealthy upstarts."

"It remains to be seen if Senator James is a swindler or was merely related to one by marriage and has delayed breaking the ties out of compassion for Haggerty's bereavement. I'm planning to dine with the senator on business. I'll see what I can discover about him."

She realized that Paul was pleased to be entrusted with such a mission by his arrogant brother, that for his aged father's sake Paul wanted to make himself useful to the company, provided doing so did not interfere with his personal agenda. It struck her for the first time that nothing had ever been permitted to interfere with Paul's agenda. He arranged his life to suit himself and convinced everyone else that they agreed with him. No one minded, least of all Miranda: Paul was such a delight to know, to live with, to look at.

Miranda hoped Cynthia's infatuation with Steven would soon be over, that it would not lead to frequent contact between her

husband and her lover. That could be dangerous and, in ways she did not care to examine, offensive.

Sex was such an awkward process! Surely the Almighty could have come up with a better arrangement! How could such a ridiculous business inflame the senses and ignite the heart? Lovemaking was ludicrous, but Lady Burdon was right: "Oh, how it was sweet!"

Miranda had no idea how—or if—she would respond when she and Paul were alone that night. She was not a qualified Jezebel. Intimacy with two men in the same week flew in the face of every value ingrained in her by family, society, religion, and her own meticulous nature.

She could tell Paul she was tired after the journey from Liverpool, that she had a headache. But that would only put off the inevitable.

Yet she managed to talk companionably with her husband while she wrestled with her conscience, while she wondered fervently what he and Steven had found to say to each other in Walford's luxurious railway car.

When Cynthia and Price returned from their walk, all four Cunninghams went upstairs to their suite of four bedrooms and a salon, furnished in a style that recalled Hobart's overdecorated drawing room without the personal gewgaws. They said good night in the salon.

What am I going to do? Miranda was thinking as Rooney helped her to undress and prepare for bed while Paul went to his bedroom to change.

She could not refuse him. There was no valid reason to refuse without telling him why.

And she could never bring herself to tell him why.

But she had changed so much and Paul was a perceptive man and might sense it anyway. There was a second woman in her, recently released, a woman she still did not know and could not yet control.

———— • ————

Paul, waiting impatiently for Miranda's maid to leave, had never experienced this overwhelming meld of love and desire before. Even on their honeymoon he had curbed the force of his passion for her.

"You mustn't jump on the girl as if you were Attila the Hun," his father had warned him before the wedding. "Miranda looks like a woman, but she's still an innocent girl, so you will be polite and save your acrobatics for the kind of women who appreciate them."

Then and ever since, Paul had disciplined himself to be very gentle and tender with his wife; he kept under rigid control his desire to explore her luscious body more completely, to go beyond the limitations of acceptable marital relations. The conventional wisdom restricted a gentleman to modest caresses of his nightgowned wife, followed by a discreet raising of her gown and then by penetration and consummation in the missionary position.

The whole thing was to be accomplished as quickly as possible and with as little embarrassment to her as could be managed. Ardor, that sloppy business, along with its lickings and snufflings in the dark, its grunts and groans of lust and climax, were better left to domestics and laborers or to the decadent rich and painfully poor who neither toiled nor spun but found diversion in vice. A man could easily buy the kind of woman who would let him satisfy his more animal cravings.

Tonight Paul's hunger for his wife was all the more amazing because they had been married for twenty years. Her body was familiar to him, but tonight he was as eager as if he had never possessed her before. That troubled him: He was not of a turbulent nature.

He was content to lead a quiet, scholarly life far from the madding crowd. He believed in the seventeenth-century credo that man was a noble savage, that pure womankind existed to calm his primitive side and impure women to absorb what could not be calmed, and that the ills of mankind were curable by a social contract among people and the state based upon the Bible and good conscience.

And yet he sat there, priapic and almost panting for coitus with his wife! As soon as he heard the maid leave he knocked on the communicating door.

"Come in," she called softly. She was already in bed. He turned his back to hide his erection while he took off his robe, then sat down on his side of the four-poster.

"Are you tired, darling?" he asked.

"No," she said.

He got under the covers beside her and put his arms around her. Her satiny skin and fresh scent excited him even more. He turned her face up to his and kissed her ardently, his tongue exploring her mouth, his lips nibbling hers.

There was an urgency in him she had not sensed since their honeymoon, but then he had been controlled about it and now he was not. His insistent mouth on hers aroused her. And the way he held her, as if he could not get close enough. She was drenched in desire, his and hers, and when his hand went under her gown and touched her breasts, she felt herself falling into the maelstrom of sexual desire.

Lie quietly, she warned herself. *Be the way you always are with him.*

"I want you," he whispered, and everything changed between them.

He had never kissed her with such hot desire, never pulled off her nightgown and tongued her nipples until they were rigid, never touched her intimately, sighing with pleasure at the silkiness of her. She did not pull away from him. She could not.

He was too eager to be astonished when "here," she said, "here," and showed him where his touch excited her. Soon her breath came in little moans of rapture and her body arched and trembled with pleasure.

He did not wonder what had provoked such sudden heat in him, or her unbridled response to it. This was not the time—the time might never come—to perceive that there was something smoldering in *her* that had set him on fire and not the other way around. He was swept away by her sensuality. He was beyond thought.

He went more deeply inside her and her hips rose and circled to his rhythm. It was then that he felt, for the first time from her, that long shudder that happened so rarely in women and then usually in the kind who were paid to pretend it. A wave of power surged through him, erupted from him, and he felt for a split second that he would die—willingly—of sheer delight.

They slept afterward, too amazed to talk about it.

When Miranda woke the next morning, Paul was not beside her. She could hear him in his own room and wished he had stayed with her, that she could have wakened in his arms. She lay between the soft linen sheets and tried to think clearly.

It puzzled her that their marriage had been so successful without deep sensuality on either side when, as had now become obvious, they were both sensual people! She wanted to talk to him about that. She wondered if he had ever let loose that side of himself before last night. She wondered if he had a mistress and the thought of it was painful. He was *her* husband, *hers*!

She rolled over and lay there looking at the brocade canopy over the bed. Last night she had intended to be the same wife he knew, to behave in bed as she always had done. But she was no longer the wife he knew. Once started on that sublime ascent, she could not make herself stop short of the summit. She could not lie there quietly and submit.

She felt like an actress dominated by the character she had brought to life. The other woman had taken over and she could not quiet the rocking of her hips, the sounds she made, the way she held him and touched him and responded when he stroked her. She could not stop until she got to that place where his kisses and caresses had promised to take her so many times before and never had.

Most frightening of all, she was not sure whether, last night, she had reached it with Paul or Steven in her mind. Perhaps she had betrayed them both.

Paul opened the door slowly. "Ah, you're awake," he said. "Coffee's just arrived."

He came to take her hand and bent to kiss her, stroking her hair as he always did in the morning. But he was avoiding her eyes. She sensed that he was embarrassed by their abandon the night before, that he preferred not to mention it. But there had been nothing shameful in it! The only shame was in her betrayal of him, and he knew nothing about that.

They had their coffee, she propped on pillows in lace-trimmed slips piled behind her in bed, he sitting by her side with a newspaper as a shield between them.

For a moment she was keenly disappointed that they had made passionate love for the first time in twenty years of marriage and were still too embarrassed by it, too enslaved by convention, too distant from each other to acknowledge and enjoy it.

But if it's acknowledged, she reminded herself, *it might have to be explained. He might suspect what happened, he might insist that I tell him.*

She thought suddenly of her sons and knew she and Paul could never talk about it. Spoken words, hanging in the air, risked discovery, and Miranda knew she would rather die than have her children discover what she had done.

And she could not face telling Paul. Nor could she say that she had suffered a temporary madness that was over now. That would have been another lie: if she never saw Steven James again, it would not be over. He was what she would recall of passion for the rest of her life.

More than that, Steven had restored her youth in a mere few days. She had been like a house shuttered up and aging, and he had opened the shutters and let the sunlight in.

Instinct told her that sooner or later Paul would guess how she had learned what she knew, what she wanted. But he would never confront her because he could not bear to know the answer.

So it was a mutual decision, even though unspoken. It sprang from a warning in the marrow of their bones that to speak of it would be to destroy their marriage, and marriage was no idle episode. It was a sacrament, a solemn pledge, the linchpin of society. It was for life.

"Where would you like to go today?" he asked, putting aside the paper and reaching for his pipe.

"I hadn't even thought about it."

"It's a lovely day," he said, lighting up. "I thought we might all drive out to the country and lunch there." The tendrils of aromatic smoke reached from him to her.

"I'd like that," she said, slipping easily into their habit of leaving certain things unsaid. "I'll have my bath and be dressed by—when?" She glanced at the small carriage clock her maid had placed on the bedside table. "Ten."

He kissed her lips and left her to her morning rituals but not before she felt in his kiss that today would be charged with expectation of what the night would bring.

———— • ————

"One of the main differences . . ." Lady Burdon announced, sipping tea from a porcelain cup between phrases, "between the Yankees and ourselves is that American millionaires work. The Sloanes go to their store . . . the Vanderbilts go to their New York Central offices."

She leaned forward to let the count light a mild cheroot for her, the first of the three she smoked each day. They were seated before an open fire in the morning room of her mansion in St. John's Wood. There were traces of a hearty breakfast on the cloth-draped

table between them: eggs, bacon, kippers, cheeses, fresh butter, pre-serves, a variety of hot buns and breads and biscuits, and a Georgian silver teapot on its oval tray, flanked by matching sugar bowl, spoons, and creamer.

Lady Pat, as her friends called her, found her morning room more inviting than the vast rooms where her guests gathered. Its ceilings were as high, its dimensions as perfect, but it was not fashionably paneled and accoutered with dark wood and plush.

The colors in this room were her favorites: grass green and white with touches of coral and turquoise in the pillows and the fringe on the draperies. The two wing chairs they sat in were softly cushioned and covered with green silk brocade, not the stiff, slippery horsehair the past century had favored; the lamps and mirrors were carefully placed, the shades chosen to create a sunny glow no matter how gray the weather beyond the draperies might be.

"And what are your latest conclusions about European aristoc-racy?" Jean-Baptiste asked, vastly amused, as always, by her conversa-tion.

Lady Burdon made a ritual of preparing two more cups of tea before she answered. Her houseguest, she reflected as she passed him his cup, looked at least a decade younger than his forty-odd years. He was nattily attired, as always, and his cheeks had a healthy glow after a brisk, early morning walk.

No amount of expensive tailoring, fine leather boots, or perfect manners could make him as handsome as Alastair or as charismatic as Senator James, but he had an attractive face and a charming manner. His kindness shone from his eyes. He reminded her of her second husband, the one man she had truly loved among three spouses and a score of lovers between marriages.

Intellect shone out of the count like the aurora borealis, and Lady Pat was sure that at the end of the day it would win Miss McAllister, in whom the baroness had taken greater interest since their arrival in London a week before.

Settling back in her chair, she answered his question. "European aristocracy spends most of its time fornicating with its friends' spouses or murdering various species of wildlife, depending upon the season."

He chuckled. "Surely you don't disapprove of lovemaking, Patricia."

They looked at each other and smiled, she recalling a few weeks in her forties and he her kindness to a virile but virginal Jean-Baptiste still in his teens. They were friends now, but the memory of that encounter still warmed them both.

"Hardly," she replied. "although 'the position is ridiculous and the pleasure transitory.' But I did not mean love. I meant fornication for its own sake—which is a horse of quite another color—together with blood sports pursued as a way to pass the time."

"For an earl's daughter, you take a dim view of us."

"Deservedly so. We've been the most pampered and privileged people since the fall of Rome and, as a result, we've had the time to become the most cultivated. But we're sliding rapidly downhill because the vigor fostered by work has been weakened by generations of inherited wealth."

"Really, *ma chère*! People have been predicting the demise of the aristocracy for centuries and it has yet to crumble. Ordinary people want kings. Not too long after beheading Louis XVI we French crowned an emperor! George Washington was invited to be king of the colonies that had just fought a war against the very idea of monarchy. So much for democracy."

She tilted her head like a wise old bird. "Probably because humankind is totally unready for democracy. Men are far too selfish, vindictive, and violent to govern themselves."

"On that last I agree. But rest assured that no matter what happens in America, democracy hasn't got a chance in Europe. Traditions run far too deep."

"Ours date back to the Magna Charta, but you French are a politically unstable lot," she said with a twinkle. "Every time a gov-

ernment falls, the Parisians take to the barricades. As for the Germans, they still worship trees and believe in Valhalla."

"And you British believe that when he is needed, King Arthur will return from Avalon!"

She nodded. "Probably carrying the Round Table."

"But I'll warrant that the monarchies will be alive and well when the year 2000 arrives," he said.

"When it does, we'll have Charon row us back across the Styx from the land of the dead to have a look. We'll see then which of us was right."

They finished their tea and sat in companionable silence for a few moments until the count asked, "How would you cure this lamentable decline of the aristocracy?"

"New blood."

He recrossed his legs and waited for her to elaborate.

"We're inbred," she said. "The best families have been intermarrying for centuries. We're losing our vitality. Look at Walford!"

"There's nothing wrong with Walford that life won't soon cure," he said.

She harrumphed. "He dabbles in opium and bisexuality, looking for thrills. He's like Dorian Gray!"

The count shook his head. "Youthful high jinks," he said. "For that you may blame his father's refusal to let him *do* something. The young fellow's got a good grasp of world affairs. He ought to go into politics."

"I agree that our young lords should go to work," Lady Burdon said, nodding her head vigorously. "But does he? No! He's off in search of an heiress."

"First things first, my dear. His family needs money desperately. And it appears he's found it done up in an attractive package."

"Jean-Baptiste, we've agreed that Miss Cynthia doesn't give a rap for him—and won't until the senator is out of her dreams."

He looked bleak, and Lady Burdon, noticing, went on. "But she is not your concern. The similarly smitten Miss McAllister is. You must woo her until you win her." She cocked her head again, watching him.

Lady Burdon and the count had spent several afternoons and an entire evening in Kitt's company since their arrival in London. Lady Burdon was concerned about Kitt's unhappiness and admired her determination to hide it. But the older woman's experience had proven to her that the only real cure for a woman's unrequited love was to find a man who loved her more.

The count, wreathed in clouds of tobacco smoke, frowned as he answered her question. "You honestly advise me to marry a textile manufacturer's daughter from the wilds of North America? I admit the girl is fascinating, a brilliant scholar with a unique kind of beauty. But my feelings aside, would my family and friends accept her?"

"Do you care?"

He shook his head.

"Well, there you are, then. Fortunately you needn't worry about marrying money, although the girl is comfortable and, I gather, will be more so in several years time."

The count sighed deeply. "She hardly knows I'm alive, much less that I care for her. She's as electric as that gorgeous mane of hers. In many ways she reminds me of you."

"In my salad days." Lady Pat touched her lips with a damask napkin. "I hope yours is not the kind of love that vanishes when gratified!"

"Never!" he said, smiling at her.

She nodded. "I ask because Miss McAllister is a person of value. She is a marvelously spirited young woman and no fool, just the wife for a jaded dilettante like you. She would never bore you to death."

"I appear to bore *her*."

"That's because you seem struck dumb whenever you're near her. It is not an Adonis who will captivate her now, you know; she's

been in love with one of those and been hurt by him. It's kindness and trust and an intellect to match her own. Be patient."

He nodded.

"It's bound to come right," she said, smiling. "All in the fullness of time."

"Time is of the essence," he mused, his eyes on the sculpted ceiling, where nymphs and satyrs gamboled in bas relief, their privy parts draped in streamers of painted silk. "My family keeps reminding me that I owe them an heir."

"Miss McAllister is a healthy woman in her twenties, at a comfortable remove from the grave. If you apply yourself, you can get three children without killing her."

"*Bon Dieu!* Two will suffice if they are boys. I want her as a wife, not a brood mare."

Lady Burdon rose and shook out her skirts. "Then come along. Your future countess is waiting for us at Brown's. We're all three driving to Hampton Court for luncheon."

An exultant smile transformed his face. "And you arranged it! What a wonderful woman you are." He took her hand, bowed over it, and kissed it. Then he followed her out of the morning room, his mood considerably brighter than it had been only moments earlier.

Seventeen

"Wonderful, isn't it?" Kitt said.

They were looking back at Hampton Court, a stately, imposing palace of once rosy-red brick, now darkened by time. They had recrossed the drawbridge and stood beside the Maze that was near the Lion Gate, all of it dwarfed by the soaring parapets.

"My favorite palace," Lady Burdon said.

"Another of the homicidal Henry's trophies," the count added.

"Nonsense, it was a gift from Cardinal Wolsey," Lady Burdon corrected him. "The cardinal didn't have the sense to avoid out-splendoring the king."

"So Hampton Court was—temporarily—a ransom for his priestly head," Kitt said. "What a vicious man Henry the Eighth was."

"This is why the enchantress, Anne Boleyn, haunts this place?"

"No, Count, Anne Boleyn stalks the Tower," Lady Burdon said. "With her head tucked underneath her arm."

"It's the ghost of Catherine Howard in the Haunted Gallery here," Kitt said. "Wife number four, pleading to see the king. She was sure he would spare her, if only she could see him. He had never

been able to resist her, so the old rake wouldn't look her in the eye, but he must have heard her wailing in the corridors of Hampton Court Palace. She was beheaded, but her ghost still pleads for mercy."

"Do you believe in ghosts, Miss McAllister?" the count asked.

"My head doesn't, but my instincts do. Imagine Catherine's terror! It couldn't just evaporate. Why wouldn't some of that colossal woe remain inside the walls that first felt it?"

"I often wonder," the count mused, "why the same is not true of love?"

"What do you mean?" Kitt asked, observing him with fresh interest.

"Only that hauntings are usually associated with violence or anguish or death. I don't know of any castles warmed by the ghosts of great love."

"Probably because love is not stronger than death," Kitt said, "And anguish is."

"You contradict the Song of Songs, my dear," Lady Burdon said. "I believe you are a skeptic."

Kitt smiled suddenly, a neat, quick, abbreviated smile. She knew she was a hopeless romantic. If she gave a different impression to these astute friends, so much the better.

The count admired her flash of a smile. The *dentition* of Americans was *superbe*! It could not be the appalling food they ate, accompanied by gallons of muddy coffee—rather than wine to aid the digestion—so it must be the water. Or perhaps, as Lady Pat insisted, it was the mingling of bloodlines in America that gave its citizens their outrageous vigor, their ever-increasing height, their rude good health.

"Does romance displease you?" he asked Kitt, again admiring her coppery hair and her slim figure. She was tall but as deftly turned as a Frenchwoman.

"Outside of novels, poetry, and operas, it's of questionable significance," she said.

"But what would life be without romance?" he asked in alarm.

"Amusing, intelligent, and untroubled," she returned.

"We must try to convince you otherwise." The count tapped his forehead with a finger as if to awaken inspiration *"Ça y est!* Tomorrow we shall visit the Tower of London and look for Anne Boleyn. She was intelligent *and* passionate."

"And another victim," Lady Burdon clucked. "Like Catherine Howard."

"They both committed adultery," Kitt said rather sharply.

"They were *charged* with it," Lady Burdon replied. "And there are worse crimes."

"Not for a queen," d'Yveine said.

"What are some worse crimes?" Kitt asked.

"An unforgiving heart. A narrow mind." Lady Burdon waved an imperious hand. "But we must stop philosophizing and think about luncheon."

The inn they chose was charming and thoroughly English, as was its cuisine. The menu that day was clear soup, brook trout, roast beef and Yorkshire pudding, followed by a chocolate trifle and a savory. The wines were good and the trio thoroughly enjoyed one another's company.

Kitt's first days alone at Brown's had been utterly miserable. She had tried to argue herself out of her low spirits, as she had done so often in the past, but logic had not worked this time. Being alone in a foreign city had not helped. She had even begun to dream of the embracing walls of home.

She tried visiting museums and found herself drifting and dreaming of Steven. She looked for him at the hotel, but over a week had passed and she had yet to see him. So she had been grateful for the invitations from Lady Burdon—to take tea in St. John's Wood, or to go for a drive, or to visit the shops.

The outings made her feel much better. Lady Burdon was good company; she seemed to have been everywhere and done everything. Her mansion was fabulous and her interests extensive.

"I'm quite certain," Kitt had told Lady Burdon one day as they were riding in the Row, where all of fashionable London turned out to see and be seen, "that you'd have liked my mother and she you."

"Were we so alike?"

"Both beautiful, although my mother didn't have three husbands—or such a salty wit." She had waited while Lady Burdon acknowledged an acquaintance passing in another carriage.

"My mother married for love," she said, "even though her family disowned her for it."

"Fortunately I was not disowned when I did that," the older woman said. "But love is not the best reason for marriage."

"I sometimes feel that I know my mother through her books," Kitt said dreamily, ignoring Lady Pat's last remark. "I made Papa teach me to read when I was four so that I might communicate with her through her favorite books. It was my mother who nurtured my love of reading. Books were my companions, my sword and buckler against life's trials."

And very effective until I met Steven James, she almost added.

She was tempted to confide in Lady Burdon about him. The most worldly woman she had ever met, the lady had taken Kitt under her wing, a welcoming place where interesting people gathered. But it was not easy for Kitt to admit to anyone what a great fool she had been.

The two women were frequently joined in their excursions by Lady Burdon's houseguest, the Count d'Yveine, and Kitt had come to like him more and more. He was very clever; literary allusions did not go over his head. He was a sophisticate but a kindly one and did not seem as self-centered as most men. Even his face with its regular features was more attractive than it had seemed when she first met him. And what she had taken for romantic attention aboard ship, she now realized was simply continental gallantry. Toward Lady Burdon he showed a brotherly affection that was very touching.

All of that was why, over luncheon at Hampton Court, she eagerly agreed to accompany the count and Lady Burdon to the

Tower of London the following day. They were planning their visit, when their animated discussion was interrupted by the Cunningham party's arrival at the same restaurant.

———— • ————

" 'O frabjous day,' " Lady Burdon crooned to d'Yveine that night when the two of them were back in the morning room having cognac and a last smoke in front of the fireplace.

"What kind of day?" the count asked, puzzled.

"One of those marvelous nonsense words from Lewis Carroll," she explained. "And this day has been as *frabjous* as going through the looking glass. That little drama at the restaurant was very revealing."

The count agreed. "The senator's three lady admirers were glacial with one another."

"I wonder if Mr. Cunningham suspects."

The count swirled the golden liquid in his snifter and inhaled the perfume of Napoleon brandy. "I think not. He is besotted with his wife, and a man in that condition doesn't want to have such suspicions."

"Do you suppose his wife and the senator have been meeting in London?"

"Impossible to say, dear lady, without seeing the lovers together. But we shall have the entire cast here on Thursday evening, provided Senator James accepts your invitation."

"He won't refuse. If they aren't meeting, how could he possibly miss the opportunity of seeing her again?"

"And if they are meeting?"

"My answer is the same." After a pause, Lady Burdon resumed. "Mr. Cunningham is a charming man. Handsome too."

"Apparently not enough of either to stop his wife from straying."

"My dear Count, that just shows how little men know about

women. It isn't how men *look* that attracts women. It's something in them that calls to the same thing in us. For men, on the other hand, appearance is all. If a woman is beautiful, she need not be very much more."

"Not at the start, perhaps."

"But it's how love starts that matters! Who cares about how it ends? If it isn't from boredom, it's always some mawkish nonsense or a flagrant *delictum* that's happened countless times before to millions of others."

"It feels like the first time," the count said, "when a *delictum* happens to you." He covered a yawn and rose from his chair. "I'm for bed. Thank you, dear friend, for another delightful day."

He bowed over her hand and withdrew, and she sat on, transfixed by the flames in the fireplace, remembering the first time certain things had happened to her.

————— · —————

Lady Burdon's invitation reached Steven the following day, after he returned from a meeting with Raymond Steele.

During the week just past, Steven had begun trading to recoup some of the losses Gus had arranged. He had purposely drawn on the letter of credit Gus had insisted on giving him; he wanted Gus to know he was up to something.

Raymond Steele had been helpful, providing Steven with pointers for operating in foreign markets and arranging introductions to men who provided venture capital or, for a fee, knew where to get it. They were all gentlemen, although some of more recent vintage than others.

"If the nouveaux riches chafe under Britain's rigid class distinctions," Steven said to Steele one day over lunch at a pub, "they take pains not to show it. More than that, although they live in great comfort, they avoid the opulence of the aristocracy. That, I suppose, is in order not to look pushy."

"Not one of the men you've met is an Augustus Haggerty," Steele said. "He flaunts his wealth."

Steven didn't give a tinker's dam about Haggerty's breeding. He was still furious with Gus.

"He's a diamond in the rough," he replied moderately. "But it's clear that Britons are not as proud of their self-made men as Americans are."

Steele nodded. "Americans have a different standard of success."

"You mean money?" Steven asked, feeling his hackles rise. Steven often criticized his country's shortcomings at home but he had discovered he didn't like to hear anyone do it abroad. "I don't entirely agree," he said. "After all, how much more could I buy with fifty million than with twenty?"

"What's your point?"

"If I had twenty million, I'd keep right on working to make more. Once a man's reached a certain point, it's the challenge of the game that matters—the game, not the candle."

Steele laughed. "But in America it isn't *how* you play the game that matters, it's whether or not you win. On the playing fields of Eton it's the other way round."

"They're not called perfidious Albion for nothing," Steven said. "Britons are just as fond of money as anyone else."

"Agreed. But they have such different ideas. Americans idolize daring and sheer guts more than quiet courage. Americans make heroes of rascals like Haggerty—and social arbiters of tradesmen-turned-gentlefolk, like the Astors."

"Maybe we do, but not all English heroes were King Arthurs. Some of them were possible child murderers like Richard III or lady-killers like Henry VIII. Lancelot cuckolded his dearest friend."

"But Lancelot was French and the French will do anything to needle the English." Steele tapped Steven on the back affectionately. "But you're absolutely right. The English are not called perfidious Albion for nothing."

Both men laughed and went on with their lunch of cottage pie and ale.

"If you're really serious about politics," Steele said nonchalantly, "you'd do well to cut your ties with Haggerty."

But before he did anything, Steven wanted to turn Gus's chicanery to his own advantage. He was trying to decide just how. He would not demand Haggerty's political influence as the price of silence: Steven wanted to cut the connection, not reinforce it. If he revealed what Gus had done, it would cost the little man his seat on the New York Stock Exchange. But that would be too cruel a punishment: Gus without the market would be like a ship without a sail. It might cost Steven his political future as well.

Steele and Steven parted after lunch and Steven found a cab and was well on his way to Brown's before he abandoned the idea of a little high-class blackmail. No man could be involved in an open scandal and get to Washington—or stay there. So he could never take Gus to court. It was too great a risk to himself.

What Steven ought to do once he'd made another few million was to marry the right kind of girl—Americans preferred married men in government—and build a political career on his own, as far removed as possible from Augustus Haggerty.

But there was another risk: Miranda. She was a good deal more dangerous than Gus. Having met—and, dammit, *liked*—Paul Cunningham that day in Walford's railway car, Steven had firmly renounced any thought of seeing Miranda in private again when—if— she called to arrange it, as she had promised.

Easier said than done! He missed her painfully, as if a limb had been lopped from his body. The sweet warmth of her was always in his mind and just out of reach. The thought of holding her made his body and what was left of his heart ache. Sometimes he believed that nothing he accomplished in life would be fulfilling without her.

——— · ———

He felt hollow by the time he stepped down from the hackney, paid the driver, and walked into Brown's. At the concierge's desk he was given a hand-delivered envelope of heavy cream-colored vellum. Wondering what it could be, he tore it open.

Lady Burdon! For next Thursday evening. It was the invitation she had promised on the trip from Liverpool—and Miranda and Paul would certainly be there!

Steven knew he shouldn't go. But he must! The very thought of seeing her again was too great a temptation to resist. He stood at one side of the concierge's desk, tapping the invitation on his free hand, aware he was losing his battle to stay away from her.

Abruptly, Steven changed his mind again about Thursday evening. He would not go. He crossed the lounge to go upstairs to his room, so deep in thought that he did not notice Kitt McAllister, who had been watching him since he entered the hotel.

Kitt knew what the envelope contained. She had received one just like it. It was all arranged: the count would come to collect her and escort her to the party.

Count d'Yveine! So clever, so attentive, so comforting. But all she wanted was the man who had just walked through the lounge without even seeing her!

Eighteen

Cynthia's face lit up as she entered Lady Burdon's drawing room on Alastair's arm. Lately when she walked into a theater or a restaurant her eyes darted nervously, searching for Steven's face, but tonight she was thoroughly dazzled by the vast room, its islands of richly upholstered chairs where small groups clustered, its miles of Persian carpets, its crystal chandeliers, gorgeously sculpted ceilings and moldings, and the life-size paintings that hung on the walls, among them several portraits in oil of Lady Burdon.

"There are nudes of her in an upstairs gallery," Walford said, watching Cynthia closely as he said it.

Cynthia remained unflustered. She knew Walford took a naughty pleasure in shocking her, as her brothers did, and she was not to be shocked. "I can see why she was a belle in her youth," she said.

"Oh, she still is," he said.

"Surely she's not pursued by suitors at her age," Cynthia laughed.

Walford smiled. "There's many an old gentleman would love to

marry her, but she's had enough of connubial bliss and prefers solitary splendor."

"In this house I can understand why," Cynthia said.

Walford glanced down at her again. "Grand, isn't it?" he said,
and, when she nodded, he added, "Almost as grand as Inderby."

"So you've told me," Cynthia replied airily.

"You've only to say the word and my lady mother will invite all
three of you for a weekend in the country." He inclined his head to
indicate Paul and Miranda, just behind them. "I'd really like you to
come."

"Perhaps when we return from Cairo," Cynthia said casually,
her attention still on the room and the handsome, sumptuously
dressed people gathered in it.

Walford, disappointed at being put off yet again, was forced to
admit that elusive or not, American or not, she was an exquisite little
thing and it would be no hardship to marry *her* along with her
money, to dress her in the latest fashions and show her off. The
problem lay in persuading her to marry *him*.

Walford was a roué but he was not a fool: he knew she was
bewitched by the craggy-faced, broad-shouldered Senator James, to
whom he privately referred as Dan'l Boone. Unless James could be
upstaged by British glory, tradition, and a title, Alastair did not stand
a chance. He decided to have his mother extend the invitation to
Mrs. Cunningham, never mind Cynthia's wish to put it off. Cynthia
was too good a catch to lose by inaction.

Miranda saw Steven the moment he entered the drawing room, as
if they were still connected by that invisible cord that had first
drawn them together. Both of them made casual conversation
with other guests as they moved slowly but irresistibly toward each
other.

It seemed to take hours, but at last they were standing in one of
the many small alcoves in the drawing room, the nature of their

conversation camouflaged by the party smiles they wore like Greek masks.

"These have been the most impossible two weeks of my life," she said.

"Mine too."

He had not expected to be so shaken by the mere sight of her. His decision to be judicious began to crumble.

"We're taking a terrible risk, just talking like this," she said.

"I know that, but we must talk. Can't we meet somewhere alone?"

"No," she said, smiling brightly.

A force stronger than what was right and reasonable began to overpower him.

"Miranda," he said urgently, leaning toward her. "Come away with me! We won't go back to the States. We'll live here in England or in France. I don't care where, as long as we're together."

"I can't do that," she said. "I wanted to, but I can't."

He gazed at her in astonished silence.

"And I can't see you anymore," she said, her voice shaking. "I can't go on like this!" Her words seemed to pour out as they had the first time they were alone together. "All this time I've been in bed with two men. It starts with him . . . and then I think of you . . . and I can't hold back and then he *is* you. It has to stop."

She looked away, clasping and unclasping her hands. "And now he can't hold back either. It's never been like this between us. I want you all the time . . . and he wants me all the time."

"I don't want to hear it!" he said sharply, wincing from the first vicious pang of jealousy he had ever experienced.

"It's worse to live it."

"I know that. That's why you must leave him."

"I love him too much to do that," Miranda said. "He's a wonderful man."

"How can a woman love one man and desire another?"

"You know I feel more than desire for you."

"Then why?"

"Because one of us has to be sane. On the ship I thought you would be, but now . . . Steven, I can't let this . . . fascination we have for each other ruin all our lives: yours, mine, Paul's, and my sons'. I think I knew that the moment I saw Price on the pier at Liverpool. I couldn't bear to have my sons hate me, hear filthy things said about me. And Paul and I have had twenty years together. How can I throw that away?"

She glanced around to see if anyone had heard them, was watching them, and then she smiled again, a ghastly smile this time, wrenched from the lines of torment in her face.

"But you can do *this*! Knowing what we are to each other, you can say good-bye and never see me again?"

"I must!"

"You say that here, but if we were alone together . . ."

She was quiet for what seemed a long time, tacitly agreeing that what he said was true. It was only the code of civilized society that kept her from leaving with him right then, finding a bed in this vast hive of rooms and shutting out the world forever.

"But it isn't only that," she said softly. "I love you in a way I will never love anyone else." She looked at him ardently, as if memorizing every plane and angle of his face. In her eyes he saw passion and tenderness and the anguish of good-bye even before she turned away from him. He almost followed her, but decades of convention held him back.

From across the room Paul noticed his wife and the senator. Glad to see her enjoying herself, he was about to check on Cynthia, when something made him turn back.

A chill began to crawl like a centipede along his spine. There was something in the way they looked at each other, spoke to each other, resisted an obvious yearning toward each other, that told him what he had suspected since that first wild night with Miranda.

Someone had taught her what she knew now, had shown her what she wanted, had taken her where Paul never had. She in turn had taken Paul so far beyond anything in his experience that he had deliberately ignored what he could not face: Miranda had a lover. His perfect wife had been unfaithful to him.

Now Paul knew who her lover was, and it almost broke him. Rage immobilized him, helped to hold him together, or he would have left this place, left her, and never turned back.

Then it occurred to him that Miranda might be planning to leave *him,* to desert him for her lover! He went from hot anger to utter desolation to the cold determination never to let her go. No matter what she had done, he *would not* let her go! He was desperately in love with her! He had loved her from the start, but in the protective way a husband loves a wife. Never had he felt the naked need that she had recently aroused in him. Aroused and satisfied.

Ironic, he thought, that at forty-two, an age when the novelty of marriage had long ended and most men strayed more seriously, he should have found his temptress at home. What she had done was unbearable—but it must be borne because she was his. He wanted her and he would keep her, as much for how she enhanced his days as for how she electrified his nights.

They could stay together only if neither of them referred to what had happened to her. Or to what was happening between them as a result. Above all, they could never speak of Steven James.

He saw her walk away from the other man, her expression and her body movements both negative and final—or was that just his own wishful thinking? He was wretched because he cared only that she stay with him, be his wife, delight him with what the other man had taught her.

How, he wondered, had he, Paul Cunningham, so easily become a voluptuary?

How had he developed an unquenchable thirst for just one woman?

He knew how. He had been married to her for more than

twenty years, had sensed and ignored that side of her nature all that time. He closed his eyes and heard her voice, saw her smile, imagined the soft swelling of her breasts under his hands, the long, smooth length of her legs, the paradise between them, the touch of her fingertips on him, her mouth, the sweetness of her. He felt her enclosing him, moving with him, sighing with him. She was his wife!

He went to reclaim her.

Kitt no longer heard what d'Yveine was saying. She had managed for a while to reply to his remarks, but as soon as the exchange began between Mrs. Cunningham and Steven, she heard nothing at all. Her senses spun out toward the couple, a web she tried to cross to hear what they were saying.

With a sinking heart she saw how strong the bond was between the lovers. He appeared to be pleading for something and she was refusing him. After a while the nods and smiles they had been using to hide the pull between them were forgotten. Kitt turned her head to see who else might be observing. Cynthia was. And Mr. Cunningham was.

Kitt shuddered—for Steven's sake she hoped the nature of their involvement was not as clear to the others as it was to her—and then she looked again at the scene in the alcove. She saw Miranda turn from Steven and walk away. She saw him almost follow, then restrain himself by force of will, shaken by Miranda's desertion.

That was when Kitt knew there was more than lust between them. It came to her with frightening clarity that those two people loved each other, and her heart ached for them. She had been sick with despair for her own dashed dreams; now she was worried about their ruin if the scandal got out. They were not evil, either of them.

She made a small sound and her hand went to her mouth.

The count, who had been standing at her side, took her arm

firmly and led her across the drawing room and into the "small" dining room, where a table that ordinarily seated thirty had been moved against the wall and was laden with a superb buffet. Small tables and chairs had been scattered about the room, and Jean-Baptiste sat Kitt down on a chair and went to a sideboard for a tot of cognac. He returned and handed her the glass.

"Here, my dear. Drink this. You are very pale."

She took the glass and sipped it, shuddering from the strong liquid but grateful for its heat in the cold pit of her stomach. She sipped again and nodded to the count as the nausea faded.

"Shall I fetch a doctor?" he asked.

"Thank you, no. I'm better now. You've been very kind."

"Young ladies frequently feel faint."

Kitt looked at him squarely. "I've never felt faint in my life."

"Then it must be that you have *le coeur gros.*"

"A heavy heart? Yes. My past sorrows just caught up with me."

"Why was that?"

Kitt sighed. "Has it never happened to you that a word, a sight, a sound, a melody, suddenly brings together every hurt you've ever felt? The lives gone, the moments wasted, the undiscovered loves?"

He patted her hand. "My dear, you are too young to have such gloomy thoughts."

"I'm twenty-five."

"Ancient!"

"That depends upon one's point of view." She didn't regret her candor. She did not care if she sounded as bitter and hopeless as she felt. She went on. "To Miss Cynthia, for example, her aunt has one foot in the grave."

"But we know that isn't so," he said, his expression conveying more than concern.

She looked at him searchingly and he nodded briefly, telling her that he knew a great deal more besides. She blushed deeply and turned away from him.

"And I'm an old maid."

"*Chère demoiselle,*" he said gently. "You are not. Lady Pat was your age when she married for the first time."

"That beautiful woman? But why?"

He shrugged. "It was her own choice—as it must have been yours. If you've had few suitors, it has been because you wanted none. Men sense these things—some of them at any rate. They are as much afraid of a rebuff as anyone else."

She gazed at him, confounded. It was not the kind of thing sophisticated gentlemen said to females of any age.

He saw her confusion and smiled. "People send out messages, you know, which others receive. It's a bit like the wireless. Trust me. I swear on my honor that I am not as foolish as I look."

How very kind he was! "I don't think you are foolish in the least," she said.

His smile was almost boyish. "Then may I presume to ask you a question?"

"Provided I may presume to leave it unanswered."

"But of course," he assured her. "I am curious about your name. Why did your parents choose to call an innocent babe Kitt?"

She smiled. "My name is Louisa Kittredge McAllister. Kittredge was my mother's maiden name. After she died and my aunt Louisa, for whom I was named, came to live with us and look after me, I was called Kitt to avoid confusion."

"Ah," he said. "I see. But since there is no confusion between us, may I call you Louisa?"

"If you like," she said.

"Now, finish your cognac," he suggested, "while I tell you about Patricia's collection."

The count waved a hand that included the carved panels of the dining room walls, the silver and vermeil cups, bowls and serving dishes on the table, the hand-embroidered Madeira cloth draped over the table, and the matching, four-branch crystal candelabra placed at intervals along its length. He talked amusingly of where and how Burdons past and present had come into possession of these

treasures, until the cognac was gone. Then he escorted Kitt back to the drawing room, where laughter and conversation made a pleasing rumble.

Kitt searched the room. Miranda was talking to Lady Burdon, Paul Cunningham at his wife's side. Steven James and Raymond Steele had their heads together. Lord Walford and Lewis Wendall were standing at one of the windows. Kitt could not find Cynthia Cunningham.

Cynthia stood on a small platform in the retiring room reserved for ladies, while a maid sewed a loose garland on her skirt. Cynthia had ripped it herself because she needed time to think.

To begin with, she had noticed a change in attitude between Miranda and Paul since their reunion and she wondered about its cause. They had always been a companionable couple, talking and laughing together while so many married people had little to say to each other, but now there was a new quality to their companionship that disturbed Cynthia. More than once she had surprised her uncle consuming Miranda—it was the only way she could describe it—with his eyes. And they spent a lot of time at the hotel while Walford squired Cynthia about.

Cynthia had been virtually certain that the lovers had not met again until tonight. But after seeing them together, she decided she might be wrong. Apparently, no matter how closely she was watched, Miranda was capable of duplicity. Either way, after this evening Cynthia had no doubt that the senator was still spellbound by her aunt.

It infuriated Cynthia beyond bearing! She was determined to separate Steven and Miranda, even if it took some egregious behavior to do it. Miranda stood between Cynthia and the man she loved, and Miranda must be set aside no matter what it took.

In the meantime, Cynthia would hang on to Walford, just in case.

"Thank you," she said to the maid. "That will do nicely."

The maid gave a little bob and went back to her place near the door. Cynthia fluffed the tiny curls around her face and used a rice paper on her perfect nose, admiring the room's reflection in the glass as she did so. Even this room was magnificent!

She imagined what it must be like to be mistress of a mansion like this. It might be wiser to spend a weekend at Inderby before the trip to Cairo. She wasn't the only wealthy American debutante in London, and it would do no harm to make an impression on Walford's parents before their need for money made them less choosy.

But she put that plan aside when, returning to the drawing room, she saw the senator heading for the door. She went directly to him and spoke softly.

"I must talk to you about something very important."

"What is it?" he asked.

"Not here," she said, shaking her head slowly. "Why not take me to tea at Brown's tomorrow. That's a good excuse, although the truth is I have something far more important than orange pekoe to discuss with you."

That seemed to rattle him. Maybe he was wondering if she wanted to talk about Miranda. Well, he deserved to be rattled! When they were married she would see that he never had the chance to stray. Once she had him, she would never let him go.

"I'll come to the Bristol for you at four o'clock," he said. "And now I must leave. Good night, Miss Cunningham."

"Until tomorrow, Senator."

She watched him go and wondered if Paul had noticed his wife and this man together tonight. But in almost every French novel she had read, the injured spouse was the last to know.

She went to find Walford.

Nineteen

Steven arrived at the Bristol in a hansom cab punctually at four o'clock the following afternoon. During the brief ride to Brown's he and Cynthia made conversation about their respective sightseeing adventures in London, although he could tell from the way she smiled at him and the flush on her lovely face that she had something far more personal in mind than monuments. He wondered what on earth it was.

Was Cynthia the one who knew about Miranda and himself?

He decided she knew nothing. She would not have spoken to him if she knew, much less have asked him to take her to tea. Miss Cynthia was not as seraphic as she looked, but there were certain things too shocking for her to handle, and her aunt's affair was one of them.

They bowled along the clean, quiet streets of Mayfair with the afternoon shadows lengthening. There was that atmosphere of order, culture, and decency the British Empire's capital inspired.

"What a beautiful city," Cynthia said.

"Yes, it is. Far more beautiful than any of ours."

"Ours have strength," she remarked.

"But this city has character."

"Which do you think is more important. Senator?"

He smiled. "I have no idea. And it depends upon whether you're talking about people or cities. And here we are at Brown's."

Steven had reserved a table in the lounge, a preferred meeting place for elegant ladies and distinguished gentlemen. The lounge was almost full, the air redolent of steaming tea, the fresh fragrance of cut flowers in vases, the scent of the women's perfume.

Footmen circulated with trays of watercress and cucumber sandwiches on thinly sliced white bread. Others carried baskets of hot scones dripping with fresh butter, or petits fours and fruit tarts and a variety of biscuits and sweetmeats.

Cynthia went on talking idly, *like a cat playing with a mouse,* Steven thought. Impatient, he finally asked her what she wanted to discuss.

"Something I can offer you," she said boldly, seeming suddenly much older than she was.

He was intrigued. "And what might that be?"

"Myself," she said, demurely now, watching him from under her lashes.

He was taken aback. It was an extraordinary thing for a young lady to say.

When he did not respond, she blushed furiously and added, "I mean as an influence on Uncle Paul if you need one. I know that Cunningham's is now considering sharing certain real estate interests with you."

"I've already discussed the preliminaries with your uncle," Steven said. "The rest must wait until I return to New York and confer with my associate."

"I would suggest that you leave your associate out of this."

"I appreciate your advice," he said indulgently.

She felt patronized, like a child. "But you have no intention of acting on it!"

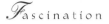

"My dear Miss Cunningham, I think you must leave my business to me."

She was furious that he didn't take her seriously. He would have listened to Miranda's advice! But she must not show the full extent of her anger. Men didn't think ladies had any anger in them. "I think you should know that my father disapproves of Mr. Haggerty."

"Most people do. But I thank you for warning me and I'll bear it in mind when I meet your father in New York."

"Are you about to leave for New York?" she asked with barely disguised alarm. "I thought you were going to travel."

"I haven't decided," he said. But he knew he would not go home while there was any chance of Miranda's being in London.

After a brief silence Cynthia was impelled to make another bold suggestion. "Why not come to Cairo with us? I'm sure my aunt and uncle would be delighted to have you join us."

His eyes flickered, and she knew she had struck a nerve. Cynthia was right! Miranda had ended the affair last night, but her lover had not. He would probably welcome the chance to try again in Cairo. But this time Paul would be there and Steven would turn to Cynthia for solace.

She knew it was a gamble—men always wanted what they could not have—but she was prepared to take it. She wanted him beyond anything she had ever dreamed. If he had asked her to elope with him that very moment, she would have done it.

But he was shaking his head. "I really haven't the time."

So even if the affair *was* over, he was not ready to turn to Cynthia. He didn't even think of her as a substitute. It was humiliating.

No man had ever failed to respond to her coquetry, not even men old enough to be her father. She suddenly had an inkling of what it must be like for a woman to be less than bewitching, to be plain or old and obliged to wait for a man to notice she was alive.

She looked at him woefully, her huge eyes glistening with tears at the shock of her first rejection.

"Miss Cunningham, what is it?" He leaned forward anxiously, concerned for her and painfully aware that it was scandalous for a young lady to cry in the lounge of a hotel.

"I'm so miserable," she said. "And no one will help me."

"I will if I can," he said, trying to soothe her. "Tell me what's wrong."

She hesitated, wanting him to know a few practical things that might influence him, then whispered. "I'm being forced to marry."

"Walford?"

She shook her head. "It doesn't matter who, although he's at the top of their list. Anyone of good family will do. The man needn't even have money," she said, and added, "I have plenty of that. But that's why Papa sent me away with Aunt Miranda, on a marriage safari! It's so degrading!"

"I'm sure your aunt and uncle would never want you to marry against your will."

"You don't understand! They're the ones who most want me to marry! If Miranda doesn't succeed, my father will be furious with her and . . . well, she and Uncle Paul . . . depend upon my father." She took a handkerchief from her purse and carefully blotted the corners of her eyes. "Financially," she whispered as if it were a dirty word.

From a young girl it was vulgar at the very least. Steven, newly amazed that she would mention money, didn't believe everything she said, but some of it had the ring of truth: Miranda had told him about Charlotte's curse and their demeaning search for a mate who would redeem the family's honor.

He didn't doubt for a moment that a man like Hobart Cunning-ham would use his only daughter to that end, whether she was willing or not. He felt sorry for Cynthia. She was manipulative and

spoiled, but she was also young and vulnerable and so very, very beautiful.

"I'm sorry, but I don't see what I can possibly do to help you," he said kindly.

She shook her head, her messages delivered, and pursued her strategy. "Nothing. Just take me to tea once in a while. It's a comfort not to be lectured all the time."

They were still talking when it turned six o'clock. She could be very charming when she chose, but Steven thought they had been unchaperoned long enough. "It's time I took you back to your hotel," he said, rising.

"May we have tea again tomorrow?" she asked.

Steven, mindful now of the calculation behind Cynthia's maidenly facade, said he would send her a note as soon as he had an afternoon free.

When he left her at the Bristol, Cynthia went upstairs to tell Miranda about her coup. She knocked on her aunt's bedroom door and Miranda's muffled voice asked who it was and told her to wait. Annoyed, Cynthia went to her own room to remove her hat and jacket and smooth her hair before returning. This time she was permitted to enter.

"I'm just out of the bath," Miranda called. "Sit down. I'll be right there."

Cynthia sat down and waited impatiently for her moment of triumph. A few seconds passed before she noticed the rumpled bed and a pungent odor in the darkened room, its draperies already closed against the dusk. It was an unfamiliar odor—part sweet, part acrid.

There was a streak of light under the door to her uncle's adjoining room, and suddenly Cynthia knew that when she knocked they had been in that rumpled bed together, that the strange odor came, somehow, from marital relations. In the afternoon! After last night's scene with her lover!

Miranda appeared wearing a quilted silk robe, her hair covered by a towel turban. Even in that outfit she looked elegant as she crossed the room and slipped behind the draperies to open a window.

"Strange time of day to have a bath," Cynthia observed when Miranda reappeared and went to her dressing table.

Miranda sat down and pulled off the turban, letting her luxuriant dark hair tumble down around her shoulders.

Cynthia had to admit she was breathtaking with her hair loose. No wonder she could wind Uncle Paul around her little finger. And she probably let him see her naked! No one had seen Cynthia naked since she was out of diapers. Even when she bathed, a sheet was stretched across the tub for modesty's sake and her maid held a large towel well above eye height when Cynthia got out of the bath.

"Is that what you came to tell me?"

"No," Cynthia said—to the idea of Miranda naked as well as to Miranda's question. "I came to tell you I've been having tea with the senator."

"That's very nice, dear," Miranda said as if Cynthia were four years old and had announced she'd spent the afternoon making sand castles. "Did you go alone?"

"Since you and Uncle Paul seemed otherwise occupied, I did."

Miranda flushed slightly and picked up her hairbrush. "You should have taken Baxter."

"Oh, for heaven's sake! It was broad daylight and the lounge at Brown's Hotel was crowded."

"It isn't comme il faut. I have no objection, but your uncle will."

"I'm not planning to tell him. And you certainly don't tell him everything, so that's all right."

"Well, you've brought me your news. What now?" Miranda brushed her hair.

"I asked him to come to Cairo with us."

Miranda looked even more disapproving than she sounded. "Really, Cynthia! It is not your place to extend invitations to anyone, particularly not a man."

"In any event, he refused." Cynthia smiled thinly. "Of course that won't stop me from trying again, either before we go or after we return. After all, I'm young. I have plenty of time to wait for him."

Miranda felt as if the girl had turned into a Harpy, one of those mythical creatures with a woman's head and the body and sharp talons of a bird of prey. Cynthia was a female fixed upon a mate, coldly reminding Miranda that age must step aside, that youth would be served.

"Let me tell you one of the more brutal facts of life," Miranda said, meeting Cynthia's eyes in the mirror. "It amuses you to tell me I'm growing old, but so shall you. Your skin will crinkle like plissé and your pretty baby curls will thin and turn gray. Your hands will betray you first with spots and ropy veins. So if you're strong enough to live to a ripe age, those will be your rewards. You can drink the waters from Saratoga to Baden-Baden, but if you live, age will come. No matter how strong and beautiful you are today, you'll have to face tomorrow."

Cynthia sprang to her feet, her eyes still fixed on her aunt's. "You're horrible to say such things to me!"

"But these are things you ought to know. They might make you less mean and hard."

"I hate you, Miranda!" Cynthia said, bursting into tears before she ran from the room.

Miranda sat where she was, the brush poised in midair. "Hate me or not, it's true," she whispered softly. "Unless you meet a man like Steven James and burst into bloom again."

Her sons, her husband, and a still, small voice within had made her renounce Steven, but he had given her the passion of her life. When other matrons gathered to talk dreamily and wistfully of engagements announced and honeymoons taking place, Miranda would relive those days aboard an ocean liner, not so long ago, when she was young.

Twenty

*M*ary Frances Alton, dressed in her best, sat on a small settee in Kitt's hotel room a week later and talked hurriedly, as if it would hurt less that way. She kept her hands cupped over her face and her voice was muffled. Her body was tense, elbows pressed close to her sides.

"He didn't bother me the whole time we were westbound for New York," she said in a strained whisper, "and I thought it was over. Then he started again on the way back and this time he . . . got what he was after."

"Oh, no!" Kitt breathed.

"He did me twice." Mary Frances shuddered. "I'll never forget how it felt to have him pounding inside me like I was some kind of bug he wanted to squash." She stopped and drew a few shuddering breaths before she went on.

"Some of the officers knew. I could tell by the way they looked at me, as if they were thinking to do me too. They didn't even try to stop him, the animals! If he'd uv let 'em, they'd uv stood there and watched."

"Oh, no!" Kitt wailed.

"Oh, yes. He bragged as how he told 'em all about it, how they laughed and called me dirty names. I didn't know what to do except jump in the ocean, but I didn't have the spunk for drowning."

She dropped her hands and looked entreatingly at Kitt. "I look different, don't I? That's why I'm scared to go home. Mum'll know just lookin' at me!" She covered her face again with hands that shook. "That's why I came straight here."

Kitt went to sit beside her and put an arm around the trembling girl. "You were right to come to me." She rocked the slight figure. "I'm sorry, Mary Frances. I'm so very sorry."

"Do I look different?" The girl's brown eyes searched Kitt's.

"No. You look just the same."

"I *feel* like a dirty rag."

"Hush, Mary Frances. *He* is, but you're nothing of the kind." Kitt stroked Alton's hair. "I'm going to order some tea and then we'll decide what to do. What time are you expected home?"

"Now. The train from Liverpool just got in. I told my brother Denny I had to drop off a petticoat you forgot, but I don't think Mum will believe that."

"I'll send your mother a note saying I've asked you to stay an hour or so and do a few things for me." Kitt rang for service. "Take off your coat and hat. There are fresh towels if you want to wash your face, and the ladies' is just through there." She sat down at the writing table.

Mary Frances removed her hat and placed it carefully on a low table. She had dressed in her best to come to Brown's, a two-piece gray suit modestly trimmed with black braid under a loose black coat, a gray felt bonnet trimmed with black and white ribbons, and a brand-new pair of gloves she had been unable to resist when she and Maizy shopped along Ladies' Mile in New York City.

That had been a happy day. It seemed like years ago.

Today she had been afraid Brown's Hotel would not let her in, that everyone could see she was damaged goods.

"What's the address?" Kitt asked just as a porter answered her ring. The envelope was addressed and dispatched and tea ordered. Kitt came back to the settee and took the girl's hand in hers.

"One thing's certain," Kitt said. "You can't go back aboard until that man's been discharged. I'll go to the shipping line and see to that myself."

Mary Frances shook her head violently. "If he were discharged on my account, they'd all gang up on me. I can't do that."

"Then you can't go back at all!"

Mary Frances began to cry, her speech losing more and more of its polish. "And me as worked so hard to get where I am. It ain't fair!"

"It's unbearable!" Kitt agreed, her face flushed and angry.

"But I must work, miss. My family needs the money."

"We'll find you better work, where you won't be in danger all the time."

"But there's Maizy and them other girls. For all I know, they been done too. It ain't summat a girl talks about."

"That's what's so unconscionable, that it probably does happen all the time. But you must stop speaking as if it were your fault. He's the criminal!"

There was a knock at the door and tea was brought in on a tray. Kitt poured for both of them, putting plenty of milk and sugar in Alton's, and watched the girl warm her hands on the cup while she sipped gratefully at the hot liquid.

Kitt was far more shaken than she showed. A fierce urge to protect this girl swept over her. Mary Frances had no recourse that wouldn't reveal her own shame or put her at risk from men who would attack her, then deny everything and back each other up. Girls like Mary Frances had to submit or lose jobs they needed desperately.

It was unbearable!

She would not turn to Steven this time. Since the night of Lady

Burdon's party she had caught only a few glimpses of him. Once he was having tea in the lounge with Cynthia Cunningham; another time he was on Albemarle Street, walking with Mr. Steele. He had not noticed Kitt in the lounge—Cynthia seemed to have his full attention—and he and Mr. Steele had bowed politely when they passed on the street while Kitt had walked briskly by with only a nod of recognition and a smile so artificial, it made her face ache.

She should have escaped and started on her travels, but she was too demoralized to contemplate seeing Florence and Rome and Pompeii alone. Nor could she bring herself to leave London while Steven was still there. Even so, had it not been for Lady Burdon and the count, she would have booked passage home by now. But she couldn't rely on her two new friends indefinitely.

Sometimes she longed to be back in her own house with mementoes of her mother and father and Aunt Louisa all around her. Then she would remember the dull life of a spinster in a small Connecticut town. The years would stretch bleakly before her, empty save for church socials and Independence Day picnics. There would be Christmases and Easters alone or with neighbors who felt obliged to include an old maid in their family celebrations.

She had to *do* something, something of value. It was not in her nature to do nothing or even to suppose that nothing could be done. There were only two times nothing could be done: in the face of death or when you loved someone who didn't love you. To Kitt these circumstances felt remarkably similar.

Stop moaning for now, she told herself firmly. *This is nothing to do with you, it's to do with Mary Frances!*

An idea struck her almost immediately: She would speak to Lady Burdon, who could certainly find work in her enormous mansion— or among her many friends—for another servant!

It annoyed Kitt that she must always seek help from other people, but she had no choice.

—— · ——

The hot sugared tea had helped to revive Mary Frances. A hint of color returned to her chalk-white face. New compassion swept over Kitt to mingle with her outrage and harden into resolve.

She turned to Mary Frances and said, "I'm going to take care of this, I promise you. I know someone who will help—and if she can't, she knows a gentleman who will."

And if neither Lady Pat nor the count could do anything, she would do it herself!

"But how, miss?" Mary Frances was always practical.

"I can't tell you that until I speak to the lady in question." She sat back, thinking hard. "In the meantime, you must go home."

Mary Frances shook her head. "I dassn't. Our mum will know for sure."

"Nonsense, Alton. And what if she does? She's your mother!"

"She'll say it was me," Mary Frances said in a high, nervous voice. "That I was too familiar like. My pa'll beat me. He always says it's a girl's fault when she gets herself treated like dirt." She shook her head. "No, I can't go home."

For a moment Kitt was at a loss, but she thought quickly. "Very well, then, you needn't go home to stay, but you *must* show your face this afternoon. I'll go with you and say you're being considered for a position as a lady's maid and must wait until after dinner to meet the lady. After that it'll be too late for you to go home alone, so you'll have to stay with me."

"A lady's maid?" Alton raised her head, caught by the possibility that her nightmare might lead to her dream.

"I'm not sure what sort of position the lady or her friends can offer you, but whatever it is will be better than going back aboard that ship! Come now, we must get ready."

Fifteen minutes later they were in a hansom cab headed for an area near the London docks.

There were squalid neighborhoods in Branford, Connecticut, but they were nothing like the dingy rows of houses Alton had grown up in. These were the essence of age, warped and pocked like centenarians. They were attached houses, two rooms up and two down with a privy out back and small, grimy windows at either end. The entire area was black with city soot and the smoke from coal-powered stoves.

The neighborhood swarmed with children, a flock of whom followed Alton and Kitt into the house. They seemed separated in age by no more than a year. The front room was cramped to start with and had been made even more so by two bedsteads that probably slept three or four children each and an ironing board assembled from a plank propped on the backs of two chairs and covered with a blanket. The walls were water-stained and patches of mold flourished in the corners.

Kitt was not shown the rest of the house, but she knew it, too, must reek of fish heads and boiled cabbage, of infrequently washed human bodies crammed into tight quarters, however hard the mother might work to keep it clean.

Mrs. Alton was a tall, spare woman wearing a dark stuff dress and a worn apron, her brown hair bundled into a careless knot atop her head. Mary Frances had inherited her mother's hair and eyes, but the daughter's features were finer and there was not yet the network of lines that covered Mrs. Alton's face.

She looked briefly at Mary Frances, satisfying herself that her girl was healthy, then turned a stern face to Kitt.

"This is Miss McAllister, Mum," Mary Frances said. "I met her aboard the *Sylvania.*"

Mrs. Alton nodded briefly and offered Kitt a chair, whisking away invisible dirt with the towel tucked into her waistband.

"Will you take a cuppa, miss?" she asked with the same stiffness Mary Frances had displayed when Kitt first met her.

Kitt accepted although she was already awash in tea. "I'm sorry

to burst in on you like this," she told Mrs. Alton, "but I'd just heard about a good position for Mary Frances, and there was no time to send a second note."

Mrs. Alton nodded, her wariness diminishing slightly. She had been suspicious of that first note, fearing her daughter had been persuaded by some crafty madam to visit a "hotel" that was really a brothel.

When her daughter arrived at the door in a hansom, loudly heralded by a troupe of neighborhood children, Mrs. Alton had set her iron on the piece of scrap metal she used as a trivet and gone to the door. She half expected her girl to emerge dressed in red satin and black lace with her face painted and a blowsy whoremistress in attendance, ready to offer money in return for Mary Frances's apprenticeship as a prostitute and no questions asked.

The sight of the tall, sedate young woman who accompanied Mary Frances changed all that. Miss McAllister was a lady. Mary Frances looked quite the lady herself, which made her mother both proud and anxious as she went about fixing the tea.

"So there's persons as wants Mary Frances workin' for 'em," she said after she had served tea in thick, chipped cups and returned to her board. The fresh smell of ironing mixed with the other smells.

How, Kitt wondered, had Alton learned to be so crisp and neat? Then she remembered: since she was eleven, Alton had been in service with a wealthy family. There the girl had been required to wash every day and to keep her clothing spotless, two almost impossible achievements in this place with no running water and no privacy. And in that same upper-class house Alton, with her sharp eyes and ears and quick intelligence, had improved her speech, learned which forks to use and how to dress with more taste than money.

"Of course, the lady must meet Mary Frances before she decides," Kitt explained, "but she is engaged until about eight o'clock this evening. I thought it wiser for Miss Alton to stay with me after the interview than to come home alone so late at night, and I expected you would want to meet me first." She smiled. "And here I am."

Mrs. Alton, pleased to hear her child called "Miss Alton," nodded her agreement briefly. "And if Mary Frances suits, when'll this lady be wantin' 'er?"

"I'm sorry, but I won't know that until after the interview either."

Another nod. Then a pause while the cooled iron was exchanged for one that had been reheating on a small black stove. When the iron was in motion again, the mother asked, "Why yer takin' such an interest in my girl?"

"Oh, Mum!" Mary Frances gasped at the ungracious question.

"No sass from you," her mother ordered, waiting for Kitt's reply.

"Because she's so very good at what she does. And I like her."

Mrs. Alton snorted. "The gentry don't bother with our sort outta likin'."

Kitt met the woman's eyes. "Maybe not the gentry in England, where everyone accepts his place and agrees to stay in it. But I'm American, and in America it isn't where you come from that matters, it's where you end up. Americans are people who want to get ahead."

"Better mind they don't trip over their own feet gettin' there," Mrs. Alton remarked.

There was a short silence.

"Yer of an age to be married," Mrs. Alton said to Kitt, making her daughter gasp with embarrassment again.

"But not of a mind to be," Kitt lied calmly.

Mrs. Alton grunted. "Bein' lumbered with a husband and family is enough to keep a woman out of the mind to be, but by the time she knows what she's in fer, it's too late. The harm's done. Still, it ain't nateral for folk to live alone." She looked squarely at Kitt, then

gave a little smile. "Yer young yet and bonny. Yer may change yer mind."

Kitt smiled back. "In any event, Mary Frances will stay with me tonight," she said. It was a statement, not a question.

The woman nodded. "Long as she remembers as 'ow she ain't no Yankee to be gettin' ideas above 'er station."

"I'll remember that," Kitt said, rising and offering her hand. Mrs. Alton looked surprised but took it briefly.

"Thank you, Mum," Mary Frances said.

"Well," her mother explained to Kitt, "I'd rather have 'er workin' on dry land than on them boats with their 'eathen doin's."

"Yes, so would I," Kitt said, and whisked Mary Frances out of the ramshackle dwelling and into the waiting hansom.

"I'm sorry" was the first thing Alton said when the door had been closed. "That's how she is."

"She's a fine woman," Kitt told her while the hansom drove back to the West End. "She protects her family. It's a relief to meet someone who says exactly what she thinks. And she had every right to question my motives."

"Just looking at you should have been enough," Alton said. "There's no young lady looks less of a white slaver than you."

They both laughed heartily at that. It relieved some of the nervous tension of the afternoon. When they reached the hotel, Kitt dropped Mary Frances with the suggestion that she take a nap before what might be a long evening. Then she directed the cab to take her to St. John's Wood and sent her card in with the request that Lady Burdon spare her a moment if it was at all possible.

Twenty-one

"Have you become a placement agency for domestics?" Lady Burdon asked.

They were alone in the morning room, the count having gone to his club. Lady Burdon had no other callers that afternoon and had welcomed Kitt with a warmth she did not show to everyone.

"At the moment," Kitt said, "this girl is my only client, but I could easily be persuaded to take on more. I'm sure most agencies don't bother to investigate the people who require servants. If the address is respectable, the people are assumed to be."

"But in your view a good address is no guarantee?"

"Not always." Kitt chose her words carefully, reluctant to disclose more of Alton's story than necessary. "I met her aboard the *Sylvania,* where she was a senior stewardess—and she accomplished that in little more than a year after she was hired. Before that she worked her way up from kitchen maid to lady's maid in a private house and learned a great deal about appearance, deportment, and manners from observation. Brushed up her speech too."

"She sounds very enterprising."

"She is!" Kitt said enthusiastically. "And bright. She deserves better than she's had."

Lady Burdon lit a thin cheroot. "Sherry?" she offered. Kitt nodded and her hostess poured two glasses of amontillado from the crystal decanter on the side table. The pale sherry gleamed inside the crystal, delicate and limpid. "What could be safer than working on a ship?" Lady Burdon asked, savoring a sip.

Kitt's glow faded. She hesitated again before she said, "A swine of an officer was after her and threatened to have her sacked unless she gave in."

Lady Burdon's expression was one of disgust. "And did she?"

"She would never give in," Kitt said, evading the truth without telling a lie. "I asked Senator James to help and he put a stop to it, but apparently only while the senator was on board." She shook her head. "It started again soon after and if she stays aboard that officer will go on tormenting her."

"The man must be punished," Lady Burdon said firmly. "And publicly too, to shame him before the world." She snorted. "An officer and a gentleman indeed!"

"What about her?" Kitt demanded, her eyes flashing. "Why should she be shamed at all? But she would be. People always assume . . ." Kitt's voice trailed off.

Lady Burdon nodded. "Ah, yes, of course. As if women want men to violate them."

"I'm determined she shall not go back. I can't offer her money. She's too proud. I'd send her to school if I could, but she wouldn't accept that either. So the next best thing is to find safe employment for her. And here I am, begging you to take her on as a lady's maid or to find someone who will."

"I can think of several places, but she'd start as a parlor maid at best."

Kitt frowned. "No, a lady's maid is what she wants to be. That's a modest enough ambition in life; why should some ruthless male set her back? Please keep thinking, Lady Pat."

Lady Burdon considered while she drank her sherry and finally said, "I do know someone who needs a maid and something of a companion. The lady—who could have been a teacher—would take pleasure in feeding a hungry mind and in having the company of such an admirable young woman as you say this is."

"That's wonderful!" Kitt said. "Who is the lady?"

"You."

"I?" Kitt was astounded. "But I don't need a maid!"

"Oh, but you do. You cannot go traveling about by yourself until you're a lot older and considerably more dilapidated than you are now. Yankee or not, it simply is not the done thing. And you are far too young and inexperienced to be safe in foreign parts, particularly among the Latins, who are notoriously hot-blooded, especially toward women with titian hair!

"I'm not suggesting that you make a bosom friend of her, but you need a congenial companion or you'll soon be headed for that backwater in Connecticut, where you will embroider altar cloths and wash the feet of the poor on Maundy Thursdays. You'd be miserable in such a life."

Kitt shook her head in wonder. "How did you know I was thinking of doing just that—and dreading it too?"

"I'm a sorceress, how else? But at my time of life sorcery is a mélange of experience and common sense. How much longer would you have stayed on in London all alone? I'd have had to insist that you move into this house, and with Jean-Baptiste in residence it would not have been proper."

Kitt's green eyes widened in surprise. "I can't thank you enough for even considering such an invitation—which, by the way, I could not have accepted, your houseguest notwithstanding." She got up and paced in front of the fire. "I don't know why I didn't consider asking Alton to stay with me. I'd love to tutor her. She has a quick mind and a hungry one, as you put it."

"And you could continue her lessons during your travels. Think how stimulating it would be to show her the wonders of the world."

"It would be fascinating," Kitt said. "But before I go traveling I must do something to protect girls like her."

Lady Burdon puffed on her cheroot. "I didn't think you had a burning desire to do good works."

Kitt sat down. "I'm no Lady Bountiful. You mustn't think I see myself that way. But the idea of staying in the circumstances one is born to infuriates me! Even worse, people meekly agree to be victimized by the class above them."

"It's a system that has worked well for centuries, my dear. You mustn't forget that most of us take pride in doing the best we can with what fate has given us. There's nothing wrong with being the best farmer, tinker, chimney sweep, or laundress."

Kitt nodded. "Her mother is like that. Still, it's hard to believe the place Alton comes from when you see what she's made of herself. She'd have continued, too, except for that loathsome brute. There has to be a way to keep women safe, even if it means dragging the truth out into the open."

Lady Burdon's interest sharpened. "Doing that would upset several applecarts."

Kitt smiled. "I think you like upsetting applecarts."

"It has its moments," Lady Burdon agreed, then paused. "Are you a suffragist?"

Kitt tilted her head to one side and pondered that for a moment. "I'd prefer not to label myself."

"You will be labeled, nonetheless. In this world a person is what others say she is."

"Well, we shall soon see what I am," Kitt said. "I'm angry enough to break a few windows on Oxford Street."

"At least you've solved the immediate problem of your Mary Frances."

"You did that, Lady Pat. I don't know how to thank you—for this and your many kindnesses to me."

Lady Burdon smiled fondly. "Come now, you exaggerate. I merely stated the obvious."

"The obvious is the last thing I tend to see." Kitt was thinking of Steven now. She wanted to talk about him but asked instead, "Have you seen the Cunninghams since your party?"

"I dined with them a few evenings ago. With Walford."

"Is he still courting Cynthia?"

"With little success, to judge from her cool reaction to him. But Alastair is a tenacious fellow. I gathered he might accompany them to Cairo—or follow on shortly after they leave London."

"And when will that be?"

"Next week, I believe. Yes, next week. Where does the time go?"

Kitt got out of her chair. "It's late. I must tell Mary Frances the news."

"I'm sure she'll be delighted."

"She may faint dead away unless she eats something soon." Kitt smoothed her skirts. "D'you know her dream is to serve the mistress of a great house with no one above her on the domestic tree but the butler, the housekeeper, and the cook. Being my maid won't be quite the same thing."

"If your aim in life is to make *her* dream come true, you must marry a great man."

Kitt laughed. "Not likely."

"Then find a dream of your own." Lady Burdon held up the lorgnette she rarely used and studied Kitt. "What would you say if I told you that marrying a great man would not be difficult?"

"I would say you'd had too much sherry. And I can't see myself falling in love with a great man."

"Love is not required to make a good marriage. You American girls make far too much of it—but not your clever millionaires who marry for the same reasons ours do: property and heirs to inherit it."

"Mrs. Cunningham didn't marry for either reason," Kitt said heatedly.

"Mrs. Cunningham is a special case."

They sat in silence for a moment. The clock on the mantel chimed seven.

"I must go," Kitt said. "I'll bring my new companion around to meet you when it's convenient."

"I'm perishing of curiosity, so make it soon."

"And I'd like to meet some of your suffragist friends."

"What makes you think I have friends among those Amazons?"

"You're not the only sorceress in London." Kitt smiled affectionately and hurried off. She had been on the brink of revealing her feelings for Senator James and his for Miranda. Lady Burdon was so easy to talk to.

What had she meant when she called Miranda a special case?

When the carriage pulled up to Brown's Hotel, the commissionaire helped Kitt out and she went quickly upstairs to tell Mary Frances her news.

"Now that that's settled," Kitt said over dinner, "I've just had another brilliant idea."

Mary Frances stopped her fork in midair. "My stars, miss, how many can a body have in one day?"

"I've decided we should move to a flat. I have business in London that will keep me here for a while and a flat will be more comfortable than any hotel."

"Oh, Miss Kitt," Mary Frances said, her face wreathed in smiles at the prospect of "doing" for this lady. "That would be lovely."

"We'll start looking tomorrow."

"It's all happening so quickly."

"Not at all. When you have a great idea, act on it!"

"All the same, I can't believe any of it," Mary Frances breathed.

"You'll believe it once we've moved. Now finish your dinner."

The hotel had provided a trundle bed for Miss McAllister's maid and they retired early, both of them weary from the events of the day. But they were up and dressed when morning tea arrived at seven o'clock and Kitt wrote a note to Mrs. Alton while Mary Frances fixed her hair as she had done on the ship.

"What a relief to have you back!" Kitt said. "But what am I to call you?"

"Alton is proper," Mary Frances said.

"Then Alton it is," Kitt said, closing the envelope and addressing it. "I've told your mother you're working for me and we'll call round in a few days. Now let's order breakfast and be on our way."

The chief bellman had hired a carriage for them and recommended an estate agent. They set off in high spirits. It was one of London's golden days with sun flooding the freshly swept avenues and a breeze so mild it might have been heralding spring.

"London is my favorite city!" Kitt said.

"Not Paris?"

"It's odd, I know, but I don't much like Paris," Kitt said. "My father used to say France is too beautiful a country to be wasted on the French."

Alton laughed. "And Rome?"

"Rome *is* splendidly pagan, even with the Vatican watching over it," Kitt said after a moment's reflection. "It's a toss-up between London and Rome, but I think London's my first choice. It's so *civilized,* so sure of itself, so serenely powerful. That's because the sun never sets on the British Empire."

"It sets on the London docks," Alton said flatly. "There's a lot of London that isn't so civilized."

The brougham stopped on Oxford Street at a two-story building with a handsome facade. A delicate bell tinkled as they went inside to what looked like a small salon with rugs, chairs, and walls in the same sickly shade of green.

They were greeted by a corpulent gentleman in striped trousers and a cutaway who glided toward them, his folded hands resting on his belly, his round face beaming like Humpty Dumpty's.

"Good morning, dear lady. May I be of service?"

"I am Miss McAllister," Kitt said, willing herself not to laugh at the gentleman's unctuous manner. "Brown's Hotel will have rung."

"Indeed, yes. We have many American clients. I am Mr. Purdy." He led them to the rear of the large room and bustled about placing chairs—one discreetly behind the other—for the two young women who avoided the merriment in each other's eyes.

"I should like to rent a furnished flat in Mayfair for at least six months," Kitt said.

"Excellent! We have several listed." He cleared his throat. "How large an establishment do you require?"

"We shall require at least two bedrooms, probably three."

"A modest dwelling, then." He looked like a large, disappointed baby.

"Not all Americans are flamboyant, Mr. Purdy. Let us say I require something between a tent and a mansion, with indoor plumbing."

It took him a moment to perceive that this was in part a pleasantry. Then he chortled and cocked his head to one side, his chins rolling to rest on his stiffly starched collar.

He opened a folder on his desk and described his listings as if they were state monuments of the greatest importance. Kitt chose three and, politely but firmly refusing Mr. Purdy's offer of a clerk to accompany them, Kitt and Alton set out to visit them.

By lunchtime Kitt had rented a charming flat on Dover Street with three bedrooms, a water closet and a bath, a sunny drawing room, and a dining room that could seat ten. The kitchen was modern with a coal stove, twin sinks, and painted wooden cabinets.

Everything was provided except linens, "so it will be a day or two before we can move in," Kitt told Alton when they had returned to the hotel. "But why do you look so worried?"

"It must be costing you a fortune," Alton said.

"Not more than I can afford." Kitt said it firmly, but she would have to ask her father's executor to release some of the money Sam had left in trust until she turned twenty-eight. That had been to protect her from fortune hunters marrying to get their hands on her money, but Sam had fully expected her to be married well before now.

The strong-featured face of Steven James crossed her mind and she resolutely pushed it away. She had more pressing things to do than languish over an impossible love or wonder how she could love him despite what he had done.

"Tomorrow we must shop for linens," she told Alton. "And the next day we'll see your mother and Lady Burdon. Then we'll pack our things and move."

"It's like a dream," Alton said.

"It will soon become very real," Kitt replied. She sounded practical and down-to-earth, but quite suddenly she felt prophetic.

Twenty-two

The carriage left the county road and bowled along the serpentine drive of Inderby, the family seat of the earls of Inderby since 1595. Cynthia and Miranda sat facing forward with Paul opposite. Behind them was another coach bringing the two maids, Rooney and Baxter, and Paul's valet.

Luggage was strapped atop the two carriages. It was only a weekend visit, but that meant at least four changes a day: breakfast, luncheon, afternoon, and dinner dress.

"And no repeats," Cynthia had reminded her aunt.

Miranda watched Cynthia closely as they rode through the park. The girl had behaved with sweetness and light after their last angry exchange, but Miranda was not fooled. Cynthia resented her aunt, kept the viscount guessing, and continued her pursuit of Steven.

It was her way of dealing with the unfamiliar pain of rejection. She probably dreamed of a proposal she would refuse for the sake of refusal. But a proposal from the senator would never come, no matter how many times Cynthia persuaded Steven to take her to tea.

"I just caught a glimpse of the house through the trees," Paul said after they had been on the drive for several minutes.

"Imposing?" Miranda asked.

"Very." Paul glanced at his niece. "Aren't you curious?"

Cynthia nodded. "Of course. It's all Walford talks about."

Paul smiled. "How are you and Walford getting on?"

"I'm not sure," Cynthia said. She spoke directly to her uncle, excluding Miranda. "Sometimes he's great fun and sometimes he's constrained and even pompous."

"People have moods," Paul suggested. "And the British aristocracy have more moods than anyone else. By American standards they're distant and formal, even supercilious."

Miranda wondered what her husband would say if she told him how close and *in*formal Alastair was with Lewis Wendall. Paul would be horrified that she even knew of such repulsive practices, as if mere knowledge could taint her.

He had no such misgivings about exploring the frontiers of marital sex. It excited both of them to experiment, but lately the essence of their encounters had changed. Paul did not spend the night with her unless they made love. It was as if he were rewarding her with his presence if there was sex and punishing her by his absence if there was not.

She wanted to pinpoint when this behavior had begun; she puzzled over it almost constantly before concluding that it was the night of Lady Burdon's party. He must have seen her talking to Steven in a way he considered inappropriate. He had not mentioned it, no doubt because it might cast a pall over their newly discovered passion.

At least it seemed highly unlikely that she would have to tell him about Alastair's perverse habit. Even supposing that Walford wanted to marry Cynthia, his parents would be reluctant to have an American daughter-in-law. It all depended upon how desperate the earl's financial situation was.

"Suppose he were to request my permission to propose?" Paul asked his niece, his words interrupting Miranda's reflections.

Miranda replied without thinking. "You would have to refuse."

"Have to?" Cynthia questioned. "Why?"

"Yes, why, my dear?" Paul echoed. "I like Walford. Don't you?"

"He's very attractive, but he's not the right man for Cynthia." Miranda knew it was a feeble excuse even as she said it.

Cynthia bristled. "That's for me to decide. To hear you talk, no one is right for me. Not the senator and not the viscount."

"Look!" Paul said, diverting them from a dangerous conversation. "There it is!"

Inderby, appearing through trees as old as England, was a monument in red brick and stone. Its many windows glinted in the mid-morning sun, and when at last it came into full view, it was awesome in its stateliness.

"It *is* marvelous, isn't it?" Cynthia breathed.

It was the image of that England which some of the former colonists so admired, as if a part of them regretted ever having declared their independence. England was what America's patrician classes revered and copied, as they copied French fashions, and Inderby was the essence of England.

"Extraordinary," Miranda agreed, aware that Cynthia was given to romantic imaginings. The girl was gazing at the enormous house, so many times rebuilt and enlarged. It had over seventy rooms, only a dozen of which were used by the family. The rest, Walford had told them, housed paintings and collections of china, porcelain, and sculpture gathered from the four corners of the earth. The rooms were opened for guests on great occasions, "like engagements, weddings, and christenings," Alastair had added, watching Cynthia.

Miranda knew Cynthia was picturing herself as mistress of this fabulous domain. As a child Cynthia had always been the heroine of any tale she read or imagined, the queen of all she surveyed.

A chill went through Miranda: most girls would be sufficiently impressed by this place to marry for it, but only a few would be foolish enough to think it could replace love or, at the very least, affection. Cynthia was one of the few.

Miranda turned once more to the window, trying not to worry about an impossible situation she might never have to face.

Where the trees ended, carpets of lush lawn rolled toward the mansion like an emerald sea. Lawns, she had read somewhere, thrived on English mist and centuries of care; these were dotted here and there with copses of elms, with groves of laurel and copper beech, with the Palladian temples and small Grecian villas that had been called "follies" during the eighteenth century, when they were the rage. The mansion itself was surrounded by luxuriant shrubbery, so smoothly clipped it looked unreal.

"I'm impressed," Miranda said.

"Don't let *them* know that," Cynthia whispered as the carriage drew to a halt before a wide flight of stone steps. Footmen were already there to open the carriage door and hand the travelers out, while another contingent directed the second coach to the service entrance.

———— · ————

Moments before, Alastair had turned from the window of the small drawing room and announced to his parents that the carriage was in sight through the trees and would arrive in five minutes.

Cyril, fifteenth Earl of Inderby, finished the article he was reading in the *Times* before he put down the newspaper and rose from his favorite wing chair. He was a slender man, somewhat taller than his son and heir, and not nearly as handsome.

His dull brown hair, now graying, was neatly parted on the left and combed slickly back from his high forehead; his hazel eyes were large and intent under heavy lids; and his other features were narrow and neat except for his bushy eyebrows. He had a small mustache but was otherwise clean shaven and looked every inch the soldier he had been in his youth.

The earl had been the third son in his family. He always knew he would inherit nothing from his father—primogeniture was the

law in England—and with two older brothers between him and the title had therefore taken up a military career. He had succeeded to the title at his father's death only because the two older brothers had predeceased him. He still remembered his third-rate status as a small boy. His resentment of his own son's privileged position was irrational but strong.

Aside from that, the earl was nostalgic for the excitement of battle. The country was no place for a man in his prime, as the mistress he kept in London kept telling him.

"Come, my dear," he said now to his wife. He always called her his dear, although he had long since forgotten that he had ever loved her. "We must welcome our only hope."

The countess stopped working on her tapestry, set the frame upright, and was helped up by her son, whose face and coloring were almost mirror images of her own. Lady Caroline had been the loveliest girl presented at court in her year and had expected of life exactly what it brought her: marriage to a nobleman, three children—one of them this favored son—an unassailable position in society, and no experience whatever of poverty, ugliness, or vice beyond what appeared in the Bible.

She had invited the three Cunninghams because her husband had ordered it, but she could not understand how the family could be so desperate for money that her son had to marry an American for it.

"Surely there are wealthy English girls," she had protested.

"Not many and not wealthy enough to handle our debt."

"Look how Jennie Jerome turned out," she had warned her husband, who harrumphed, his usual response to her unsolicited opinions. Since that was typical of husbandly responses among her acquaintance, it did not trouble her.

The countess's main concern was that Alastair should marry well; therefore a bumpkin from the colonies would not do. It saddened her that her son seemed eager for the match. She had always been first in his affections, ahead of any of the young ladies he knew. She reminded herself to be patient. This visit would surely prove that the American girl was not suitable.

"Thank you, darling," she said to Alastair for his helping hand as she arose. To her husband, with the smile that once had made him melt with love, she said, "Cyril, dearest, please do not be naughty. If Alastair must sacrifice himself, it is our duty to make it as pleasant for him as possible."

There, she thought. *I cannot be more sympathetic to his plight than that!*

"But I've told you, Mother," Alastair assured her. "It's no sacrifice."

She reached up to pat his cheek. "You're a fine, brave boy, darling. I'm proud of you." Then she smoothed the skirt of her dark blue silk dress and shook out the lace frills at her neck and wrists. One graceful white hand patted her upswept hair before she took her husband's arm and advanced with both men across the faux marble and trompe l'oeil columns of the entry hall just as the great oak door was opened by the butler.

The tall woman she saw coming through the door made the picturesque countess feel small, pale, and insipid, but she could not acknowledge such feelings to herself and they were transposed into immediate dislike. Lady Caroline was nothing if not socially correct, and she gave the smile she reserved for guests who had never been invited before.

"Mother, Father, may I present Mr. and Mrs. Cunningham?" Alastair said. And to Paul and Miranda, "My parents."

The American woman's smile was dazzling. So was her husband's. They were a striking pair, the brunette in a handsome suit of deep raspberry that shouted "Paris!" and the fair-haired man tailored in Savile Row. Lady Caroline felt suddenly dowdy in her blue silk and lace ruffles and disliked Mrs. Cunningham even more.

Then the countess turned her attention to the girl standing just behind her aunt and uncle. Alastair had gone on and on about how lovely she was, but Lady Caroline, eternally the belle of the ball, had not taken him seriously. Now she was obliged to.

The girl was breathtaking. She was small, dainty, and quite perfectly made. Her manner was modest and attractive and so was her pale blue cashmere dress under a sable cape. But the countess was not taken in. Behind that seraphic face and those heavenly blue eyes she could sense a spoiled, willful girl who had dug her talons into Lady Caroline's beloved son.

Well, she should not have him! Lady Caroline would see to that. For the moment, she invited them all into the small drawing room for an aperitif before luncheon and they strolled in together, two families apparently delighted to have met.

———— . ————

Cynthia closed her eyes when Walford kissed her. They were walking alone on the loggia after dinner and she had permitted the liberty because she was curious about how it would feel. The kiss had been light and brief and her reaction neutral.

"I'm sorry," he said when it was over.

"No, you are not," she replied. "But I accept your apology."

Walford looked down at her. She was given to making unexpected remarks like that; it was part of what made her far more interesting than most girls her age. Insipid girls were the reason he preferred older women, conversationally and sexually.

"Where do we go from here?" he asked.

She gestured at the loggia that ran along the south side of Inderby. "We have two choices: east or west," she said.

"I wish you'd be serious once in a while," he returned, but he took her arm through her sable wrap and they resumed their walk.

"Do you really?" she asked. "Wish I'd be serious?"

"I suppose not," he admitted ruefully. "I rather like you the way you are."

"Do your parents?"

"Yes, of course. Who could resist you?"

They looked at each other. They both knew the answer to that, but they never mentioned Steven James. It only piqued Alastair's interest in this lively young lady that she cared for "Dan'l Boone" more than she cared for the sixteenth earl-to-be.

Alastair was of an uncommon nature in more ways than one. He could not resist experiment, particularly of the risky kind. He was not attracted by what came easily and, for him, most things did. And he'd be damned before he'd marry one of the dull daughters of the nobility to save his birthright, when there were heiresses like Cynthia to be had. A gentleman, after all, had to spend some time with his wife, and Alastair was easily bored by most respectable women.

Cynthia had never bored him, and he would not allow her to be respectable in bed.

"What shall we do tomorrow?" Cynthia asked.

"Ride in the morning if it's not raining."

"I didn't bring riding clothes. And I'd rather play chess."

"Chess it will be."

She glanced at him. "Are any other guests expected tomorrow?"

He shook his head.

"What a pity," she said, "now your parents have seen I know which utensil to use at table and don't drink the water from my finger bowl."

"I had already assured them of that," he said, and they both laughed. "Still," he went on, "I'm sorry you got the impression that you are being vetted."

"Oh, for heaven's sake, Walford!" she said, shaking her head. "What else is this about?"

"Assuming it is, how would you feel about it?"

"I haven't the faintest idea," Cynthia replied. "And it's getting cold out here. Do let's go in and see what they've found to talk about."

Once more she had eluded him and once more he was intrigued.

———— · ————

"What do you think now?" Paul asked his wife when she was in
bed that night. Her bedroom was paneled in patterned blue China
silk with matching hangings and draperies. The ceilings were
molded and gilded in the baroque style, like the Walford railway
carriage.

"I think we're being patronized by the mother and tolerated by
the father," Miranda said.

"Cynthia too?"

"Oh, they like Cynthia. They can like her because she doesn't
count for anything but money in this equation and never would,
even if she were foolish enough to marry him."

"But young Walford seems thoroughly smitten."

"What Walford seems may be very different from what he is."

Paul shook his head. "I cannot fathom your dislike of him."

"He reminds me of Hobart. If the price is right, anything is
acceptable."

Paul, still standing at the foot of the bed, studied her. "I'd hate
to think Hobart—or anyone, for that matter—could influence your
likes and dislikes to such an extent."

Several moments of silence passed. Miranda yawned. "Lord, I'm
tired. Making conversation with these people isn't easy."

"Then you must sleep." He came to the bedside and leaned over
to kiss her forehead.

"I'm half gone already," she murmured. "Good night, Paul."

"Good night, Miranda."

She closed her eyes and listened as he went through the communicating door to his own bedroom. There it was again: no lovemaking, no love. But she was certainly not entitled to complain.

She wondered, as she often did, what Steven would say to all of
this.

———— • ————

Steven James was the focus of his father-in-law's thoughts as well.

"What's the boy up to?" Augustus Haggerty asked himself. On his desk in New York was the latest report from Raymond Steele. It said Steven had virtually abandoned the mission to raise capital and form an offshore company with it. That was bad enough, but Gus was more perturbed by other matters.

For one thing, Steven had drawn upon the letter of credit to its limit and, according to Steele, was speculating heavily in European markets.

For another—of which Steele was unaware—Steven had revoked Haggerty's power of attorney the day after the *Sylvania* docked at Liverpool. Haggerty was no longer free to manage Steven's portfolio. Copies of the legal revocation papers had arrived just the day before, but there had been no personal word from Steven to explain his action.

Not that Gus needed any. Obviously the boy was a lot angrier than Gus had anticipated and the crossing had not cooled him down. As for the grand gesture Gus had intended to make—replacing all Steven's losses as soon as he had proved his point—the appropriated letter of credit was more than enough to cover Steven's losses and had stolen Haggerty's thunder.

Gus was alarmed. He'd intended a good jolt to shock Steven out of his apathy, but now it appeared he had gone too far.

Not only had he lost control of Steven, but he might lose Steven altogether and he could not tolerate that.

"*No!*" Gus said, his pink cheeks turning crimson, tears dimming his eyes. "He's my son! He's all I've got besides a lump of money, and what good's money with no one to leave it to, no one to miss you when you're gone and cry at your wake?"

He picked up the telephone on his desk and, when his chief clerk answered, told the man to book him on the next steamer for England.

"And make it a fast one," he ordered. "I'm in a hurry."

"What do you suppose," Lady Burdon asked the count as the carriage drove them to the Savoy for dinner, "will come of the Cunninghams' weekend at Inderby?"

"Trouble," Jean-Baptiste replied. "Alastair is ready, but I doubt his mother will be. She dotes on the boy. In her opinion, only a royal princess is good enough for him."

"But in the end Lady Caroline must do as Inderby tells her. The whole affair will depend upon how much Miss Cunningham's father is willing to pay."

"I'm glad I have no such problem."

Lady Burdon patted his hand. "Now that your young lady has decided to stay on in London, you'll have time to court her."

The count sighed. "Why is it that one collection of atoms evokes love and another does not?"

"Ah," said Lady Burdon. "People have been asking that question since the Garden of Eden."

Twenty-three

When the footman had deposited their baggage in the rented flat, Alton made tea from supplies they had already stocked, and the two young women sat in the parlor together, relishing the privacy of their new home.

"We did the right thing," Kitt said.

"Yes, Miss Kitt, you certainly did."

"As soon as we're settled in, we must have Lady Burdon and the count to tea."

Alton was reflective. "That man grows on a body. He may not be the prince out of a fairy story, but he has a lovely face."

Kitt nodded agreement. "It isn't important what people look like. There aren't that many men in the world who are considerate and handsome too."

There was a silence. They both knew of two who were—and that Miranda was not content to be married to one of them.

"There's His Lordship," Alton said, mentioning another.

"Lady Burdon thinks Miss Cunningham will marry him."

"And a good thing too," Alton remarked. "They deserve each other, both of them bossy as they are."

"And both of them beautiful."

Another silence. Neither of these two young women had ever felt beautiful and consequently believed they had no right to expect the attentions of handsome men.

After tea they unpacked, their spirits rising again, and after a supper of poached eggs on toast and rice pudding, they were feeling very much at home.

It's a new leaf, Kitt thought when she was in her bed. *I can make a fresh start.*

Kitt knew she had made a total fool of herself over Steven James. During the week before the move, she had retreated, abruptly and quite unconsciously, into the persona of a spinster devoted to good works.

The fringe of curls popularized for so long by the Princess of Wales was long gone from her forehead, and she gravitated once again to her dark-colored dresses with sober trim. The earrings and bracelets had been put away and she wore nothing more elaborate than a cameo and small pearl ear studs.

Lady Burdon noticed but said nothing to Kitt. To the count she remarked that his chances had definitely improved.

"Explain, if you please," he asked her, "why it should be easier to woo a little nun than an animated young woman."

"Piffle. This austerity is only temporary. She can't smother her nature. She'll soon realize she wants more out of life than crusading."

"And turn to me?"

"If you're clever enough to be there."

"I don't see why you must help her to become a campaigner," the count said querulously.

"Because the sooner it's over, the sooner to sleep. If she had to do it on her own it would take her years to get where she's going."

"Where she thinks she can go," he temporized.

"No, Kitt will hang on until she does what she's set out to do. Then she'll have time for you."

"I begin to fear for my happiness as husband to such a woman."

"When did common sense ever get the better of love?"

The count smiled in that charming way he had and did not answer. He was French, after all, and supposed to be an expert on love, although sometimes he was thoroughly puzzled by women. Still, if Lady Pat approved of what his Louisa was doing . . .

Lady Pat had agreed to invite a large group of suffragists to a tea the following week to introduce them to Kitt.

"Mind you," she counseled Kitt, "they'll expect you to support the suffragist cause, but their ranks include women who represent many other grievances of our sex. It will be up to you to get them involved in the particular cause you've decided to support."

If all went according to plan, introductions to more militant groups would follow the meeting and, after Kitt had joined several of those groups and given a few public speeches, she would ask her sponsors to arrange interviews with presidents of shipping lines, with government officials, with anyone who had influence in the travel industry.

"Build a better mousetrap," she told Lady Burdon, "and the world will beat a path to your door."

"I devoutly hope not!" Lady Burdon said in mock alarm.

"Maybe I don't have a better mousetrap," Kitt went on, "but I have a story that will make them sit up and take notice. It amounts to legalized assault on helpless girls!"

"That will get their attention," Lady Pat observed. "Sex always does."

Kitt, who had long since grown accustomed to Lady Burdon's blunt observations, agreed.

It was from Lady Pat she learned the Cunninghams were about to leave for Cairo by way of the Paris Exposition. "And high time too! If that girl keeps running after Senator James, Walford will never ask for her."

From the count Kitt learned that Steven was to stay on at Brown's Hotel indefinitely. It was a mixed blessing. It disturbed her to know he was so close, although still out of reach. But with Cynthia gone, Kitt could dream of chance meetings that turned into teatime tête-à-tétes, of teatimes that led to dinner invitations.

With Miranda gone as well, it would be easier for Kitt's dreams to expand. Kitt had almost forgiven him for falling in love with Miranda. She was less successful at forgiving Miranda for falling in love with him.

———— • ————

"I don't know how we colonials have managed to survive in such cramped quarters," Cynthia said, laughing. The three Cunninghams were having breakfast in the parlor of their suite at the Bristol while, in the bedrooms, the servants finished packing for the voyage to Cairo by rail, coach, and steamer. With a short visit to the Paris Exposition added, it would take them over three weeks to reach Cairo.

"I take it you find Inderby more to your taste," Paul said.

"Infinitely."

"The question is whether you fancy Alastair as much as his house," Miranda said. "He goes along with it."

Cynthia's features took on a haughty cast. "I'm aware of that. I was merely admiring his property."

"It isn't his yet," Paul reminded her.

"But someday Alastair will inherit," Cynthia said, tossing her head.

"And his wife will be Viscountess Walford until that happy event and Countess of Inderby after it," Miranda observed.

"A consummation devoutly to be wished, don't you agree?" Cynthia replied.

Miranda and Paul exchanged a glance.

"Do *you* wish it?" Miranda asked.

Cynthia shrugged. "I needn't decide until he proposes."

"You ought to be prepared because he *will* ask for you if he thinks you'll say yes." Paul hesitated. "Will you?"

Cynthia's sophisticated air melted like new snow. "Oh, Uncle Paul, it's so confusing." She got up and went to him, perching on the arm of his chair and talking in that way she had that excluded Miranda. "I still think I'm in love with someone else."

"But has the senator shown any romantic interest in you?" Paul asked in a strained fashion that made Miranda avoid looking directly at him.

"I know he likes me but he seems to have other things on his mind. Anyway, how do people know if it's love or only fascination?"

Paul's fair skin flushed. "You had better ask your aunt," he said. "Women know far more about love than men do." He excused himself and went downstairs to settle their bill, leaving his wife and his niece together in a thickening silence.

"Is that true?" Cynthia said at last. "That women know more about love?"

"Some of us have more time to devote to it. But do we *know* more? Hardly. That's a fiction men have invented. If they can claim to be ignorant about love, they needn't concern themselves with its consequences."

"Does Senator James know about love?"

Miranda looked at her niece steadily. "He is not a subject for discussion between us."

"Because you say so?" Cynthia approached her aunt, her hands curled into fists. "Except for you, I'd be engaged to him by now! He's the one I really want."

"But he doesn't want you. And you're not really in love with him, Cynthia, or you couldn't even consider Alastair with all his lands and titles. You've been thrown off balance because Steven didn't fall at your feet the way most men do. And you're using Walford to get even with him."

Cynthia turned away. "I don't know what I'm doing," she cried in real confusion. It made Miranda want to comfort her, until Cynthia went on. "And I don't know how you could go from his bed to Uncle Paul's without a second thought!"

"You can't begin to know what my thoughts are. You're a child, Cynthia, but it's time to grow up now, to stop blaming people for not playing the roles you've assigned them in your romantic fantasies."

"I know what you want, Miranda. You want me to marry Walford and stay safely here in England, far away from *him,* so you two can carry on together in New York!"

"Another fantasy. As it happens, I think it would be a great mistake for you to marry Walford."

"So I've gathered, but why?" Cynthia turned on her angrily. "Tell me why!"

"It's your money he wants, not you."

Cynthia's face twisted. "It isn't! Not entirely. He's in love with me."

"He couldn't be," Miranda said flatly.

"He's kissed me!"

Miranda digested that before she said, "You should not have permitted it."

Cynthia was impatient. "Aunt Miranda, this is 1900, not the Middle Ages! There's a lot to be learned from a kiss."

"Really? What?"

"How a man feels about you."

"If a man is still breathing, he has the same response to any woman he kisses."

Cynthia still stood over her. "I don't know why I even talk to you, much less listen to anything you say." She turned abruptly and left the parlor.

Miranda covered her face with her hands and hoped she wouldn't fall apart. It was unnerving to feel both anger and sympathy for Cynthia, but she did. Those outings Cynthia wangled with Steven were almost as disquieting as the girl's interest in Walford's pedigree and property.

Thank heaven they were leaving for Cairo in an hour! It would give Cynthia time to reflect.

"And me," Miranda whispered. If they had stayed in London for one more day, she knew she would have called Steven, just to hear the sound of his voice.

But she would have been unable to stop at that.

By the time she returned from Cairo he would be back in America, and by the time Miranda reached New York, he would be in Albany and someday, if Haggerty had his way, in Washington.

And then? Would they ever meet again?

——— · ———

When the Cunningham party boarded the train for Paris later that evening, Steven was sitting opposite Gus Haggerty in the dining room of Steele's club. Steele had suggested it as a meeting place and had promised Haggerty to arrive at least fifteen minutes late.

"That way you two'll have time to talk," Steele had said. Steele had no idea what Haggerty had done to make Steven James sore as a boil, but it was clear that the senator was furious with his father-in-law. Steele and Haggerty had already met, and the Irishman knew as much as Steele did—"the bare essentials," Steele had called them with a grin—about Steven's affair with Mrs. Cunningham during the voyage and Miss Cunningham's determined pursuit of him ever since.

Gus and Steven were both punctual and greeted each other with near-British formality at the club. They were shown to their table, where they ordered two whiskies. Steven covered his anger while Gus admired the walnut paneling and the carved, vaulted ceiling of the dining room, the paintings of famous members past and present,

and the massive silver serving pieces on rolling tables presided over by white-gloved waiters and stewards.

"Mighty fancy," Gus said, trying an opening gambit before they got to the main event.

But Steven was impatient of pretense. "What do you want, Gus? Tell me before Steele gets here."

Gus slapped the linen-draped tabletop with his napkin. "What do I want? Why, to see you, lad! To talk to you, make sure you understand—"

"I understand all too well," Steven cut in. "You must think I'm an idiot. You'd have to, to suppose we could take up where we left off after what you've done."

Haggerty was stricken, genuinely so, Steven would have sworn. "Ah, Steven darlin', can't you forgive a lonely old man for a foolish mistake? Haven't you made your own share of them?"

Steven nodded. "And I'll probably make a lot more, but I don't intend to repeat any. So whatever it is you're selling, Gus, you'll have to peddle it elsewhere."

The older man's face twisted like a disappointed child's, but his blue eyes studied his son-in-law carefully. Gus was almost as good at reading people as he was at reading balance sheets.

"I didn't want to lose you," he said. "I've been very lonely all by myself without you and Alicia. But you've changed, son. What's happened?"

Gus thought that surely it wasn't anything as unimportant as his affair with Mrs. Cunningham! He was probably in love with the niece who looked so much like Alicia, and he'd be troubled by that.

"You damned well know what happened," Steven said, but he avoided Gus's eyes.

Gus shook his head. "No, it's more than me. With all your sorrows you still had a bit of the boy in you the day you sailed from New York. I don't see that boy anymore."

Steven was surprised at his perspicacity. His rancor softened, but all he said was "I lost my faith."

Gus snorted, drawing glances from the neighboring tables. "Surely you had none in me!" he said. "You always said I was a pirate."

"Toward others, not to me."

Gus drained his whisky at one gulp. "So it's not what I do, it's who I do it to! What kind of standard is that?"

Steven shrugged. "It doesn't matter, Gus. Even if I believed you only wanted to teach me a lesson, I wouldn't want to be connected with you again."

"Why not make that decision after you've heard what the deal is?" Gus, desperate to keep their attachment alive with money if not love, felt he would be forced to play his high card now.

"Because it isn't the deal, Gus, it's you. You don't want to work with me, you want to own me. It's not an associate you're after, it's a son. And one who's willing to be your puppet."

Gus gazed at him, speechless for a moment. Then he nodded. "All right, it's true what you say. You're a lot more to me than a friend or a partner. You're my last chance at a son. Is it such a fearful thing for a man to want?"

"No, but I already have a father. And I'm my own man, Gus. You've never accepted that."

Gus nodded sadly. That was true, also, but it was equally true that this was not the engaging, high-spirited young man he had known. Whatever had happened to Steven, it was not all Gus's doing.

"I should have caught on," Steven said, "when you arranged for me to marry Alicia. In your eyes that made me a Haggerty."

"And what's so terrible about that? You were as eager for the match as I was! It was a good marriage. You're mourning my poor little girl still."

Steven started to speak, then remembered whose fault it was that Haggerty's little girl was dead. He took a deep breath and let his anger go. Aggravating as Gus had been, there was no point in telling him the wretched truth about his own tepid feelings for Alicia or in

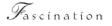

blaming his father-in-law for helping Steven to do anything he wanted to do.

The fact was that he was equally disgusted with himself for not having looked before he leapt into marriage, as his sister had advised, and for having been so easily misled by his own ambition.

"And what of your political career?" Gus asked. "You can't suppose you can go it on your own?"

Steven half rose, visibly furious again, his torso thrust forward as he leaned on his hands, although his voice was low in deference to the other diners. "You bastard! I knew you'd threaten to withdraw your support if I refused to be your substitute son! Well, do it, then, and you can go to the devil for all I care. I'm finished being Haggerty's boy. If I want to get to Washington, I'll get there on my own."

"Mother of God!" Gus was astounded. He reached out to put a hand on Steven's arm. "Listen to me. I meant no threat. Why would I withdraw my support? I'm devoted to you, Steven. I'll do anything you want, to prove that." Gus's face shone with obvious sincerity.

Steven drew a deep breath. "Then stop trying to run my life."

"I never meant . . . but never mind. I'll do whatever you say, only don't let this come between us," Gus pleaded, sure now that this had more to do with Steven than with Gus himself. He thanked God and all the saints that he hadn't mentioned the Cunningham women. "Dammit, here comes Steele. Look, son, what's between us is none of his affair. Now, calm yourself, there's a good fella. It won't hurt you to listen to the deal I have in mind. No need to make any decisions one way or the other." He looked at Steven, his face creased with apprehension.

Steven sat down, amazed at his own raw temper, feeling slightly foolish as Steele joined them. It was hard to be angry at Gus for more than five minutes and impossible for Steven to sit in judgment on him.

The waiters soon descended, carved thick slices from the huge roast of beef, which was kept piping hot inside a silver cylinder with a sliding top. The three men were served boiled sprouts, carrots, and potatoes along with wedges of Yorkshire pudding, dollops of grated, creamed horseradish, and the rich, red juice of the beef. When the service was complete, the wine steward filled the glasses and the staff withdrew.

Steele put a generous piece of beef into his mouth and chewed it with relish. "Well, now," he said to Haggerty after he had swallowed it. "Where do you plan to make all this money?"

Haggerty's blue eyes darted from Steele to Steven. "Panama," he said.

Steele and Steven regarded each other, then turned back to Gus. "You can't be serious!" Steele said.

"If the great de Lesseps couldn't repeat his Suez triumph and build a canal across the Isthmus of Panama," Steven exclaimed, "what makes you think you can?"

"I don't plan to build it," Gus said. "The U.S. government does. So if it fails, the government bears the burden, not private investors."

"Then where do private investors fit in?"

Gus smiled. "In the corners, like always. Look, the government builds a canal, someone's got to administer it. That means people. People have to live somewhere and eat something. That means construction contracts and import concessions to anyone with an inside track. And how do you get the inside track?" Haggerty raised his hand and rubbed his thumb against two fingers. "Money," he answered himself with satisfaction. "But we must do it now, while the official line is that a canal can't be built."

"But can it?" Steele persisted. "The French company went bankrupt in '79. Worked like slaves for seven years and lost twenty thousand men to tropical diseases."

"That's right," Steven agreed. "Panama's not a nice, dry desert like Suez. It's a pestilent swamp; de Lesseps proved that. What happens if a big ditch is still impossible and no contractors are needed to house the workers? We'll have bribed ourselves into a dead end."

"Then we'll have lost only our initial, very modest investment." Haggerty popped a brussels sprout into his cherubic mouth and chewed it. "But you're not looking at the big picture when you talk of dead ends," he said.

He leaned forward in his eagerness. "That canal *must* be built and necessity is the mother of invention. America's determined to keep European influence out of the western hemisphere with the Monroe Doctrine and suchlike. And what's the one thing that could stop her? I'll tell you: distance. The country's too vulnerable with its coastlines three thousand miles apart."

Gus attacked a small potato before he went on. "The Spanish-American War showed us that supplies from New York had to go all the way around South America to get to Los Angeles. Now, aside from mail and communication, where does that leave the military on one coast when the supplies are on the other?"

Haggerty ate a piece of beef while the other two waited impatiently. "And then there's trade! With the West Coast and the Far East. That canal will be as busy as Broadway! Someone's got to supply the ships for it."

"But the U.S. will have to fortify any canal it may be able to build," Steele said. "What makes you think the British Empire will give up that treaty? The one that guarantees the canal zone's neutrality?"

"Treaties are written on paper," Haggerty said. "Paper can be replaced. They're considering a new treaty right now."

"You've done your homework," Steven said with reluctant admiration.

Haggerty nodded. "I try," he said, looking hopefully at Steven. "Sometimes I'm not as careful as I ought to be."

The conversation continued and Steven's interest sharpened in spite of his vow to stay away from his father-in-law. But there were many other decisions to be made before he could take a chance like this.

Still, it was a tempting proposition and the three men talked on until it was past eleven. They arranged to dine together again the following evening and resume their discussion then.

Twenty-four

*H*aggerty, who was staying at the Savoy, wanted a bit of night life; he and Steele went off in a hansom to gamble and then finish the evening at a brothel.

Steven waited until their hansom pulled away. He decided to walk back to Brown's and did not hail the next cab in the rank waiting across the street. There was a fine drizzle, but Steven had grown accustomed to London weather. He liked walking late at night through the quiet, misty streets with their atmosphere of substance and order.

There was a comforting solidity, he reflected, about a country already arrived at the height of empire. In America there was the turbulence of a country striving to get there.

Steven hoped America didn't arrive too soon. It took time and experience to provide a solid base for expansion. He was concerned that his country, with her energy and eagerness, would construct a glittering superstructure before it had a firm foundation and as a result would rise quickly but soon collapse. But then, other great empires of the world had taken centuries to build, only to disintegrate in a matter of years.

But he was certain the British Empire would endure, would go on colonizing and cultivating the godforsaken corners of the world. Oddly enough, worldly, sophisticated London often reminded him of Greenhill Farm and the days of his youth. There was no bustle at Greenhill—or here in Mayfair—as there was everywhere in New York City at all hours; nor did he sense the constant stir and scheming he had found in Albany and would surely find, multiplied one hundredfold, if he got to Washington.

He was not naive: He knew the same plotting went on in Whitehall and on Threadneedle Street. But it was done with the polish of long practice.

"If it takes a dash of hypocrisy to make life so pleasant," he murmured as he walked, "that's little enough to pay."

But America was bold and brash, like Gus Haggerty.

"Dammit," he said, shaking his head when he thought of Gus. The man knew how to get to Steven, how to persuade Steven that his affection was genuine, that he had learned his lesson and would never allow his need to push him past the line again.

But there were people—and Gus was one of them—who were obsessive about those they chose to love. They demanded an equivalent return of their feelings and would often cross the line to get it.

More and more, as the hours without Miranda stretched into days and then weeks, Steven wondered if she was his obsession. His separation from her had made him see that he needed to change his life entirely or he would never be free.

Now it struck him that he could best do that by settling permanently in England. He had made his first fortune on the American market; there was no reason he couldn't expand it on the London Exchange and the Paris Bourse.

"And I'd be far away from Gus," he told himself, "even if I do decide to gamble on the Panama Canal."

He would also be far away from Miranda, and that was more to the point and much harder to accept. He replayed their last conversation at Lady Burdon's over and over in his mind, amazed that

Miranda, after her refusal on the ship to end the affair, could have told him good-bye so abruptly and so finally not very long afterward. Evidently she loved her husband more than she knew.

But she was the shape and sight and sound of love to Steven, and now, having found it, it was not in his nature to let it go without a fight. He would not leave London before she returned and he had another chance to persuade her.

His heart leapt at the thought that she might agree to stay with him—and sank at the possibility that she might not. It angered him. He was not accustomed to denial.

If she rejected him, he would definitely stay on here. There was no way he could live in the same city as Miranda and not be with her. Here he could reshape himself and be—almost—the man he had been before he met her, his heart defended, his passions restricted to his groin and his life complete in and of itself, not lonely and bland without the magic presence of one woman.

His solitary thoughts were diverted when he passed a storefront on Oxford Street that was being used tonight as a meeting place. Large blue letters on a white banner over the door proclaimed this to be a gathering of the Women's Political Union.

Through the glass front of the shop, he was astonished to see Miss McAllister step up to the small platform at the back of the store.

———— · ————

She was surrounded by bolts of cloth, glass button cases, spools of thread, racks of ribbons, and trimmings neatly wound on large wooden bobbins, fitting forms discreetly covered by swaths of muslin but hinting at female curves beneath, and all manner of sewing paraphernalia. Her presence eclipsed all of it as she folded her hands on the small lectern and acknowledged the scattered applause with a nod and a bow.

Steven made a generous contribution to the basket at the door, not recognizing Alton, who held the basket, although Alton recognized him. He went inside to listen, careful to stay half hidden at the back of the shop lest Miss McAllister see him and be unnerved by the unexpected presence of an acquaintance.

He didn't know he was impelled by his need to be in the presence of someone who knew Miranda, someone who had been a part, however remote, of the happiest days of his life. He was glad to see Miss McAllister, curious about what she was doing there and eager to talk to her. He wondered where she had been for the last few weeks.

He noticed the starkness and severity of her dress, but it could not diminish her personality any more than that red hair could be eclipsed by her hat.

It was while she was thanking her small audience for giving her the opportunity to ask their help that he recognized Lady Burdon and the count, two more from the *Sylvania* crossing. Miss McAllister had surely seen them, but recalling their first meeting, he remembered that there was very little that could intimidate this remarkable young woman.

He wondered briefly what the two aristocrats were doing in such an unlikely place, but he focussed his attention on Kitt when he heard her say "legalized assault on women." The words were followed by a small gasp from the audience at this questionable choice of words.

"I am obliged, however reluctantly," Kitt went on, "to tell you what happened aboard one of our proud passenger liners. A young woman of excellent character and pride in her profession as a senior member of the staff was relentlessly pursued by one of the ship's officers—whose job, I remind you, is to protect those weaker and less advantaged than himself.

"She resisted him repeatedly, even when threatened by him with dismissal without a character if she did not surrender. Intercession by a concerned passenger held him off for a while but soon he renewed his hunt—and this time he trapped his quarry and had his way."

A hum of indignation filled the room, but Steven could not tell whether the audience objected to what the officer did or to the bold way the speaker described it. But Kitt would not let them escape with a pale euphemism. She persisted when the hum faded.

"He raped her," Kitt said, her green eyes blazing. "Brutally and repeatedly, he raped her."

A hubbub arose in the audience and a slim, sallow chap standing near Steven began scribbling frantically in a notebook. His garish tweed suit and Loden cape were not a gentleman's attire but they were a clue to his profession. Steven had been pursued by the Fourth Estate when he was a stock market wunderkind and had developed a sixth sense for reporters.

"Press?" Steven whispered while the room still rippled with shock.

The man nodded. "For the *Daily Review*. Never heard that word used in mixed company before—nor spoken by a lady, not even one of these crazy suffragists," he said. He wet the point of his pencil with his tongue, wrote for a few seconds more, then looked at Steven.

"A rare bird this one." He glanced at the flyer in his hand. "Miss Kitt McAllister. A Yankee." He shook his head. "Doesn't look like a dried-up old maid either, not with that hair. She could be a looker if she'd wear a bit of color, spruce herself up."

"She's an exceptional young lady," Steven bristled, resenting the man's crude assessment of Miss McAllister and her possibilities as a "looker."

She was speaking again.

"I've come here tonight because women must have the right to report such situations as the one I've described without being blamed for what is clearly not their fault. Having the vote will give us a better chance to protect them, but I've come to ask your help and your advice until that happy day arrives. I'm a stranger in your admirable country and I have no idea where to begin.

"I want to protect decent young women trying to make an honest living. I cannot stand by and allow them to be victimized by the men—gentlemen, so-called—who are their superiors in rank but not in character."

She paused for a moment, gathering them in.

"I will be obliged for anything you and your organizations can suggest, and these terrified girls will be grateful."

She was so clearly sincere, so obviously intent upon justice that her unfortunate language was immediately forgiven—she was not, after all, English—and an avalanche of helpful suggestions began, along with invitations to join several groups, as Lady Burdon had predicted.

Steven saw the count and Lady Burdon exchange a congratulatory glance, as if they had contributed to Kitt's success. Steven wondered if they had and, if so, in what way. They joined the applause when it began, and Steven applauded with them while the reporter made his way toward the podium, the better to interview Kitt when the meeting ended.

Steven very much wanted to talk to her, but this was no time for a conversation. She was besieged by her audience and he left the shop to resume his solitary walk to Brown's.

Once there, he went to the bellman, asked for paper and pen, and wrote a message for her. Sealing it, he returned it to the desk and asked that it be delivered to her room.

The bellman sucked in his cheeks. "The lady has left us, Mr. James," he said mournfully. "About a week since."

Steven was taken aback. "Did she leave a forwarding address?"

"No, sir, she did not . . ." His sentence seemed unfinished.

Steven found a sovereign and passed the coin across the counter.

"Her maid comes every few days to fetch the post," the bellman said in a conspiratorial whisper.

"Then will you deliver this to her maid next time she comes?"

"At your service, sir," the bellman said.

Steven went up to his room, still thinking about Kitt McAllister and the strange turn her plans had taken. He had supposed she

was in Rome or Florence by now. Instead, she was giving rousing speeches about the problem she had brought to Steven on the ship!

He remembered which newspaper that reporter represented and made a mental note to buy a copy the next day.

Then he got into bed, turned out the light, and thought about Miranda.

———— • ————

When several days had passed with no reply from Miss McAllister, Steven again consulted the bellman.

"The letter was delivered, sir," the bellman assured him. "At least, it was given to the lady's maid."

Something in the man's tone caught Steven's attention. "What do you mean by that?"

"I can't say what happened to it after the maid got it, sir, now, can I?"

Steven eyed him skeptically. "What do you think might have happened?" he asked, passing another coin across the counter.

"It might have been torn up," the man said, skillfully pocketing the money. "Mind, I'm not saying for a fact that it was, but it could have been."

Steven frowned. "When is the maid expected again?"

The bellman glanced up at a clock on the mantel across the room. "Very soon now," he said.

Steven nodded, took a seat just inside the lounge, and picked up a newspaper to conceal his face. The minutes passed very slowly with guests and visitors coming in and out until, finally, a neatly attired young woman entered and went to the bellman, who nodded and greeted her with the exact amount of cordiality accorded a lady's maid. She took the small packet of letters he gave her, glanced through them briefly, then put them in her purse, nodded at the bellman, and left. The man glanced at Steven with a wink and

Steven followed her out of the hotel, keeping a safe distance between them until she reached Dover Street.

There she stopped briefly, tore one of the envelopes to bits, scattered them to the wind, and then continued along the street to one of the residences.

When she had gone inside, Steven waited five minutes before he retrieved several scraps of his note and went into the building. The small entry boasted an alabaster vase of fresh flowers reflected in a gilt-framed mirror over a half-moon table. The parquet floor was highly polished. Near the inner door there were three small strips of white pasteboard, each with a name neatly inked in script.

MCALLISTER was one of them.

Steven left, puzzled over why Miss McAllister's maid would have destroyed his note.

On his way to a luncheon appointment the next day with an investment banker Steele had introduced, Steven passed a florist near Green Park and ordered a dozen yellow roses, with instructions that they were to be delivered to Miss McAllister herself, not to any of her domestics.

On the card he wrote:

> *I heard you speak at the Women's Political Union and*
> *was very much impressed—and surprised that you are still*
> *in London. I hope you'll allow me the pleasure of calling*
> *on you soon. Steven James.*

A thought struck him: Miss McAllister had had no maid on the *Sylvania.* Maybe she had rescued the stewardess after the girl was attacked. And maybe—Steven's face felt hot—it was the stewardess who had found out about him and Miranda and was trying to protect her new employer from a rogue male.

If she didn't reply, he would know his suspicions were correct.

——— • ———

Two hours later Kitt stood in the parlor of the flat, holding the roses and smiling tenderly while Alton carried in a crystal vase half filled with water.

"Aren't they lovely?" Kitt breathed as she trimmed the stems with a pair of kitchen shears and placed them one by one in the vase.

Alton shrugged. "I wonder how he found you, miss." She wondered as well if the matter of the notes she had destroyed would ever be discovered. But it was her moral duty to protect Miss Kitt from that man! From the look on her mistress's face that would take some doing.

"Will you let him call?" she asked.

Kitt hesitated, then shook her head. "There's no point. He's in love with Miranda. I told you how they looked at each other at Lady Burdon's that night. It wasn't just a cheap romance, Alton. But he needs a friend, and friendship is not enough for me."

Alton was sympathetic but relieved. She went to fetch the books they were studying while Kitt finished arranging the flowers. Soon they were absorbed in their lessons.

Kitt, listening to Alton conjugate French verbs, knew she must not reply, not even to thank him for the flowers. She must stay away from him and eventually she would forget how much she loved him.

If she could stay away from him.

———— · ————

"See here, Alastair," the Earl of Inderby told his son at breakfast the next morning, "the situation's serious. This matter must be brought to a swift conclusion."

"You make it sound as if he were buying a cow," Lady Caroline said with a thin, forced laugh. "The person he marries will be a member of our family. We can't keep her out in the stables, more's the pity, and that is why we must make no mistakes."

"This is a far more important transaction than any cow could be," the earl said, glaring first at his wife and then at his son. "The only mistake would be to let her get away."

"I intend to marry her before someone else does," Alastair said. "I've booked passage to Cairo and will ask her uncle's permission to propose to her directly I arrive."

"You'd have saved a deal of money by asking her when she was here," his father grumbled.

"She might have refused me here."

"Tut," Lady Caroline said. "She was overwhelmed by Inderby."

"It needed time to sink in," Alastair replied, polite but not particularly interested in his mother's opinion.

"Surely you don't think she'd refuse you!" his mother protested, torn between pride in her son and jealousy toward his future wife, no matter who that might be.

"It's hard to tell," Alastair said. "She's elusive. Not like any girl I've ever met before." He felt an erotic twinge at the memory of that chaste kiss. "She thinks like a man."

Once more his mother pounced. "How terribly unattractive! Yet you sound as if you actually admire her!"

"I do, rather," Alastair said. "She's clever as well as rich, and she's very beautiful."

"Splendid!" his father said, helping himself to smoked haddock and shirred eggs from the trays the butler presented. "If her uncle likes you, what she wants does not signify."

There was silence in the room until the butler and his minions had served everyone and withdrawn.

Then, "I cannot bear it!" the countess protested.

"Come now, my dear," her husband said in the same tone he would have used to a small child. "We must yield to necessity."

"But she may not be worth it. You have no idea how large her dowry is!"

"Very large," Alastair said.

"That is a matter for negotiation between her father and myself," the earl said impatiently, abandoning all pretense of regard for

Lady Caroline's views. "I'm sure we can reach an agreement without your assistance."

Alastair turned a piece of dry toast in his graceful fingers. "Perhaps her father will come here to discuss her dowry while we are in Cairo."

"Excellent idea. I shall have Truscott contact him"—Truscott was the earl's solicitor in America—"as soon as you tell me how she receives you in Cairo."

The countess shook her head in dismay. "An American!"

"That is no longer shocking," the earl said testily. "Do you know how many American heiresses have married titles in the last twenty years?"

"More than ten?" Alastair offered.

The earl shook his head, still addressing his wife. "Dozens!"

Privately Alastair didn't care how many English aristocrats had married money to preserve their lavish way of life. He had decided aboard the *Sylvania* to marry Cynthia Cunningham, and if he could not charm her, then he'd damn well charm her father and marry her whether she liked it or not.

The uncle was already on his side. Why the aunt was not remained a mystery. It was certainly not on moral grounds. She had indulged herself lavishly with the senator, from what he had heard.

Even the prospect of a reluctant bride did not dismay him in the least. On the contrary, it rather excited him. If Cynthia still fancied Senator James after she had produced several legitimate sons for Walford, she could bloody well take him as a lover.

But if she did, Alastair promised himself, he would call the senator out and kill him.

"When will you leave?" his father inquired.

"Tomorrow. The Cunninghams are stopping in Paris for a few days to visit the exposition, but I'll go directly to Cairo by way of Italy and be there to welcome them when they arrive."

"Well done, my lad!"

Lady Caroline wept into her tiny handkerchief.

Book

Three

Twenty-five

The train chugged slowly toward the Cairo terminal, a steel cocoon about to burst from its sudden inner agitation. There was a flurry of movement as passengers, roused from the somnolence of travel, began to gather their belongings and to peer out of the windows, calling to one another. The men's hair was tossed by the wind, the women's ribbons fluttered.

A hum sounded in the distance; it was difficult to identify and increased in volume as they neared the impressive stone station. The train stopped. The cocoon opened and began to discharge its pullulating cargo.

Leaving their first-class carriage, the Cunninghams were precipitated into a world of unaccustomed color, movement, noise, and smell, of porters, beggars, hawkers selling beads and souvenirs, snake charmers, jugglers, conjurers, pickpockets and—unmentioned—prostitutes and thieves.

"It's incredible!" Miranda said, her eyes sparkling at a sight as different from Manhattan and Mayfair as any she had imagined. "It's like the *Arabian Nights!*"

Paul watched her, stimulated by her eager response. There was an ingenuous quality about her now. Oddly enough, sexual sophistication made her seem younger, not older or worldly or jaded. She was more beautiful than ever, a joy to behold—until he remembered how and by whom she had been transformed. He had that reaction every time he looked at her, and it was difficult to take his eyes away from her; impossible, therefore, not to rage inwardly. Even while he raged, he desired her.

Now he made himself smile and say, "No matter how many times I see it, it's always exciting."

"What language are they speaking?" Cynthia asked, her sharp ear tuned to the babble on the platform.

"There are dozens of dialects, but they can all communicate in Arabic, and French is a second language here in Cairo."

"Since Napoleon's advent?" Miranda asked. "Is there anywhere in the civilized world, apart from America, that tyrant didn't go?"

"Don't be too angry with him. We owe the Rosetta Stone to him—and one of the best excavations of the Sphinx."

Paul chose two of the porters who now clustered around them. The men gathered up the hand baggage and hung it on the harnesses of shabby belts and heavy cords they were wearing. It was incredible that they could move at all, once laden, but they set off toward the station entrance with the three Cunninghams in their wake.

"Look at their poor, skinny legs," Miranda said. "It's shameful that they work like beasts of burden. Why doesn't the railroad supply them with carts?"

"Now, Aunt Miranda," Cynthia chided. "They seem perfectly content. You can coddle the poor when we're back in New York. For the moment, just enjoy the spectacle!"

The noise in the terminal was climbing to an ever higher pitch as new passengers swarmed to fill the seats just vacated, while the arriving travelers headed for the streets and whatever form of transport suited them. There were military men and Anglo-Indian civil servants traveling between India and London. There were women in

veils and men in scarlet fezzes, merchants selling silks and spices, pashas with entourages, and ordinary tourists. Over it all hung the pungent scents of Arabia.

Then the beggars closed in upon the newly arrived travelers, clamoring for handouts.

As the Cunninghams neared the arches leading to the street, Cynthia felt a tugging at her skirts and, looking down, saw a scrawny child who might have been anywhere from eight to twelve years old. His skin, stretched tight over his bones, was covered with sores, and his eyes were crusted with the yellow discharge they exuded. Flies buzzed around him. A sickly, sour stench emanated from him, and from his mouth when he opened it crocodile-wide. Cynthia felt sick when she saw that he had no tongue, only the raw red stub of one.

Nauseated, terrified, she turned her head, closed her eyes, and stood absolutely still as if to will him away. Miranda and Paul, following the porters, did not notice her absence for several seconds. Then Paul stopped and called something to the porters. "Stay here," he told Miranda, and she watched him hurry back to Cynthia.

"Get him away from me," the girl shrieked to her uncle. "Get him away!"

Paul took some money from his pocket and, staying at a distance from Cynthia, held it out to the boy and spoke brusquely to him in Arabic. But the child did not relinquish his hold on his goddess. He stared up, dazzled by the richness of her, the fair skin, the beauty. He stroked her dress as if hypnotized by the feel of the silk. He sniffed at it once or twice.

"Get him away from me!" Cynthia pleaded again, her voice rising, about to crack.

Just as the child released her skirts and grabbed for the money Paul was offering him, a handsome ebony walking stick appeared and jabbed at the boy, making him turn and run.

Paul extended a hand to the newcomer. "What are you doing here?" he asked.

"I came to meet your train," Lord Walford said.

Cynthia, hearing his voice so near her, turned swiftly and flew into his arms.

"Come, Cynthia, this will never do," her uncle said, but gently, with a smile in his voice. "You can't embrace Lord Walford in public no matter how grateful you may be."

"I'm delighted," Walford said.

Cynthia relinquished the viscount, who took her arm. "I beg your pardon, Lord Walford," she said. "Thank you for prodding him away."

"It was Mr. Cunningham's largesse as much as my stick that did it."

"He was so *repulsive*," she quavered. "And he had no *tongue*."

"Of course he had," Paul said firmly, taking her other arm. "It's a trick they have of rolling it back and then bruising it with a stick so tourists will react exactly as you did and pay more to get rid of them."

They walked back to Miranda and the gibbering porters.

Cynthia was still trembling with fear and disgust. Walford had never seen her shaken and vulnerable before, and it affected him in a way he neither recognized nor understood.

He bent toward her and spoke soothingly, deliberately avoiding Miranda's cool greeting. If Mr. Cunningham and Cynthia were pleased to see him, Mrs. Cunningham clearly was not. He reminded himself that with Miranda he must not cross the line that separated charm from flirtation, but he was hanged if he didn't find her damned seductive!

"There's a carriage waiting for us and a wagon for the luggage," he told them, patting Cynthia's hand. "The hotel *bagagiste* will see to the trunks."

"I'm very much obliged to you," Paul said.

"Not at all, sir. It's all laid on by Shepheard's."

The ladies were handed into the carriage and the gentlemen supervised the luggage as it was peeled off the porters and placed in the wagon, piece by counted piece.

Inside the carriage, Miranda was convinced the girl was not pretending. She dampened a handkerchief with lavender cologne, taking both from a small pouch she carried suspended from her wrist, and held the handkerchief to Cynthia's forehead.

"Better?" she asked after a moment.

Cynthia nodded and looked out the window. "Why do you suppose Walford came out to Egypt?"

"To ask you to marry him."

"That's what I think too."

Miranda frowned. "And after the way you welcomed him, he'll expect to be accepted."

Cynthia gave a faint smile by way of response.

"You're not going to marry him?" Miranda said incredulously.

"I don't know yet."

"Then why did you do it?" Miranda demanded. "Throw yourself at him?"

"Because he was nearer than Uncle Paul—and he was so *clean*."

"And so cruel."

"Cruel?"

"There was no need for him to prod that poor child like a mule! The boy had let go of your skirt and was reaching for the money. It *was* cruel."

"Walford says the only way to deal with wogs is to beat them with a stick." Cynthia turned to look directly at her aunt. "What have you got against him, anyway, aside from the fact that he admires me?"

"Hush, they're coming. This is not the time to discuss it."

The two men got into the carriage and it left the station for Shepheard's Hotel.

———— · ————

"Shepheard's Hotel," Paul told them as the carriage rolled alongside the Ezbekiyah Gardens, "like everything else in Egypt, has a fascinating history. The building was used as a headquarters by Napoleon during his Egyptian campaign."

Walford chuckled. "Before that it was a harem." He watched Cynthia.

"How exotic!" Cynthia said.

"And how typical of Napoleon," Miranda put in, "to choose a harem."

"Oh, it's been very proper for a long time," Paul said. "It became a Swiss hotel in 1841 and has been a center of European life in Cairo ever since."

"It has a famous veranda, hasn't it?"

"Yes," Walford said. "It's on Ezbekiyah Boulevard and everyone goes there for tea—unless they go to Groppi's near the Choubrati Promenade—to see and be seen and to gossip."

"You seem quite familiar with the city after only a few days here," Paul remarked.

"I was here before on my grand tour," Alastair explained.

"Did it mesmerize you as it did me?"

Alastair considered. "In many ways, yes, but I must confess that I know nothing about archeology and very little about ancient Egypt. Ah, we have arrived."

The concierge and a team of footmen and porters were waiting to hand the ladies down and collect their belongings. In moments they were inside the high-ceilinged lobby of the hotel, which had enough velvet, damask, gilt-framed mirrors, and Oriental carpets to exude luxury and opulence. Cairo was called the pearl of the Middle East and Shepheard's the pearl of Cairo.

Miranda and Paul were shown to their rooms while Cynthia accepted Walford's invitation to tea on the famous terrace. They sat in rattan chairs, screened from the sun by a striped awning.

"Are you all right?" Walford asked solicitously after tea had been served.

"Much better," Cynthia said.

"Perhaps you'd like something a little stronger than tea. You're still pale and your hands are shaking."

"More from embarrassment than terror."

"Embarrassment?"

"Over the way I flew at you—like Jo flies at Laurie in *Little Women.*"

"I haven't read *Little Women.* But I didn't mind it at all. In fact, I enjoyed it very much."

"The circumstances *were* extraordinary," Cynthia persisted, her tone noticeably cooler. "I'm sure you understand that."

"Quite. I understand you were not yourself." But he seemed crestfallen.

It was precisely what Cynthia wanted and she began to tell him about their visit to the Paris Exposition. They compared notes about the long railway trip to the western Mediterranean and then the voyage by ship to Alexandria and by train from there to Cairo.

"Are you tired?" he asked.

"Yes. I think I'd better have a rest."

"Shall I see you this afternoon?"

She smiled. "I don't see how you can avoid it. In any case, my uncle would like you to dine with us this evening," Cynthia said as she started up the stairs, throwing the viscount a crumb and making a mental note to inform Uncle Paul of the invitation he had not extended.

Alastair smiled and accepted with alacrity before parting from her at the broad staircase. He watched her walk up, back erect, head high. He had watched his sisters being drilled by their governesses with books on their heads when they were girls, but his sisters did not have Cynthia's grace or her glowing beauty.

Damn the girl! he thought, half angry, half admiring. *She knows how to keep a fellow guessing!*

He wondered if she had an ardent temperament, but that was something else he wouldn't discover until he married her.

———— • ————

Glasses tinkled in the dining room over a susurrus of conversation. Shepheard's boasted French cuisine as well as Swiss chambermaids and a branch of the Thomas Cook agency. The agency had reshaped travel for a great part of the world, providing a touch of civilization in the farthest reaches of the Empire and organizing excursions and guides people could not have arranged on their own.

"We should be grateful that it's not yet high season for the trippers," the viscount told them, deboning his smoked trout with the dexterity of a surgeon. "Now that the liners go directly to Alexandria, there are hordes of tourists from Christmas to early spring."

"Where shall we go tomorrow?" Cynthia asked, including Alastair in their plans with a glance of her vividly blue eyes.

"Giza," Miranda said.

"Oh, yes! The pyramids and the Sphinx!" Cynthia said eagerly.

"And tea at the Mena," Alastair added.

"Shall we go on camels?" Miranda asked.

"On horseback," Paul said. "I'll arrange it."

The fish course was cleared and a gigot d'agneau served.

"I brought a few copies of the *Daily Review* to show you," Alastair said. "One of our steamer companions is raising quite a rumpus in London."

The three Cunninghams stiffened imperceptibly while they waited for the viscount to tell them who it was.

"It seems that our Miss McAllister has been giving the most shocking talks to women's suffrage groups," he said.

"Why doesn't that surprise me?" Miranda asked of no one in particular.

"I didn't know she was a suffragist!" Cynthia said.

"She is not, according to what she tells the newspaper. But she *is* using the suffragists as a platform for her demands."

"And what demands is she making?" Paul asked. He had met Miss McAllister only twice, each time briefly: once on the train from Liverpool to London and again at Lady Burdon's soiree. On both occasions she had not been talkative, but he had been struck by the force of character she tried to hide under a docile exterior.

"She wants to protect the women who work aboard liners," Alastair told them.

"From what?" Cynthia asked.

"The unwelcome advances of the officers," Alastair said delicately.

"Isn't that just like Kitt?" Cynthia said. "But I thought she planned to leave London for Italy."

"Apparently her plans have changed. She claims she'll stay in London and go on making speeches until the shipowners agree to put it all in writing."

"She'll do it too," Miranda said.

Cynthia said nothing, but her frown conveyed her concern that Kitt was still in London and, as far as the Cunninghams knew, so was Senator James.

"She has a variety of supporters," Alastair said. "According to the *Review,* the Count d'Yveine and Lady Burdon always attend her speeches and that American senator—James, isn't it?—has been seen in the audience as well."

There was a general silence at the table, each of them concentrating on the meal as if it were essential to their very survival. Paul soon changed the subject to their plans for the next day and, when they had finished dinner, they took coffee in the lounge while a small orchestra played selections from operettas.

Alastair had been maliciously pleased to see all three of his companions thrown off balance when Senator James was mentioned— which could mean that Mr. Cunningham was aware of his wife's delinquency. Walford was convinced that Cynthia was still infatuated with the man, and it appeared to the careful observer that Mrs. Cunningham was still fascinated by him.

Alastair wondered if the luscious Miranda might be in need of sexual comfort, then upbraided himself for relapsing into habit, for although he was accustomed to having hordes of women eager for his attentions, he had not come to Cairo to amuse himself!

Alastair knew he must move even more quickly than he had anticipated. If Steven James decided to visit Egypt in pursuit of the aunt, heaven knew what might happen between him and the niece. Lovers did the most asinine things just to get even.

———— · ————

Paul, wearing silk pajamas and a robe, stood near the window of his bedroom, listening to the sounds of Cairo. Strains of music from the European orchestra floated up and, in the distance, a plaintive native love ballad seemed to wail a reply. The moon, almost full, shed its radiance on the sleeping stones of Cairo.

Paul was smoking a last pipe. Walford's mention of Senator James had unsettled him, but if he were completely honest, he would have to admit that he was perpetually unsettled lately.

There were moments when he was on the brink of confronting Miranda, of telling her he knew what had transpired between her and her lover and, more important, demanding that she tell him exactly what her feelings were for the man.

"And for me!" he muttered, furious and tormented. "Do you love me still? Did you ever?"

He felt like a fool. He knew he should talk to her, but he could not bring himself to give voice to the unspeakable, or a form to the phantom who always seemed to share a bed with Paul and his wife. Most of his solitary moments were spent pondering unanswerable questions about feelings and sensations he had never experienced, subtleties of soul and body that had never troubled him before.

What made her so irresistible that he was willing to tolerate her betrayal of him rather than risk a separation by speaking of it? What

was there about her that made him crave to bury himself inside her? What was the nature of this savage, carnal need that went by the name of love?

He could only conclude that love was erotic need directed at and deeply fulfilled by one woman. Lust was satisfied on any woman. Sex with almost any woman was pleasurable, but sex with Miranda was sublime because he loved her. She gave all of herself. She held nothing back.

Had she been that way with *him*?

What did she feel toward her newly enamored husband? What did *she* crave that made her open herself so shamelessly to him, urge him on with her hands and her mouth, arouse him and tantalize him and make him erupt with such primal force?

He knocked his pipe empty and went into the bathroom. He was in a state of arousal but he cleaned his teeth and had a quick shave before he put out the lights and went into his wife's room.

She was asleep, lying on her back with her hair billowing around her, one arm flung over her head. He stood there for some time, enchanted by the sight of her, wanting to possess her profoundly, physically and emotionally and without the shadow of her lover between them.

Maybe, he thought suddenly, if he made love to her while she slept he could banish the other man—or find out whether she dreamed of *him* each time Paul held her in his arms.

He pulled the covers down gently. She was wearing one of her silk nightdresses, gossamer and delicate. He could see the globes of her breasts and the roundness of her thighs through the fabric. Slowly, not wanting to awaken her yet, he lifted the silk.

She stirred briefly but did not waken. He took off his robe and pajamas and knelt by the bed, his head pillowed on her thighs, his face turned toward the center of her that so seduced him. It was too dark to see, but he felt his way with the tip of his tongue until he found the place that most aroused her, touching lightly at first, then more firmly until she was half awake, breathing quickly, making sounds of pleasure. Her legs parted, her hands came down to encircle his head. She said something he could not understand and her body arched and then he was on her and in her, first grasped and then drained by the soft, moist heat inside her.

In that moment she was all his—and in the next, he was all hers.

Panting after his colossal release, he lay carefully on top of her and knew he would never confront her. He could not risk losing this divine passion, not now, when passion should have been fading between them but had only just begun.

That he owed this rapture to another man's teaching enraged him enough to kill, but it soothed Paul to remember that Miranda was his and would always be his. He withdrew from her body gently, kissed her, and, covering them both against the chill night air, held her in his arms until she slept again.

He lay awake. She had said something, cried out at the height of her pleasure, but what had it been? A wordless sound or a name? And if it was a name, was it Paul's or—he could barely bring himself to form it in his mind—Steven's?

Stop it! he warned himself. He knew it was becoming an obsession. Sometimes he felt himself sliding down an inky black shaft that led only to disaster. Why be haunted by a question to which he already knew the answer? But the answer alone was not enough to cure him. He wanted her anguish, her remorse, her penitence. He wanted to hear that from her.

Twenty-six

The morning was cool and the sun barely up when they set out. It took them over an hour on horseback to reach the pyramids of Giza and the Great Sphinx, and there was still a hint of chill in the air although the sun had risen and would soon be as warming as a quilt.

They were at a distance from the Great Pyramid, the largest of the three colossal structures clustered at Giza. The sun—worshipped as the god Ra by the ancient Egyptians—cast a red-gold glow over the great limestone blocks of which the pyramids were built.

"No wonder they worshipped Ra," Cynthia said, looking at the radiant stones.

The sun gave inner life, as well, to the immense recumbent statue that seemed to guard the pyramids. They approached the mysterious, brooding Sphinx, sixty-six feet high, its full length estimated at two hundred feet, although only its head and the great paws were exposed by the latest excavation. The implacable sands had always reclaimed past excavations of the giant figure, and there had been times when even the head had not been visible.

"It has a Mona Lisa smile," Miranda said when they were looking up at the face. "I wish I could see as far ahead as those eyes do."

"It's a man's face," Cynthia said. "That of the pharaoh Chephren, who succeeded Khufu, the one the Greeks called Cheops."

Alastair shook his head in amazement. "The things you know!" he smiled. "You remind me of Miss McAllister."

"I am not in the least like Miss McAllister," Cynthia said tartly.

"The Egyptians believed in fate, didn't they?" Miranda said dreamily.

"Pagan nonsense," Cynthia snapped, fixing her aunt with a cold stare. "Fate is an attempt to absolve you of guilt. It doesn't."

"If it exists, it's a mitigating circumstance!"

"No, it's just a lame excuse for doing anything you like."

The two women had forgotten what the ancients believed and were arguing heatedly about something else. The two men were listening to the intense exchange in silence, Paul impassive, Alastair intrigued.

Miranda and Cynthia stopped speaking abruptly and they all turned back to the Sphinx.

For many minutes the four of them sat transfixed, their horses and their native guides as quiet as they were, staring at a monument carved to commemorate a god-king whose death was not the end of life but merely a passage to another plane of existence. Then Paul flapped his horse's reins and started toward the Great Pyramid at a walk.

Cynthia refused to go inside it.

"I can't bear being closed up in dark places," she said.

"You may not stay out here alone," Paul told her firmly.

"I went inside on my first visit," Alastair said. "I'll stay with Miss Cunningham." He looked off to the distance, narrowing his eyes against the sun. "The Mena is not far. We'll wait for you there."

Paul and Miranda dismounted and left the horses with one

guide, while the second guide accompanied them into the tomb. Cynthia and Walford soon arrived at the luxurious hotel, tranquil in the early morning, and were shown to the shaded terrace and served lemon squash. In the distance the three pyramids sat in splendid isolation.

"It's the height of effrontery to drink lemon squash so near the one remaining wonder of the world," Cynthia said.

He nodded. For a while they sat in silence, mesmerized by the vast desert around them, the timelessness.

"It's fascinating, isn't it?" Cynthia said in a low voice.

"Not nearly as fascinating as you are," he replied.

"Walford, can't you stop being a beau even in the shadow of eternity?"

His dazzling smile disappeared and he had the grace to color slightly. "You're the darndest girl!" he said. "Why won't you flirt?"

"In most cases it's a waste of time."

"Is ours like most cases?" he asked.

"No. Neither of us has any illusions about what the other wants."

He sat in silence for a while. "That makes it seem rather sad."

"Then let's not talk about it."

"But I must know . . ." he began, hesitated, and then continued. "Tell me if there's any point in my asking your uncle's permission to propose to you."

"My uncle can't give you permission. My father is the only one who can. To give his approval he would first have to meet your father and then, provided things were arranged satisfactorily between them, to meet you."

Walford frowned. "But you must have a preference of your own, one way or the other."

"Oh, certainly—but very little choice, as you well know, so there's no point in talking about my preference."

"For the love of heaven, Cynthia! Must you be so brutally honest?"

"No." She smiled. "But I prefer to be."

"Because it rattles me?"

"I don't really know why. Possibly because it isn't what's expected of me."

"And heaven preserve you from doing or saying the expected!"

She agreed and they both relaxed. She thought he would pursue the subject of marriage, but he did not and she was half grateful for that. She would have liked a little more ardor, no matter how she tried to discount its importance and keep him from the pretense of it, but she was not yet ready to make the most important decision of her life.

The news of Kitt's having stayed on in London had been bad enough; that she was becoming a tabloid celebrity was worse. Worst of all was the fact that Steven seemed to approve of such appalling behavior.

Did Steven admire her? Women envied Kitt's self-possession and intellect even while they considered it unfeminine, but men admired it and admiration could so easily turn to love!

And Kitt could marry whom she pleased. She answered to no one but herself. It was the one freedom Cynthia really coveted.

Still, Cynthia appeared calm and unperturbed as she sat among the ruins in decorous silence with her thoughts thousands of miles away and a longing for Steven in every fiber of her being. She wanted to watch him walk and hear him talk, to imagine his mouth against hers and his arms around her.

Why couldn't she feel that way about the urbane and handsome man who wanted to marry her? Walford was too good-looking to be real: his golden hair, his heavily lashed eyes almost as intensely blue as her own, his aristocratic nose and his splendid physique, slender but strong, like illustrations she had seen of Michelangelo's *David,* suitably shielded by a fig leaf.

Aside from that, he was clever and witty and he made her laugh. Life with him would be a constant round of parties, hunts, balls, theater, shopping, travel, gorgeous clothes, and resplendent jewels.

Cynthia would be the leader of her "set." And mistress of that house! She had not been inside the Inderby mansion in London, but from all reports it was equally magnificent and in need of repair. Her money would refurbish everything.

She smiled at Walford and sipped her drink.

Walford knew he had been outmaneuvered again. This girl had the most uncanny ability to speak her mind and still tell him nothing. Despite that—maybe because of it?—he found her tantalizing. He had a sudden impulse to lean forward and kiss her mouth as he had done that night at Inderby.

He felt a sudden leap inside him at the prospect of bedding her. He thought about it often, thought of stroking her silky white skin, the pink buds of her nipples, the softness of her small, round breasts. In his imagination his fingers slipped between her legs and he heard her gasp of shock, the cringing away of her body and his own insistence, superior strength, and ultimate domination of her. He heard her cry of pain when her virginity was ruptured.

"Tell me more about the pyramids," he suggested. He didn't give a hang for the damned pyramids, but he needed to get his mind off sex.

———— · ————

At the hotel's *dîner dansant* that evening, Walford was surprised to find himself jealous of Cynthia's popularity with the young men visiting Cairo on their grand tours. Had it been a cotillion, her dance card would have been completely filled.

Sitting with Paul and Miranda Cunningham at a small table in the lounge, Alastair had to watch her dancing and laughing with a succession of partners—any one of whom could be a potential suitor and all of whom must have more money to offer her than he did. He knew he must bring this marriage scheme to fruition and soon.

For a while he made conversation with Cynthia's aunt and

uncle, but when Miranda turned in her chair to speak to the dowager at the next table, the conversation lapsed. After a while Alastair sighed, attracting Paul's attention.

"You seem troubled. May I help?" he inquired.

"I want to marry her," Alastair said.

"I see," Paul said. "And she?"

"Damned if I know! I've asked her if there was any point in getting your permission to address her, but she told me that was up to her father."

Paul nodded. "It is."

"But you could put in a good word for me."

"Of course," Paul assured him, finding Walford appealing in his eagerness.

"She suggested that he might come to England to meet my father and then come out here, just as we return from upriver, to meet me."

Paul, knowing how Hobart would react to this high-handed arrangement of his time and schedule, looked doubtful. "My brother is a very busy man who dislikes travel intensely. It would be unusual for him to go to London, much less come out to Cairo. Of course, Cynthia is his only daughter and that might persuade him. If you like, I'll send a letter to explain the situation and ask him to wire his reply about where we might meet."

Alastair accepted eagerly just as Miranda turned back to them and Cynthia was delivered to her family like the crown jewels by a stubby young man with a mop of dark curls and cheeks so pink they might have been rouged.

"It's been a busy day," Paul said. "It's time to retire."

"May I stay on for a while?" Cynthia coaxed, smoothing the satin-faced lapel of her uncle's evening clothes. "Walford will chaperone me."

"His is not the sort of chaperonage I had in mind." Paul smiled. "Now, come along. There's a great deal to see tomorrow, and I won't have you missing any of it because you're tired."

Paul shook hands with Walford, the ladies said good night, and the Cunninghams went upstairs, each to a separate bedroom, although Paul went into Miranda's as soon as her maid left.

She was in bed, propped up by pillows, studying a map of the Nile and the cities along its shores.

"I find it amazing," she said, "that the Nile rises in the south and flows north to its delta on the Mediterranean. And that Lower Egypt is in the north and Upper Egypt in the south."

"It confuses everyone but the Egyptians," he agreed. "I have some news for you. Walford wants to marry Cynthia."

"So he's asked her at last," she said softly. "That means the earl approves."

"I told him—as did our forthright niece—that Hobart was the man in charge." He told her about his conversation with Walford, but Miranda wasn't interested.

"It's impossible!" she said. "She must not marry him."

"He's young, healthy, good-looking, and titled."

"He'd be marrying her for her money."

"And she would be marrying him for his title."

"And you find nothing questionable about the total absence of love, even affection, between them?" she demanded.

"I think there *is* affection. They enjoy each other's company. But not everyone is as fortunate as we," he said.

What he said should have been a reason to rejoice, but it sounded like a reproach. They gazed at each other. Miranda hid her apprehension, although her pulse beat suddenly faster. Lately, for some reason, she expected each day that he would confront her; yet their lives proceeded along customary paths—except when they made love. Then they were as intent upon exploring unknown territory as any archeologist.

She remembered waking up the night before to his incredibly intimate caresses, and her senses stirred. She almost invited him into bed now, but she had never done that. Taking such an early initiative would be crossing a line of acceptable behavior well before they were in the throes of erotic pleasure, when nothing mattered but sensation.

But she was responsible for Cynthia. She said, "No, she cannot marry him. It's out of the question. You mustn't write to Hobart."

"Why on earth not? She couldn't do any better and it's just what Hobart wants for her. Why refuse because you've taken a dislike to the boy? Irrational passions are so unlike you."

There was another heavy silence between them, as if he were on the brink of demanding how that other, even more irrational passion, had come to be.

Miranda drew a deep breath. "The 'boy,' as you call him, likes boys," she said.

Paul stared at her in disbelief. "Not according to his reputation! And I've seen how he looks at women. I've seen how he looks at *you!*"

"Maybe he thinks I'll be fooled or flattered into approving of him."

"Possibly even into being tempted by him?" Paul asked heatedly.

"Tempted? By a pederast?"

"Women are tempted by all kinds of men."

Again they were no longer discussing Cynthia's marriage, but their own, and Miranda could not face it.

"Let's suppose Walford can satisfy himself with both sexes," she said. "Let's suppose he's incapable of love and marries mainly for money, for heirs, and to protect his reputation. That's all very well for him, but what of his wife?" She shook her head. "It could be an appalling experience for a girl like Cynthia. Just imagine—"

He cut her off. "That's a terrible accusation to make against Walford! What proof have you?"

Another silence stretched between them. She was reluctant to talk about the ship, but there was no way to avoid it.

"It was obvious to me," she finally said, "that he was carrying on with an American man during the crossing."

"Which one?" Paul demanded. "I'm under the impression there were several American men aboard."

She ignored the implication. "Lewis something-or-other. He and his parents were in Walford's railway carriage from Liverpool to London. What difference does it make who he was?"

"Did you witness any aberrant behavior?"

"Of course I didn't. But I could tell by the way Lewis looked at Walford that there was more between them than there should have been. And I wasn't the only one who sensed it. Lady Burdon did too."

"Lady Burdon, I hear, loves to stir up trouble. And even if what you suspect is true, it is not a serious obstacle to marriage. Young men often indulge in experimentation of that kind until they marry and settle down."

"Did *you*?" Miranda asked.

"That is neither here nor there," Paul said frostily.

"Oh, Lord," Miranda murmured. "Do our sons?"

"It's not the sort of thing a father asks his sons. But if you throw a group of adolescent boys together with no outlet for their clamoring instincts, they're almost bound to explore with one another."

"Walford is no schoolboy," Miranda said. "He's twenty-five. He can have almost any woman he wants. If he seeks sexual contact with males, it's because he wants it, because he's perverse by nature."

"Miranda, you're making a tempest in a teapot. In any case, Hobart must be notified of this proposal."

"And about His Lordship's evil inclinations?"

"I'll cross that bridge if and when I come to it."

"And of course Cynthia has nothing to say about it."

"I hear your women's organizations speaking!" he said. He had said that before, but indulgently, not in anger. "Cynthia has refused suitors since she came out and she'll refuse Walford if she so chooses."

"And if Hobart insists?"

"You're borrowing trouble again! She may be perfectly willing."

"If she is, it's because Walford's titles and estates dazzle her!" Miranda said stubbornly. "They would outweigh her judgment. Besides, what does she know about homosexuality?"

"Nothing, I devoutly hope, as once was the case with you."

Miranda began a hot reply, then thought better of it. He had come very close to linking her knowledge of perversity to her newly acquired techniques in bed. She shrugged. "If you won't tell Hobart about Walford, I will," she said before returning to her map.

Her defiance astonished Paul. She had never been backward about telling him what she thought, but neither had she been stubborn and indignant as she was tonight. She had been the perfect wife, never demanding, never denying, a comfort to him in every way. Even her interest in women's groups, while it shocked his family, had not created any serious difficulty in their personal relationship.

And she had never threatened to go above Paul's head in dealing with his brother!

He stood there, looking at her while she pored over the map, and the tension hummed between them.

"Lately," he said at last, "I simply don't recognize you."

She glanced up at him. "I'm the same person I've always been. It's the situation that is unfamiliar."

He stood where he was for several moments, on the verge of shedding some light on "the situation" before he went to the communicating door between their bedrooms. He hoped she would call him back and apologize. Once she would have, so their day would not end on disagreement. Now he was unsure of what she might do about too many things.

"Good night, Miranda," he said.

"Good night, Paul."

He left. There was nothing else he could do.

"This has got to stop!" Miranda murmured to herself when the door had closed behind him.

It was time to accept the obvious: almost everything Paul had said tonight applied to their own marriage or hinted at her adultery. How much longer could they go on talking to each other on two levels?

Paul was not a fool. He certainly knew from her behavior that there had been someone—maybe he thought several someones— who had launched her onto erotic seas. He had said nothing because this aspect of his wife made her as utterly irresistible to him as Steven had been to her.

She found it perplexing that Paul had developed such an enormous appetite for sexual adventure but still refused to discuss any aspect of sex with her, still demanded that the conventions be observed, that he make the overtures and she merely respond to them.

For him the act remained an unmentionable subject, wrapped in the silence of shame, the performance of which, until the night before, began between decorous sheets and continued in silence for as long as could be managed.

For her it was not only a supreme pleasure but a way to get close, to get through, to blend her deepest self with another human being's. There was nothing hidden and nothing disgraceful about that. It had been that way with Steven because he was uninhibited even when the lovemaking was over. She could talk to him about anything—and they had known each other for only a few days, not for twenty years!

Paul loosed his sensuality only in the act. He was one of the civilized people who made rules about love, drew curtains around it, tried to ignore the messier aspects of its physical expression. But it had a profound effect on everything in life in one way or another.

Miranda believed that wars had been fought over the craving of a man and a woman to possess each other, that lives had been sacrificed and kingdoms lost, convention defied and honor abandoned in the name of love.

Why didn't Paul demand to know the truth from her? There could be only one explanation: his pride would force him to divorce her as a result, and he still loved her. More important, he was *in love* with her.

"And I love him!" she whispered, turning out the light and burying her head in her pillow.

But she was *in love* with Steven. She might never be able to define it, but she knew that a subtle difference existed between those two states, one as sweetly heady as springtime but the other as intoxicating as wine. Even people who had not experienced either condition accepted the premise that they existed and that there was a difference between them: love could make you happy, but falling in love could drive you mad.

In her mind's eye she saw Paul's wonderful face, and her heart ached for him. She felt an overwhelming nostalgia for the years they had shared, untainted by inconstancy or suspicion. She needed her memories and for more than half her life her memories had been shared with him. She couldn't hurt him more than she already had.

So she would never tell him. No matter what he said or did or asked or insinuated, she would never tell him. No matter how heavy her conscience, she would have to bear the weight of it alone. That was her punishment, and only those acquainted with guilt knew how subtle and cruel a punishment it was.

Twenty-seven

"You're looking very fine," Lady Burdon said as the footman helped Kitt into the carriage. "That deep plum color suits you."

The door was closed, the footman resumed his place on the box beside the coachman, and the carriage rolled on.

"Thank you, Lady Pat," Kitt said with an affectionate smile. "You are very chic as usual."

"One must be chic when driving in the Row." The older woman's tone was often ambiguous. She observed the customs of her time, but she mocked many of them. Driving in the Row was a mindless activity, but she did it regularly, dressed to the nines. To-day, under a warm cloak of ocelot, she wore a suit of steel-blue wool and an amazing hat of the same fabric trimmed with pale blue silk cabbage roses.

"But it *is* peculiar to call a place Rotten Row," Kitt remarked, "and then make it fashionable for society to dribble back and forth, showing itself to the same people who dribbled along yesterday."

Lady Burdon smiled. "I like the way you describe our quaint little habits."

"Forgive me, Lady Pat. I'm impatient to know when I'll have that interview, and it makes me cranky."

Lady Burdon nodded and the roses bobbled, even under the restrictive veiling that tied beneath her chin to anchor the creation. "I had a reply from Sir Harry Blenkinsop. He will see you at ten o'clock on Tuesday week."

"Wonderful! I can't wait," Kitt said, clapping her hands.

"Take Alton with you: Sir Harry is a stickler for form. And don't be surprised if he chucks you under the chin and suggests a course of waters at Bath. Sir Harry thinks all feminists suffer from ill health—or that they're dotty."

"I know I'm acquiring a reputation as a crazy old maid."

"No, you're far too attractive. In any case, we Brits have a fondness for crazy old maids—think of the Virgin Queen, who was also a redhead, by the way—and a healthy respect for eccentricity. That sets us apart from almost every other society on earth."

"Except the American South," Kitt reminded her. She had known Southern girls at college. "There have always been eccentrics and dotty old maids by the bushel in the South. Since the War of Secession killed off so many southern men, there are even more of them. But I'm not in the least eccentric. I just want to be myself."

"Tut, my child. This would be an impossible world if people went about being themselves, acting on their impulses. Our species is not benign."

"True, but certain members of it are very kind," Kitt said, patting Lady Burdon's hand.

"Rank sentimentality."

"Not at all. And you are only one of many reasons why I shall stay on in England."

"Another reason, I take it, is still Steven James." Lady Burdon nodded to friends in a passing brougham while Kitt composed herself. She no longer had any secrets from Lady Burdon, but any mention of the senator threw her off balance.

"You know I haven't replied to any of his notes and I haven't acknowledged his flowers," she said when Lady Burdon had settled back. "I don't know why he keeps sending them."

"Because you don't reply! It's the nature of men to pursue women, particularly elusive women. You should ask him to tea one day and tell him why you're eluding him! Get it out and over with and he won't be sending notes and flowers."

"You can't mean I should mention his affair with Mrs. Cunningham!"

The older woman reconsidered. "No, you can hardly do that. It would be far too honest and it would get straight to the heart of the matter, and that isn't the done thing. But you might refer to *Miss* Cunningham and see what reaction you get, particularly now that Walford's gone to Cairo to bag her."

"I half expected the senator to follow the viscount."

"After the aunt or the niece?"

"Either," Kitt said gloomily. "Or both."

Lady Burdon shook her head. "He's not that bad a lot. Furthermore, the senator doesn't care a rap about Cynthia. He likes looking at her because she is glorious to behold."

"So is the senator," Kitt said.

"Agreed, although not in the same way as Walford and Cynthia's uncle Paul, either of whom could have stepped out of a Gainsborough. The senator is very male and pure colonial, however well mannered. No wonder Walford calls him Dan'l Boone."

"I shudder to think what Walford calls *me*. He considers all Americans bumpkins—except for Cynthia."

"But, my dear Kitt, Americans *are* refreshingly rustic. Your girls are tall, healthy, and individualistic. Your men are rugged, charming, and brawny. *Our* young people, on the other hand, tend to be languid and effete."

Kitt laughed. "Treason!"

"It's truth, not treason. As is this: you might find that on your next meeting Senator James will have lost much of his power to enchant you. A man you hardly ever see can acquire many imaginary qualities, while familiarity only reduces the romantic glow."

"That doesn't bode well for marriage."

"I was talking about a tea party, not a wedding," Lady Burdon shot back.

"Remember what happened at the Boston Tea Party," Kitt said. "Invite him to tea," she murmured. "I'll have to think about that."

"You have thought about it quite enough. You must do it." And they both went back to nodding and smiling at familiar faces.

When Kitt got home she wrote a note to Steven and asked Mary Frances to take it to Brown's Hotel.

"Oh, Miss Kitt, it's trouble, I can feel it in my bones."

"Nonsense. Shrinking from all contact is childish—and rude, after all the roses he's sent."

"All the same, he's trouble."

But Mary Frances recognized the determined expression on her mistress's face and hurried off to deliver the invitation.

Steven's message the next day said he would call at four o'clock a week from Tuesday if that was convenient. It was the same day as Kitt's appointment with Sir Harry Blenkinsop.

———— · ————

On that Tuesday afternoon Kitt answered the door herself and they smiled tentatively at each other until she offered her hand. The touch of his palm against hers made her tingle.

"Please come in," she told Steven cordially. "It's nice to see you again."

Steven placed his hat and stick on a bench in the foyer and handed his overcoat to the silent young woman, soberly dressed, who came to take it, the same one who had torn up his notes. She avoided looking at him directly.

He followed Kitt into the parlor, which seemed smaller to her when he was in it. He was even taller than he was in her thoughts of him. She indicated one of the wing chairs near the fire for him and took the other, settling her black skirt and ruffled white silk blouse as she sat down. There was a handsome cameo at her neck, and her copper-colored hair was swept atop her head in a puffy "cottage loaf" favored by the American girls Lady Burdon admired.

Kitt knew she looked attractive, but Steven looked even better than her fantasies. So much for Lady Pat's theory.

He overwhelmed her just as he had when she first set eyes on him. It was his physique, tall and muscular, his abundant wavy hair, his dark eyes, the tiny indentations at the corners of his mouth. And it was his unassuming manner and his engaging personality, the courtly way he treated women without putting the barriers of gender between them. It was every detail of him and the totality of him that captivated her. And she had never met a man so easy to talk to.

"I must apologize for my rudeness in not acknowledging those lovely flowers," Kitt began. "I've no excuse, but I've been very busy lately."

"I know," he said. "I've heard several of your speeches. Real rousers, all of them. I'd supposed you to be revisiting the ruins of Pompeii, so it was a shock to find you making the natives restless on Oxford Street."

Kitt laughed, unable to quell her delight in having him so near and overjoyed by the oblique admission that he had thought about her. "You should have stayed to say hello after the meetings disbanded. Lady Burdon and the count often do."

Kitt hesitated a moment. She had fully expected him to sail for New York after the Cunninghams left for Cairo. But he was obviously waiting for Miranda's return and at the thought Kitt's exhilaration faded considerably.

"How does it happen that you're still in London?" she asked him.

"I have business," he said vaguely, dashing her hopes. "My father-in-law's here as well," he added, and hope rose again that he might have legitimate reasons to stay that had nothing to do with Miranda. He looked at the fire. "I'm thinking of settling here permanently."

"Here in London?" She was amazed. Did the lovers plan to stay on together, to live openly in sin? "Why?" she asked, then reddened as she realized how rude her personal questions must seem.

He did not seem to mind. "I feel at home here."

"But you must live in America to be elected to office!"

"Lately I'm not sure I want to hold office."

She was astonished. On the ship he had wanted it very much. Or was he preparing to renounce his political future for Miranda?

"Oh," she said, her inner glow now entirely gone. "I thought you were fixed on a political career."

"I was a successful investor before Gus—my father-in-law—got me appointed to the state senate. The market is just as exciting, and a man can call his soul his own. That isn't true in politics."

Alton, arriving with the tea tray, set it down on the round table between the wing chairs. "I'll fetch the scones straightaway, miss," she said, reluctantly retreating again with a backward glance at Steven James as if he might suddenly change his shape and acquire a tail and a pitchfork.

"She makes tea as only the English can," Kitt said, pouring.

"Who is she?"

"Her name is Alton and she's my companion. Do you prefer cream or lemon?"

"Cream and sugar, please. I'm beginning to enjoy tea myself."

"Yes, it grows on you. But tell me more about your plans. Would it be a complete break with home?"

"It's too soon to say. I'll have to be an expatriate a little longer before making a final decision, but I've written to my sister to start making some preliminary arrangements for me." He took the tea she passed him, saying, "Now it's your turn. Will you be starting on your travels soon?"

"Not until I've accomplished what I set out to do here." *I hoped to make you love me,* she thought, wishing she had the courage to say it.

What she said was "There must be a clear standard of conduct on all ships and a clear punishment if it's breached. If people won't behave civilly of their own accord, they must be made to."

"Your maid, then, is the girl you were defending on the ship."

Kitt looked anxious. "I've never said so, and she would die of shame if I did, although she's very grateful to you."

"What for? From what you say in your speeches, it still goes on on all of the liners."

"Yes, but you tried. I always wondered how you managed to stop it without knowing the names of the two people involved."

He shrugged. "I told the captain I'd seen and heard overtures from an officer to a stewardess that were both threatening and unwelcome. He must have passed the word that there was a colonial aboard and we are said to respect women more than any other country."

She was silent, looking troubled. Her concern for her protegée was touching. He leaned forward and put his hand on her arm. "I would never betray a confidence, Miss McAllister."

"No," she said softly, "I don't believe you would."

Her green eyes were clear and shining, the most unusual green eyes he had ever seen, their vivid color encircled by a band of blue. He watched the worry in them fade and felt suddenly very concerned for her. He leaned back in his chair, taking his hand from her arm.

"You must call on me if I can help in any way," he said.

"I may have to. It won't be easy to have those regulations adopted."

"Those regulations should apply to more than ships' officers, certainly."

"Of course, but ships are a start."

"Will getting the vote for women help?"

"It will help us to influence legislation and give us some re-course when the rules are broken. But sooner or later suffrage is bound to become law, so that needn't be my primary goal. Of course, I work with the suffragists. I speak at their meetings and in turn they help me to get the attention of the right people."

"People in general are paying attention to what you say."

"Many of them because of the lurid subject matter," she said scornfully. "As if I would speak of such loathsome behavior for their entertainment!"

He sipped his tea, admiring her for not mincing words. No maidenly euphemisms for Miss McAllister! If it was rape, she called it rape. That red hair of hers was to be taken seriously: she had a tempestuous nature. He was surprised this had never struck him before.

"Have the suffragists lived up to their side of the bargain?" he asked.

She nodded. "I've met some captains of industry who tell me they're sympathetic—and then are remarkably slow to act. Lady Burdon helps too. She arranged the meeting I had this morning with the president of the Excelsior Steamship Lines."

"Blenkinsop?"

"Yes, do you know him?"

"I've met him a few times." It had been in connection with Gus's plan to reap riches from the Panama Canal, which sounded better and better to Steven the more he looked into it. The Excel-sior Lines had some older vessels in dry dock that could be bought at a reasonable price to transport supplies and laborers to Panama while the canal was abuilding and goods for the administrators and their families when construction was complete.

"But Blenkinsop's one of those stuffy Brits," Steven said. "Strikes me as the kind of man who would froth at the mouth at the very idea of women voting."

"He is and he did. He told me I was outrageous and unwomanly and needed a keeper. I told him I did not care to be kept."

Steven chuckled. "Did he dare to offer further advice after that?"

"He said a woman's place was in the home, where she would be safe as well as quiet."

"And . . . ?"

"I said women should be guaranteed safety when they traveled on ships, whether as passengers or attendants. He said I was pert and disagreeable but he had learned to expect that from Yankees."

"Good Lord! What happened next?"

"I said that every one of my disagreeable Yankee friends and travel agents would be strongly advised to avoid the Excelsior Line until something was done to control its officers, and that if nothing was done, I would say the same thing in all my speeches." She nodded with satisfaction. "That was when he began to see the light."

Steven threw back his head and laughed heartily. "I wish I'd been there to see that old rooster try to take *you* on," he said. "What did he say he would do about fixing things?"

"Call a meeting of his ships' captains and lay down the law— which in his opinion ought to be enough for me. I asked to attend that meeting. He refused. I mentioned my cordial relations with the press, who print every word I say, and he reconsidered."

"Good for you!" he applauded. "I must write to my sister about this. One day perhaps you'll meet her."

"I would very much like that. Do you suppose she'll come to visit if you settle here?"

He shrugged. "She might. But what made you decide to start your crusade here?" he asked her. "Why not in America?"

"Because my crusade, as you call it, sprang from an incident aboard a British liner," she said, "and the people concerned are British. But I have other reasons similar to yours. I like London and I plan to stay on as well. There's so much to see and do: politics, history, architecture, the arts. I want to see some of the 'shires and visit Scotland and so much more! And I have no family back home." She glanced at him inquiringly. "As you do."

She was certain that if he set up illicit housekeeping with Miranda, it would gravely disappoint his family. She wondered if he had considered that. She guessed he had but that it changed nothing for him. He was too deeply in love.

So was Kitt. No matter what he had done or intended to do, she still loved him and always would. There wasn't a mean streak in him as there was in some men. It was his passions that were wayward, not his character, not his heart. She wanted to be the object of those passions, but if that could not be, she wanted to know his heart.

The scones arrived and Kitt poured more tea. They talked about some of the people they'd met and the places they had seen since their arrival aboard Walford's private railway car.

Before he left he invited her to dine with him at a French restaurant off Regent Street on Friday evening.

When he had gone, Kitt curled up in the chair, aglow over the dinner invitation. She mentioned it when Alton came in to clear away the tea things.

"It's nice to see you so pleased, miss," Mary Frances said in a tone that clearly conveyed her distrust.

"Oh, Mary Frances, I've explained it to you! It wasn't some cheap affair between those two. They love each other! And love has nothing to do with reason, I know that now. How can I blame him for what I feel myself?"

"But where does all of that leave you?" Mary Frances asked morosely.

"I don't know," Kitt said.

"Begging your pardon, Miss Kitt, I'd say nowhere."

Kitt shrank farther into her chair. "But what he wants is impossible, and I want to be here when he accepts that. He'll turn to me if I'm right here in London."

"Not if he's living with the lady," Alton said dolefully and, shaking her head, carried out the tea tray. She had done all she could for the present. Now she could only stand by until Miss Kitt's pipe dreams dissolved, as dissolve they certainly would.

———— · ————

It was a belle epoque restaurant: pale green brocade hangings tasseled in gold and deeper green plush upholstery, gilt-framed mirrors and paintings, ornate lamps and silk-fringed table draperies under crisp white linen cloths.

Kitt wore a black velvet gown that set off her creamy shoulders as a jeweler's box sets off ivory. Diamond drop earrings framed her face, and, apart from her opal ring, were her only adornment.

Steven was delighted with her. He had always thought of her as a woman of great intellect and courage, but tonight he was aware of the female in her. She was more than pretty and definitely not a girl. She was a unique and very attractive woman.

"May I say how charming you look?" he asked when they were seated and he had ordered champagne. "And how unusual those earrings are."

"Thank you. They were my mother's."

"She's no longer living?"

"She died when I was almost five."

"And your father and aunt died fairly recently."

She was surprised that he would remember.

"You listen well," she said.

"Claire taught me how," he explained. "She wanted to be a teacher. When she married instead, she practiced her skills on me. Listening was one of the first things she made me learn, and I've profited in many ways as a result."

Claire would be crazy about you, he thought, and realized for the first time that he often judged women by what Claire would think of them.

"I wanted to be a teacher too," Kitt confided. "But my father was lonely. He thought four years at Bryn Mawr were enough, and so I went home to him."

"Did you regret it?"

She nodded. "Very much, but not as much as I loved him. I couldn't let him be lonely."

The maître d' came, his starched collar creaking as he wrote on a leatherbound pad. Steven consulted with him and ordered: caviar, consommé, sole Véronique, quail *aux fraises des bois* stuffed with rice, almonds, and capers, a selection of vegetables in butter sauce. "And then we'll see," Steven ended. "Please send the wine steward."

"*Bien sûr,* Monsieur," the maître d' said. He left them with a bow and a flourish, his waxed mustache vibrating with satisfaction at a job well done.

"If you'd dictated a sonnet, he could not have recorded it more carefully," Kitt said, laughing.

"He takes his work very seriously."

"It's the sure way to succeed." She flashed him a searching glance. "Will you really give up politics?"

He was surprised by the sudden change of subject. "Yes, I think so. Why do you ask?"

She tried to restrain herself, but failed. "I simply don't understand how you can throw away the chance to do something important."

And make yourself the object of censure such as you've never experienced from your doting family!

"Politics isn't the only way to do important things, you know."

"For example?" she asked abruptly.

"Investment has an enormous effect on the whole world."

"The market?" she scoffed. "Do you really believe that moving bits of paper from one account to another is important in the grand scheme of things?"

"My dear Miss McAllister! Countries grow, towns are built, em-

ployment is created, the standard of living rises, the economic structure of a nation expands—all because of those bits of paper."

"I don't see how!"

"They represent investment capital. Without investment there
would be no progress."

"The market is gambling, pure and simple."

"Not simple and not pure. Progress may not always be the motive, but it is frequently the by-product. Suppose I were to tell you
that because of an investment plan now under consideration our
country may soon be stronger, better defended, with a larger population, bigger and better cities, finer schools . . ."

The wine steward presented himself, dressed in a black tailcoat
and trousers with white tie and vest and a small, flat silver cup on a
chain around his neck so that he might sip the wine before it was
poured into glasses and remove anything not up to scratch.

"I owe you another apology," Kitt said when the steward had
departed.

"What for?"

"Questioning your decisions." She knew that a woman like Miranda did not criticize a man's business life unless she was his mother
or his old-maid aunt.

"Not at all," he said. "It's what Claire does."

But you are not Claire, he reminded himself. Claire's gray eyes did
not flash with challenge. Claire's skin was not as smooth as cream.
Claire's mouth did not have a small dimple at one corner that he had
a sudden desire to kiss.

But I am not your sainted sister! she almost shouted at him. She
had no desire to be seen by him as sisterly no matter how much he
admired Claire. She wanted him to look at her as she had seen him
look at Miranda Cunningham.

She gathered her wits and was very entertaining for the rest of
the evening, even the slightest bit flirtatious. She accepted an invitation to the opera and a late supper the following week and smiled

warmly when he left her at the door, but Mary Frances, who opened it, could tell from Kitt's face that the outing had not lived up to her expectations.

"And nor will *he,*" Mary Frances muttered as she locked the doors and put out the lights. "She's the best there is and there's no man good enough for her—excepting maybe His Worship."

It was how Mary Frances privately referred to the count, and she was as resolved as Lady Burdon—although they had never actually said it in so many words—that if Miss Kitt married anyone, it should be the Count d'Yveine. He was a fine man and devoted to Miss Kitt. Why did people always want what they couldn't have? And, half the time, shouldn't have because they'd only suffer from it.

Alton was waiting impatiently for the Cunninghams to return from Cairo. This cozy flat would see very little of the senator after that, and Miss Kitt would have to accept that she would never be to Senator James what he was to her.

She stopped for a moment outside Kitt's door, ready to knock and see if she was needed. But her instinct told her that Miss Kitt did not want company, not even to help her out of the black velvet gown. Miss Kitt wanted to be alone with her misery.

The gentry! Mary Frances snorted as she went to her own room and undressed quickly. Half the nobs she'd come to know were in love with the wrong people and the other half were out in Egypt mucking about with dead folk! Lady Burdon was the only one of the lot with common sense.

She got into bed and turned out the light, wondering what it was like inside a tomb.

Twenty-eight

"My stars, is it really you?" Bertha Seeley bore down upon Miranda and Cynthia on Shepheard's famous veranda and stood over them with a proprietary air.

Cynthia's brows arched. Miranda was able to smile thinly and to greet the woman who immediately settled herself in the third of five chairs at their table.

"I knew I'd find you here," Bertha said, fanning herself vigorously. "We just got off the train from Alexandria and I'm parched, my dears, absolutely parched."

"Have some cool water," Miranda offered.

"Water?" Mrs. Seeley was horrified.

"It's bottled," Cynthia assured her.

"Oh, really?" Mrs. Seeley eyed the carafe with a little less loathing. "Can you trust these people? I prefer my bottled water poured from a freshly opened bottle. I'll wait for some coffee. They *must* boil the water for that." She raised an imperious hand to beckon the steward, ordered coffee and some cakes, and then leaned confidingly across the table, stretching her long, thin neck like a bird of prey.

"When did you get here? What have you seen? How long will you stay?"

"Please, Mrs. Seeley, one question at a time."

Bertha Seeley smiled at Miranda. "I'm just so happy to see old friends."

"We're leaving tomorrow," Cynthia said in a manner that utterly denied friendship with such a person as Bertha Seeley.

"Back to England so soon?"

"No," Miranda replied. "We're taking a kind of houseboat—it's called a *dahabiyeh*—upriver. We may go as far as Thebes."

"Good heavens! That's in Greece!"

"There is a Thebes in Greece, but this one is in Egypt," Cynthia said. "It's near the Valley of the Kings, where so many of the pharaohs are buried."

Bertha shivered. "I confess I don't understand this preoccupation with the dead. It's morbid."

"It's history," Cynthia said tersely.

"Yes, well, if I were you, Miss Cunningham, I'd turn my attention to current events."

Cynthia repressed her temper with difficulty.

"What has happened?" Miranda put in quickly. "Is there a war? Or has Queen Victoria passed on?"

The waiter appeared and set down a plate of cakes and a small china cup and saucer. He poured some strong, thick Turkish coffee into the cup and Mrs. Seeley added sugar and sipped the mixture before she replied.

"Nothing as earthshaking as that! Just a little gossip about Miss McAllister and the senator."

"Gossip?" Miranda echoed with a warning glance at Cynthia to remain silent. "I sincerely doubt that."

"Oh, it's nothing really wicked. Just that he goes to hear her

make those naughty speeches of hers and they've been seen dining together and at the opera. They dine alone," Mrs. Seeley went on, nodding her head significantly, "although she takes her maid along when they sit in a box at the opera."

"Thank the Lord for small mercies," Cynthia said tartly. "Heaven alone knows what horrors people might commit in a box at the opera."

"Cynthia, not everyone appreciates your sense of humor," Miranda said, hoping their guest had no further revelations to make about Steven and Kitt.

Cynthia had been famous for her tantrums since childhood and had been on the brink of one since the Atlantic crossing. It was unthinkable that she should have it on Shepheard's veranda. The one thing that kept her from exploding was the potential glory of marrying Walford, who would certainly flee if she made a spectacle of herself in public. But what would Cynthia do when Miranda told her such a marriage was out of the question?

Bertha Seeley took another sip of the thick, sweet coffee and tittered. "Oh, I'm sure it's all quite proper, but Miss McAllister *is* making a name for herself with those speeches."

"We're aware of that," Miranda said.

"You've been in touch with her?"

"Not since we left England, but we've had some of the London newspapers."

"But they don't tell you *how* she speaks! The *words* she uses. No newspaper would dare to print them."

Cynthia shook her head, feeling as if she had just been drenched with cold water. "I can't imagine Kitt saying anything vulgar," she said.

"How about"—Mrs. Seeley lowered her voice and circled her mouth with her hands to hide her lips from Cynthia and the other guests on the terrace—"r-a-p-e?" she spelled to Miranda.

"Perhaps she should not have said that," Miranda agreed.

"If it's what happened, what else should she call it?" Cynthia demanded almost rudely, remembering how Steven had admired Kitt's wit and personality and now must admire her courage.

Why was I such a lady? Cynthia berated herself. *Why didn't I just tell him I want him, that I'm his, body and soul.*

But that cliché, however stirring it was in novels, sounded very much like servitude. Cynthia accepted what had always been so, that women legally belonged to men: their fathers until they married, their husbands until death, the male members of the family if a woman were widowed.

But it was not that kind of legal ownership that gave Cynthia pause. It was emotional bondage, whether it was the consequence of love or of fear. Cynthia was not given to fear. She was not drawn to women who were.

Her mother came to mind and suddenly she wondered why Elsie drank to excess. Was it to hide her fear from Hobart? Hobart was a difficult man, but he had never raised his hand or his voice to his wife or his children. Why was she afraid?

Mrs. Seeley's voice jarred Cynthia from one of her first unselfish insights. "They were right after all," Bertha crowed, her eyes on the far side of the terrace. "Lord Walford *is* here!"

She watched Walford approach and said to Cynthia out of the side of her mouth, "What a clever girl you are! And here I thought you were in love with the senator!" Her voice rose to a startling pitch. "Dear Lord Walford! What an absolute delight it is to see you. Do sit here near me. My husband will be along at any moment, and we can have a good old-fashioned natter, as you Britishers say."

Walford, however startled he was by her, behaved with his habitual grace, glancing at Cynthia as if to ask what this unappealing woman had said to make Cynthia look so white. Even her delicious lips were pale. He wanted to kiss them into their usual rosy state.

Her aunt seemed in command of herself, but to the eye of a practiced libertine like Walford she was not. Walford had decided early on that Miranda Cunningham was not as cool as she liked to appear. She had a warm nature, to put it politely, and it had come as no surprise to him that she had been *aux prises* with the senator, whose nature was, if anything, even warmer.

Walford had often imagined Miranda and himself in the act, her dark hair damp with perspiration, her full breasts thrusting upward, her hips rising, falling, circling, pumping and her sex creamy wet, clasping him, milking him. It aroused him in a way entirely different from fantasies of deflowering a virgin like Cynthia.

When he turned back to Mrs. Seeley his eyes were wide and dreamy. Mrs. Seeley told her husband later that he was the image of a young aristocrat in love.

———— • ————

The Cunninghams and Alastair left the next morning aboard a rented *dahabiyeh,* a luxurious sailboat preferred over the faster steamers by fortunate people with time and money to spare. It was lavishly furnished and provisioned with delicacies and with crew and deck servants including a cook, a steward, and a couple to clean the travelers' quarters. The staff, apart from the Cunninghams' valet and two maids and Lord Walford's man, had been hired, the crew signed on, and the boat stocked by a dragoman engaged by Paul to supervise such matters.

There was an acceptable wine cellar, card tables and games in the lounge, and even a piano in the dining room. The boat had a flat-bottomed hull, the better to negotiate the sometimes shallow waters of the Nile, and there were enough staterooms for a party twice the size. The conventions were observed by having the women's quarters on the port side and the men's to starboard.

After luncheon they spent the afternoon on the canopied fore-deck, enjoying the Nile's breezes, listening to Paul tell about his team's recent discovery, and watching a panorama that had not changed for centuries.

Crops glistened in the sun, the shimmering fields of barley dotted with multicolored wildflowers. Women washed children and laundry alike in the waters of the Nile, and men tended the crops on its fertile banks, replenished every year when the river rose and deposited its rich silt to give the land those nutrients that made the Nile valley one of the most prolific in the world.

The weather was balmy, neither hot nor cold, although temperatures in the desert could drop to zero at night and rise well above one hundred degrees during the summer. The tourists on the riverboats traveled in a close approximation of their customary comfort, or, as was the case with the Cunninghams, in luxury.

After tea and a rest, they changed for dinner and gathered in the salon with its plump settees and chairs. It was decorated in a style Alastair called "tacky English."

"How very stuffy you are," Cynthia told him.

"Not at all," he protested, smiling. "Tacky's all the rage in warm climates. Even at home people are beginning to abandon Victorian for country chintz."

"Are you planning to follow suit and redecorate Walford Hall?" Paul joked, accepting a glass of pink gin from the steward.

"Not if I know the pater," Walford said. "He considers every tear and scratch sacred."

"But suppose he left the choice to you?" Miranda persisted.

"Then I would leave the details to my wife."

"Let us hope your wife has excellent taste," Paul said.

"Oh, she has. I'm certain of that."

There was a silence in the salon at the inference that he already knew who his wife would be. Paul sat down and crossed his long legs. Miranda glanced at Cynthia, who was too self-possessed to blush. She certainly knew how to handle Alastair.

The girl had changed markedly since the day Miranda called to tell her about their European jaunt. Then she had been childlike in her eager anticipation, charming when she had danced around her room. She had fallen in love with Steven like a princess in a fairy tale, but she had grown up quickly when she learned he was her aunt's lover. That had been a terrible blow to Cynthia.

I've been too wrapped up in my own problems to pay much attention to hers, Miranda thought, and wondered what it was that had given Cynthia such poise. It could not have been wisdom or compassion: Cynthia was too young for the first and far too selfish for the other. Perhaps it was simply a preoccupation with self. She was untouchable because she was untouched.

Miranda hoped her niece would deal realistically with the truth of Walford's perversity: after all, she was not in love with the viscount. Miranda knew she must have it out with Walford soon. He was entirely too certain that his proposal would be accepted. But not even Hobart would want his only daughter and favorite child to marry a homosexual!

What a waste of a handsome, healthy, virile young man! And yet there were times when Miranda caught Walford looking at her with a clearly sexual message. She was not mistaken: it was the kind of message any woman would understand.

Lady Burdon had called him democratically dissolute; she wished the wise old woman were here right now. It puzzled Miranda that Walford could carry on with Lewis Wendall, charm his way into Cynthia's good graces, and lust after *her* all at the same time.

She could have asked Steven how such a thing could be; she could not ask Paul. She had gone as far as she could go with her husband on that subject.

She shook off her somber thoughts and turned to Paul to ask, "Where shall we be tomorrow?"

"In the morning, Saqqâra," he said.

Walford smiled at Cynthia. "And what shall we see there?"

"The step pyramid," she replied. "So called because it's constructed in receding levels, somewhat like a wedding cake."

"How intriguing," Walford said.

"It was the first stone building in the world," Paul said, "and its architect was Imhotep, who was so proud of his creation that a special god was created for it."

"I would like to have a goddess created in my honor," Cynthia said.

"That's sacrilegious, I think," Alastair said, obviously amused by sacrilege.

"It wouldn't be if I were an Egyptian queen," Cynthia said.

"But you aren't." Paul laughed. "You're an American Cunningham, which is not nearly so splendid."

"Hobart wouldn't agree," Miranda said dryly.

There was another silence. They all knew that Paul had written to Hobart and they were all waiting for his reply. Depending upon what that was, they could continue up the Nile for more than a month or return to Cairo. Either way it would be a difficult situation. Young girls did not normally travel in the same party with an unattached male, whether or not a marriage was in the offing.

Miranda was determined to put an end to this impossible situation before it went too far—and with Walford's reputation as a rake and Cynthia's rebellious streak, it might very easily do that.

The irony of it was that the situation had come out of trying to please Hobart Cunningham, a man she could not abide. Hobart had been asked if Walford might accompany them up the Nile and had wired his approval before they left Cairo.

She must find an opportunity to speak to Walford privately, to warn him off and make him believe she would tell Cynthia about his peculiar sexual bent unless he left their party immediately.

"And in the afternoon?" Cynthia was asking.

"To the tomb my group discovered," Paul said. "Not far from Saqqâra."

"Uncle, you know I can't bear being underground."

"With your permission, sir, Miss Cunningham and I might visit Memphis. There's a marvelous statue of Ramses the Second there."

Paul nodded without turning to his wife. "Very kind of you." He glanced at Cynthia. "Take your maid with you," he said.

"Of course, Uncle Paul," Cynthia replied, smiling sweetly. Her blue eyes met Walford's with a flash of mischief, and Miranda knew that she would take Baxter only so far, then park the maid somewhere and profit from another chance to be alone with her suitor.

Twenty-nine

Miranda and Paul followed their escort through the labyrinth that led to a recently discovered burial chamber.

"They've done a lot since I left," Paul said. He was enthusiastic, as he had been before he met the ship at Liverpool, before one kind of wall between husband and wife came down only to be replaced by another.

The corridors smelled dry, as if baked by a different kind of sun. Little whorls of dust punctuated their footsteps, and feeble oil lamps, strung on wire along the corridors, seemed to guide them backward in time.

They came to the burial chamber where the dead queen had lain undisturbed for over three millennia and the escort lighted their way with a torch down a sloping path and through an archway. The chamber itself was unlit to protect it from smoke and its by-products, suspected of being harmful to the long-sealed contents of the tombs. The man produced two candles and, after lighting them from the torch, held the bottom of each one to the flame until it softened enough to adhere to a shard of rubble he found on the floor.

Their attendant conferred briefly with Paul in Arabic and, with

a bow to them both, left, taking the torch with him. The candles cast flickering shadows that to Miranda seemed to resonate with other presences.

The chamber was approximately ten by twelve feet, its walls covered with painted figures. Taking her hand and moving closer to the walls, Paul showed her slaves, merchants, tax collectors, judges, scribes, physicians, farmers, all going about their respective occupations, a pictorial history of this queen's people.

Tablets, or *stele,* inscribed with the picture-writing called hieroglyphs narrated the main events of the queen's life. Oval cartouches carried her insignia.

"All in all, it's a wonderful record of how people of all classes lived thousands of years ago," Paul said as Miranda studied the walls. "The artwork is interesting too. The Egyptians didn't use perspective. If you look at a profile, the eye appears as it would look head-on. But the colors were once brilliant. Look there! You'll see traces of the reds and yellows: red for men, yellow for women."

"Oh, yes! I can see the colors now!" Miranda said, holding her candle higher to peer at the painted figures. "What a shame they faded."

"We're hoping they can be restored," Paul said.

"And these?" Miranda gestured toward several clusters of pottery neatly stacked in the corners.

He pointed to one group. "Those are called mummy jars and contain the organs and entrails of the mummy, preserved for use when the spirit returned to the body. And those in that corner are jars of oil, urns of grain, and wine, pots of cosmetics, and toiletries."

"What cosmetics did they use?" She was curious about how women of antiquity enhanced their beauty.

"Soda instead of soap for the bath. Perfumed oils afterward. Henna to dye their fingernails. Rouge for their lips and cheeks. Kohl to accentuate their almond-shaped eyes. The men shaved their heads and wore elaborate wigs. The women used false braids and curls."

"Apart from the kohl and the hennaed nails, that's not so different from our powders and perfumes, our fringes and 'rats,' " Miranda said. "What kind of clothes did they wear?"

"Linen, mainly, because of the heat. Women wore long dresses, the men wore skirts."

"No corsets," Miranda said.

"No, they wore as little as possible."

Without warning, Miranda was back in her stateroom on the *Sylvania* and a man she hardly knew was unbuttoning her dress, removing her petticoats, loosening her corset and the repression that went with it. She felt the same trembling of her body, the same unquenchable desire she had felt then. She felt his mouth against her skin.

She had thought it was under control, that she could keep those memories hidden until she wanted to take them out. She had not summoned these intimate thoughts of Steven. She had no idea why they had suddenly materialized in a mortuary temple. She was shaken by them and she pushed them away.

Paul was walking around the silent room, climbing over whatever blocks of stone had been left when the smaller rubble was removed for examination.

"Nothing major has been taken away," he explained. "We want the site uncontaminated in order to learn as much as possible. In the past, too many tombs have been plundered."

She hardly heard him, still unnerved by that sudden, searing memory that left her legs weak. She looked for something to say. Finally she asked, "How can people who still believe in the afterlife have so little respect for their ancient dead?"

But she did not listen to his reply. She had supposed time was working its magic to dim the edge of that other love, that it had begun to fade. She was both dismayed and elated that those memories were not gone from her mind or her body.

Paul's voice had stopped. Miranda turned to the catafalque that stood in the center of the candlelit chamber, dominating it. She moved to the sarcophagus and leaned against its outer vault of stone. The slab that was its cover had been removed to expose a highly polished wooden case carved to simulate the folds of a royal robe and decorated in gold and turquoise.

Moving her candle toward the head, Miranda gasped. A beautiful face looked up at her. The pupils of the eyes were of black obsidian bordered by blue glass inlay and surrounded by pure white limestone. The large, expressive eyes were outlined with black to simulate the kohl used by the queen in life. The lips were full and sensual, the brows heavy, the nose small and straight. She seemed about to speak, so intense were those eyes, so real.

"If she was anything like this, she was lovely," Miranda said.

"Much good it did her," Paul replied wistfully. "According to the inscriptions we found, she was only sixteen when she died."

"How terribly sad," Miranda said softly. She reached out but did not touch the gleaming wood. "And her body's inside? Preserved?"

He nodded. "We think so. This seems to be a typical nest of coffins. The stone sarcophagus, then this ornate wooden coffin, then a simpler one of wood or papyrus, and finally the mummy wrapped in bands of linen the priests had soaked in their secret herbs and spices."

"I hope her little life was joyful." Miranda felt the tears well up in her eyes and trickle down her face. "I hope she was happy, that she was in love."

A sudden gust of wind swept through the chamber, extinguishing both candles. The lamps in the outer labyrinth cast hardly any light into the chamber.

"It must have been as dark as this when the poor little thing was entombed," Miranda sighed with an inexplicable ache in her heart, "as lonely and dark as it's been for thousands of years."

She shivered with a distant cold, as if the young queen had sent that whisper of wind to say that her life had been brutally short, that her journey back to her body had been interrupted and her rest disturbed by presumptuous mortals who would be dust themselves soon enough.

"Paul?" she whispered into the darkness, suddenly terrified by the phantoms in this place.

"I'm right here," Paul assured her, believing he understood the tremor in her voice. Tombs often had a strange effect on people, even on experienced archeologists. They felt guilty when they intruded upon the dead.

"Where could that wind have come from?" Miranda wondered, her voice hushed.

"The diggers probably opened another room and caused a sudden draft. You mustn't let your imagination run away with you."

"What shall we do?"

"Stay here with the baby queen until our man returns. No point in stumbling over those stone blocks."

But the blackness seemed to thicken, to smother her. "How long will the man be?"

"If he doesn't come soon, we'll leave, slowly and carefully."

"And the labyrinth?"

"It's lit and I know the way back. Trust me, darling."

It had been weeks since he called her that, even in bed. "Paul," she pleaded, "come to me. Come and hold me. *Please.*"

He was there in seconds. His arms went around her and his cheek was pressed to hers.

"Why are you crying?" he asked.

"She was such a tragic little thing, for all her beauty and her rank."

They stood together in the drenching darkness which, for Miranda, was definitely charged with a life of its own. The very air seemed to change, as if there were more occupants than the three of them, for the queen was as alive to Miranda as Paul and herself. Did those painted figures on the walls come to life in the dark? Were they summoned by those royal eyes?

"Life is so futile," she said. "And death so final."

"Perhaps not," he said gently, stroking her back. "The Egyptians didn't believe that. Neither do we."

"That's only a pathetic effort," she said. "We deny death, make up stories about it, celebrate it, create ceremonies to make it less fearsome—but it still lies in wait for everything that lives."

She felt the weight of it, the enormous finality of it, the ineluctable fact of it. It made life seem all the dearer, all the more to be lived with as much jubilation as anyone could seize and hold.

To have and to hold from this day forward, forsaking all others was what she had promised Paul. She had broken her promise.

"I'm sorry," she whispered.

"For what?" he asked with something in his voice that warned her not to say what the darkness tempted her to say, warned her again not to tell him what he already knew.

"For her, the queen," Miranda said instead. *For us,* she thought. "Did she leave a king behind?"

"Yes, she did. And two children."

"How cruel that was," she said—and knew it was not principally death that parted a man and a woman, but words, spoken and unspoken, that lay like barricades between them, responsibilities that chained them and mistakes that engulfed them as inexorably as any tomb.

Panic clutched Miranda again until Paul said something; later she could never remember what it had been. The mere sound of his voice stopped her panic, reassured her as it had been doing for twenty-one years. He had only to speak and she felt safe. He had only to smile and she felt loved. When he took her hand she felt strong.

She had loved him for a long time as a friend and husband and the father of her sons, and now she loved him as a lover too. How strange it was that the very reason for their new erotic relationship now kept them at a distance from each other.

They stood together in silence, suspended in a void as if they were up among the stars. To her they seemed like two disembodied souls wandering like phantasms through the ether, their breaths mingling somewhere in the space—how immense it seemed—between them.

She put her head back and kissed him. She went on kissing him, softly and hotly, as if a kiss were the most profound of physical intimacies. She kissed him hungrily, tasting him, nipping tenderly at his lips with her teeth, soothing the little bites with her tongue. Surrounded by death, they were defended by desire.

"I want you," he whispered, as aroused as she was.

"Yes," she said.

"Here. Now." He pressed her down on the carved and lacquered casket.

"Yes!" she said again. His right hand lifted her skirt and stroked her thigh. She moved her body to meet his hand—and then she felt him pull away from her.

"Paul . . . ?"

"Hush, Miranda! I hear voices."

There was a shout outside and a babble of words she could not understand. Quickly they arranged their clothes. Seconds later a figure appeared in the arched entrance carrying a lighted torch and the darkness ended.

They walked sedately out of the tomb, avoiding each other's eyes lest they betray themselves, leaving the queen behind but taking desire with them, an ache not to be satisfied until hours later when, at last, they were alone.

Then she clung to him with avid little whispers of passion while, outside on the moonlit deck, Cynthia and Walford strolled.

Cynthia, on Walford's arm, was thinking furiously. Fate seemed to be leading her toward marriage with Alastair.

Steven clearly did not want her—the only wrenching rejection she had ever known. It was made worse by his recent association

with Kitt McAllister. Whether or not it was romantic for him—
Cynthia knew that it was for Kitt—it was public, and that could
make Cynthia a pathetic figure.

Humiliation was far more painful to endure than unrequited
love.

There was one sure way to avoid public shame: marry Walford
and have the kind of life she'd always planned before she met Steven
James.

"A penny for your thoughts," Walford said.

"I was just thinking of what we saw today at Memphis."

"I'm shattered," he said. "I hoped you were thinking of me."

She sighed. "Walford, you know I don't like that kind of chat."

"Well then, I'm damned if I know what to say to you."

"It seems to me that we talk for hours."

"But not about anything that matters."

She deliberately let a few seconds go by before she answered.
"Talk about what matters, then."

"Will you marry me?" he said immediately.

"You know it's not for me to say."

"But would you if you could?"

They had stopped walking and she leaned against the polished
railing of the boat and gazed at him. The moon was full on his face.
How handsome he was! How almost angelic. But there was something behind that angelic appearance, something wicked that both
fascinated and frightened her.

"Would *you* if you could?" she asked him.

"Marry you? Hang it, Cynthia, I've asked you over and over."

"Because your father told you to."

"Partly. I'd be in all kinds of trouble if I married without my
father's permission, just as you would."

"In your case, the trouble would last only until he died," she
said. "The estate is yours by law."

"He's in excellent health," Alastair said. "But if I were free to
marry any girl in the world . . ."

"Alastair!" she said. "I don't expect any dramatic declarations. Just tell me the truth."

"I'd rather marry you than any other girl I've met."

"Why is that?"

"You're jolly good fun, Cynthia, aside from the way you look. And we do get on together."

She turned away to contemplate the river once more. He put his hands on her shoulders and she felt his lips brush the nape of her neck. A tingle went through her, tantalizing and exciting. She turned back to him.

"Kiss me," she said.

His mouth came down on hers. Her arms went around him and she let her lips part under his. He gasped and drew her closer.

"Say you will," he demanded.

"Yes," she said. "I will marry you."

"Hallelujah!" he said.

She liked the way he held her. Her cheek rested in the curve of his neck and he rocked her gently.

"We'll be splendid together," he said. "You'll see."

"Let's hope our fathers think so." She stepped away from him. "It's late, Walford. I must go in."

"Another kiss."

"Tomorrow," she said, and left him, knowing nothing was decided until her father and his decided it.

Walford stayed on the deck and smoked a cigar. He could not have described what he was feeling: He had never experienced this combination of tenderness and desire before.

Cynthia would be a perfect wife. They would be together always and that was comforting. Strange, that the very idea of tying himself to one person for the rest of his life had once made him rebellious. Now he could not imagine life without Cynthia.

She was the most beautiful creature he had ever seen. She was clever and witty and not taken in by the pap other girls liked to hear from men. She was not like other girls at all. She was a challenge. He even considered the possibility that he was in love with her, but he abandoned it immediately. He did not believe in love. He threw his cigar overboard and went to his cabin.

But he could not sleep. He was thinking of how delicious her mouth was when he kissed her. A sweet desire aroused him and, thinking of Cynthia this time, and not of her aunt, he relieved himself and then lay in a haze of release and anticipation. He dozed and was almost asleep when he heard the soft tapping on his cabin door.

"Come," he said.

The dragoman opened the door. He was a light-skinned Egyptian with large liquid eyes and an unctuous manner that Alastair despised, even though he expected inferiors to fawn.

"What is it?" he asked the man.

"Does Your Lordship require a woman?"

"Good God! Did you stock a few prostitutes in Cairo?"

"Alas, no, sir. But there are girls in the local villages."

"No," Alastair said. The idea of a smelly native did not appeal to him at all.

"A boy, then?"

"No!" Alastair rasped, disgusted. "Damn you, man! Get the devil out of here!"

"Yes, Your Lordship. A thousand pardons, Your Lordship."

The door closed behind the dragoman and Alastair flopped back against his pillows. He had half a mind to take a stick to that bastard's hide! How dare he offer Alastair a boy?

And yet, he knew that a year before, even six months, he'd probably have taken a village girl or a local boy, maybe even one of each, just for the sheer debauchery of it. Sex had always been a sport to him, like cricket or hunting, even more enjoyable with the sauce of vice. He had experimented with it as he still did with varieties of wine and spirits, cigars and tea, tailors and bootmakers.

It struck him now that he might give the wrong impression to other people because of his looks and his promiscuous habits. But Alastair was damned if he'd be labeled a faggot, not for a few, usually drunken, forays into other men's bodies. He had never permitted a man to enter his.

"I'm not a faggot," Alastair said to the empty cabin. "I never was."

He was not an introspective man and made no attempt to examine why he should suddenly give a hang what anyone thought.

"But it's probably all to the good," he said aloud. He punched his pillows. "When I've married Cynthia no one will ever mistake me for a nancy boy again."

He drew up the covers and went to sleep.

———— . ————

In the morning a Thomas Cook agent arrived as they were finishing breakfast to deliver a wire that had just missed them in Cairo:

ARRIVE DECEMBER 3 BRISTOL HOTEL
STOP BE THERE STOP H CUNNINGHAM.

The message electrified the party, much as they tried not to show it. Paul was pleased, Miranda visibly anxious, Cynthia and Walford self-conscious, like two children who know they are being discussed by their elders.

Paul went to consult his timetables with the dragoman.

"We can have another morning on the river before we put about for Cairo," he said when he returned.

"Will we have any time there to visit the bazaar?" Cynthia asked. "We missed it entirely the last time."

Paul assured her they would have two days in Cairo before boarding the train to Alexandria to catch the next steamer across the Mediterranean.

Thirty

It was not until the second day in Cairo that Miranda found an opportunity to speak to Walford, and then it was in the bustle of the bazaar. The place was crowded, noisy, and exotic and emitted a thousand smells, some of them decidedly unpleasant.

Paul and Cynthia were in the street of the glass vendors while Miranda and Walford, a few streets over, were looking at rugs.

"I'm not in the least interested in rugs," Miranda said to him when they were quite alone.

He looked at her inquiringly.

"What I have to say," she went on, "is repugnant to me, but I must say it to protect my niece."

"Protect her? Not from me, certainly!" Walford was taken aback. "My intentions toward her are completely honorable."

"It is your intentions toward boys like Lewis Wendall that trouble me," Miranda said.

His handsome face froze. "I don't know what you're talking about," he said.

"Yes, you do. I can't let Cynthia's life be ruined because of your unorthodox preferences."

His blue eyes regarded her steadily. "Assuming for the sake of argument that you are correct, such experiments are commonplace and temporary."

It was what Paul had told her, but she remained unconvinced. "For schoolboys, perhaps, but for a grown man about to marry for money, I don't believe it is temporary."

"You are insulting, Mrs. Cunningham. I honestly love Cynthia."

"I don't believe that either, not for a moment."

Underneath the tanned skin he was pale with anger. "And why do you suppose your beliefs will carry any weight in this affair?"

"I shall tell Hobart, and if it doesn't stop him from swapping his daughter for a title, I shall tell Cynthia."

His expression changed abruptly from hauteur to supplication. "No! Please don't do that!"

He might have been one of her sons trying to keep a secret from his father, but she knew she mustn't be moved by that. "I'm sorry, but if you persist in your suit, I must tell her."

"Cynthia won't know what you're talking about."

"I'll find a way to explain it to her."

"But she's already promised to marry me!"

Miranda shook her head. "That is not binding and you know it. Her father will decide, not Cynthia. You were wrong to ask her before getting permission from her father."

"But her father has no reason to reject me!"

"I can supply one," Miranda said.

"You'd ruin my life with a lie?"

"I won't have to, provided you withdraw your proposal."

Walford turned away and pretended deep interest in a small silk prayer rug for several moments while Miranda stared at a fringed, circular mat in jewellike colors.

"Mrs. Cunningham," Walford said, holding up the prayer rug as if to show it to her. "I don't think you are in a position to cast any stones, not in light of your affair with Senator James."

Miranda flushed painfully and leaned against a pile of rolled rugs, trying to draw a deep breath. "Don't threaten me," she said in a low voice.

"You have more to lose than I do," he said. "If it became common gossip—and I would see that it did—your husband would divorce you."

She looked at him steadily, saying nothing.

"You would lose everything."

"We are not talking about my marriage," she said sharply, "but about the one you're planning."

He shrugged. "You don't believe me, but I love Cynthia. It's a great surprise to me too." He looked so bemused that she almost believed him. "I never expected to fall in love, but there it is. I want to marry her for more than her fortune."

"But would you marry her without it?"

He shook his head. "I am not at liberty to consider only my feelings in the matter, any more than you are in the other matter. I do want to make her happy and I'm prepared to mend my wicked ways in order to do that. Fortunately, the vice you refer to is not one of mine."

"Is blackmailing me evidence of your improved character?"

"It's precisely what you were doing to me."

Rage made it difficult for her to breathe, but she nodded an acknowledgment and a look of reluctant admiration touched his face.

"You have far more courage than one expects to find in a beautiful woman," he said.

"I'm immune to flattery, Lord Walford."

"That was the simple truth. So is this: if you make any unfounded accusations to prevent my marrying Cynthia, I shall reply with an accusation against you that is well founded and easy to prove."

She knew this was no idle threat: he would do exactly as he said.

She wanted to protect Cynthia, but the price would be too high. She was mortified at this new proof of her selfishness, but she had no choice.

"She doesn't love you," Miranda said.

"She will, in time."

"You have a high opinion of yourself."

"I know women—and how to please them in many ways."

She turned her head abruptly, as if she could not tolerate the sight of him. To him, she looked magnificent standing there, her bosom swelling, her face white, her back straight as a ramrod.

"Mrs. Cunningham," he said entreatingly, because he did admire a strong adversary, "couldn't we simply trust each other?"

"About what?" Cynthia's voice said behind them.

"About a choice of carpet for Mrs. Cunningham's foyer," Walford lied smoothly. "She likes this one, I prefer the other. But there's a third somewhere that I think combines the good points of both."

Paul, coming up behind them, looked at the carpets. "Whichever you prefer," he said to Miranda. He saw her white face in full light. "Are you ill?"

She took a scented handkerchief out of her pocket and pressed it to her forehead. "I'm feeling a little faint. It must be the heat and the noise. I think I'll go back to the hotel, but you three must go on. I don't want to ruin the outing for you."

Cynthia and Walford went off to visit the Citadel and the tombs of the Mamelukes, but Paul insisted upon going with her to Shepheard's.

"What happened?" Paul asked when they were alone in Miranda's bedroom. Rooney had unlaced her and she was lying on the bed in a white cambric peignoir, drinking iced lemonade with a cool cloth on her forehead.

"It's nothing serious. I'll be fine if I rest awhile."

"I mean, what happened between you and Walford?"

"Nothing at all. We were looking at rugs."

Paul sat down in the armchair beside the bed. "Miranda, both of you were furious, and it had nothing to do with rugs."

She did not reply.

"I hope you realize that my brother wants this marriage," Paul said. "He wouldn't be traveling all the way to London otherwise."

"I know that," she said. "But he wouldn't have come at all if you'd told him the truth about Walford."

"Miranda," he said impatiently. "It is not a matter you are qualified to judge. In any case, the subject is obscene, particularly from my wife."

"Cynthia ought to be protected from such obscenity."

"I want your word that you will not discuss Walford's youthful peccadilloes with Hobart!"

She looked at him for a long moment, almost as if she did not recognize him. "I don't understand you. You're not the kind of man to sacrifice Cynthia on the altar of Hobart's social ambitions. You're much too principled to do it even to curry favor with him for yourself."

"To what purpose would I curry favor with my brother?"

"To spend half your life out here, doing what fascinates you. If Cynthia marries Walford, Hobart will be in your debt."

"You're being dramatic. If I thought Walford threatened Cynthia's happiness in any way—"

She interrupted him. "To begin with, Cynthia is not in love with Walford."

"She certainly likes him enormously. Maybe that's a better basis for marriage than the unrequited love she imagines she feels for another man."

In another moment he would have said Steven's name.

"Maybe it is," she said, backing off.

He drew a deep breath. "Then you agree to let it drop?"

"Paul, I have the most horrible headache. Can't we discuss this later?"

"Of course," he said, getting up immediately. "I'll leave you to rest. But there is nothing to discuss. I will be obeyed in this."

He went out and she was left to consider all of it: her warning to Walford, his to her, Paul's blindness to Cynthia's predicament. And Paul's demand that she obey. He had never done that before.

Or was Paul furious with Miranda because he could not resist her? So furious that he would deliberately reject whatever she said to keep her in her place?

She had no choice but to wait and see what developed in London. The two fathers might detest each other on sight. Hobart was easy to loathe and the earl's preoccupation with rank would make Hobart resentful.

If she could not ignore Paul's insistence that she say nothing to Hobart, there was always Cynthia.

———— · ————

On the railway trip to Alexandria, Walford racked his brain trying to think of some ploy other than blackmail to keep Miranda quiet. He was amazed she had the temerity to allude to homosexuality and blackmail, much less discuss them. And he had to give her high marks for admitting that she was as guilty of a blackmail attempt as he.

She feared his threats. He feared hers. They were at an impasse.

Walford concluded that his best defense was a good offense. If he could compromise Cynthia, the question of his sexual inclinations would be academic. Once compromised, Cynthia would have no recourse but to marry him. It would be the act of a cad, but since he planned to marry her anyway, what difference did that make?

Having made that decision, the question of where and how was the next problem. She would be too inaccessible on the train to Alexandria and during the boat journey across the Mediterranean.

The same would be true on the long rail journey from Italy to the Channel. But they would break the fatigue of constant travel with a few days stay in Paris, and there was no place better suited to intrigue than Paris.

"It will be an adventure to see that city with you," he told Cynthia when they were on deck during the crossing from Africa to Europe.

"We'll only have a few days in Paris. Is that enough time for an adventure?"

"Absolutely, if one knows where to go and what to do."

"And you're one who knows."

He smiled and nodded. "You'll see."

"Where would we begin?"

"By escaping from your aunt and uncle."

She laughed. "That's impossible."

"Not if you help."

"What could I do?"

"Well, let me think a moment." He looked out to sea, pretending to reflect. "You could say you have a headache and refuse to accompany the three of us to Napoleon's Tomb."

"That would be a pleasure," Cynthia said. "I've had enough of tombs to last me a lifetime."

"All right, then. We now have you alone at the Ritz with a mythical headache. I am with Aunt and Uncle Cunningham, but only for an hour. I spill some wine on my shirt and hurry back to the hotel to change."

"And then what happens?" she asked, joining the fun.

"We go to Montmartre."

It was a mythical place, the soul of "Gay Paree," slightly naughty and very different from the palatial hotels and residences of the Right Bank, where convention was revered if not practiced. In Montmartre people sang, laughed, embraced in public, danced to the music of guitars and accordions and, in the spring and summer, sat under parasols on the Place du Tertre while they drank wine and watched strolling singers, jugglers, and artists who did charcoal sketches and silhouette cutouts. *La vie de bohème* made the senses keener: The sky was bluer, the clouds whiter, the wine sweeter. Love and music made an intoxicating combination.

Alastair had it all planned, but he kept the details to himself. First they would walk on the cobbled streets and see sidewalk displays of art, a perfectly innocent pursuit. They would stop in a café for wine and Alastair would contrive to keep Cynthia out until well after dark. That was all it took—several unchaperoned hours with a man of Walford's looks and cavalier reputation in a notorious section of this libertine city—to compromise a young lady's good name. He need go no farther than that.

But I wish I could! he told himself, looking at her profile on the small steamer's deck. He wondered if her unusual curiosity could get the better of her upbringing, if he could persuade her into one of the small hotels that rented to lovers by the hour and initiate her into the mysteries of sex. Sometimes he thought she was cold, but the way she kissed him that night on the Nile had been very warm indeed.

She was so totally unpredictable! She might very well decide to satisfy her curiosity with the man she was about to marry. Or she might go off in a huff at the very suggestion. But he was sure of one thing Cynthia would never do: scream and faint. Any more than her Aunt Miranda had in the bazaar.

"Does that kind of adventure appeal to you?" he asked Cynthia now, looking down at her with that innocent smile he could summon at will.

"I'll tell you what I think when we get to Paris."

"Fair enough," he said, hiding his frustration that she had eluded him once more. He had been accustomed to having his way before he met her. He decided he would have to wait until he had her where she could no longer elude him. No matter how clever she was, in bed she would yield or be taken.

His anger passed as quickly as it had come. "Shall we go inside

and have a sherry?" he asked. He offered his arm, she took it, and they crossed the deck of the steamer and went into the salon, a glorious pair watched by every passenger there.

"Act as if they were the gods come down from Olympus," one bewhiskered merchant grumbled to his wife, his eyes following the couple.

"A scurvier lot never drew breath," she sniffed.

"That's the truth," he said. "I know who he is, but who's the girl?"

"The Yankee heiress he wants to marry."

"Good Lord! At this rate all the British nobility will be married to Yankee women." He shook his head and returned to his week-old *Times* and she to her *Tatler* while, across the room, Walford and Cynthia joined Miranda and Paul.

A tall woman with bushy brown hair and an enormous bosom sat down at the piano and began to play Chopin waltzes, leaving all four of them free to listen without making conversation.

Walford was thinking about how he could turn an outing to Montmartre into a seduction. The three Cunninghams were thinking of Steven James.

Thirty-one

Steven was in a hurry. He had spent more than an hour with his tailor in St James's and he did not want to be late for his meeting with Blenkinsop. Sir Harry, a master at business, was also a stickler for social form, fond of saying things like "punctuality is the politeness of kings." Steven knew the remark wasn't original. He would ask Miss McAllister whose it was when he saw her that evening. Miss McAllister was a mine of information.

Sometimes, when she was not so . . . so *removed* from him, he wanted to hug her.

He found a cab rank and got into the first one, giving the cabbie an address in the City. But he was not thinking about his meeting. He was thinking about Miranda.

A hot wave of longing swept over him, only to be replaced by shame when he imagined for the hundredth time what his sister would say.

"If you love her," Claire would protest, "how can you ask her to become an outcast, a social pariah? To leave her sons, her family, her country?"

"As long as we have each other," he murmured to the distant Claire, "we'll have all we need."

"You're talking like a schoolboy, not a grown man. Even lovers cannot live in isolation from the rest of the world." He could hear Claire's voice, heavy with derision.

And it was true. Miranda and Steven would have to live in the shadows of society, in the demimonde of divorced women, actresses, mistresses and their keepers. It was an untenable position for a decent woman whose only crime was to have fallen in love. With the right man but at the wrong time. He glowed at the thought of seeing her again, and then the light faded when he imagined whispers about her as "that Cunningham woman." Even if someday he could marry her, she would always be "that Cunningham woman."

But he loved her! And she loved him! She might have been remorseful enough to send him away right after she was reunited with her husband and—a far more compelling reason for remorse, Steven was certain—her son. But their separation must have been as painful to her as it was to him, as if a chunk of himself had broken away. By the time she returned from Cairo after weeks of routine domesticity, she would be ready to listen to her heart.

Without warning he found himself wondering what Kitt would think of him if she knew. Steven had cringed more than once at that possibility, but had concluded that if she did know, she would not be seeing him at all. Independent as she was, she could not receive an adulterer. It was yet another reminder of what Steven and Miranda would face.

Kitt *did* seem more remote, more guarded than she had been aboard the *Sylvania*. Still, she rarely refused his invitations and seemed happy to see him. He had noticed that he missed her if he didn't see her for more than a day or two—but what did he miss? He pondered that as the cab rumbled toward the City. Until recently, women had attracted him simply because they were women: innocent or worldly, sweet or clever, strikingly beautiful—like Cynthia and Miranda—or subtly so, like Kitt.

He pictured her, tall and trim in her severely elegant clothes. Tonight they were going to hear *La Bohème* and then on to supper at a Gypsy restaurant, Tzigane, that was all the rage. Opera was beginning to grow on Steven in the same way tea had, and Kitt's utter delight in music increased his own appreciation of it.

They would be alone at Tzigane, just the two of them. A maid was not required in a restaurant. To the Victorians, food was such a total preoccupation that no other appetites could obtrude.

He was looking forward to those hours alone with Kitt. And then Miranda's face flashed upon his memory again and he felt torn between loyalty to his true love and the comfort he took in the uncomplicated fondness he felt for Kitt.

The cab stopped and, with some difficulty, he turned his attention to business and got out.

——— . ———

Sir Harry was almost enthusiastic when he greeted Steven in his office, which was decorated in serious shades of brown.

Sir Harry Blenkinsop himself was amazingly tall. Steven was unaccustomed to men who soared above him, and this one tried to equalize things by keeping his head permanently cocked to one side or the other, as if to bring himself down to the level of those puny mortals with whom he conversed.

They discussed the ships he wanted to sell, trying to reach an agreement on how many and how much. Gus Haggerty had gone back to New York, but he was as reluctant as Raymond Steele and Steven were to buy any of the six battered vessels Blenkinsop offered, not in their present condition. On the other hand, buying them elsewhere would cost a lot more. Blenkinsop, after all, was their partner in the canal deal. Steven was there to negotiate a better arrangement.

"The others have decided not to buy any ships at all," Steven said.

"Then how will they have the use of them?" Blenkinsop scoffed, blinking at Steven like an incredulous owl.

"We prefer to lease them from you."

Blenkinsop's face took on something approaching a patronizing smile. "Why would I consider that? Ownership leaves me lumbered with the costs of dry dock, skeleton crew, and provisioning. If the syndicate buys them, my costs will be reduced to my share of the operation."

"Sir Harry, those ships will have to be refitted if you want to sell them to anyone—even to lease them to our group, come to think of it." Steven smiled ingenuously. "You're too canny to pay good money for ships in their condition, especially if you're your own customer."

Blenkinsop offered Steven a cigar, grunted when Steven refused, and went about the business of clipping it, moistening it, and lighting it, regarding Steven with narrowed eyes.

"Look," Steven said to break the silence, "the costs of dry dock are already yours. You can't expect to be relieved of prior commitments. But as soon as we start operations, all of your expenses will be shared. And at the end of the day you'll retain ownership of a number of seaworthy vessels."

"After refitting them and then paying a share of leasing what I already own?" Blenkinsop, behind a cloud of blue cigar smoke, resembled a pale ectoplasm more than ever. "What do you take me for, Mr. James?"

"A man with a good head for business. If you refuse to lease, we'll have to look elsewhere for our ships. In that case, the Panama Canal project will no longer be open to you."

"Come now, Mr. James, let us not be hasty." A flush appeared on Blenkinsop's bleached cheeks, and Steven knew he had won. The prospective profits were too enormous to be turned down over the cost of refitting six ships!

They went on bartering until they reached agreement on the terms for leasing six vessels—all to be refitted at Sir Harry's expense—to the group.

"Which, by the way, may be growing," Blenkinsop said. "I'm expecting someone from New York who will probably be interested, and when he's interested you know the deal's a good one. Do you know Hobart Cunningham?"

"By reputation only," Steven said with sudden, irrational apprehension. Steven had nothing to fear from Hobart, but from what Cynthia had hinted that day at Brown's, Miranda might. "But I'm acquainted with his brother, Paul."

"The grave digger?" Blenkinsop tittered, then began to cough, and this time his face went red. When the paroxysms ended, he took a few breaths of smoky air and gestured toward a tray of bottles and glasses. "Whisky," he gasped, and waved Steven in that direction, indicating that his guest should help himself as well.

Steven poured the whisky and brought it to Sir Harry, who sipped carefully until his coughing stopped.

"Now, where were we? Ah, yes, Hobart Cunningham. I'm not clear just how he heard about our project, although I know he has sources in London and Paris. Perhaps it was your father-in-law who told him." He studied Steven attentively.

"He *was* my father-in-law," Steven said. "Apart from my interest in the Panama Canal, I know nothing about Haggerty's activities."

"Ah? Well, that's not the only business Cunningham's on. He's got a girl with a fortune and he wants to swap them for a title. He's coming over to settle the terms of her dowry."

So Cynthia finally gave in, Steven thought, remembering her tears when she told him she was being forced to marry. He felt vaguely responsible for not having rescued her; her superficial resemblance to Alicia had always been a disturbing reminder of his irresponsible marriage. But what could he have done for Cynthia? And how had she made him feel it was his obligation to do anything?

"I take it the groom-to-be is Lord Walford," Steven said.

"How did you know that?" Blenkinsop demanded testily.

"I met Walford and Miss Cunningham on the *Sylvania*. He seemed taken with her right from the start."

Blenkinsop nodded, soothed. "In the old days these things were

~~~ ~~~ about 'em in the gutter press, along

Allister woman. I don't hold

apers, not even when she's a

ven a sly wink.

good friend of mine," Steven

g she does is out of convic-

rased his smirk. "Met her on

olitely.

Kitt with this man. Not long

furiously.

hia would come back to Lon-

ched with eagerness to see her

the decision they would have

to ma...

———— · ————

Kitt and Lady Burdon walked briskly in Green Park, careless of the chill November wind that sent the leaves eddying around their feet. They had discovered another shared preference: cold weather.

"I understand our friends are returning from Cairo," Lady Burdon said after ten minutes of companionable silence.

Kitt was dismayed. "I thought they planned to stay there for at least another month." *I need more time with him,* she thought frantically.

"So they did. But Miss Cynthia's papa is en route to London, and that must mean Walford's popped the question."

"Maybe her father is coming on other business."

"In that case, he would not have called her back to London!

No, the word about is that Mr. Cunningham will be meeting with
the Earl of Inderby to thrash out the knotty question of her dowry
and the announcement will be made shortly after Miss Cynthia
arrives."

"What if they don't agree about the dowry?"

"Then the Cunninghams will steam back to the colonies and
Walford will find himself another heiress."

"The dowry is a barbarous custom," Kitt said, trying not to
think about what would happen when Steven and Miranda were in
the same city again.

"Actually, it's quite sound," Lady Burdon said. "When a man
marries a woman he thinks he's doing her a favor; but if she has a
dowry, the score is evened."

"Not if he has control of her fortune as well as her person."

"I doubt Papa Cunningham will allow Walford to control all
the money. He'll insist that a portion be set aside for his daughter."

"If Walford and his family are as hard up as you've told me,"
Kitt remarked, "there must be a lot of money involved."

*Maybe they won't agree about the dowry! Maybe Cynthia and Miranda
will go back to Egypt!*

"Fortunes," Lady Pat agreed.

"I'd rather be loved for myself," Kitt said.

"Wouldn't we all!"

"You were."

"In my second marriage, yes. But the other two worked quite
well even though they were business arrangements."

"I can't imagine sharing a bed with a man I don't love."

"There is a rule for that. Close your eyes and think of England.
It works."

They had reached the deserted bandstand where, in the spring
and summer, an orchestra played. It was empty and silent now.
Dried leaves and twigs scudded across the path and the day that had

seemed invigorating to Kitt moments before was mournful and bleak.

Miranda was coming.

At the prospect Kitt felt unaccessorized again. She was without the provocative dark eyes and the brunette splendor of Miranda. Her body was devoid of Miranda's lavish curves and imposing presence. Nor did she have Cynthia's seductive beauty and the assurance that went with it. If Kitt seemed self-assured, it was because, through close observation, she had learned to act that way. Kitt would have given everything she had to be what was deemed a beautiful woman in 1900, even her dependable, steadfast intelligence. It was cold comfort now.

"You're thinking about the senator and his lady," Lady Burdon said.

Kitt blushed. "How can you tell?"

"Your expression is a remarkable blend of affection and rage. The affection must be for him, so I conclude that your rage is for Miranda Cunningham."

"For the situation, not for the woman. It's astonishing, but I still like her." They walked on in silence for some minutes before Lady Burdon spoke again.

"I've always wondered how you found out about those two."

"Alton told me."

"I see," Lady Burdon said. "Alton is a good friend. She told you the morning we disembarked at Liverpool, did she?" She smiled at Kitt's amazement. "Before that morning you were very spirited. In the railway carriage to London you were like a lost lamb. Then you put on your prison clothes and became a feminist."

"I've always been a feminist."

"On a far smaller scale, you must admit, and arrayed in brighter colors."

But Kitt was on another track. "It's a shock to learn that my feelings are apparent to everyone," she said.

"Not to everyone. Most people are too preoccupied with their own feelings to notice anyone else's."

There was another silence before Kitt asked, "Does the count know?"

"Yes."

"That explains why he's been so kind to me," Kitt said.

"Not so. The count is much taken with you, apart from kindliness."

It was a comforting thought. Kitt said, "I like him too."

"Enough to marry him?"

Kitt almost laughed. "I wouldn't dream of it."

"He's a decent, charming, cultivated man. Why not?"

"Apart from the fact that I don't love him, it's an impossible idea," Kitt said. "The count is a French aristocrat, and my father was a textile manufacturer in what you both still call the colonies."

"Which makes you a colonial textile princess in love with the son of a colonial dairy farmer. But, of course, that sort of thing doesn't matter in America, where every girl's dream is to marry a prince."

"It matters in France. And in England as well."

"Jean-Baptiste doesn't care what people think."

"But his family cares. And I would care, although it would be a challenge to beat them at that game. But you're mistaking his kindness for serious intentions."

"I know him far too well to make a mistake of that kind," Lady Burdon said firmly.

Several moments passed before Kitt said, "I suppose you and the count have had a jolly good laugh over my infatuation."

"Not at all! Since he is also infatuated, he sympathizes and he is patient. He knows that the senator's heart is not free. I'm not sure you do."

"I do," Kitt said.

"And may never be."

Kitt nodded.

"But you'll wait until he's sufficiently miserable without the gorgeous Mrs. Cunningham to seek comfort from you."

"Yes. But he may never be without her."

Lady Burdon shook her head. "Eventually they'll part. When remorse flies through the door, love flies out the window."

Kitt was silent, hoping that was true.

"And after waiting for what may be years," Lady Burdon said, "you would think yourself lucky to marry a man who loves another woman."

"I could change that! I know I could!"

"Nonsense! You marry a man as he is, not for the alterations you hope to make in him. Men never change; they don't see any reason to change. You'll just become a shrew, snipping and clipping at him like a demented tailor, and he'll find solace elsewhere."

It was Lady Burdon who stopped walking this time. She turned to Kitt and took both her hands. "Listen to me, my dear. In every marriage there is one who loves and one who lets himself be loved. If my years have taught me anything, it is this: be the one who lets herself be loved. For you that is impossible with Mr. James but not with Jean-Baptiste. You would have a contented life if you married him. Contentment is more rewarding and longer lasting than mad infatuation."

She clasped Kitt's hands for a moment. "Here I am, trying to make you listen to reason, when what you want is the delirium of love."

"I know I must give it up," Kitt said, surrendering to logic. "I hoped for more time to make him see the light, but if she comes back now . . ."

"I'm sorry, my dear Kitt, truly I am." Lady Burdon patted Kitt's cheek with great affection. Then the two women walked on.

———— • ————

La Bohème burst like a tidal wave over Kitt, exposing feelings she had concealed since she was small. The news of Miranda's return, combined with the yearning inspired by the music, had reduced her to despair. She understood how much he loved Miranda and how, because he loved her, he could not destroy her. But even if he did give her up, that didn't mean he would ever turn to Kitt.

Some of Kitt's despair had been distilled into exasperation toward Steven. How could he be so blind to what Kitt felt for him? It was in her voice when she spoke to him, in her eyes when she looked at him, in the air between them. No one was immune to love, not even if it was unrequited. Even the gods want to be worshipped.

Look at me! Kitt pleaded with him silently. *Why can't you look at me the way you look at her, just for a moment, and you'll see what's waiting here for you to take.*

It seemed to her that he must hear her, that the music would open a door and let her into his heart.

If she hadn't come back so soon, would you have come to see me differently? Would you have whispered to me in the half dark? Would you have kissed me?

But now, with Miranda crowding between them, he would never turn to Kitt, would never even suspect the passion she felt for him. It was beyond bearing any longer and, Kitt had decided, she would no longer bear it.

She felt bitter at her own pretension. As if the choice were hers! Very soon now Steven would forget Kitt was alive.

He would arrange a rendezvous with Miranda. They would meet and make love. The idea of them together made Kitt tremble with jealousy.

She turned her attention back to the stage lovers who sang so rapturously of parting in the springtime. How insipid their love seemed by comparison with her own anguish! Tears of sorrow and resentment filled her eyes and trickled down her cheeks while the

music and the voices and her lonely hunger for love—*his* love—
threatened to demolish her.

When the curtain fell, there was a hush before the applause
began and then it was thunderous. Steven leaned toward Kitt and
offered his handkerchief.

"Are you all right?"

"Of course." She ignored his handkerchief and took her own
out of her small beaded purse. "I always weep like a fountain in the
third act."

"It was very moving," he said, "but I had no idea you were such
a romantic."

"Well, I am," she said with some asperity. "Even feminists have
feelings."

Something in the way she said that moved him. "I never meant
to imply you didn't. And I don't think of you primarily as a feminist."

Kitt could not control herself. "Then what am I to you?"

"A friend," he said earnestly. "A very good friend."

She got to her feet. She did not want this disparaging "friendship" that cast her heart and soul aside and did not go beyond a
handshake.

"Will you have a glass of champagne before the last act?" Steven
asked, puzzled by the momentary flash of hot anger on her face.

She nodded and, with a word to Alton, they stepped into the
corridor. "Why wouldn't I be romantic?" she demanded.

"You're too practical for sentiment."

"One thing has nothing to do with the other."

Mercifully, there was too much of a crowd to allow a conversation in the corridor, and by the time they reached the bar, Kitt had a
grip on herself while Steven went for the drinks. He returned with
two glasses of champagne and they moved away from the crush of
people.

Her face was flushed and her temper raw, but she was in command of herself, enough to make appropriate conversation about the unhappy love story they had been watching on the stage.

———— · ————

For the first time Steven was aware of the admiring glances she drew from other men. She did not look austere tonight. She was wearing a gown of ivory satin embroidered in gold thread, a gown that hugged her bosom and showed her white shoulders. Her luxuriant hair glowed like silk under the crystal chandeliers. She was like a golden apple, at once tart and sweet, crisp and succulent. He wondered how she would look with her hair loose and tumbling onto her creamy shoulders.

It was not the first time he had imagined her like that, but it was the first time he did so consciously. He realized how very attractive she was each time he saw her. He especially liked to watch her speak at public meetings, where she seemed even taller than she was. Her voice was commanding but not strident, and she had a contagious fervor. It was no wonder that she roused the people who came to hear her.

"What a delightful surprise," Lady Burdon's voice said, and they turned to greet her and the count. Steven was annoyed by this trespass into their evening. The count's open admiration of Kitt—he called her Miss Louisa—irritated Steven, and he was relieved when the warning bell sounded and the two couples separated.

"Why is Lady Burdon so fond of that man?" Steven grumbled on their way back to the box.

"He's a dear man and very clever," Kitt said. Already fond of Jean-Baptiste, she could have kissed him tonight for his gallantry toward her. It eased her pride to have Steven see that she was not a "feminist friend" to all men.

Steven barely heard the final act. As soon as the final curtain fell, he whisked her out of the opera house and into a hansom. "To the Tzigane," he told the driver. He turned to Kitt and smiled. "I hope you like Gypsy violins as much as you like Puccini."

———— • ————

Kitt's emotions were once more aroused, this time by music of a different kind. If it lacked the purity of Puccini, it made up for that with the raw feeling that poured from the violin strings, the sheer, lovely, maudlin romance of it.

They ordered a peppery veal dish to be served over rice, and a bottle of heady red wine. When the wine was opened, tasted, and poured, they leaned back to listen. Kitt closed her eyes, her lashes casting shadows on her cheeks.

She was still shaken by the stupidity of human relations, by the social conventions that kept people from revealing love or pain or anger, while it was perfectly acceptable to gossip, to belittle and snicker and criticize and hate.

". . . and I've just finished it," Steven was saying.

"I beg your pardon?"

"You said *Wuthering Heights* was one of your favorite books, and I finally bought a copy and read it."

"Too 'romantic' for you?" But she was pleased that he would read a book because she liked it.

"On the contrary. I found it very touching."

"I'm sure it was Heathcliff who moved you most."

He nodded. "He was doomed from the start, like a character in a Greek tragedy. There was no way for him to escape his fate." He looked at her. "Doesn't he move you?"

"Not much," she said, suddenly angry with her most adored fictional hero. "He suffers, yes, but not as much as Isabella does at his hands."

Isabella's fate in the novel had struck a chord inside Steven. Like Alicia, she had married a man who did not love her. "She should not have married him," Steven said as if he were speaking of Isabella Linton, the fictional bride, when in fact he meant Alicia Haggerty James.

"She married him because she loved him," Kitt returned. "He married her out of selfishness and injured pride," she went on.

"I don't see that," he said earnestly before reminding himself that they were discussing a novel. "Or, at least, that's not the whole story. It was as close as he could get to the world and the woman he really wanted."

"He had no right!" Kitt said heatedly. "He had no right to marry one woman to get to another!"

"People make terrible mistakes," he said, remembering Alicia and his son, pale and cold in that coffin.

"He knew what he was doing! That is what is unforgivable."

Steven heard in that a second indictment, this time of his affair with Miranda and the destructive course he wanted Miranda to follow.

"Knowledge is no guarantee of wisdom," he almost pleaded.

"At least it should guarantee restraint."

They looked at each other. He could almost feel her distaste.

"You've guessed, haven't you?" he said, referring to his marriage.

"Yes." She meant Miranda.

"But you don't understand."

"I understand that it wasn't some passing fancy, no matter how suddenly it was born. I know you truly love each other. I could see that at Lady Burdon's party. But you will ruin her life if you persist. How can you do that to someone you pretend to love?"

He turned to her, first confused and then appalled when he understood her true meaning. He had never told her about his marriage: she was referring to Miranda! He was horrified that she knew.

"Shocks you, does it?" she said, reading it in his face. "That I know love when I see it? Do you suppose you're the only person on the planet capable of love like that? You're not, you know. But you may be a scoundrel—like Heathcliff!—ready to ruin a woman's life—and your own—and a few others—for something that simply should not be. I never would have believed you could be that selfish, that shortsighted. I thought . . . ." She searched for a word. "Better of you than that," she finished.

They sat looking at each other as if they had never met before. Then she reached to take up her purse. "I would appreciate it if you'd take me home now. I couldn't possibly swallow anything."

He nodded and called for the bill. He paid it, then took her arm and escorted her to the street, where the commissionaire hailed a cab for them. They got in and sat in complete silence until they came to Dover Street, and he dismissed the cab and took her to her door.

"I'm sorry, Kitt," he said, saying her name aloud for the first time.

"So am I, Steven."

They both wondered, when each was alone, what the other was sorry for.

Kitt, with Alton's shoulder to lean on, was dry-eyed but racked with sadness. "I've stopped," she whispered to Mary Frances. "I've been fooling myself long enough, but now I've stopped."

"It's better this way, Miss Kitt," Alton said, stroking Kitt's shoulder and holding her hand. "He's not a bad man, but he's not for you and there's an end to it."

Kitt nodded. "But *why* isn't he for me? I'm a woman. I'm not ugly. I make him laugh. We get along so well. *Why* isn't he for me when I'm so much for him?"

"There, Miss Kitt," Mary Frances crooned, rocking her. "Nobody knows the answer to that. It's his loss, don't you see, not yours."

—— · ——

Steven, shattered by Kitt's candor, dreamed that night of Isabella Linton/Alicia Haggerty/Miranda Cunningham and the harm he had done to all of them, sins of commission or omission, it didn't matter; one sort was as bad as the other. It never entered his mind that he had done any harm to Kitt.

Thirty-two

Hobart was pleased to have reached London a few days before the Cairo contingent would arrive. He had things to do, not least of which was to visit a lower-class bordello. The stewardess he had commandeered aboard the ship had been far too tame for his taste.

He was met at the railroad station by his man in London, Tedley, a small person with a monocle and a mustache. Tedley fiddled constantly with the monocle and chewed on the mustache, but he knew how to keep a sharp ear to the financial ground and, as the carriage rolled toward the Bristol, he swiftly put Hobart in the picture regarding the Panama Canal venture.

"They've called the syndicate Tri-Panalco," he finished.

Hobart shrugged, unconcerned with the name of the project. "If I go into this thing, I don't want my name linked to Haggerty's," he said.

"It might not be possible to avoid that," Tedley warned, although, like everyone else, he was nervous whenever he couldn't deliver what Hobart Cunningham demanded. "This fellow James is

a stickler for staying legal. But we might find someone to front for you."

"And who the devil is James?"

"Senator Steven James."

"Him?" Hobart hooted. "He won't be a senator much longer unless he goes back where he belongs. What's he doing here?"

"Speculating in the market, as far as I've been able to discover."

"And still hand in glove with Haggerty, I'm sure."

"The consensus is negative. They've fallen out. They're both investing in Tri-Panalco, but there the connection stops." Tedley cleared his throat. "He came on the same ship that brought Mrs. Paul and Miss Cunningham."

Hobart glanced at him sharply. "And? Come on, man, spit it out, I haven't got all day!"

"It appeared Miss Cunningham was much taken with him. They saw each other frequently before the family left for Cairo."

"Was there gossip?" Hobart's eyes narrowed.

"No, sir. People just wondered which of the two men Miss Cunningham would choose."

Hobart leaned back. He was wondering why Miranda had not written to him about this—or Paul either, for that matter. Then he shrugged and put the question aside. Obviously Miranda considered the viscount a better match and had turned Cynthia in his direction. Hobart could not object to that.

He turned back to business. "I'll decide who, if anyone, will front for me when I've seen all the details of the scheme."

"Of course, Mr. Cunningham. I've brought the particulars with me." Tedley patted his breast pocket. He was certain Haggerty and James would see right through anyone Hobart used as a front, but for the amount of capital Hobart could invest, Gus would look the other way—and persuade Steven James to do the same.

"Now tell me about the earl," Hobart ordered.

By the time they were nearing the Bristol, Hobart knew more

about the extent of the earl's misfortunes, including the size of his overdraft and the value of his lands and holdings, than he had been able to learn in New York.

"All they know is fox hunting and pig sticking," he said. "The market completely escapes them."

Tedley looked uncomfortable at this description of the class he had been brought up to revere.

"I'm told," Hobart went on, "that Lady Caroline is reluctant to have her son marry an American."

Tedley, looking even more uncomfortable, confirmed this. "She is an overfond mother," he explained. "I don't think any girl he chose would really please her completely."

Hobart brushed the countess aside, as he did all women, including his wife, when he had no physical use for them.

The one exception was Miranda, he thought, looking out of the carriage window. He was eager to see her again, to watch her walk, to hear her voice—even when she contradicted him or ignored his veiled attempts at seduction. Maybe that was the trouble. Maybe she didn't appreciate the extent of his passion for her.

He was welcomed by the hotel manager and ushered to the suite reserved for himself and his family.

Once Tedley and the staff had withdrawn, Hobart left the salon of the suite and walked to the bedroom Miranda and Paul would occupy. It seemed to him that the air was suffused with her already, with that total female quality in her that so enraptured him.

"What does my archeologist brother know about passion?" he muttered, scowling at the sight of the bed.

But she had helped to find the perfect bridegroom for Cynthia! He would be very generous with her to show his gratitude. Perhaps his approach to her had not been gallant enough. He resolved not to growl and grumble at her as he did at other women, and not to refer to his power over Paul's purse strings. But, as if mocking his good resolutions, his sexual fantasies of her had grown all the more ferocious since their last meeting.

He read over the Panama Canal notes Tedley had given him, then bathed, dressed, and went down to dinner. He detested dining alone, and as soon as he had finished he took a cab to an address recommended by a colleague and, choosing a buxom brunette, spent a few vigorous hours acting out his fantasies.

"Now, there's a proper savage," the buxom brunette said when she came slowly down the stairs some fifteen minutes after his departure.

"They're all savages," the madam replied, yawning. "What d'you think you're here for?"

"Not to get done like a bunged-up chimbley." The girl winced as she sat down on one of the overstuffed couches.

"Take him to court, then," the madam cackled. "File your petition."

"File it? It's so sore I can't 'ardly touch it wif a powder puff."

The women guffawed while Hobart, going back to the Bristol, reviewed the offer he would make to the earl the next day.

———— · ————

"Stay upstairs," the earl instructed his wife when the crested coach bringing Hobart down from London came rumbling into view at the bottom of the drive. "I'll call you when we've settled everything. If we cannot agree, there's no point in your meeting him at all."

"I have no wish to meet this American primitive."

"Goodness gracious," the earl growled. "The fellow doesn't wear buckskins and carry a bow and arrow! Now, go upstairs. Mr. Cunningham and I have important business to conduct."

"I hope you cannot reach an agreement," Lady Caroline said, and rustled away a few moments before the butler opened the heavy, carved oaken door of Inderby to that odious girl's odious father.

"Welcome, Mr. Cunningham!" the earl said. "I hope you had a pleasant journey."

"Very comfortable, I thank you." Hobart gave his overcoat and hat to the butler, revealing his bald head and elegantly clad body, then shook the earl's extended hand.

So this is a blueblood, Hobart thought, noting details of the earl's appearance and in particular his lordly manner. *I suppose he pisses wine instead of water!*

Sharp-looking devil—no wonder he's rich! the earl decided at the sight of this tall, wickedly handsome man whose baldness only made him more intriguing. It was clear that in the colonies, money didn't care where it went. The earl had no use for American democracy. All that tomfoolery about equality! You had only to look about you to see that men were not equal! In England the lower classes recognized their betters. Everyone knew his place and stayed in it. That was what made the Empire great!

He led his guest into the library, with its intimations of time and tradition, of centuries of Inderbys. If Hobart had one faint streak of envy in him, it was for a family tree as noble and solid as the earl's, for the pomp of his heritage borne out by the portraits of forebears that hung on every wall, by the suits of armor and the trophies the earl's ancestors had brought back from every corner of the British Empire, all of it a reminder that they were the lords of creation.

Hobart decided on the spot to build a mansion on upper Fifth Avenue worthy of the Cunninghams. He had always ridiculed as middle-class the notion of outdoing his peers in anything but money and power. Now that his former social position was about to be brilliantly restored, he would put society in the shade with bricks and mortar, stained glass and imported tapestries, a house like this one with young Lord and Lady Walford in residence at least several months of each year.

Hobart took a seat, accepted a glass of champagne, found it superb, and confronted the earl. "I understand your son wants to marry my daughter."

Inderby, startled by this abrupt plunge into such a delicate subject, merely nodded. Caroline was right. The fellow *was* a primitive.

"I take it he has your permission?" Hobart persisted with a wolfish grin.

Inderby was flustered. "Provided you and I reach an agreement on other matters, he has my blessing."

"My daughter's dowry is why I have traveled so far." And without further ado, Hobart named a vast figure.

The earl, even though the phlegmatic blood of Englishmen idled through his veins, almost gasped, but with great effort managed instead to say calmly, "That would be acceptable, depending upon how the funds will come to us." His solicitors had urged him repeatedly to ask that—"assuming Your Lordship prefers substance to colonial real estate."

Hobart took a slim notebook from his breast pocket and read off a list of securities, real estate holdings, utility monopolies, railroad rights of way, gold bullion, and cash in the new gold-backed certificates. "One tenth of the total will be entirely under Cynthia's control," he said, closing the notebook. "A woman with a nest egg makes a better wife."

"Of course, of course," the earl hastened to agree. It all seemed perfect—too perfect, he reminded himself. "We had hoped to meet Mrs. Cunningham," he said, suspicious of why Cynthia's mother had not accompanied her husband to London. Madness? Hereditary disease?

"My wife is recovering from surgery at present," Hobart said with convincing concern. "Women's problems. She grows stronger by the hour and she will attend Cynthia's wedding, as will my sons and brothers and their families."

"I devoutly hope so," the earl said.

Hobart paused. "Of course, you have the advantage of me."

The earl, thinking that, of course, an English aristocrat had the advantage over almost everyone else on earth, asked, "How so?"

"You have met my daughter. I have not had the honor of meeting your son."

The earl chuckled. "You'll like him. Everyone likes Alastair. He's a good chap. Goes on about politics and industry more than I like, of course. Has an itch to make his mark in the world."

"A laudable ambition," Hobart said, his interest in his prospective son-in-law quickening.

The earl frowned. "He has no need to make his mark. He's not a fishmonger, after all! He'll inherit the title, the land, and the estate. Property is what makes a gentleman, not plebeian ambition."

"Certainly," Hobart said, privately deciding to have a serious chat with Alastair. The earl himself had little talent for business: his present circumstances were proof enough of that. It was galling to turn a fortune over to a financial ignoramus, and if the son showed any aptitude for handling money, Hobart would encourage it.

Hobart's eye wandered to a trio of portraits hanging over the mantel of the huge fireplace. The earl might be muddle-headed about business, but he had a very clear image of his place in the world, something his deep roots gave him, and he had to be respected, even envied, for that. "Are those your sons?" Hobart asked.

The earl nodded proudly, although his face was sad. "The one on the left is Avery. The one on the right is Arthur."

Both were dark-haired and comely, like their father, but otherwise unremarkable. And since they were both dead, Hobart turned his attention to the center portrait of Alastair, Viscount Walford.

He gazed piercingly at the fair young man. He was handsome—almost beautiful. His face had an expression of aristocratic hauteur, of proud self-confidence. The shoulders were square, the bearing relaxed, the attitude that of perfect authority.

"Striking," Hobart said. *They should have called it "The World Is His Oyster,"* he thought. Physically, Walford was as breathtaking as Cynthia. They would probably produce astonishingly beautiful children. But Hobart so relished the idea of being grandfather to a future earl that he would have agreed to the match had Alastair resembled the hunchback of Notre Dame.

Cynthia would one day be Countess of Inderby and the reflected glow would make the Cunninghams stars of New York society. Even Charlotte's curse was powerless against a title. And Elsie *would* attend her daughter's wedding, regally dressed and sober, if she had to be chained to her bed until the great day arrived.

"They'll make a magnificent couple," Hobart went on, and the earl agreed, waxing poetic over Cynthia's beauty.

All that remained was to seal the agreement. Hobart decided not to hold it up until he met Alastair. The viscount had been thoroughly investigated and everything Hobart had learned assured him that Alastair was a well-set-up fellow who sowed his wild oats like any healthy man, even if in an eccentric fashion from time to time. Everyone knew the English had a bit of the faggot in them, with their clipped accents and their lah-dee-dah manners.

"It seems to me," Hobart said, "that there is little left to do but to congratulate each other."

Inderby, almost dizzy with relief at the enormous amount of money soon to flow into his empty coffers, agreed again.

The control of this relationship had clearly shifted to Hobart: even blue blood paled by comparison with so much money. But as the two men talked, a subtle kinship began to emerge. They had much in common, if not in background and specific interests, then in temperament and personality and in their opinions of men, women, and horses.

Both men were ruthless, although the earl had English charm to camouflage it. Both were obsessed, Hobart by money, the earl by rank. Hobart saw things in the realm of finance that other men did not see; he saw sonnets in a balance sheet.

Inderby was devoted to protecting his way of life and passing it on to his heirs; to that end he was faithful in his attendance at the House of Lords, Buckingham Palace, Ascot, and the hunt. He lived by the code of his kind, and that was all God and his sovereign required of him.

Through all of his financial troubles he had been certain that his Anglican God smiled upon the nobility and would send him a miracle to save the estate from ruin. And here was that miracle in the form of Hobart Cunningham, lofty, bald as a Christmas turkey, but an impressive man nonetheless and as right-minded as the earl himself with respect to basic beliefs. It would be difficult not to appreciate him for what he was.

Then it was time for a toast before luncheon and the earl sent for his wife.

Lady Caroline, entering the library with a chilly expression on that face so like her son's, expected to meet a mountebank, but she was totally unprepared for Hobart Cunningham. His presence was overwhelmingly male, but there was something sinister in his temperament that rolled across the distance between them and washed over her with the chill of sorcery. Most men did not recognize the devil in Hobart, but women did.

"My dear," her husband said, "may I present Mr. Hobart Cunningham. Mr. Cunningham, Lady Caroline, my wife."

The touch of his palm against hers and then of his lips on the back of her hand sent a cold flash through her. She was overcome by the power the man exuded.

All of the men she knew had power, even if it was only the power of their gender; but gentlemen held it in check to avoid frightening the fair sex. This man did not bother to hide it. She felt a combination of dread and breathless expectation such as she had never before experienced.

She had no other way to give it form than by the metaphor of helpless surrender, and there was only one kind of surrender with which she was familiar.

"You have a beautiful, charming daughter," she said formally, having to say something.

"And you a handsome and charming son. The earl and I have agreed they'll make a splendid pair."

"I am delighted to hear the news," she said as if just learning the engagement was official, although she had known it as soon as her husband sent for her. She still found the idea of Alastair's marriage intolerable, but this man was as intriguing as the Black Knight of legend. She felt like a maiden besieged in a tower, like one of the Sabine women just before the rape. When Hobart Cunningham looked at her, she felt as naked as Lady Godiva.

Hobart's eyes probed hers. She colored and lowered her lashes and then he knew the reason for her confusion, even if neither of them recognized how close fascination is to repugnance, as love is to hate or sacrifice is to egotism.

Well, he thought, *it never hurts to be on cordial terms with one's in-laws.*

She was not the type who usually appealed to him: She was small and fair and tight, even demure. But Hobart had never bedded a countess, and it aroused his curiosity. She would be naive about such matters, and he relished the idea of shocking her, but her seduction could wait until the knot between their children had been securely tied.

He had no doubt whatever that she would succumb.

Over luncheon the earl talked about their children's travels in Egypt. His wife discussed arrangements for the engagement announcement and the party to be held there, at Inderby. Hobart listened and approved, delighting in his surroundings and in the obvious blend of attraction and aversion he aroused in the countess.

". . . to know your brother and his wife," the earl was saying. "A charming couple."

"Delightful," the countess confirmed with a curl of her lip that did not escape Hobart. The countess was not fond of Miranda. "I cannot imagine her attending board meetings in her husband's place," she went on, "but I was assured she does."

"Only as a favor to him," Hobart said. "He's a devoted scholar and she does what she can to make his research possible."

"I've promised to introduce him to the head of the Archeological Society," the earl said.

"He'll be much obliged to you."

"I'm afraid I don't know any ladies who sit on boards of directors," Lady Caroline pressed on. "But London is full of crusading women who might interest Mrs. Paul Cunningham."

Hobart savored his wine. "Cunningham women do not crusade."

"I so admire the feminists' courage," the countess persisted with a little sigh. "I just don't understand what it is they want."

"The vote!" the earl barked. "What will they do with the vote when they don't know one end of an issue from the other? The next thing you know, they'll be wanting to choose their own husbands."

Hobart laughed. "My daughter was not brought up on such nonsense."

"Hear, hear!" the earl said, raising his refilled glass again. "Women need managing. That's what men are for."

Hobart exchanged a secret smile with Lady Caroline, who drew her breath in sharply, fluttered her fan, and smiled in shameful anticipation of being managed.

You can't hold a candle to Miranda, Hobart wanted to tell her. *She's ten times the woman you are.*

And in just a few days he would see her!

Thirty-three

Hobart was waiting when the travelers entered the lobby of the Bristol. Cynthia flew into his arms and hugged him, kissing his cheek. He returned her embraces. It was a rare display of affection between them, but she *was* his only daughter and she *had* done her duty, so he felt well disposed toward her.

"How's my girl?" he asked her. "Lovelier than ever, I see."

Smiling and blushing, she released him and he turned to the others. "Paul," he said, clapping his brother on the shoulder and vigorously shaking his hand. "You're looking very well. Egypt agrees with you far more than Wall Street ever did."

It was Hobart's invariable double-edged greeting when Paul returned from a dig. Paul smiled and nodded. That was his greeting, although this time Hobart seemed genuinely pleased with the lot of them.

"Miranda" was all Hobart said to her. His eyes quickly catalogued her black wool cape, lined and bordered with black fox, and the large black hat that set off her velvety skin. She was lush and ripe, even more so, it seemed to him, than on the day she had sailed from New York. Venus in furs.

He leaned forward to kiss her cheek and caught the light perfume that so excited him. For one intoxicated moment he was tempted to embrace her passionately in front of all of them. . . .

"And this," Cynthia said, jarring him back to reality, "is Lord Walford."

Hobart made a swift inventory of Walford's supremely attractive person. "I saw your portrait when I visited your father," Hobart said. "It doesn't do you justice."

Indeed, it did not. Walford's smooth complexion had been kissed by the sun god of Egypt, and his clear blue eyes were even more startling against the bronzed skin and the golden hair streaked with platinum. His shoulders were broader than they had been when he sat for the portrait, and although he was an inch shorter than Hobart and Paul, he was a fine figure of a man. His manner reflected aristocratic assurance when he shook hands with Hobart. He had been born with it.

"I was much younger then," he said. "I'm honored to meet you, Mr. Cunningham."

He could charm the britches off Queen Victoria, Hobart thought. But then, so could Cynthia.

Hobart sent the ladies upstairs to rest, assigning Paul to accompany them, and invited the viscount to have a sherry in the bar. It was not the way one met with a prospective son-in-law, but neither man cared and both were in a hurry.

——— . ———

"Your father and I have reached an agreement," Hobart told Walford as soon as they were seated and the sherry poured. "I propose a toast to your engagement, of which I heartily approve."

Walford smiled his most engaging smile. "Thank you, sir. I was very anxious about that."

Hobart nodded. "So was I. In a way, I still am."

Walford waited, saying nothing.

Hobart liked a man who knew when to keep his mouth shut. "If you will pardon my candor," he said presently, "it upsets me to throw good money after bad. Your father seems to have done nothing about protecting his assets and now finds himself with virtually none."

Walford chewed his lip. "It's true that the pater hasn't got much of a head for business," he said, reflecting that Hobart would have thrown money down a sewer to get his daughter a title. Walford was unconcerned about the marriage—that was a certainty now—but he wondered what Hobart was after, although he knew better than to ask.

"Do *you* have a head for business?" Hobart asked slyly.

Ah, thought Walford exultantly, *so that's what he wants.* It was what Alastair wanted too.

"Better than his," he said without recourse to false modesty, "although I'm seldom given the chance to show it."

"I could give you the chance," Hobart said. "I could make it a condition of the dowry that its funds are to be managed by you." Both men knew that as long as the money was forthcoming, it made little matter to the earl who managed it. Hobart offered Alastair a cigar.

Like Indians smoking before the massacre, Alastair thought, and refused it: Cynthia disliked the odor of cigars and he was determined to please her up to the moment they were married, at which point it would be her duty to please *him.*

"And who is to manage me?" Alastair asked, smiling again.

Hobart grinned.

Walford considered that for a moment. *My God, the things one does for England,* he thought. "For how long?" he inquired.

Hobart shrugged. "For as long as you feel the need of assistance from me. A clever man knows when to seek advice, and you are a very clever man."

Alastair nodded briefly, acknowledging the compliment and accepting the terms. He had always resented his father's uninspired control of the estate and everything on it; it would be exhilarating to have the shoe on the other foot.

"I wouldn't want to embarrass the pater," he said, glancing at Hobart.

The devil you wouldn't, Hobart thought. *You'd pitch him into the Thames if he stood in your way.* He was even better pleased with his future son-in-law than he had been with Alastair's father. Inside this golden boy was a crafty young man who, like Inderby, would do anything to get what he wanted; Alastair surpassed his sire in that he wanted a future as much as a past.

"Your father will be glad to be relieved of the burden," Hobart assured him, "and we'll take care not to embarrass him."

"Then I would like very much to learn from you."

They sipped their sherry and talked on about finance for a while, particularly about Tri-Panalco. Alastair asked intelligent questions, which gratified Hobart enormously, but the viscount had no reaction when Hobart mentioned the participation of Senator James.

That kindled Hobart's curiosity. The two had met aboard ship, so why had the viscount not mentioned it? Had James been a possible roadblock to this marvelous match, as Tedley had inferred? Was he still? Hobart would have to lay down the law to his headstrong daughter. Young girls were skittish: seeing the senator again might even make Cynthia think she could change her mind, as she had been known to do. Hobart filed the senator away for a more thorough investigation.

When Hobart and Alastair left the bar an hour later, Cynthia had not been mentioned. Walford had not declared his love for her and Hobart had not noticed that omission. Cynthia was irrelevant except as the instrument of their merger.

They made arrangements to dine that evening, and then Walford went back to Inderby House in St. John's Wood, the family's London mansion. Hobart watched the carriage pull away from the Bristol and, with a thrill of anticipation, went upstairs to see Miranda.

———— · ————

He found the family having coffee in the salon of their suite. He stood in the doorway, smiling benevolently upon Miranda.

"You look like the cat who ate the canary," Paul said when he noticed his brother in the doorway. Paul was not blind to Hobart's libidinous admiration for Miranda, but his response had always been to ignore it; now he was enraged even though he knew Miranda disliked Hobart intensely. If she was capable of adultery with one man . . .

Cynthia had put down her cup and was waiting for her father to render his verdict. Miranda was intent upon adding another drop of cream to her coffee.

"I like this fellow you're going to marry," Hobart said. "He's no fool."

Cynthia's joy was clear, but restrained. "I'm glad that's settled!"

"No fool and a Greek god too," Miranda said, putting down her cup and saucer as she intercepted a warning glance from Paul. "Coffee, Hobart?" Without waiting for an answer, she filled a cup from the graceful silver pot and set it down for him on the serving table beside her.

"A girl can as soon marry a handsome man as a homely one," Hobart said.

"Or a rich man as a poor one," Miranda returned.

"Aunt Miranda does not approve," Cynthia said.

"Her approval is not required, although it would be welcome," Hobart said, going to get his coffee. "And I was just about to congratulate you on a job well done." He looked down at Miranda, admiring her posture, her grace. Next to Miranda, Lady Caroline had no piquance at all, just a watery appeal, rather like English coffee.

Even Cynthia, he thought, turning again to his daughter, *has more spice than sugar in her.*

"I had nothing to do with it," Miranda said.

"Have it your own way," Hobart said, still standing near her while he sugared his coffee. "But you did sail off with her in September and by December she's engaged to marry into the English nobility. I am obliged to you." He bowed, reached for her hand, and held it to his lips. He felt her pulling away from him.

"But why don't you approve?" he asked her, dropping her hand.

Cynthia answered for her. "She says he's marrying me for my money."

"Any reasonable man considers money when he marries," Paul put in.

"You didn't," Miranda said, smiling at her husband. "I was one of the poorer Prices."

Paul nodded, enchanted by her smile. He had not seen her smile in quite that way for months. It was one of the things that had so charmed him over the years of their marriage, that sweet, warm, confiding curve of her mouth. He remembered it welcoming him home; he remembered it across the candlelit dinner table from him; he remembered it over their sons' heads when the boys were small.

He was startled to realize that despite her treachery and the turbulently carnal relationship between them that had sprung from it, he still loved her as tenderly and protectively as on the day he had proposed. It shook him, this all-encompassing love he had for her. It could not be written off as mere eroticism. Love was not that simple. It was made of so many, many things.

He could not stomach his brother's fawning on Miranda or Hobart's pretended "gratitude" toward himself and her. He preferred Hobart cold and heartless, true to his real nature.

"I think I'll stretch my legs," Paul said, rising suddenly and muttering, "I need a walk after all that traveling." He retrieved his overcoat, hat, and gloves as he went through the foyer and was gone before anyone had a chance to comment.

Cynthia got up too. "I'm going to have a bath and a rest." She went to her father and stood on tiptoe to kiss his cheek. "I'm so glad you're pleased with me, Papa," she said, and glided away to her bedroom.

When Hobart sat down, there was only the serving table between him and Miranda. He stirred up the sugar in his cup between sips. "What's all this nonsense about not approving of Walford?" he asked pleasantly. "He's healthy and clever, apart from his extraordinary looks. She could do a lot worse." He paused. "Is there anyone else she fancies?"

Miranda made an impatient gesture. "She doesn't love him, but that isn't why I'm against the marriage. The point is that he doesn't love her."

Hobart threw back his head and laughed. "Miranda, you sound like a schoolgirl. He doesn't have to love her! He has to treat her with respect in public and give her the protection of his name and title—along with a few sons." He looked at her obliquely with his cold, granite-colored eyes and shook his head. "Love!" he scoffed.

"What about the way he treats her in private?"

A lubricious grin broke across Hobart's face. "For example?"

Miranda was reluctant to speak with him of sex, but she had to protect Cynthia. "This extraordinarily handsome man carries on with other men," she almost whispered.

He stared at her as if she were mad. "That's neither here nor there," he said. "The misadventures of youth. I knew all about it. But it's nothing that need concern us now."

"That's what Paul said."

"Paul says intelligent things upon occasion."

She rose suddenly, her fists clenched, her voice low. "It could be terrible for her, don't you see that? She's so innocent! Or he may never consummate the marriage . . . normally. How would she know?"

He eyed her suspiciously. "He'll consummate the marriage, all right. He needs heirs like anyone else. What makes you so sure the fellow's a real queer? Did you try to seduce him and fail?"

She looked at him with icy contempt.

He waved a placating hand. "A joke. In poor taste, I'll admit. But how do you know?"

"It was obvious to me from the way he and a younger boy behaved on the ship—and equally obvious to a lady whose experience and worldliness I trust."

"What would either of you know about such matters?" Hobart inquired. "What would any decent woman know?"

Miranda ignored the question. "Maybe it wasn't even his fault when he was little—he's so beautiful! But he's not a defenseless child any longer. Now it's something he chooses to do."

He put down the cup and saucer and leaned back in his chair, his large, blunt-fingered hands resting on his thighs. "And you consider it your duty to save Cynthia from this fate worse than death?"

"I consider it *your* duty," she said.

He rubbed his whiskers. "In ancient Greece it was considered desirable for friendship between men to include a physical connection. And both were usually married with families."

"This is not ancient Greece. What would New York society say if your son-in-law's perversity became known? And don't tell me you don't care. You care desperately. It's why you're selling Cynthia: for a title."

"Be quiet!" he snapped. "I forbid you to judge my motives. And I forbid you ever to speak of this again. With anyone. Do I make myself clear?"

When she did not reply, he shook his head. "There," he said. "You've made me scold you again. And I'd vowed not to. Miranda, look at me."

After a long while she did.

"I've had the fellow investigated thoroughly. There were a few incidents, but every young man has to let the badger loose from time to time."

"With badgers of the same sex?"

He was annoyed. "In the main, this one consorts with women."

"In the main!" she said derisively. "And you think Cynthia would be untroubled if she found out about the exceptions? You amaze me. I didn't think you could ever amaze me again."

He leaned forward eagerly. "When did I amaze you before? Tell me."

She shook her head.

"You know what I feel for you, that's it, isn't it?" he said, his sharp-featured face hovering as close to hers as he could get. "What I've always felt since the moment I met you. I wanted you then. I still do."

"I'm your brother's wife!"

"He need never know."

Her dark eyes narrowed and she got to her feet as if to flee although he had not moved. "You *are* despicable."

"For God's sake, woman. Look at yourself! You're a Venus and you're married to a man who's probably never even seen you naked. You pretend you're a hothouse flower, but *I* know"—he pounded his chest—"that inside you're a volcano."

Now he did take a step toward her. "Miranda," he purred. "I can make you weep with pleasure. I can do things to you that you cannot imagine. Let me."

She moved away from him.

"Do you understand what I just said to you? Or must I sugar-coat desire and say that I love you?"

She shuddered and, calling out for her maid, she swept past him and out of the salon.

He watched her go. She had not rejected his passion, only his offer to call it love. He would try again.

She was trembling when she reached her bedroom. If Rooney had not been there, she would have burst into tears to release the tension within her. Instead, she began to pace back and forth in the room, wringing her hands.

"Mrs. Paul?" Rooney begged. "Are you ailin'? Shall I send for a doctor?"

"No," Miranda whispered. "I'm just on edge."

Rooney went to the dressing table and poured a glass of water from the crystal decanter. She added several drops from a small bottle and a lump of sugar, stirred the mixture, and took the glass to Miranda.

"Here," she said firmly. "A little laudanum is what you need." It was a concoction of opium and alcohol, commonly prescribed for pain and, in the case of women, for the many disorders blamed on nerves or female hysteria.

"I can't sleep now!" Miranda protested. "I have to go to dinner."

"You can't go to dinner twitchin' the way you are! I only used a drop or two, just to soothe your nerves. Please, Mrs. Paul, dear. You look so pale."

Miranda took the glass and drained it, then allowed Rooney to get her out of her travel suit, loosen her corset, and settle her on the chaise under a soft quilt. "I'm right here if you should be wantin' anythin', ma'am," Rooney said. "Now close your eyes and let the medicine work."

Miranda closed her eyes. In a little while the narcotic blunted the jagged edges, but Hobart's face still floated before her. She grimaced and a faint taste of bile rose to her throat.

But what right had she to moral outrage? He had only invited her to do out of lechery what she had already done out of love. But no matter what the motive, the act was the same and the betrayal. That was her dilemma: her guilt.

It was always there. Every morning it awakened her like an in-

fant demanding to be fed. All day long she carried it with her, between her breasts or on her back or in the hollow caverns inside her. And at night she took it to bed with her, half hoping and half fearing that Paul would come to her and blot it out with *his* hunger and *his* need and *his* suffering. She knew he felt demeaned because he *could* not and *would* not resist her. That was his dilemma.

But they belonged together, of that she was certain now. She could as little bring herself to abandon Paul as he to abandon her. She did love him—that had never changed, although the expression of it had—but she prayed fervently she would not ever see Steven again. She would have to send him away, but how could she when the mere fact that he was somewhere in London, only a few miles away, kept her in a permanent state of feverish anticipation? Food nauseated her. She wanted only to sleep.

But could she avoid Steven? He and Hobart were involved in the same venture together. They would probably run into each other in the course of Cynthia's engagement celebrations.

Of all the terrible tricks destiny had played on her life and Steven's, surely a business connection between him and the Cunninghams was the most unexpected and the most fiendish!

Miranda sat patiently that evening while Rooney dressed her hair. The maid's chatter was soothing since it required no thought, and the feel of Rooney's hands brushing and pinning her hair helped to relax her.

"I think I like you best in black," Rooney said when she had finished. She shook out the wide lace-trimmed bertha of Miranda's dinner dress. It framed her shoulders with the same tiny pleats of the dress bodice, as delicately tucked as a baby's christening gown. "But then, you can wear any color the good Lord made."

"Except puce," Miranda said.

Rooney smiled, pleased to see her mistress in better spirits. "There isn't a woman alive who can wear puce."

There was a knock on the door, and Cynthia's voice asked permission to enter. Miranda nodded and Rooney went to let her in. She floated over to Miranda in a gown of palest lilac, looking like a vision.

"Look!" she said. "An engagement gift from Papa." She ran her fingertips over a necklace of amethysts and diamonds and showed the matching bracelet and earbobs. "Aren't they splendid?"

"Lovely," Miranda said. "They make your eyes look like Parma violets." Cynthia was more spectacular than ever. It pained Miranda that her happiness would be short-lived. No girl, especially not this one, should have to face the shock that awaited her. And no girl should consider marriage in total ignorance of what it normally entailed. There, at least, Miranda could help.

"Thank you, Rooney," Miranda said to her maid. "You may go."

Rooney dropped a curtsy and left, closing the door behind her.

"Cynthia, I want to talk to you."

Cynthia scowled. "Are you going to tell me horror stories again?"

"I only want to tell you something about the physical side of marriage, so you'll know what you're getting into and whether or not you can consider making love with Walford."

"Yes, I can."

Miranda was surprised, then realized what Cynthia understood making love to be.

"There's more to it than a kiss," she said.

"Well!" Cynthia said with interest, seating herself in a chair near Miranda's. "Do go on."

"Do you have any idea at all about male anatomy?"

Cynthia hesitated. "I know more or less what's under those fig leaves at the museum. I grew up in a houseful of brothers, don't forget, but I saw them in the buff only as infants. One assumes *that* grows as the boy grows. But what has that"—Cynthia searched for a word—"that apparatus to do with marriage?"

Miranda told her.

"It gets big?" Cynthia said in wonderment. "And hard?"

"Hard enough to penetrate you."

"Where?"

"Down below," Miranda said. "Between your legs."

"Does it hurt?"

"It may hurt the first time, and you'll probably bleed a little. After that, no, it doesn't hurt."

"But what a revolting idea."

"I suppose it can be with the wrong man."

"And how, pray, does one find out who the *right* man is before it's too late?"

"A man who loves you enough to please you in every way will try to please you in that one."

Memories of forbidden nocturnal explorations when she was a girl flooded back, and Cynthia turned deep red, recalling the sensation her busy fingers had produced. Suddenly she glared at her aunt.

"Is that what you did with *him?* Let him put himself inside you?"

"That's what sex is. It's how love and children are made."

"Do you have a baby every time you do it?"

"No. The possibility is there, though, unless you're already pregnant."

"Do you mean a husband would want to do that when his wife had a great belly?"

"Probably not toward the end, out of concern for the child. But husbands want sex when you least expect it."

"And wives must oblige?"

"It's part of marriage—it can be a very pleasant part. And if a man loves you, he can usually tell when you'd rather not."

Cynthia sat bolt upright in the satin-covered chair and seemed to be thinking furiously for a while before she said, "And you don't think Walford loves me enough to know or care what I want. That's it, isn't it?"

"That's part of it."

"I could just tell him."

"But sexual relations aren't the only relations to consider. Married people don't make love all day. They have to like each other when they walk or dance or sit by the fire or talk about their dreams and their children."

"Walford and I can talk for hours without a stop."

Miranda nodded. "Yes, I know, he's a clever, interesting man."

"I think I'd as leave talk with him as have him do *that* to me."

"You can't separate sex and marriage. They're both part of the package. It's a better package if love is part of it too."

"Then *why* are you so set against *Walford*? He loves me, I know he does."

I can't tell her, Miranda agonized. *Not tonight. She's had enough for one day.*

She glanced at the carriage clock on her dressing table. "We're late. We'll talk again soon."

Cynthia nodded, relieved although still curious. Then she said, "Have you heard from him yet?"

Miranda shook her head. "And I hope I won't."

"I don't believe that."

"Oh, I want to see him, I don't deny it. But I hope I won't."

"Why not?"

"Because of Paul and what it's done to him."

Cynthia's eyes widened. "You mean Uncle Paul knows?"

Miranda nodded. "We've never discussed it, but he knows."

"Poor Uncle Paul," Cynthia said, walking toward the door. "Poor Aunt Miranda."

Cynthia stopped and whirled around. "I don't have a grain of sympathy for you! Paul was betrayed, not you!"

Miranda sighed.

"Besides, you can't love two men at the same time!" Cynthia protested.

"But I did. I do. And when you're married to a man like Paul,

adultery is the most shameful, saddest, loneliest thing in the world. The only good time is when you're with your lover. The rest is hell." Miranda took Cynthia's arm and gently steered her toward the door.

"I don't understand," Cynthia said, suddenly more confused than judgmental.

"I'll try to explain it so you'll never have to experience it."

Aunt and niece went down to the lobby together.

$\mathscr{T}$hirty-four

$\mathscr{L}$ady Burdon's smaller dining room was filled with rows of gilt chairs, each of them occupied by a well-dressed woman. The women varied in age from thirty to seventy or more, but all of them were married or widowed and most of them would have had a difficult time explaining the real reason for their presence there to their disapproving families. This kind of thing was not the province of virtuous women.

They had come to listen to the notorious Miss McAllister read a report on her recent meetings with the Excelsior Shipping Lines, on whose board of governors several of their male relations sat. The men had been outraged by Miss McAllister and her demands, although they had conceded that there was nothing for Excelsior to do but to comply.

"You'd think she was advocating murder!" the younger ladies said among themselves. "How can they be so critical of a valid cause?"

"Because its champion is a woman," the older women explained.

They all felt perfectly safe in coming to Lady Burdon's for "tea."

Lady Burdon might be given to outlandish opinions from time to time, but she was a social arbiter, distantly related to the royals, and eminently respectable.

The women's faces were wreathed in smiles and they applauded the news Miss McAllister brought them. All of their demands had been met and working women would be protected on the high seas by officers of the Excelsior Lines, who would answer for any infringements of propriety. No female staff members could be discharged without a hearing before her colleagues of both sexes.

"But this is one small battle," Kitt warned them when the applause died away. "The war goes on. We must see that the sudden gallantry of these former sea wolves"—her tone provoked laughter—"is so loudly praised by the press that the other lines will be forced to follow suit."

She went on speaking, but the Count d'Yveine already knew what she planned to say, having listened to her the evening before in Lady Burdon's morning room.

"She doesn't look well," he whispered now to Lady Burdon from where they sat at the back of the room. He looked worried. "She looks strained."

"How would you look if you had just abandoned a beautiful dream?"

"Is that what she told you before she left last night?"

Lady Burdon shook her head. "Not in so many words, but it's in her face. She has what someone called a 'speaking countenance.' And she has not seen *him* since their evening at the opera."

"Not like her to quit a battle, is it?"

"*Cher ami,* there are some battles in life that one should quit as quickly as possible."

"*Ma pauvre petite,*" the count murmured, gazing anxiously at Kitt. "For her happiness I would forgo my own."

"*Ça,*" said Lady Burdon, "*c'est l'amour.*"

"*Oui,*" the count agreed, his large brown eyes lingering on Kitt as she ended the meeting with a request to see the committee briefly after tea. Two footmen pulled back the sliding doors to the drawing room and fifty women began to drift off in that direction.

"You must propose to her as soon as possible," Lady Burdon said under cover of the general movement in the room.

"Surely not! She needs time to get over him."

"If she gets over him, she won't have need of you! She is vulnerable now. She needs devotion and admiration and support. Given too long on her own, the wound will heal, a scar will form, and she'll be a confirmed spinster—and you know how stubborn she can be."

He offered his arm. "She reminds me of you."

"Nonsense," she said. "I am the most docile and biddable of creatures. I always listen if people have something worthwhile to say."

"Alton told me something frightening just before the meeting began: that Louisa talks of returning to Connecticut."

Lady Burdon turned to him, consternation on her face. "She must not be allowed to throw away her life in that poky little backwater! All the more reason for you to declare yourself at once. Promise me you will!"

He hesitated. "I am not a bold young lover, Patricia," he said wistfully. "I never was."

"You are young in your heart and I remember you as a bold lover. But in this life you must go after what you want, whether it's a woman or beer and skittles."

He was about to ask her what skittles were, when a group of ladies interrupted them. Left to himself, the count looked around the vast room until he found Kitt.

She saw him approach and was glad of it. Apart from her father, she had never known a man as kind as the count. But she wondered what her mother had felt when she eloped with Sam McAllister.

Her mother, after all, had defied the Kittredge clan and been disowned by them. She had surely been motivated by more than a need to bask in the warmth of one man's esteem after being rejected by another. Surely Kitt's exquisite mother had never been rejected by anyone.

Then, too, esteem was a far cry from what Kitt felt for Steven, what she wanted him to feel for her. But esteem was more dignified than languishing for a man who loved someone else. Esteem was infinitely less perilous than love.

On the other hand, if she would never know the heights of the grand passion with anyone else, wasn't it better to live alone?

"An encouraging meeting, as always," Jean-Baptiste Rouel said as he reached her.

She could not resist asking, "What would you say if I held such a meeting in France?"

He smiled. "There would be no audience. Frenchwomen have different ways of getting what they want."

"From shipping lines? How would a Frenchwoman go about that?"

He chose from a footman's tray of tea sandwiches, but she refused. It worried him. She was becoming far too thin.

He said, "She would prevail upon her husband to prevail upon the shipping line directors."

"How would she prevail upon her husband?"

"With honeyed words and admiration. With his favorite dinner." He paused. "As Delilah prevailed upon Samson until she cut off his hair," he added.

"But that is taking the long way round! It's like needing someone to intercede between you and God." Theology was a favorite subject of discussion between the French Catholic aristocrat and the Protestant daughter of a Yankee mill owner. Kitt shook her head impatiently. "Why can't people simply say what they mean? Ask for what they want?"

"For fear of rejection," he said simply.

"Better to tell the truth and shame the devil," she replied.

They both accepted tea from another footman.

"I take your point," he said, "but board directors are not God."

"They can be to the Altons of this world."

"Touché," he said, smiling at her affectionately.

"Now that I've made my point, I suppose I must apologize for being so argumentative," she said, touched, as always, by his indulgence. "And unmaidenly," she added archly. "Please forgive me."

He tilted his head, studying her. "You are not unmaidenly, *chère demoiselle.* You are quite perfect just as you are. You are Louisa."

She would have been a fool not to hear what was in his voice, not to see what was in his eyes. It was wondrous to be loved. It would have been infinitely delightful to rest her head on his shoulder, to feel his arms around her and know that he would be there always to love her and care for her.

Lady Burdon swept up to them. "Kitt, there is a lady here whom you should meet." She indicated an imposing dowager on the other side of the room. "You already know Lady Harper, who will introduce you."

Kitt thanked her, excused herself to the count, and went off.

"What were you talking about?" Lady Burdon demanded.

"It seemed to be religion but it was actually about love and sex and truth."

"Did you ask her to marry you?"

"Of course not!" The count was indignant. "A man does not propose marriage in a crowd."

"Better here than never! Suppose she packs up and leaves?"

"She doesn't seem in great haste to leave England. Perhaps Alton is mistaken."

"Jean-Baptiste, you have no imagination! Didn't you hide your misery and threaten to return to France when she was seeing the senator?" She did not wait for his reply. "Kitt has no wish to see the happy couple together—nor to celebrate Miss Cynthia's engage-

ment. But she might stay on if she could announce an engagement of her own."

"She isn't that petty!" he argued. "She's far too intelligent to react like a schoolgirl to someone else's happiness."

"At moments of high emotion, one's generosity of spirit deserts one." Lady Burdon lowered her voice. "I've just heard that Lord Harry has involved himself in business with Cynthia's father and Senator James. That puts the senator and the Cunninghams rather too close for comfort."

"Do you think the lovers will dare to meet?"

"They are bound to be invited to the same parties more than once."

"Will you invite them both?"

"Of course."

He was dismayed. "Will you warn Kitt she'll be dining with both of them?"

"Naturally. If she is engaged herself, perhaps she will come. And if she isn't, she may be gone to the colonies before I need to warn her! You must *do* something."

The count nodded his compliance.

"As soon as possible," she insisted. She watched him stride purposefully in Kitt's direction and crossed her fingers behind her back. She had suffered great losses in life: three husbands, one of whom she had loved with all her considerable heart, a son dead of pneumonia at the age of four, and several lovers dear enough to make her reminisce on winter evenings before the fire. Her two remaining sons were properly devoted, but they were, quite correctly, involved with their own families. Besides, they were entirely too conventional for her.

She had never had a daughter. She was determined not to lose Kitt, who was all she had hoped her daughter might be.

Then she went to rejoin Lady Blenkinsop and find out more about this new Anglo-American company.

The tension in Blenkinsop's office the next morning was thick. Hobart had declared that the amount of money the earl was about to invest should make him the majority shareholder in Tri-Panalco. Steven had just rejected the offer.

"There is no point in our setting up an offshore company to avoid the Sherman Act unless it remains under American control," he said.

"Isn't our present majority shareholder American?" Hobart asked, "and therefore subject to the Sherman Act?" He glanced at Steele, who had been silent.

"No. Mr. Haggerty has withdrawn as president of the parent company," Steven said.

"In whose favor?"

"In mine," Steven said, "since I plan to make England my permanent home and will not be subject to the antitrust laws."

"Did you plan to tell us about this new development?" Blenkinsop inquired, his head tilted as he studied Steven.

"I just have. It was only decided this morning." Steven turned back to Hobart, to whom he had taken an instant, virulent and, it was clear, entirely reciprocal dislike. Paul Cunningham, to Steven's relief, was not present, but he could not help wondering why Hobart had kept Paul out of this meeting and brought the viscount but not the earl: both father and son were ready to make huge investments in the company. Steven had no doubt that it was with Hobart's money.

"Furthermore," Steven went on, not in the least perturbed by Hobart's hostility, "the bylaws of the parent company clearly state that there shall be no majority shareholders in its offshoots."

Alastair spoke for the first time. "How can there be such an investment as we propose without the transfer of shares?"

"You would be issued nonvoting shares," Steven said.

Alastair nodded. The senator was too clever by half.

"As long," Hobart was saying, "as Lord Walford has access to the parent company's books."

"Of course," Steven said to Walford, deliberately ignoring the implied insult.

So, Steven thought. *He's protecting himself while monitoring his daughter's dowry—which is exactly what Haggerty wanted to do with me.* Steven looked at Walford, whose expression said clearly that he had nothing to do with Hobart's affront.

The viscount was very much impressed by the American. He had been impressed by him aboard the *Sylvania,* but mainly as a rival for Cynthia's fortune, until he realized that the senator was not interested in marriage.

"Then we are agreed," Steven said, in a tone that would tolerate no further discussion.

And there it was: Hobart must either yield or be locked out of a potentially enormous profit. After a tense moment, Hobart nodded. The gains would outweigh even this outrageous agreement. Walford breathed a sigh of relief and glanced at Steven with a little nod of admiration.

The American seemed even more attractive now, Alastair reflected, not only because of his financial and legal expertise but also because of his rugged good looks and his muscular body. Here was one Yankee Alastair would not patronize. Nor would he ever refer to him again as "Dan'l Boone." He was a man whose regard Alastair wanted and that was a novel experience. It was usually the other way round.

He was pleased that Steven was going to reside in London and looked forward to a closer association with him growing out of their business connection. Alastair liked being around him. He could quite understand Cynthia's earlier crush on him and Miranda's affair with him.

"Then I think that concludes this discussion," Blenkinsop said. "May I offer you gentlemen a drink?"

Steven and Steele accepted. Hobart and the viscount refused, saying they were expected to take the ladies to lunch. They took leave of the others and went out to find a cab.

————— · —————

"Stubborn bastard, our senator," Hobart said as soon as they were in the street.

Alastair shrugged. "If he can use the law rather than be abused by it, where's the harm?"

A hansom picked them up and was directed to the Ritz. The two got in.

"I'd have thought you'd dislike an upstart American," Hobart said. "Especially one who was a rival."

Alastair glanced at him. "For what?"

"For Cynthia's affections, my boy! I understand they saw a lot of each other aboard ship and were often together here in London. Before your engagement, of course."

Alastair, refusing the cigar Hobart offered, lit a cigarette. "One can't avoid other passengers on a ship. She's engaged to me now, so it makes no odds how often she saw him before that."

"Whatever happened to jealousy?" Hobart asked with more sarcasm than curiosity. "What happened to knights and their ladies fair? To duels at sunrise?"

"Went out with Napoleon," Alastair said. "All that stabbing and shooting made a mess about the place."

"So you're not concerned with the senator's attentions to Cynthia? Or hers to him?"

I'll be damned, thought Alastair. *The old devil knows about his daughter's crush on the senator but not about Miranda's affair with the man!*

"Not anymore," he said. "A girl's entitled to a choice, especially when she's a girl like Cynthia. And now she's made it."

Still, the idea that Cynthia might have imagined herself in love with Steven James—or why would it concern her father?—had begun to rankle. It had been a small impediment at the start, easily overshadowed by titles and charm. But was the impediment completely gone?

It struck Alastair that for the first time in his life he might be second choice. The notion was like a barb in his flesh. He had to know what Cynthia felt for the tall, dark American.

There was only one sure way to find out. His plans to seduce, or, at the very least, to compromise Cynthia had come to nothing: Miranda had not allowed the girl out of her sight in Paris. But their betrothal was official now, part of the dowry had been turned over, and that made them as good as married in the eyes of the world. Alastair had great faith in his powers of seduction, particularly of virgin debutantes.

At that moment it became more than a whim to get Cynthia into bed. It was essential to his ego. He must not, at all costs, get her pregnant before the required two years of a society engagement had elapsed, but there were many ways to satisfy himself. He almost smiled. She wouldn't know the difference.

"From what you've heard, what do you think of this Haggerty?" Hobart was asking.

"A bog trotter but a crafty one," Alastair said. "I gather the idea for this pyramid was his. I'd rather have him with me than against me."

"And the handsome senator?" Hobart's eyes narrowed as he scrutinized his companion closely.

"Honest as the day is long," the viscount said easily, "which could be his saving grace or his downfall."

"And Steele?"

"Someone's errand boy. I haven't figured out whose."

"Mine," Hobart said, and burst into laughter at the expression on Alastair's face. "My boy," he said, clapping the younger man on the shoulder, "it's a pleasure to know you."

Alastair smiled faintly. He had correctly evaluated Hobart Cunningham and liked him less and less as the days passed. But Hobart was ruthless in getting what he wanted—most of the time—and Alastair admired that. Alastair had always learned from the people he despised. In the case of Steven James, he could learn from someone he liked.

———— • ————

Cynthia looked more beautiful than ever at luncheon, and to her fiancé that was very beautiful indeed. Apart from her Yankee accent, which a tutor was already beginning to eradicate, Cynthia was perfection. She really *was* like a Dresden figurine, small and graceful and pink and white, with a full, sweet, rosy mouth and an adequate bosom as far as Alastair could tell. It was impossible to know for certain: a female's curves were so often augmented by puffs of satin tied around her bosom, or her hips by ruffles sewn into her corset or her chemise.

"Did you have a nice morning?" Cynthia inquired dutifully.

"Very rewarding," Alastair said. "I saw our old friend Senator James." He watched carefully, but there was no significant reaction from either Cynthia or Miranda.

Damn women, Alastair thought. *A fellow never really knows what they're thinking!*

"And how is he?" Paul asked, his tone conveying no more than polite interest.

A cool customer, Alastair thought. *He must know he's a cuckold, but I'd bet a packet he still sleeps with his wife.*

"He's planning to stay on in England permanently," Hobart told them, watching Cynthia for a telltale blush. But if his daughter had been partial to the senator, she appeared to be over it.

"And so, I think, is Miss McAllister," Cynthia said, picking daintily at her food. "I heard it somewhere."

"And who is Miss McAllister?" Hobart demanded.

"I wrote to you about her, Papa. One of our shipboard companions. She's that crusader for women's rights who raised such a stir."

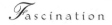

Hobart turned sharply to Miranda. "Was it wise to let Cynthia associate with a radical feminist?"

"Oh, Aunt Miranda wasn't to know," Cynthia said airily. "Miss McAllister wasn't a crusader aboard ship. She took up the cause only when she got to London."

Hobart, mollified, returned to his luncheon.

"I wonder," said Alastair, "what there is about this climate that makes some of our women so militant?"

"Do you disapprove of women who demand their rights?" Cynthia asked with her customary sauciness when she spoke to Walford. Today it angered him.

"Crusading females are offputting in the extreme," Alastair said, turning to Hobart. "Don't you agree, sir?"

"Entirely," Hobart announced. "Wouldn't have one in my house."

"All the same, we shall have Miss McAllister at Inderby," Cynthia said sweetly. "She will be invited to our engagement party. You can meet her then, Papa."

"I liked her very much," Miranda said before Hobart could protest.

"I hope you don't intend to make a habit of her," Alastair said to Cynthia, who immediately put enough food in her mouth to prevent her replying.

What a clever little vixen it is, he thought. *It'll be a pleasure to tame her.* For the moment, he had to be content with her silence as the conversation turned to other matters.

———— · ————

Hobart, still annoyed from the morning meeting, cornered his brother as soon as he could.

"What do you know about Steven James?" he demanded.

Paul blanched. "What do you mean?"

"I'm told Cynthia was seen with him a great deal before you went to Cairo."

"They met on the ship and had tea together a time or two here in London," Paul said, relieved beyond measure that Cynthia, not Miranda, was the focus of Hobart's concern. "She fancied herself in love with him when she arrived in Liverpool."

"And he didn't return her affections? That's odd. Most men can't resist her."

"Obviously he can, since it came to nothing," Paul said. "And then she was overwhelmed by Inderby."

"But why did James squire her about if he wasn't interested, why continue his acquaintance with our family? Was he looking for information?"

"What on earth about?"

"Business," Hobart snapped. "Maybe some plot he and that fellow Haggerty are cooking up."

Paul nodded, grateful for a way out of this perilous discussion. "That could account for it. Very astute of you to see it."

"Little brother," Hobart said expansively, "in business one has to keep one's guard up. I'll have a word with Cynthia about her sins. Fortunately there isn't a thing she could have told him." He paused, frowning. "But Miranda could."

"Dammit, Hobart, what a thing to say! You know she wouldn't!"

"No, of course not. I spoke hastily. Come along now, let's have a stroll before it's time to dress for dinner."

But the senator's "friendship" with Cynthia nagged at Hobart. He would have Tedley investigate it more thoroughly, and only when he had all the information would he confront Cynthia with it.

He was beginning to feel uneasy about the long engagement dictated by social custom. Steven James was as attractive in his way as the viscount in his. Alastair was just this side of beautiful; Steven was as virile as a gladiator. Alastair was born with a silver spoon in his mouth, Steven with a milk pail and a talent for making money.

Both young men were intelligent, ambitious, and smart as all get-out. Any foolish young girl might have trouble choosing be-

tween them—although James, apparently, had not made a bid for Cynthia and had no wish to be chosen.

That brought Hobart back to square one. If Steven didn't want the girl, why had he been attentive to her? It could only be to keep up his contacts with the Cunninghams and that could only be for information.

Hobart kept chewing it over in his mind as he walked with his brother. It was not what he considered a major concern, but it would nag at him until he put it to rest. He was not a man to let things nag at him.

In the meantime, and despite the stumbling blocks Steven James put in his way, he had what he wanted: a silent partnership in what could be a huge moneymaker with no risk to himself or his reputation if, because of that crook Haggerty, anything went wrong. And he had a daughter about to marry into one of the fine old families of England. What Hobart still wanted was his brother's wife and, one way or another, he would have her too.

Book
Four

Thirty-five

Cynthia stood on the fitting platform at Worth, being measured, while Miranda watched from a comfortable armchair. There was a nervous gaiety about Miss Cunningham that Madame Hortense, one of the couturier's supervisors, put down to elation over the girl's coup. The viscount was a great catch; no one thought his naughty reputation anything but glamorous for a handsome bachelor.

As for the bride-to-be, she was rumored to have a great fortune and Madame Hortense was in raptures over her face and figure. Madame was an angular woman with an equine face, "who looks," Cynthia had told Walford, "as if she's about to poke in my pockets to find a carrot."

"*Soie* for the *fiançailles*," Madame Hortense now suggested with a heavy French accent, although she had been born in Bayswater. "Satin for the *robe de mariage*."

"Won't satin be heavy for spring?"

"Not at Inderby!" Madame Hortense said. "An English spring is usually cool, and those massive old buildings can be frigid. Either way, satin is traditional." She rested her chin on three of her extended fingers. "With Miss Cunningham's exquisite eyes we must have a touch of blue for the engagement gown, *n'est-ce pas?*"

"Yes," Cynthia said. "Love knots."

"Love knots are not *comme il faut,*" Madame Hortense protested. She turned to Miranda, as if for confirmation.

"Whatever you like, Cynthia," Miranda said.

Hortense almost clucked her disapproval but, mindful of who she was and who they were, she went on directing the fitting, wondering what the world was coming to when young girls were indulged in this way. Love knots on an engagement gown! The implications! Entirely too suggestive!

The measuring over and a white silk fabric as soft as angels' wings selected for the formal engagement ball, Miranda suggested tea at the Ritz. "You must be tired after standing so long," she told her niece. "And I have something to discuss with you."

Cynthia nodded and they got into the coach Hobart had put at their disposal for the rest of their stay. It was a clammy December day, and they were glad of the carriage robes and the foot warmer— a stone bottle filled with embers—and of their furs and gloves and muffs as the horses trotted briskly toward the Ritz. London was beginning to prepare for the Christmas season, and in the gathering dusk the shop lights twinkled as they poured light across the damp pavements.

"I expect Ebenezer Scrooge to appear at any moment," Miranda said, looking at the gaily festooned shopwindows.

But Cynthia was not thinking of Dickens. "I suppose you want to give me the other half of your lecture on the birds and the bees," she said.

"I don't think either species suffers from this particular aberration."

"Goodness me, it sounds serious. What's it called?"

"It has many names, but it means the attraction of men to men rather than to women."

"But men have more in common! They are quite naturally at-

tracted to one another for sports and business and smoking smelly cigars in their clubs."

"I am speaking of a sexual attraction, Cynthia."

Cynthia's lips formed an O of surprise. Then she frowned. "But . . . I don't see how . . . or why."

"I don't pretend to know the details myself. I just know that it exists and that it is insidious because it's kept so secret."

Cynthia was silent for some moments before she asked, "Then how is it discovered?"

"By inappropriate behavior between two men. Words. Glances. Jealousy."

"And if undiscovered?"

"Many of these men marry and have children. Then they can indulge this particular vice furtively."

"Their wives don't suspect?"

"Most women are totally ignorant of normal sexual practices, much less abnormal ones."

Cynthia nodded agreement. Then there was another long silence before the girl turned to her aunt.

"How can that have anything to do with me?" she asked, her words clipped, her voice cold.

"I've been trying to tell you—" Miranda began.

"You've been trying to tell me Walford's like that," Cynthia interrupted angrily. "And that's why you say I shouldn't marry him!"

Miranda hesitated, unprepared for Cynthia's quick grasp of things, before she said, "Yes."

"I don't believe you! Women fall all over him."

"What woman could resist him? His looks are overwhelming and he is charming and witty along with his title. But I'm talking about his nature, Cynthia, not his looks and not his rank. He couldn't really like women if he prefers men. It is not what a woman wants that matters to him, but what *he* wants."

"How can you hate me so?" Cynthia demanded in sudden fury.

"Oh, don't deny it, I know you do. It's because I made you stop your filthy affair with Steven, isn't it? Now you'll do anything to even the score, even this. You're a nasty, evil, vicious woman and I despise you!"

"Cynthia, please, I'm trying to spare you . . ."

"No! You don't want me to marry a glorious young man or have a title or be mistress of those stunning houses. You can't have what you want, so you try to ruin everything for me! But I won't let you!" She held up an imperious hand when Miranda attempted to speak. "Don't speak to me. I don't want to hear anything you have to say." She tapped on the panel and the coachman opened the peephole. "Drive to the Bristol," she ordered, and the peephole closed.

They arrived at the hotel, rode up in the Bristol's lift, and separated without exchanging another word.

Cynthia was panting with anger and her effort to control it until she could be alone. She strode across her room, snatched off her bonnet, and sat in front of the dressing table, talking to herself in the mirror as was her habit when she was very pleased or very upset.

"How could I have admired that woman so much?" she demanded, rubbing the taut muscles of her neck and shoulders. "But everyone does. 'Isn't Miranda beautiful? Isn't Miranda intelligent? Isn't she a perfect wife and mother?' " Cynthia picked up a silver brush and with all her strength threw it at the mirror, cracking the glass. She sat staring at it, not really seeing it, while she thought feverishly.

This *thing* between men and women! Why was it so important? Why were people endlessly obsessed with it even if they had to discuss it in whispers or pretend it didn't happen? What possible difference could it make to her whether it was Walford who would thrust himself inside her or someone else?

But she knew there was more to sex than the act itself! She had

wondered about it for years even before she discovered how it was done. She had been beset with impulses that flooded her and vagrant desires that spread throughout her body when she danced with an attractive man, that had made her seek that release for herself that so outraged her nurse and her governess.

While she was considering all of that, her expression had changed from anger to impatience and finally to doubt. She could not tolerate the idea that any young man she favored could resist her—and none ever had—much less that he could be attracted more to another man than to her! It was a monstrous concept, difficult to absorb.

"I have to find out about Walford," she told herself. "I *must*."

But how? There was no one she could ask—no one but Miranda, who confessed to ignorance of the details herself and had offered no proof of Walford's iniquity! Cynthia's own mother, when she wasn't drunk, had only one reaction to men: terror. Elsie's terror, Cynthia suddenly suspected, might be linked to the intimacies of marriage.

She could not imagine her fragile mother welcoming sexual penetration! Elsie had done her duty, as women referred to it, because it was how children were made and it was a woman's duty to bear children, but she would never talk about sex and she would know nothing about intercourse between men.

Alastair's kisses were more ardent than any Cynthia had experienced since she made her debut and started allowing some boys to kiss her. In fact, his kisses were daring, wet, and open-lipped, his tongue probing her mouth, and she felt those strange throbbings whenever he kissed her, "down below," where Miranda said he would put himself inside her.

A thought struck her and she spoke to her reflection.

"Suppose I tell him he can do that to me now—not in so many words, but indirectly—and see how he reacts!"

She already knew he would not have proposed to her without the fortune that came with her. She could accept that; it was the way of the world. But she felt certain he was attracted to her. To be admired and desired by men was her purpose in life. It was why she *was,* why all women were.

But she would not marry a man without knowing whether he wanted her as a woman!

"I must know," she told herself fiercely. "I *must.*"

She stopped talking to herself when her maid knocked and entered the bedroom. "I didn't know you were back, Miss Cynthia . . ." Baxter began. Then her eyes grew round as saucers. "The mirror!" she wailed. "What happened?"

Cynthia, actually seeing the cracked mirror for the first time, shrugged. "It broke."

"Oh, dear, oh, dear," Baxter moaned. "That's seven years of bad luck."

"Don't be ridiculous!" Cynthia snapped. "And keep your silly superstitions to yourself."

"Yes, miss," Baxter whispered.

"Ring for tea," Cynthia ordered. "And a glass of sherry," she added. She needed something to steady her nerves, and this was no time for laudanum. On the few occasions when she had taken the opiate for monthly cramps, it had made her sleepy and right now she had to concentrate.

The challenge was to find a place where she could be alone with Walford, unchaperoned by her aunt or her maid. But Walford was nothing if not resourceful: he would find a way if she gave him reason to believe she would yield to him.

She had never flirted with him—that was what had caught his attention and kept it. She had never had to flirt! She had only to appear and men fawned upon her.

She flung herself onto an Empire sofa, seething with another kind of indignation.

Why should she, Cynthia Cunningham, marry a man who was tainted in what seemed a particularly repulsive way . . . when Steven James was still in London and unattached?

Miranda was as much beyond his reach as she had ever been, and, according to the gossips, Kitt McAllister had made no progress with him while Cynthia was in Cairo.

But Cynthia was engaged to Walford and she had to start with him. Cynthia knew how to be alluring, how to seem acquiescent and close to surrender. She had been born knowing how to send that message. What followed after she sent it was up to Walford. Whatever men did to women, he knew how to do it.

She sighed. So did Steven James!

Suddenly she sprang up and went to the desk. She snatched up her writing case and found a piece of her heavy vellum notepaper. She thought for a second, scribbled a message, and sealed it.

"Baxter!" she called to the worried girl. "Take this down to the bell captain and tell him to see it's delivered." She handed the note to Baxter, relenting when she noticed the maid's pale face. "And stop worrying about the mirror. The superstition only works if you do it accidentally, and I did it on purpose. Tell them to send up a new one. Now, off you go."

"Yes, Miss Cynthia," the maid breathed, and darted away just as the tea tray was brought. As soon as the door closed again upon the waiter, Cynthia picked up the glass of sherry and tossed it down, for all the world like an habitual drinker.

———— · ————

Steven was in the parlor of his suite at Brown's, seated at the writing desk. He was conscious that while he wrote he still waited for a sign from Miranda. He knew it would not come, even that it should not come, but he waited all the same.

He said nothing about her in the letter he was writing to Claire, and that made it difficult to explain his plans to his sister.

And now, he wrote to Claire, *I have decided to stay on in England. I always wanted to leave the farm for New York because the city was more challenging. Then I wanted to leave New York and its unhappy memories. London harbors no memories for me and is far more to my taste than New*

York City, to say nothing of this business venture that has been claiming all my time. London feels like home to me and will feel even more so when I've taken a flat of my own.

Having buried the core message of the letter there on its second page, he went on writing, asking her to close up his bachelor flat in New York and to have his clothes and a few belongings shipped to him as soon as he could provide her with a permanent London address. When he had sealed it, he went down to post it in plenty of time to make the next transatlantic mail packet—when it was able to sail! The fog outside was too thick to see more than his hand in front of his face, but he decided to walk for a while.

"You want to be careful not to get lost, sir," the bell captain warned. "A man can lose his sense of direction with naught but fog to guide him."

"I'll be careful," Steven promised, and went out into the mist. In a few moments he was obliged to use his walking stick to keep himself at a consistent distance from the curb, but he rather liked the dreamlike sensation of walking in a white cloud. He had planned to stroll around the block, keeping to the sidewalk, but he soon found himself on Dover Street, across from where Kitt lived.

He could see the light from the windows of her parlor. He missed their cozy chats in front of the fire. He missed Kitt's fiery spirit that matched her copper hair. He missed her wide fund of knowledge, the odd facts about odd things that stayed in her memory.

"More than any of that," he admitted to the muffling fog, "I miss Kitt."

He had not seen her since that miserable night. His face grew hot remembering her expression! Kitt's good opinion had become important to him, as important as Claire's, he now realized. Had he lost it forever?

"You've made a fine mess of things," he upbraided himself. Somehow his emotional life had always been at sixes and sevens and still was. Was that all the fault of "the troll who lived under the

bridge"? His little man, protecting him from any emotions he could not direct and dominate?

He was almost certain Claire would say so, but she was unaware that Steven had taken his first enormous risk in loving Miranda. And to what end? Only to give her up if she could not face the life of a social outcast, a pariah.

He looked up at Kitt's windows. He would have liked to explain it all to her, to recapture any regard for him, however slight, she might still harbor. But what on earth could he tell her?

He remembered everything she had said that night, but above all he remembered something she had asked: "Do you suppose you're the only person on the planet capable of love like that?"

It was suddenly obvious to him that she had been speaking of herself. He wondered whom she had loved so deeply and lost, Kitt with her high spirits and flaming hair. She deserved to be happy. He hoped she would be.

He turned away and, listening carefully to avoid other wanderers in the fog, he plunged through the curling mist until he found his way back to Brown's Hotel.

When he woke the next morning the fog had completely lifted and in its place there was brilliant sunshine under a crisp blue sky. When his breakfast tray was brought there was a note on it addressed to him in what he recognized as Cynthia's handwriting.

"There's a man waiting downstairs if there's a reply," the floor waiter said, and Steven nodded as he opened the envelope.

It said that Cynthia would be at the National Gallery at three o'clock, at the Egyptian exhibits. She most earnestly begged that he meet her there on a matter of greatest importance to her.

He dashed off a brief consent and it was taken by the floor waiter to be given to the waiting man. He could not help wondering if Hobart was behind this curious request, if it had something to do with the Panama Canal scheme. Hobart was despicable enough to force his daughter into marriage; he would certainly not stop at using her to spy on his business partners.

Cynthia looked exquisite in that violet-blue color that so became her. A radiant smile lit her face as soon as she saw him, and she waited expectantly as he approached, the way a girl would wait for her lover. It unsettled him.

"Miss Cunningham," he said, taking her outstretched hand.

"I wish you would call me Cynthia," she said.

"Soon I'll be calling you Viscountess."

Her smile faded. "That is exactly what I wanted to talk to you about."

He waited, hoping she was not going to speak about her forced marriage again, since there was nothing he could do to prevent it. What she did say made him even more uneasy.

"I want to know if you find me attractive."

He frowned. "You must be joking."

She turned imploring eyes on him. "No, I want to know. Please tell me the truth."

He drew a deep breath. "I don't think there's a man alive who wouldn't find you attractive. I know you're the most beautiful girl I've ever seen."

She turned to face a glass-enclosed cat of black obsidian, stylized in the Egyptian fashion, proud and eerily menacing.

"Then," she said, "if things had been different, you might have married me."

He was astounded. "Cynthia! That's not the sort of thing a young lady says."

"Why not? It's very important to me to know."

"Walford is the proper person to address on this subject."

She shrugged. "Walford wants my fortune so much, he might have convinced himself that he is madly in love with me." Her slender fingers moved back and forth along the pedestal on which the black image sat. "Maybe he doesn't love me at all." Her eyes slid in his direction. "Maybe he loves someone else."

"I doubt that. And he seems to be a good fellow," Steven said.

"Do you think he's too beautiful?"

Steven reddened. "I don't think anyone can be too beautiful. He's an unusually handsome man, but no more so than you are a woman. You'll make a very attractive pair." He wondered what she was driving at.

She shook her head, as if in confusion, then changed the subject. "He told me you were going to live in England. Is that so?"

"That is my intention."

She turned to him. "Shall we see each other?" Again her eyes were fixed on his face as if she pleaded for some response, although he could not imagine the nature of it.

"I don't move in the viscount's circles."

"But you and he are partners."

"Business is one thing and society is another, particularly for titled Englishmen." For a moment he thought she *had* been sent by her father to forage for information.

"You and I are American," she reminded him. "Titles mean nothing to us."

He suspected that was not entirely true in her case. "Then perhaps we will see each other from time to time."

"I hope so," she said as if comforted by the idea.

A silence fell between them. If she had another question to ask him, she had decided not to utter it, but he was disconcerted by her intensity.

"Shall we see the rest of the exhibit?" He offered his arm and she took it.

They walked more deeply into the Egyptian displays. Neither of them had noticed the Countess of Inderby, who pretended not to notice them as she rustled along beside two of her fashionable friends.

"I think I've seen enough of Egyptian clutter for one day," the countess said. "Shall we move on?"

Her friends agreed with her, and they moved away from the couple who had been engaged in such rapt conversation across the gallery and made their way out of the hall. Lady Caroline resolutely hid her dismay at such an improper rendezvous between a newly engaged girl and a young man Miss Cunningham seemed to know far too well.

And there was no chaperone in sight! If the couple were recognized, the news would be all over London by this evening! Lady Caroline decided to give the little hussy a piece of her mind before dinner that evening at Inderby House.

If she got nowhere by confronting Miss Cunningham, she would put the matter to her husband! And if he did nothing, she would go to the girl's father and finally to her son. She let herself hope that this would be enough to break Alastair's unfortunate engagement.

Thirty-six

Lady Burdon's gala on the first of January was an annual event in London. People had been known to put off their departures to Monte Carlo, Biarritz, and Italy in order to attend.

And on this New Year's Day there was more to the evening than to see and be seen. Young Lord Walford would be there with his American fiancée, Miss Cynthia Cunningham. Those who had not been invited to Inderby for the engagement ball the day after Christmas would finally get a close look at the American heiress.

"Too delicious," gushed the ladies upon sight of Cynthia.

"Lucky fellow," said the gentlemen, enraptured by her still-budding beauty.

"How romantic," murmured the young girls wistfully with many languishing looks at the stunning viscount.

When all the guests had arrived and been welcomed, Lady Burdon retreated to her morning room for a few moments respite. "All this delight," she grumbled to Kitt, who had accompanied her, "grates on my nerves."

"Aren't you pleased about Cynthia and Walford?" Kitt asked, holding a lighted match to Lady Burdon's cigarette.

"I'm neutral. Neither of them means a great deal to me. And you?"

"I'm neutral too."

"One of these days you might have to take sides in a social imbroglio," Lady Burdon said, "and then where shall you be?"

"Sides?"

"What if Miranda Cunningham runs off with the senator?"

Kitt's face shifted subtly into harsher lines, then she shrugged. "What an idea! I think there's very little chance that will happen."

"My dear girl," Lady Burdon said anxiously. "You're not planning to wait for that affair to run its course?"

"No, Lady Pat," Kitt said softly. "I am not."

"Then what *are* you planning?"

"I have no plans at the moment."

"You are not going back to America?"

"Someday, perhaps, but not now," Kitt said. "I considered it, but I've decided against it."

"Thank heaven for small mercies," Lady Burdon said, fanning herself with a book from the table beside her. The two sat in comfortable silence until Lady Burdon had finished her cigarette. Then she rose from her chair.

"I must wander among my guests," she said. Passing the pier glass, she looked into it, turning this way and that to check her gown of royal blue silk lavishly trimmed with black lace. A feathered decoration rode upon her head like a bird about to take flight.

"War bonnet still in place," she announced, and walked on, Kitt following her in a satin gown of that uncompromising scarlet rarely worn by redheads and never by spinsters but which became her very well. The two women parted at the drawing room, where music floated in from the ballroom: "My Wild Irish Rose," "After the Ball," "On the Banks of the Wabash." They were songs from America played in honor of the bride-to-be who, with her fiancé, moved from group to group to chat with the guests.

"Angelic, aren't they?" the count said, coming to stand beside Kitt.

"A pair of cherubs," Kitt agreed, turning to smile at him.

"Will they be happy, do you think?" he said.

She thought a moment, then nodded. "They want the same things. Don't you think that will bring them happiness?"

"Who can say? Do we know what happiness is or just think we know?"

But Kitt was in no mood for philosophy. She needed to move. She needed to do anything but stand there and wait to see Steven and Miranda, separately or together.

"Right now it would make me wildly happy to dance," she said.

"My pleasure," the count replied, and they went toward the ballroom, stopping for a brief exchange with Cynthia and Walford on their way.

"Is it my imagination," the count asked afterward, "or has her accent changed?"

"Now, now, Monsieur," Kitt chided gently. "That's to be expected after a prolonged stay in any country. I believe mine has changed too."

"Not at all!" the count protested. "Nor mine."

"You are French and therefore immune to foreign influence," Kitt declared, and continued on to the ballroom. He followed, chuckling.

Steven turned with a glass of champagne in his hand and almost collided with Paul. It was the first time they had been close enough to speak since the train from Liverpool, but neither did for the first few moments of this unintentional meeting.

"I had expected to see you at the Tri-Panalco meetings," Steven finally said stiffly.

"As I told you, I'm not much interested in business," Paul replied.

"How was your trip?"

Paul, governing his impulse to flee, said a few words about Egypt, and added, "We had planned to stay longer, but then there was Cynthia's engagement."

"I was pleased to learn of it," Steven said formally. "I'm sure she will be very happy."

Paul nodded, glancing around to see where Miranda was. She was about twenty yards away talking to the earl, but her eyes darted around the room, searching, until they met Paul's and he convinced himself that she had been looking for him. She said something to the earl and, with Inderby at her side, had already started in Paul's direction before she caught sight of Steven.

Both of the men waiting for her had to admire her poise. She looked down several times, but only as if to check her path around the many chairs and tables clustered in the drawing room. She greeted those people she knew, even stopping briefly to exchange a word with two of them. By the time she and the earl reached her husband and her lover, she was in command of herself. Just as she was greeting Steven, Hobart arrived, a welcome diversion for once.

"Good evening, Miranda," Hobart said, bowing over his sister-in-law's hand. "You are magnificent, as always."

Steven found the next few minutes almost unendurable. He wanted desperately to be alone with her, to tell her he was preparing to make a life for the two of them there in London. Instead, he had to make polite conversation.

"I understand you've delayed your departure for New York," Steven said to Hobart. The wretched man would want to take his whole family along with him, but he would not take Miranda!

"Only for another few weeks."

Steven glanced at Miranda, but she gave him no sign that the departure date was not welcome to her. He felt as if the floor under his feet had just shifted, that there was more behind her reserve than discretion. Something was terribly wrong. He glanced quickly around the circle of faces, looking for a clue.

Steven feared he would explode if he didn't touch her. He turned to Paul. "May I have your permission to dance with Mrs. Cunningham?"

Paul flushed, then nodded almost imperceptibly, and Hobart and the earl stepped back to let Miranda pass. Steven escorted her to the ballroom and they joined the dancers visible from the drawing room. Soon they moved off and were lost to the three men who had been watching them.

"Darling," Steven said softly the moment he touched her. "My darling."

"Stop," she begged. "You mustn't speak to me like that."

"I can't help myself. I've been waiting for weeks to say those words."

"Steven, nothing has changed. We'd both of us be foolish to pretend it has."

"Things *have* changed, darling. You'll be able to divorce Paul and marry me as soon as the decree is final."

"No," she said. "I cannot divorce Paul."

"Why not? You don't love him."

"But I've told you that I do," she said, her face pale and distraught. "I can't explain it, but you must believe me when I tell you that I cannot divorce him."

"No," he said urgently, beside himself. "I won't accept that. But this is no place to discuss it. Meet me tomorrow and we'll talk."

She said nothing, leaning back against his arm. He reveled in her nearness. In the midst of a crowd, unable to say what he felt, a mere look was a kiss, and that long-forbidden clasp of hands almost as exciting as making love.

The music stopped and they applauded politely. She took his arm and they walked back toward the set of sliding doors, one of several sets that had been thrown open between all the enormous rooms on this floor.

"I can't let you go!" he said as they walked. "Dance with me again."

"That would embarrass him, Steven." Her tone left no doubt that she was not to be moved.

"Then we *must* meet!" They were nearing the three men, who were no longer talking among themselves. "Miranda!"

"Yes, all right! Where?"

He gave her the name of a country tavern he had found for just such a meeting, where no one would recognize them.

She nodded. "I'll be there at four o'clock," she said. Those were the last words she said to him that evening, but he cherished them while he waited for the shining hour to come.

Miranda's jaws ached from clenching her teeth. She had supposed she was well prepared to meet Steven without making a fool of herself, but the erotic current between them was so intense that she was afraid everyone in the room could feel it. She was relieved when he moved away from the Cunninghams.

She was rescued by Kitt McAllister and the count—except that it soon became apparent that Miss McAllister had trouble looking directly at her.

Oh, my God, Miranda agonized. *Does she know too? How many people know?*

She was dizzy with apprehension. "Please excuse me," she said with the last of her strength. "I must look for my niece."

Miranda fled to the ladies' retiring room and ran into the lavatory, where she was sick. The attendant tapped at the half-open door.

"May I help you, madam?"

"A glass of water, please."

The woman, neatly dressed in black but without cap or apron, took a bottle of smelling salts from her pocket and held it under Miranda's nose.

"Shall I call someone, madam?" she asked after Miranda had moved her head to escape the pungent salts.

"No," Miranda said. "It's a momentary faintness I've had several times lately. It will pass."

The young woman nodded, helped Miranda to a comfortable chair, and went to fetch a glass of water. Then she brought a cool, damp compress to place on Miranda's forehead.

"Your color's coming back," she said after a few moments. She had a curiously flat voice and not a trace of sympathy in her manner.

Miranda, needing sympathy, lay in the deep-cushioned chair, her feet up on an ottoman and her head back. The attendant sat near her, plying a fan. She leaned over from time to time to turn the compress.

"Thank you," Miranda said. "I'm feeling better."

"You should rest a while longer, Mrs. Cunningham," the girl said.

"How do you know me?" Miranda asked.

"I was on the liner from New York. I was a chief stewardess and I took care of Miss McAllister."

Miranda opened her eyes, and a look passed between the two women. On the girl's side it was accusatory, as if she were saying "I know all about you too."

Miranda closed her eyes.

Maybe the stewardess had seen Steven entering or leaving Miranda's bedroom. Then Miranda wondered what a stewardess was doing here, and suddenly realized that this must be the girl who was raped, the one Kitt McAllister defended and was said to have taken under her wing. She felt great pity for what the stewardess had suffered, but she could only be sorry; she had no way of knowing what that experience was like.

"No one can know another person," she murmured wearily, "without walking in her shoes."

"Madam?"

"Everyone is on the outside looking in, but each of us is on the inside looking out, and whatever happens is ours to live with and ours alone."

Mary Frances, the strangled humiliation of rape always with her, nodded, this time in sympathy. Miss Kitt had given her the courage to declare what had happened to her and to reject all blame for it, but some people—including her own mother—still harbored suspicions that she had provoked it in order to profit from it.

And just look at all it had brought her! A better than respectable situation, a good life with the best of women, an education. None of it would have happened if that pig hadn't raped her. But had she wanted his attentions? No! She would rather have gone on toiling her way up than go through that!

Alton looked searchingly at Mrs. Cunningham. She was not brazen; she was monumentally sad. She was not a promiscuous woman—Mary Frances had seen enough of those on the crossings to know the type. Alton shivered.

What had this woman got from her great love affair? From the look of her, nothing but sorrow. Mrs. Cunningham had no more sought adultery than Mary Frances had sought rape. It had happened, the way love had happened to Miss Kitt. Miss Kitt said so, so it must be true, even if love was a total mystery to Mary Frances.

She devoutly hoped it would stay that way.

She reached out to take Miranda's hand and the current between them had changed. "Are you better, ma'am? Will I be fetchin' you anythin'?"

Miranda shook her head. "I'm all right now, thanks to you. I had better put myself in order and go back to the party," she said.

Mary Frances helped her up, then arranged Miranda's dress and smoothed her hair.

"Miss McAllister is lucky to have a friend like you," Miranda said when she was ready to go.

Mary Frances, with a small bob, thanked her and watched her walk down the hall in the direction of the music.

———— · ————

Kitt, dancing with the count, had been amazed to see Steven and Miranda on the dance floor and grateful that neither of them appeared to notice her. They were absorbed in each other in that way that is particular to lovers, as if the sun and everything under it had been eclipsed.

She realized that the count was looking at her with his heart in his eyes. His devotion flooded over her like a warm current in frigid water, and she welcomed it.

"Louisa?"

"Yes."

"You know I am leaving tomorrow for France."

"But not permanently."

"I shall return. But I have a question to leave with you."

"I don't understand."

"You must not answer it until I return."

"All right."

"Promise me you will not answer it."

"I promise. What is the question?"

"Louisa, I love you in a way I never thought to love any woman, and I want most profoundly for you to be my wife." He shook his head. "Don't answer."

She could not have answered. She was not so much surprised by his proposal as she was startled by her response to it. Half of her wanted to say she did not love him as he loved her, that it would be unfair to him. The other half so much wanted what he offered that she was ready to take it on any terms.

"Monsieur le Comte . . ." she began.

"You promised," he warned.

"I merely wanted to say . . ."

". . . that you are mindful of the honor I do you in asking you to be my wife, et cetera, et cetera. But that is unnecessary between us."

She was quiet for a moment. "You must have proposed often to predict my reply so well."

"I have rehearsed this declaration," he countered. "But I have never cared enough to make it to anyone else."

She was overcome by that. Her eyes filled with tears of loneliness and the prospect of an end to loneliness. She did not love him as she loved Steven, but she was fond of him and her affection was as clear and untroubled as a mountain lake in midsummer, unsullied by wanton hungers, unthreatened by desire.

"I *am* honored," she said, "and I will wait until you return to give you a reply."

People formed a circle when the engaged pair stepped onto the ballroom floor.

"Look at them," Hobart said. "I've never seen a more superb couple."

Lady Caroline nodded, although it was only her son she beamed upon. "I could wish Miss Cunningham were more discreet," she whispered to Hobart when their nearest neighbors were beyond range of her voice.

"What do you mean?" he demanded, his face clouding.

"I saw her with Mr. James at the National Gallery. They were deeply engaged in conversation and did not notice me—or my friends."

"Did your friends notice them?"

"No, I led them away."

"Perhaps they met by chance."

"No, their behavior was too intense to have arisen from a chance meeting. And Miss Cunningham was unattended."

Hobart's gaze followed the engaged pair, who were now talking to several couples. Cynthia seemed utterly content, a lovely smile on her face and all of her attention directed at her fiancé.

"I shall speak to her," Hobart said, wondering why he had not yet heard from Tedley with particulars of Cynthia's latest meeting with the senator.

"Let us hope that no one else saw them," Lady Caroline said. "It could become a matter for serious gossip. Your daughter is indiscreet."

"I'm quite aware of that," he said, and, taking her arm, led her to the ballroom. "You don't like the idea of this marriage, do you?" he demanded when they were moving to the music.

She turned crimson and seemed at a loss for words. He waited.

"Marriage is difficult enough without complications," she finally replied.

"Such as?"

"Differences in background. Or if one of them should care for someone else," she said.

"Her background is entirely suitable. And how can you gather the other possibility from one conversation in the National Gallery?"

"Had you seen them, you would have come to the same conclusion, I assure you. They were not passing the time of day."

Headstrong little bitch, Hobart fumed, furious with Cynthia. He had spoiled her, but he had not believed her capable of such a gross error in judgment.

"Lady Caroline," Hobart said, inclining his bald head. "You are a clever woman as well as a lovely one. Let us keep this matter between ourselves. I shall speak to my daughter."

"But if she cares for someone else?"

"I will not allow the marriage," he lied.

Relief flooded her. She had railed at her husband and got nowhere, but Hobart's response was as decisive as he was powerful. "You are more than kind, Mr. Cunningham, you are also considerate. I hardly welcome the humiliation of a broken engagement, but we must do what is best for our children's happiness."

Happiness be damned! Hobart scoffed silently. *I don't care if Cynthia's lost her head over the senator. She'll marry whom I say she'll marry and that is the viscount. And she'll marry him sooner rather than later.*

Then he turned his attention to compromising the insidious woman in his arms before her maternal jealousy could rob Hobart of the prize he had won.

"What a pity," he said with a meaningful smile, "that I will soon depart without having visited the National Gallery."

That curious flutter she felt in his presence, part fear and part titillation, rippled through her. His true meaning was apparent: *she* was the National Gallery he wanted to visit. With his bald head and his aquiline nose, he looked like a handsome but rapacious bird.

She thought of a painting she had seen, reproduced in one of the naughty art books her husband kept hidden in his study. She saw herself as that painting of the naked Leda, her breasts round and high, her thighs parted for intercourse with the god Zeus, who had taken the form of a swan and nestled between her legs. It had first repelled her—as Hobart had—and then fascinated her—as Hobart did—and she thought of both the man and the painting often.

"I should very much like to show you some exhibits," she said.

"And I am eager to see them."

They made an appointment to meet at the National Gallery.

"Well, then," Alastair said. "Just see where we've got ourselves."

Cynthia laughed. "I'm sure you've danced before a crowd of people before."

"Never with my future wife." He looked down at her. She was very animated tonight, almost nervous. Cynthia was a spirited girl, but she was always poised and rarely as agitated as this.

"Does that please you? Do I?" she asked.

"Wouldn't be here otherwise."

For a few moments she said nothing. Then she remembered Miranda's horrible suspicions about him and she smiled at him coquettishly. "The wedding seems endlessly far away," she said.

"The time will go by in a few winks, you'll see."

"Really, Walford, that's almost ungallant of you. You're supposed to be an impatient bridegroom."

Expertly, he reversed their direction. "But I am," he said. "Damnably impatient." She did look particularly appetizing tonight, like a meringue filled with sweet custard just waiting to be licked.

She looked steadily into his eyes. "Why must we wait?"

He had the feeling they were reading lines in a play. *What is she up to now?* he thought. "Because the rules decree an engagement interval of at least a year before we marry."

"But you don't follow rules."

"When they concern the future Countess of Inderby, I do."

She sighed. "Maybe we must wait that long for the ceremony, but must we wait for everything?"

She lowered her eyelids, and her long lashes rested on her alabaster cheeks. Her dress of virginal white was elegant, as were all of her dresses, and they never overpowered her. Her glossy hair was carefully curled and arranged, but wisps of it escaped the pins and combs as a little girl's might. She was not only appetizing; she was totally innocent, and that in itself was an enormous enticement to him.

"We're never alone," she pouted. "We haven't been, not since Egypt."

"I want us to be alone as much as you do."

"Then find a place, Alastair," she said. From a sophisticated woman it would have been a bold invitation. From Cynthia it was only a promise of stolen kisses.

He considered the girl/woman in his arms, feeling both amusement at her naïveté and arousal at the mere fact of her innocence. If they were alone together, kisses would not be enough.

She had moved nearer, and although their bodies did not touch, the silk of her dress billowed between his legs as they circled, as if he had mounted her. For the first time, he had to admit that to a surprising degree he enjoyed her company, was perhaps even the slightest bit in love with her, although he had only once felt the gallantry that was supposed to be a part of love. That had been in the Cairo station, when she turned to him for safe harbor.

Then, over her head, he caught sight of Steven James watching them. The senator was the tallest person in the room. Alastair was jolted by the suspicion that as she had on the ship, Cynthia was behaving flirtatiously for the senator's benefit, not his. He reversed his direction again, furious with her for using him to make another man jealous, and determined to punish her for it.

"Yes," he told her, moistening his lips. "I'll find a place."

$\mathcal{T}$hirty-seven

$\mathcal{M}$iranda faced Steven across the scarred wooden table between them. She had not removed her hat or gloves.

They were in the parlor of a tavern in suburban London. Upstairs there were rooms where salesmen and other itinerants stayed
when they were on the road—Miranda wondered if they brought
women here—but this private parlor, if far from luxurious, was
clean and smelled pleasantly of furniture wax. The carpet was worn
and the chintz of the armchairs and draperies faded, but with a
bright fire in the grate and green plants on the windowsills, both of
them should have been more comfortable than they were.

Steven had been talking steadily since they came in. He had
made no attempt to touch her. In the uncompromising light of day
he could see how strained she was, how distant. Had he imagined
those few electrifying moments while they danced the night before?
He couldn't believe she had changed toward him, and he was determined to share what he had come to tell her: the solution to their
problem.

"There it is," he finished. "London is not New York and
England is not America. We would not be ostracized here, except by

people we've never met and would not care to know." He stopped. She was so still! "Miranda, aren't you going to talk to me at all?"

She wanted to tell him how very dear he was to her, what a joy it was just to look at him, how she would miss him every day of her life.

What she said was "Steven, I'm going to have a child."

He sat back in his chair, astonished. He imagined an earthquake must feel like this, everything displaced, rearranged, altered.

Women rarely conceived at her time of life! His eyes were sweeping up and down her body. If it was his child, she would be about four months along, but with tightly laced corsets and those bell-shaped skirts, it was impossible to tell.

"It's Paul's," she said, answering his unspoken question. "I didn't think I could . . ." Her voice trailed off.

"But what . . . ?" he whispered. "When?"

"In Cairo. I think I even know which night."

He flinched.

She drew a deep breath. "I was asleep one night and when I woke he was making love to me. But I was greedy for it, and he was greedy for me."

He lowered his head until it rested in his hands. "Don't," he groaned. "Don't."

"I think I conceived that night, but something else happened too. Up until then, Paul was you and you were Paul. It was unbearable, the three of us in bed. I told you that!"

"Miranda, for God's sake!"

"But that night was different," she rushed on. "That night he wasn't you, he was himself, my husband, in a way he had never been before, claiming what was his. And I love him. I always did, but not as completely as I do now. I have you to thank for that."

She clasped and reclasped her hands. "We were living in a dream, you and I, a dream aboard an enchanted ship. You were wise enough to see that from the start and now I know it too."

He raised his head and saw her haunted face. It was over; he

knew that now. Her pregnancy had totally transfigured her and the nature of his love for her. She no longer belonged to him, but first to the child inside her, then to Paul.

He wanted to run from the pain he saw in her eyes, but he was too much its cause to do that. He would always miss her. She had been a sanctuary not only for his desire but for himself, a haven for his sadness, and he had to protect her, all of her, her mind and her heart as well as her body. If she had compromised the standards she was raised on, it had been for love of him, and he had to be worthy of that.

"Yes, it was a dream," he heard himself say. "But every moment of it was true for us. You would never have left your husband, but if, by some magic, we could have stayed on that ship, you would never have left me."

A tentative smile played upon her face. "Do you believe that?" she asked, hanging on his reply.

"I believe it because it's so."

Tears rolled down her upturned face, and she did not avoid his touch now. He enfolded her and kissed her wet cheeks.

"Paul knows," she said.

Recollecting Paul's behavior the night before, Steven nodded. "Have you discussed it?"

She shook her head. "But since this happened he and I seem to understand each other without words."

"I'm glad of that," he said, supposing she referred to her pregnancy and admiring Paul's restraint more than ever.

She framed his face with her hands and kissed him softly, a wistful, yearning kiss with the echo of passion in it. Then she cradled his head close to her breasts. "I'll never forget you, Steven. I'll always think of you and love you and go back inside that dream with you, just for a little while."

In the silence, fear suddenly seized him. He held her at arm's length. "Miranda, it's dangerous for you to have a child!"

"I've had two others."

"But that was years ago!"

"I never even thought of that," she said.

"It isn't too late to do something about it."

She was still again, thinking, before she shook her head. "No, that's dangerous too. Even more so."

"Not if it's done by an expert. Miranda, even if I never see you again, I must know you're still in the world, so I can hear about you and know you're alive." He shuddered, seeing Alicia's open coffin, the still, white figure holding that tiny waxen doll.

"Hush, you're being morbid," she said.

"I'm amazed Paul hasn't suggested it."

"He may when I tell him."

He was speechless for a moment. "But you said he knows!"

"I meant he knows you're my lover. But I haven't told him about the child yet. I wanted to tell you first so I could promise him honestly that you and I will never meet again."

"Good God, Miranda! Hasn't it occurred to you that this might be the last straw for him? He might not want to deal with the filthy gossip there might be about whose it is, or even the absurdity of having another child so late in life. You could avoid all of that if you did the reasonable thing."

"Would you want me to do it if it were yours?"

"Yes," he said. "*Yes!* It's you I love."

But she shook her head.

He gathered her into his arms and rocked her, that smothering guilt, all too familiar, enshrouding him. "Miranda, what have I done to you?"

"I was lucky to find you," she whispered. "I wouldn't trade one second I lived with you for the clearest conscience on earth."

"Promise me something."

"If I can."

"If you need me, in any way, for anything, if Paul is not as . . . forgiving as you think he'll be . . . you'll tell me. You'll let me help you, even from a distance."

"Yes," she whispered. "I promise."

They stayed in each other's arms for a few more moments of anguish and sweetness and the ineffable memory of passion shared. Then they said good-bye and left the tavern in separate hansoms, as they had arrived.

There was a wire waiting for Steven at Brown's, but he did not open it immediately. He stayed in the gathering darkness of his sitting room for an hour, staring at nothing, trying to put all of it together. He could understand Miranda, but Paul was unfathomable. To know what he knew and still tolerate the fact of Steven! It was unnatural. Or he loved his wife far too much to throw her to the wolves.

Steven had no appetite for dinner and he changed his coat for a smoking jacket. It was when he was back in the sitting room that he remembered the telegraph envelope and opened it.

Claire would arrive at the end of the week and wanted him to book her at Brown's and to meet her ship when it docked in London. He was overwrought and depressed after his meeting with Miranda and he looked forward to the comfort Claire would provide. He slept badly that night, and on the following morning he reserved the room adjoining his sitting room for her before he took a long walk in the cold, damp January air.

The week seemed to crawl by, and he spent as many hours as he could with the solicitor retained by Tri-Panalco, drawing up the necessary papers and following the progress of negotiations on the new Hay-Pauncefote Treaty until the day of Claire's arrival finally came.

He was disappointed to see how forbidding she looked when she saw him, but when she stepped off the gangway she smiled, hugged him, and called him "little brother" as she always did.

He collected her luggage, helped her into a hansom, and sat next to her, holding her hand. She told him about the crossing and he told her about Tri-Panalco, but he could sense a great flood dammed up inside her and she rounded on him as soon as they were alone in the little parlor.

"What is this nonsense about deserting your family and your country to live in England?"

"Did you come all this way just to ask me that?"

"Yes! Wouldn't you if I suddenly decided to become an orphan in a foreign land with no better explanation for it than a career change? What of your political career? What of you, Steven, and the rest of your life?"

"I'll be all right here!"

"I want to know why you made such a mad decision."

"And I'll tell you, but first let me order something for you. What shall it be?"

"A pot of strong coffee, if they know how to make it," she said, and withdrew to her bedroom.

He ordered coffee for her and tea for himself, then he poured a tot of whisky and swallowed it neat. He waited until she emerged, her bonnet and coat removed, her hair carefully arranged but her expression giving clear evidence of her anxiety.

"Who is she?" Claire demanded.

He shrugged. "You could always see through me. She's married."

"Lord! What an ugly business. Tell me the rest."

He told her everything, including his good intentions and his attempt to let go of Miranda when she left London for Cairo. "And it worked," he said. "Or I thought it was working. I was beginning to see a great deal of Kitt McAllister, and she's an unusually interesting person."

"And Mrs. Cunningham?"

"I told you. She had put an end to it before she left for Cairo."

"But when she came back you decided to try again."

He nodded. "And she refused again."

"She has more sense than you do," Claire said.

"She's pregnant," he said.

Claire gasped. "Don't tell me it's yours!"

He shook his head. "No, it's her husband's. For some reason our—" He hesitated.

"Your affair." She said it for him.

"It was far more than an affair. She made me understand that I wasn't uniquely responsible for Alicia's death—and my son's. No one else could do that for me." He looked at her. "Not even you."

"Steven, the woman was too infatuated to criticize you! And you wanted someone who knew all about you and still loved you in a way no sister could." She waited, and after a moment she sighed and said, "Tell me the rest."

"For some reason the time we spent together ignited a spark in her marriage that had not been there for twenty years. They've discovered each other in that way."

"And he just . . . accepted such an intimate change in his wife?"

"The reason would have been obvious to any man, but they've never discussed it. She believes her husband knows who he was."

"You speak of yourself in the third person!"

"It seems now that it was someone else, that we were two other people at the time."

"The man would be a fool to accept that—or a saint!"

He shrugged. "He's no fool. And he loves her."

She touched her handkerchief to her lips in a nervous gesture he had never seen before. "Twenty years of marriage," she said. "How old is she?"

"About forty."

"What a time of life to conceive," Claire said, shaking her head. "Do you think her husband will accept this child as his own?"

"They were away for many weeks. He'll know it's his."

"Even if he does, will everyone else? Steven, they used to hang women for adultery, or brand them or banish them. They're not much kinder to them now."

"I know what I've done to her! Don't you think I know?"

Claire's gray eyes filled with sudden tears at the look on her brother's face. "I'm sorry for you both," she said gently. "But she's a grown woman, not some silly girl. She knew what she was doing."

"I wouldn't have lost my sanity over some silly girl," he said bitterly.

"No. Your little troll has always protected you from that. But why would any of this make you decide to live here in London?"

"Before I knew about the child, I thought it would be easier for us to live together here and to marry as soon as her divorce was final. There are far fewer people who know us. Of course that's impossible now, but I could never live in the same city and stay away from her."

The waiter arrived and they waited until he had set down the tray and departed.

"Never is a long time. You must come home and try!" Claire said.

"No, it would make things more difficult for her." He looked at her contritely. "You were very good to come, Claire. I wish I could do as you suggest, but I can't."

"Oh, Steven," his sister sighed. "You waited all these years to fall in love, and then it was with a married woman who's pregnant in middle age with her husband's child." She poured a second cup of coffee and sugared it but did not drink it. "How can I leave you here by yourself? What will you do?"

"Attend to business. There's a dangerous partner in Tri-Panalco and he has to be watched."

"Who is he?"

"Hobart Cunningham."

"Not her husband!" Claire was dumbfounded.

He shook his head. "Her brother-in-law."

"You're making me very angry! Is your interest in the company an excuse to maintain some contact with her?"

He helped himself to a cup of tea. "It's really amazing how I've grown to like this stuff," he said, raising his cup to his lips.

She ignored his newly acquired taste for tea, but she knew that stubborn scowl of his from infancy. Steven had always refused to obey orders. He had to be persuaded, and that took time.

She took another tack. "I suppose the Panama Canal is an exciting project, but one day your business with it will be finished. What then?"

"The world's a busy place. I'll find another project."

She could not restrain herself. "And have canals and bridges instead of a wife and children and a home of your own! That isn't the stuff of life, foolish man! That's an invitation to loneliness and misery."

"You're probably right," he agreed gloomily. "But I can't go back to New York City now. It's where she lives."

"Run for the senate, then, and live in Washington. You can do it on your own, you don't need Haggerty." She glanced at Steven. "I read that he had returned to New York."

"And good riddance—although this canal business will be very profitable."

"Tom says America's growing like mushrooms after a rainstorm and needs control or it'll go crazy as a rutting bull." She colored at the unintended revelation that she and her husband spoke freely to each other about such earthy matters. It implied an intimacy rare between men and women in their day, married or not.

"Tom's right about that," Steven said, ignoring her blush, pleased for her and her healthy marriage. His sister had always been so understated, so nearly spartan, he had not paid much attention to the sensuality in her nature.

Even if she disagreed with him, at least she understood him.

"I'm in no mood for politics right now," he said. "I'm in the mood for a bath and a drink and dinner at the Savoy. How does that sound?"

She nodded, so grieved by his weary face that she stopped arguing. Still, she was determined to have her way in the end. He would *not* become an exile, not while she drew breath!

——— • ———

Lady Burdon and Kitt were already seated in the Savoy dining room when Steven and Claire arrived.

"Who do you suppose she is?" Lady Burdon asked, finishing her coquilles St. Jacques.

"If you don't know, she must be new in London." Kitt had suddenly lost her appetite for asperges tièdes au vinaigrette.

Lady Burdon raised her lorgnette. "Not English or French by her style," she murmured, "but she has an intelligent face. Where *does* he find these women?"

"She looks American," Kitt said. She hadn't seen Steven since the Boxing Day gala at Lady Burdon's, and from where she was sitting she could feast her eyes on him. It was not a seemly pastime for a woman about to engage herself to another man—which was what Kitt had decided to do as soon as Jean-Baptiste returned from France. In fact, this dinner was a small celebration of her decision, revealed to Lady Burdon that afternoon, to accept his proposal.

"Ah, he has seen us," Lady Burdon said with a veiled glance at Kitt. Both women returned Steven's polite nod in their direction. "I must know who she is. Would you be upset if I invited them to take coffee with us in the lounge after dinner?"

"Not at all. I'm as curious as you are."

Calling for paper and pen, Lady Burdon dispatched her invitation and received an affirmative reply. Kitt lost what little appetite she had.

Steven introduced his sister to Lady Burdon and then to Kitt.

"I've looked forward to this," Kitt said. "I've heard so much about you."

"As I have about you," Claire returned. "Your reputation has spread, even to the farmlands of Upstate New York."

"There are feminists in Ipswich," Lady Burdon said. "Why not in Upstate New York?" She glanced again at Kitt, but Kitt seemed at ease and appeared so for the rest of the evening.

"A very engaging woman," Lady Burdon said to Kitt in the carriage going home. "What do you suppose she's doing here?"

"Perhaps she missed her brother. There are ten years between them and he was mainly in her charge when he was small."

Lady Burdon nodded. "Yes, well, tonight he seems to need looking after, as he did on the ship." She turned to Kitt. "But attractive as his melancholy is, he needs a sister or a friend, and you don't want to be either."

Kitt patted her hand. "Not to worry, dear lady."

The carriage stopped at the mansion, the steps were put in place by the footman, and Lady Burdon was handed out. "I'll send Alton out to you," she told Kitt, Alton having spent the evening with Lady Burdon's maid. "Rest well, and ring me tomorrow."

Kitt waved and sat back, relaxing her guard. Steven had spoken to her this evening, but she had spoken *at* him, almost through him. It was virtually impossible for her to look at him and not give herself away. She wanted desperately to comfort him, to know what made him look so bleak, even to ask if he had seen Miranda privately. She wanted to shout at him for risking so much, for throwing away so much. She wanted to tell him she loved him.

Alton came out of the mansion and got into the carriage. Lady Burdon, allied with Alton to get Kitt safely married to the count, had just told her briefly about their encounter with Steven James at the Savoy.

Alton was worried, particularly since the count would be away for at least another week. A lot could happen in a week, especially to someone like Miss Kitt!

"Was it a nice evening?" she asked when the carriage was moving again.

"It always is with Lady Pat," Kitt said. "And we ran into Mr. James and his sister, Mrs. Harden, who is here for a short visit."

"A long way to come for a short visit," Alton commented.

Kitt thought so herself. Claire had left her husband and children to make a long voyage. Why? Steven had never portrayed her as a woman who would cross the Atlantic on a shopping spree, and her style—quality without flamboyance—confirmed that.

In moments the carriage had reached Dover Street and Kitt went to her room while Alton locked up before coming to help Kitt undress. She found her at the window, looking out at nothing in particular.

"Is it the headache?" Alton asked.

Kitt shook her head and held up a hand. It meant she was not in a talking mood.

Alton turned back the bed and plumped up the pillows. "A good sleep is what you need. It isn't every day a lady decides to marry royalty."

"He's only a count, Mary Frances. That's not nearly so grand."

"Grand enough," Alton said briskly. "And a real gent too."

"Gentleman," Kitt corrected Mary Frances automatically, getting into bed. "It's vulgar to shorten words."

"Yes, Miss Kitt," Alton said, extinguishing the gas lamp. "I wish you a good night."

"And you," said Kitt. She tried to summon up Jean-Baptiste's thin, aristocratic face, his clear brown eyes, his gentle manner. He had told her about his family's chateau south of Paris, about growing up as the only son—after five girls!—and thus the cherished heir to the title and the estates, and about his long and fierce refusal of a socially correct marriage without love, a refusal that had earned him the fury of his parents.

Jean-Baptiste was certainly a romantic, although how he managed to be a skeptic as well was a mystery. She wondered how his family would react to Kitt McAllister.

"Louisa, Comtesse d'Yveine," she murmured to herself as she fell asleep. But it was Steven who invaded her dreams again and made her toss and turn most of the night.

—— · ——

"I liked them," Claire told Steven in the lift at Brown's. "Miss McAllister is charming and Lady Burdon is right out of Oscar Wilde. How long have they known each other?"

"Since the *Sylvania*."

"An extraordinary vessel," Claire said, raising her brows. "So many dramas began aboard her."

They got off the lift and walked along the corridor to her room, where they said good night. Claire prepared for bed as quickly as she could and sighed when she was finally beneath the covers, wondering how badly Steven had burned his political bridges. She was still certain that politics was the kind of challenge that could bring him home, but the merest whiff of scandal would make a career in government impossible.

She wondered, too, if Steven would ever marry again. After the tragedy of his marriage to Alicia, Steven would not have let down his emotional defenses over any ordinary woman. A rare pity that Miranda was married and really too old for him. Claire wanted to meet her, however remote that possibility seemed.

Claire also decided to learn more about Miss McAllister, with whom she had felt an immediate kinship. Steven said he had been seeing her, and his letters had made it clear that he admired her. Yet this evening the two had been awkward with each other.

Claire fell asleep trying to work out why.

Steven was gone when she awoke late the following morning, but he had left a note saying he would be back at two to take her to luncheon. She rang for coffee, and when it was brought there was another note on her tray, this one from Lady Burdon, inviting Claire to one of Miss McAllister's lectures the following afternoon at teatime.

"Tea!" Claire protested, pouring out the feeble liquid that passed for coffee in England. "They make a religion of it." But she accepted Lady Burdon's invitation.

Thirty-eight

Claire listened attentively to Kitt McAllister, noting the composure that was unexpected in someone with such an animated personality. She was both reserved and forceful.

"Such a vivacious young woman," she said to Lady Burdon as they joined the applause. "And courageous. I admire that."

"Some people are still shocked by her," Lady Burdon replied as the room began to empty. "But times are changing. The merry antics of the Prince of Wales are easier to emulate than the virtues of his mother, much as people respect the old girl."

"I've heard many tales about Prince Edward."

"Most of them are true. His Royal Highness boasts a long list of mistresses. Some of them were received by the Princess of Wales in the approved fashion of a Victorian wife. I don't know how she managed to do that. But Victorianism is beginning to fade."

"Not in America. We are more Victorian than you are."

"That is because it was imported, and I'm told Americans are mad about imports. But here is Kitt," Lady Burdon said, turning.

"Your speech was a real rouser, my dear. Contributions will pour in."

"We must raise voices as well as money," Kitt said, greeting Claire, "or nothing will ever change."

"Mrs. Harden and I were just discussing Victorian rules and regulations."

"In my country," Claire said, "the public demands virtue—or the appearance of it—in our elected officials."

"Yes," Kitt agreed. "The senator says that politicians must fit into a mold."

"He fits no mold I've ever come across!" Lady Burdon remarked.

"He's what is meant by rugged individualism," Kitt replied, glowing.

It was how she said it—defensively, protectively, even proudly— that spoke volumes to Claire. Kitt, she supposed, knew what her feelings were; women usually did. But Steven seemed to have no idea that Miss McAllister was in love with him.

A plan began to form in Claire's mind.

"Come and sit near me," Lady Burdon invited Claire when the house had emptied, patting the seat beside her on the sofa. The other ladies had gone home in a swish of skirts and a clatter of carriage wheels on the cobbled streets. Kitt was in the library, drafting a reply to a newspaper article that referred to her as "the tempestuous but ill-advised Miss McAllister."

"How long will you be here?" Lady Burdon asked Claire.

"Only for a few days more."

"Such a short visit! Can't you be persuaded to stay?"

Claire shook her head. "I have a husband and family to consider. My sole purpose in coming was to bring my brother home."

Lady Burdon puffed on a cheroot. "And will he go?"

"I'm not sure."

"I hope that he will, not merely for his sake but for Kitt's."

There! Claire thought. *I knew there was something between those two!* But Lady Burdon's next words amazed her.

"Kitt is going to marry a very worthy man."

"I'm delighted to hear it, but what has Steven to do with that?"

"Come, Mrs. Harden, I think you're clever enough to have guessed." When Claire said nothing, she went on. "Kitt is a practical creature in most respects, but she is utterly besotted by your brother. It would be difficult not to be; he is exceptionally attractive. But his heart is elsewhere."

"I know that," Claire said.

"Ah? Well, then, you can understand my concern. Kitt has decided to accept the Count d'Yveine's proposal as soon as he returns from France, and it would be a disaster for her to change her mind because of a hopeless fascination."

"You're very fond of Kitt," Claire said.

Lady Burdon nodded.

"Even so, you have no right to meddle in her life."

The faint light of battle gleamed in Lady Burdon's eyes. "Nor have you."

"He's my brother," Claire said.

"Friends one chooses are apt to be more compatible than the relatives inflicted upon one," Lady Burdon replied. "I have grown very fond of Kitt and I will do everything in my power to protect her from her own romantic impulses."

"Perhaps her fascination, as you call it, is not hopeless."

"It is, as long as your brother's is."

"We shall see." And Claire nodded slowly, taking up the gauntlet. Lady Burdon was a formidable adversary, but Claire had an advantage: She knew Steven through and through.

They were talking about the queen's failing health when Kitt came in.

——— • ———

The rain came down in sheets that evening and Claire and Steven dined at the hotel. Claire spoke admiringly of Kitt, and from Steven's response gathered that he shared her opinion.

"Do you know the man she is to marry?" she asked him.

He looked up from his poached turbot, startled. "I had no idea she was engaged."

"To some French count or other," Claire said. "It's to be announced when he returns."

"I know him."

"Don't tell me you met him on that wretched ship!"

Steven nodded. "Who told you Kitt was going to marry?"

"Lady Burdon. I like the old dragon, but I think she's pushing Miss McAllister into this marriage."

"Kitt is not easily pushed."

"I very much doubt it's a love match on her side."

He shook his head. "What are you, some kind of crystal gazer who can divine these things? You hardly know Kitt and you've never met the count."

"Tell me about him."

"He's a French aristocrat with a philosophical bent. He's a true gentleman with a good nature and a kind heart. And he's probably the only person I've met who's more widely read than Kitt."

"Do you think he cares for her?"

"I'm sure he does."

"And she for him?"

He hesitated. "Yes, but it's difficult to say in what way."

Claire put down her fork. "It isn't difficult for me. In the ways that matter between a man and a woman she cares for you, Steven. She lights up whenever your name is mentioned. She . . . sparkles."

"You're imagining things! She's horrified by my ties to Miranda."

"So am I, but that doesn't stop my loving you. I simply cannot understand how a man can be so blind to a woman's love for him."

"Claire, you exaggerate!"

"Think about it, and I'm sure you'll conclude that I don't exaggerate at all."

He was quiet for a moment, sipping his wine. At length he asked her, "What would you have me do? I didn't love Alicia as I should have when I married her. I won't make that mistake again."

"You didn't admire Alicia as you do Miss McAllister. Alicia was sweet and pretty, all the things a submissive little wife should be. The trouble is that none of that inspires you at all. But Kitt is extraordinary! Or do you find extraordinary women offputting?"

"Of course not! She's a great friend and she's wonderful company. But that isn't love and I can't turn it off and on like electric current!"

She took his hand. "Little brother, listen to me, please. Sooner or later someone will replace Miranda. Not completely, perhaps. She'll always have a place in your heart. But I'm talking about the rest of your life. You are not a solitary man, nor are you one to be content with casual pleasures bought like cabbages. Someday you'll want someone of your own, so why not now and why not Kitt? Don't let this chance at happiness escape you because the timing is wrong."

He listened, remembering what had been lost to him and Miranda because of bad timing. "I never realized how coldly objective you can be," he said.

"Only where those I love are concerned," she said with sincerity that was not in the least cold. "Promise me you'll think it over? It will comfort me when I leave you."

"You've only just arrived! Can't you stay at least another week?"

"No, Steven, I miss Tom and the children and I'd only go on meddling in your affairs."

"If I let you meddle, will you stay just one more week? There's so much I want to show you. London is a fabulous city—and our roots are here. Please, Claire?"

She had never been able to resist him when he pleaded like that, but she was not sentimental enough to let an opportunity pass her by. "I'll stay *provided* you give me your word you'll come home before you make a final decision about where to live."

He was suddenly nostalgic for the sprawling fields of home, for the long summer days and the crystal air of winter, for the sheer space of his country. He was homesick for America, a country not even half formed, her potential still hidden. She was, like Gulliver, a giant bound by flimsy restraints, certain to get free and bestride the world one day, given her gift for industry, technology, and expansion.

America was as turbulent as Britain used to be when the Empire was forming. Order and serenity were agreeable but not as stimulating to Steven as turbulence, discovery, and new frontiers. And, quite simply, he missed the faces of his family.

"Yes," he agreed. "I'll come home before I make a final decision."

——— · ———

Several days later Mary Frances hurried from Dover Street to St. John's Wood, where she rang the bell at the service entrance. It was permissible to use the front door late at night when she joined Miss Kitt in the carriage, but not during the day when she came uninvited. Mary Frances had no desire to enter a higher social stratum. She wanted only to get to the top of her own. When Miss Kitt married His Worship she would have arrived. Lady's maid to a countess!

"But you could do so much more," Miss Kitt had insisted just that morning over their daily lessons. "You might teach or nurse or open a shop of your own."

"I'd as lief learn as teach, and I have no wish to be nursing or selling, miss," was Alton's airy rejoinder. "I like doing what I do."

"But one day you'll want to marry! And husbands can die and leave you with a flock of children to provide for. Every day I hear the most harrowing tales."

"Now, Miss Kitt," Alton had soothed. "I'll not marry, I promise you, and so I'll not be left with kiddies to provide for."

Alton had said as much to her own mother, whom she went to visit once a month.

"Yer no dummy," her mother had replied with approval. "It's naychur gives yer the itch and by the time yer sees it's a mug's game it's too late."

"Then why do women marry?"

"People's allus tellin' 'em be fruitful and multiply." She had given Mary Frances a sharp, appraising look. "Don't let me ketch yer multiplyin' without a husband."

"I'd rather eat worms," Mary Frances had assured Mrs. Alton.

Inside the service entrance, Alton greeted Lady Burdon's maid, Evans, who was having a cup of tea in the servants' parlor. Evans was about a dozen years older than Mary Frances and about twenty-five pounds heavier. That and her experience in service had given her dignity and authority. Mary Frances had far outstripped Evans in education, but she took care not to let anyone know it. It had not escaped her notice that education was belittled by those who did not have it.

This morning she carried—conspicuously—an envelope that was her excuse for coming to Lady Burdon today. Since there were frequent notes exchanged between Dover Street and St. John's Wood, no one suspected this visit was any different.

"You know the way," Evans said. "Her Ladyship is in the morning room."

Alton hung up her hat and coat outside the kitchen and said good day to Mrs. Beebe, the starched, rosy-faced cook, before she

made her way up the back stairs and along the wide halls to the morning room, where she knocked at the door.

"Come," Lady Burdon's voice said, and Alton went in and closed the door behind her.

"Good afternoon, Alton." Lady Burdon looked up from her book. "What's happened? You look about to burst with news."

Alton, like Lady Pat, did not waste time waltzing around a subject. "Miss Kitt's gone to the shops with Mrs. Harden."

"Again? That makes three times this week!" She paused. "Did they go alone?"

Alton nodded, frowning. "I do wish His Worship would come back."

"I, also, but I've just had a letter saying he is delayed for another week."

"It might be a good idea to tell him what's happening. That would hurry him."

Lady Burdon shook her head. "His pride would be so wounded that he would ignore the message and demand the messenger's head on a plate."

Alton shivered, not doubting for a moment any excesses ascribed to the aristocracy. "Himself is takin' the two ladies out to dinner this evening."

"Mrs. Harden is a very clever woman," Lady Burdon said. "But I'm a wily old bird and I shall find a way." She smiled. "Alton, thank you for telling me. You must go home now in case the ladies should return from shopping earlier than expected. I will think of a way to deal with this."

Alton waited, but Lady Burdon shook her head. "No, I can't tell you how, my dear. I don't really know yet."

"Yes, Your Ladyship," Alton said, and went out. Downstairs she gathered her things, graciously refused a cup of tea, and hurried back home to await new developments. There was nothing more she could do today but worry about how Claire Harden had managed to coax Kitt into dining with the man who had smashed her illusions like a porcelain cup.

But Steven, Claire, and Kitt never went out that evening. Queen Victoria was dead and London plunged into deep mourning.

———— · ————

"It's the end of an era," the earl said to the Cunninghams when the news reached Inderby. It would be their last visit before Hobart took his family back to America. It was a still, gray day and a blanket of fog wrapped the grounds as if in mourning for the departed monarch.

Lady Caroline nodded. "Life will never be the same."

"But she's been in seclusion for years," Cynthia said. "Why should anything change?"

"She'd begun to play a greater role again before she became too frail. And her influence was enormous," Alastair said. "She's been an icon for so long."

Hobart looked up from the newspaper he had been reading. "What kind of king do you suppose Edward will be?"

"You never know," Paul said. "History is crowded with rulers who changed radically when they came to power."

Miranda said nothing, Hobart noticed. She had been unusually quiet during this visit to their prospective in-laws. Hobart had expected to be on the high seas by now, but Alastair had convinced him that it would be unseemly to rush Cynthia away right after Her Majesty's death, leaving her fiancé to mourn alone. A subject, even a future one by marriage, had responsibilities to the monarch.

"Not that any of you give two hangs for her," Hobart had scoffed.

"But I *do*," Alastair had said firmly. "This is my country and she's the only queen I've ever known. I owe her some respect."

"You English with your manners!"

"You Americans with your lack of them!"

They had left it at that, having established a bantering personal

relationship that in no way reflected their serious business affiliation, where Alastair was the eager student and Hobart the mentor. But in this instance, Hobart had given in and delayed their departure until after the state funeral.

The doors opened and the butler entered, followed by two footmen with heavy tea trays and two maids with trolleys. There was cinnamon toast, fruitcake, pound cake, petits fours, and biscuits in addition to the usual sandwiches. Plates and napkins were provided and the trolleys presented. Miranda took some dry biscuits with her tea.

Paul leaned forward, his words hidden by the genteel bustle around them. "Are you ill?" he asked. "You've hardly eaten today—or for the past week, for that matter."

"I'm all right, Paul, thank you. I never eat between meals, you know that." She smiled. "And that's all the English seem to do."

He smiled back. "I can't argue with that." *Nor with how you look,* he thought.

Once tea had been served, conversation resumed, with the earl droning on about Victoria's days of glory, Hobart reading his newspaper, and Miranda, Paul, and Lady Caroline preoccupied by private thoughts.

"Would you like to walk?" Walford asked Cynthia, his voice very low.

"I would," Cynthia replied. "If it were not so cold."

"Wear walking boots and your fur cloak."

"Will they keep me warm enough?"

"Until we get where we're going. Then *I* will."

She looked up at him, hovering over her chair as he had aboard the *Sylvania,* and her demure expression became beguiling as naturally as a bud becomes a flower. "In that case . . ." she said, rising from her chair.

"We're going to take a turn," Alastair announced to the room.

"In this weather?" Lady Caroline frowned.

"But you told me the English thrive on this weather." Hobart smiled at the countess in the same way he had the day before in an unused room high up under the eaves. He had smiled at her protests, smiled while he gripped her wrists with one of his iron hands and did things to her with the other that her husband had never presumed to do, things at once shocking and stirring that made her chirp like a canary.

Remembering that smile and the astonishing acts that had accompanied it, Lady Caroline blushed and bent over her teacup as if she were about to read its leaves.

"Be careful," she said, warning her son of more than the weather. She had already told him about Cynthia's meeting with that large American and got the same tepid reaction from him she had received from her husband and Mr. Cunningham. "Youthful high jinks," the earl had said. "We all became friendly on the crossing" was Alastair's reply.

What would it take, Lady Caroline wondered, *to stop this marriage?* Only a full-blown scandal would do, and she was not willing to be a part of it.

She was not blind to the real meaning of her encounter with Hobart Cunningham the day before. He had not succumbed to her faded charms! He was using her seduction as a kind of blackmail and the price of his silence was an end to her interference.

What a beastly man he is! she thought. But she knew she could not resist another invitation from him. That was the worst of it. The next time, he had told her, he would undress her completely. The prospect made her tingle with anticipation.

"Don't be too long," Miranda was saying, addressing Cynthia and avoiding Alastair's eyes as was her habit.

"We shall stay well within the bounds of propriety, Mrs. Cunningham," Alastair promised archly, and the young couple left.

—— • ——

Cynthia ran up the wide staircase to the palatial room she had been given and called for Baxter to bring her boots and her hooded fox-lined cloak. She was impatient as Baxter unbuttoned her shoes and laced up her walking boots, but at last she was ready.

"Gloves," she said to Baxter, feeling warm and sensual inside the white fox. While the maid scurried about, Cynthia looked around the room, far more luxurious than some of the mansion's other bedrooms, which showed signs of neglect. It would be hers one day, this room and all of Inderby and Inderby House in London and other establishments in Ireland and Scotland she had not yet seen, all hers to do with as she liked.

She would preside over all of those walls, defensive walls so thick that no one would ever dream she had been rejected by the one man she loved and—if Miranda was right—was about to marry one who did not want her as a woman. Even if she was not clear about all the details, she felt profoundly rejected by such a possibility. Her feelings alternated between bitter anger and wounded pride. She had to prove she was desirable, no matter who was hurt by it, even herself.

Baxter handed her the gloves. "Take care, Miss Cynthia."

Cynthia was pulling the gloves on. "Of what?" she snapped.

"The cold and the snow, miss," Baxter said, flustered. She had been Miss Cynthia's maid for six years and she knew a great deal more than she let on.

Baxter didn't trust the viscount, not for a minute, any more than she trusted Mr. Hobart. In Baxter's opinion, they were cut from the same cloth, even if one looked like an angel and the other like the devil himself.

They both hid behind manners, but Baxter knew that Mr. Hobart made particular demands on his wife and that Miss Cynthia either did not know it or chose to ignore it.

"What a comeuppance it would be," Baxter had whispered to Mrs. Paul's maid, Rooney, "if the daughter married the same kind of brute her father is!"

Rooney had agreed. "But it's a comeuppance no woman would wish on another."

Cynthia regathered her skirts and floated down the stairs, Baxter forgotten. She was thinking about Walford. There had been nothing more than heated kisses between them, but Cynthia had decided that there would be more, and her heart beat a little faster at the thought. Some of that was anticipation, but more of her excitement was vindication after Steven's behavior at the National Gallery. She had virtually offered herself to him and he had pretended not to understand the offer! It only added insult to injury!

Walford had been very suggestive just then about keeping her warm. What was he going to do? Where? It was all spectacularly exciting, quite the most thrilling adventure Cynthia had known in all of her guarded, insulated life.

"Here I am," she told Walford, who waited in the hall. He looked marvelous in a tweed coat with a shoulder cape and a deerstalker cap.

He smiled at her appraisingly, helped her to raise the fur-lined hood, and tied it securely for her by its silken strings. "You'll do."

"Is that all?" she replied, disappointed by such faint praise.

"It's enough." He took her hand and pulled it through his arm. "Shall we?"

Thirty-nine

They left by a side entrance and walked across the lawn toward a thick stand of trees whose snow-covered branches reached for them like spectral arms. The snow made their footsteps inaudible, and it seemed to Cynthia that the ghosts of Inderbys past hovered around them.

"Where are we going?" she asked when they reached the forest.

"To one of the follies," he said. "One of my great-uncles used it when he visited England. I'm sure you'll like it."

Something abrasive in his manner troubled her, but she went on generating small talk.

"Where did he visit from?"

"India. He commanded one of the border regiments."

"Do you ever wish you had gone out to India or Singapore?"

"All that swashbuckling? Not I. I like my comforts too well."

Again that sharp, dry tone, as if he disliked her.

He guided her off the main path and they went some distance through the trees before a building was visible. It was of neoclassical design with six soaring columns that should have been comical fronting such a small structure but instead seemed menacing to Cynthia in the gathering darkness of the winter afternoon.

"What a strange place," she said, aware that this was the first time she had been completely alone with Walford. They had been by themselves many times before, but there had always been people within call. Now they were in a forest, blanketed by snow and mist. It added to the atmosphere of fantasy and danger and romance. She felt like Beauty in the fairy tale. Would Walford remain a prince, or would he turn into the Beast as soon as they were inside?

"It's even stranger inside," he said. They climbed the four wide marble steps that led up to the pillars. He took a set of keys from his pocket and unlocked the door, pushing it open.

"Welcome," he said to Cynthia, and swept her up in his arms.

"What are you doing?" she protested.

"Carrying you over the threshold. Isn't that what Yankees do?"

"No!" she said. "It's bad luck before the wedding. Put me down."

He ignored her and carried her through the door, then kicked it closed with an angry thrust of his leg. A thrill went through her as his head bent to hers and he kissed her roughly.

"We're not supposed to do any of this before we're married," she said breathlessly when the kiss ended and he put her down.

"We're as good as," he said, untying the strings of her hood and pushing it back. "You said yourself it seemed a long time to wait, and I agree."

"I'm not sure we were talking about the same thing," she said frostily. His manner was definitely hostile; it made her uncomfortable. She decided to avoid the subject of what came after marriage, and looked around.

They were in a rectangular foyer, far too narrow for the baroque sideboard, flanked by two bulky chairs, that furnished it. The paneled walls were of pale sea green, probably found in a French chateau, and the moldings were gold. A large mirror in an ostentatious frame hung over the sideboard.

"Extravagant," Cynthia said. "It looks like a royal foyer that has somehow been compressed."

"There's more," Alastair said brusquely, taking her hand. "Come along."

"Why are the lamps lit? Is anyone else here?" she asked him.

"No, I came earlier and lit them."

"And it's terribly cold."

"There's a fireplace in here."

By the flickering gaslight she saw they were in a bedroom as small and as inappropriately decorated as the foyer. A large, very high bed with a set of steps next to it occupied over half the space. It was covered by a spread of faded turquoise brocade which matched the window hangings. A capacious velvet chaise stood on one side of the bed, and a screen, hiding what Cynthia presumed to be a washstand, on the other.

Alastair touched a match to the kindling lying ready in the grate, and it was when the fire blazed up that Cynthia could see the painted revelers on the ceiling. At first they seemed to be the usual collection of lightly clad nymphs and shepherds frolicking in a meadow, but on closer inspection she realized that the faded frescoes were of naked men and women in pairs, trios, and quartets, engaged in acts she could not have imagined in a thousand years.

Cynthia drew in her breath, too startled to look away until she felt Walford's arms come around her from behind and his hands cover her breasts. His thumbs rubbed the centers where her nipples were. It was the kind of behavior Cynthia had needed to disprove Miranda's filthy suspicions, but she suddenly knew she did not want his ardor to go any further. It was not how she had envisioned love, not hard hands on her breasts in this musty ruin with a lewd ceiling and an atmosphere of decadence.

In an easy motion he picked her up again and climbed the bed steps to deposit her on the bed like a bag of laundry. His tall body came down over the length of hers and he bent his head to nip her earlobes and her neck.

"Walford!" she protested when his hands squeezed her breasts. "No!"

He ignored her protests and held her down, his face close to hers so that the eyes seemed enormous. She was no longer reassured by his desire. She was afraid of it.

She pushed on his chest with all her strength and he relaxed his grip on her. "How dare you bring me to this filthy place and do such nasty things?"

His beautiful face was as hard as stone. "You led me to believe you wanted to consummate our marriage before the wedding. You told me to find a place. Here it is. And that"—and he waved an arm toward the ceiling—"is meant to amuse you."

"Amuse me? You must be mad!"

He shook her, then let her go very suddenly, as if *she* had offended *him*. "You're a tease, Miss Cynthia. You're accustomed to mesmerizing men with a toss of your curls, but your wiles didn't work on Steven James, did they?"

She stared at him, aghast.

He rolled over onto his back, took a flat black onyx case from his pocket, removed a cigarette, and lit it, sucking the smoke in deeply. "You were after him like a spaniel in season aboard the *Sylvania,* but he preferred the sumptuous Miranda. In Egypt you dreamed about him. I could tell, even while you were baiting your hook for me. But he was squiring the dynamic Miss McAllister. At Lady Pat's Boxing Day ball you capered like a Piccadilly slut—for *his* benefit, not mine. And my mother saw you with him at the National Gallery. Well, I'm not accustomed to playing second fiddle to anyone."

"You *are* mad!"

He got off the bed. "You did meet him, didn't you?"

She made no reply.

He looked at her with scorn. "Do you suppose I don't know your reasons for marrying me?"

"I'm sure you do!" she shot back, sitting up and sliding off the bed. "As well as I know yours for marrying me! They don't flatter either of us and would have been better left unsaid."

They glared at each other, both breathing hard. They were sleek, pampered, and dangerous, like a pair of angry tigers in a cage.

Cynthia was furious. She had the proof she wanted: Walford was like any other man. But the way he showed it did not live up to her romantic expectations. He seemed to dislike her even while he was kissing her. He seemed to want to hurt her! She was afraid of him but she was too proud to show it.

She had climbed down from the bed and now moved toward the door. "I'm going back to the Hall," she said. "I wish I'd never met you! I shall tell my father to break our engagement and I shall tell him why."

"Do you think that old rake will give up all that goes with me over a few paintings that shocked your delicate sensibilities?" he asked, mocking her. "Or because my ardor got the better of me? You know damn well he won't."

Deep inside her, she did know it. Her eyes darted around the room as if searching its dark corners for some answer to the dilemma and finding none. Walford didn't love her. He wasn't even fond of her. She could have lived with that. She did not seem to inspire the same kind of adoration in men that Miranda did. But that Walford could bring her to this seedy love nest to couple like those creatures on the ceiling was not only depraved, it was insulting.

At a loss, she gazed at him now with childlike woe, her lips trembling and her blue eyes shining with tears. "Oh, Walford, we always got on so well. We could have gone on. Why did you have to ruin everything?" She waited for the answer to that question, looking like a little girl lost, and suddenly her rosy mouth popped open, her tear-filled eyes grew round, and she pointed at him as if she had just had a revelation.

"You're jealous!"

"Jealous?" He was incredulous.

"You're jealous of Steven James!" she repeated triumphantly. "Because I admire him."

He glared at her and was about to deny it, then stopped, almost undone by the lightning realization that he *was* jealous, not of Steven James but of anyone Steven favored, no matter in what way and including Cynthia. He turned away from her, struck dumb by this stunning discovery, and forced to confront the true nature of his feelings for Steven.

He had last seen Steven at the meeting in Blenkinsop's office and had been hoping to see him ever since. He thought about him constantly, of how clever the American was—and how unflappable—when he was cutting off Hobart's attempts to dominate Tri-Panalco, how he had shown, subtly but clearly, that he did not hold Alastair responsible for Hobart's attempts to pirate the company. Alastair admired the way he distanced himself from that rogue Haggerty, and had even, according to Steele, engineered Haggerty's reluctant return to the United States.

And Alastair lingered, with a yearning unlike any in his experience, on Steven's height, his strong body, his thick black hair, and his craggy face. Walford was well acquainted with the hot, hard demands of mere lust, and this was very different.

What a colossal irony! He and Cynthia both wanted Steven, and Steven hadn't the least romantic interest in either of them.

He felt as if a thousand eyes were watching him while the truth of his real nature flayed at his defenses and stripped him naked to the world. He could hear the jeers of the wide circle of men who had so envied him his looks and his wicked ways since schooldays. He could feel the contempt they would heap on him if this other dishonorable love were revealed. It was one thing to indulge in occasional perversion out of curiosity; it was another to fall in love with a man.

Look what they had done only a few years before to Oscar Wilde, a writer of talent, even genius, for his unnatural love of Lord Alfred Douglas! They had tried the author, found him guilty, and sent him to jail for two years! Alastair would kill himself before he let that happen to him.

He must do something to hide what even that clod of a drago-man on the *dahabiyeh* had so easily perceived, what Lewis Wendall said he had known from his first look at Alastair. How many others knew—or would know if he were not crafty enough to hide it?

He had known that night on the Nile how to quell such rumors, and it was not by infuriating Cynthia! He must marry her as soon as it could be arranged. A beautiful, clever wife would be the perfect camouflage, maybe even the cure! He needed her for that almost more than he needed her money.

It was essential that she bear his children, many of them. He had come perilously close to ruining the real affinity they had, that witty camaraderie that had convinced everyone else they were in love.

"What a fool I've been," he said almost too softly for her to hear.

"Yes," she said, trembling with regret and relief, regret that they had said such ugly things to each other, relief that the ugliness was over, that he was apologizing, that she was saved from the ignominy of a broken engagement, that all he had and was would still be hers and no one would be able to say that she had been rejected by Walford. That is what they *would* have said. It was inconceivable that she would have rejected such a superb catch.

"I'm very sorry," Walford whispered. "Can you ever forgive me?"

"I don't know," she said in a small voice. She had been watching his back as he stood in utter silence, apparently too ashamed to look at her.

He turned now and she saw the lines etched upon his face by what she supposed was pure remorse.

"Jealousy is a fearful thing," he said. "I should have known that. It's the only thing that could make me treat you as I did just now. You are so very important to me and you seemed to prefer him." He stepped forward and took her hands. "Cynthia, I need you. I'm mortified by what I did and I swear I'll make it up to you." He paused, searching for the next cliché. "I dare not ask if you still love me. I can only ask you to forgive me for my infernal stupidity and let me treat you as you deserve."

She nodded.

Gently he patted her face dry with his white linen handkerchief and, after a moment's hesitation, put his arms around her. "I'll be good to you," he said. "I swear it. I could kick myself for frightening you like that."

She did not resist but nestled against him for a moment, her pride restored, her dignity repaired, her doubts erased, before she said, "It's time to go back. We've been here too long already."

He nodded, put a screen in front of the fire, turned off all the lamps but one, and took her arm to lead her out.

——— · ———

While the engaged couple were walking, Lady Caroline, pleading a headache, had gone to her boudoir and Paul and Miranda for a drive to the village. Hobart and the earl had retired to the library to smoke a cigar and have a drink.

"Fiendishly cold," the earl said, moving closer to the fire.

"You need central heating."

Inderby chuckled. "You can't heat a place this size," he said.

"You can heat part of it," Hobart replied. "I'll look into it. I have faith in Yankee ingenuity. Right now, though, I want to discuss the wedding plans. How will Her Majesty's passing affect us?"

"There'll be a year of mourning," the earl said, "which changes nothing for us. Then there'll be the coronation."

"How long after the mourning ends?" Hobart asked.

"Not decided yet. Six months to a year."

"That's precisely our problem. If they marry before the mourning's ended, they'll have to do it quietly. If they marry before the coronation, the coronation will eclipse the wedding. That won't do. I don't intend to let this wedding be insignificant."

"But you can't go against custom, my dear fellow!"

"Queens and coronations are not the custom in my country.

Therefore the wedding will be held in Washington, D.C., in June of this year."

"So soon? Impossible," spluttered the earl, and began raising objections, each of which Hobart argued down. The preparations would take far less time in the United States, where things were done with dispatch. The entire wedding party, including the Inderbys' guests, would be transported to Washington and lodged at hotels in the capital at Cunningham's expense. The wedding would be held in the Washington Cathedral with a reception to follow at the elegant Willard Hotel.

The earl was bewildered. "Why not New York? Why Washington?"

"I have influential friends in the capital who like this kind of publicity," Hobart said cryptically. He had many friends in government whom he paid handsomely in one way or another to keep tariffs up and corporations free to form secret monopolies despite the antitrust laws. "As you must have in Whitehall."

"Do these friends have anything to do with the Panama Canal?"

"They'll pass the legislation to make it possible. Which reminds me. Is the new treaty moving forward?"

"I haven't the foggiest notion."

"Good heavens, man! You're a member of the House of Lords. Find out! If the provisions of the Clayton-Bulwer Treaty are not reversed, there will be no funds voted for the canal!"

Hobart crossed his legs, pink with indignation at such feckless behavior, but when he noticed the earl's injured expression he mastered his wrath. "In any case, it can't harm our cause to invite politicians from both sides of the Atlantic to the wedding of the year, can it?"

"No, I expect not," the earl replied tightly. He was not accustomed to mixing politics and family, nor to being addressed in that tone of voice.

"Then you won't object to a change in date? It's far enough away so no one can accuse us of a shotgun wedding."

"I beg your pardon?"

Hobart put his head back and puffed on his cigar. "A wedding under duress because the bride is in the family way."

"Good heavens!" Inderby said. "What a shocking suggestion."

"Yes, well, people love to gossip, don't they? This arrangement will make sure they can't. Fortunately we haven't yet announced the wedding date."

"The countess," said the earl, raising a final objection.

Hobart smiled. After what had happened the day before under the eaves, Lady Caroline would pose no problem at all. "I'm sure she will like the idea of a June wedding. It's traditional."

The earl nodded and poured himself another drink.

———— . ————

"But I won't have enough time!" Cynthia protested.

"You'll have enough for the basics," her father replied. They had just entered her bedroom at Inderby wearing the clothes they had worn to dinner. "Whatever you can't buy before the wedding you can find on your wedding trip."

"No!" Cynthia said petulantly. "I want my year. I want all the parties and balls and luncheons and teas. I want to be married in the Abbey."

"I don't propose to argue the point," Hobart said in the tone that usually silenced objections. "You'll marry in June in the Washington Cathedral and I will hear no more about it. Everyone else is in favor of it."

That was not entirely true. Miranda and Paul seemed not to care either way and Lady Caroline was resigned, not enthusiastic. Walford, however, had been delighted, as befitted an eager bridegroom.

"I am *not* in favor!" Cynthia insisted again.

Hobart surveyed her as he clutched the lapels of his jacket. "Cynthia, you try my patience. I heartily advise against that."

Cynthia, bolstered by Alastair's declaration that he loved her and in possession of proof, however frightening, that he desired her, raised her chin and shook her head.

"Don't you defy *me,* my girl. The sooner you're married, the better for all of us. You almost got yourself unengaged as it is."

"What do you mean?"

"You were seen with Steven James at the National Gallery."

Cynthia flushed. "His miserable mother told you that!"

"Indeed she did. She told Walford as well. I don't know how you got around him—he was fuming before your walk this afternoon—and I don't want to know. But you are not to see James again, do you understand me?" He paused. "Cynthia?"

She stood near a chair, clutching its back. She looked like a crushed flower. Tears filled her eyes and spilled over onto her cheeks. "I love him, Papa," she said hopelessly. "More than I'll ever love Walford."

He waved that away. "Love Walford, Cynthia. He is where your future lies. James had ample opportunity to ask for you if he'd wanted to."

She glared at him.

He crossed his arms over his chest and stood surveying her. "What did I do," he asked of the room at large, "to deserve such a daughter? Why can't you be a lady like your aunt Miranda?"

"Lord, how I hate you," Cynthia exploded.

"What did you say?"

"I said I hate you. You're a brute. You don't care how people feel as long as they obey you."

"You're right about that," he said. "Now go to bed."

"Is that how you talk to Mother?" she demanded. "Is that why she's so terrified of you? What do you do to her that makes her drink?"

He took two steps forward and slapped her face with his open hand. "How dare you talk to me like that? If we were at home I'd lock you up on bread and water for a week. As it is, I'm warning you to do as I tell you and to convince everyone it's by your choice or I'll ship you to a lunatic asylum for the rest of your life. Do you understand me?"

Cynthia's face, neck, and bosom were stained deep red with bitter anger. She looked for a way to shatter her father's illusions as brutally as hers had been shattered.

"Of all women to cite as an example, you choose Miranda!" she said scornfully. "She's in love with Steven James too! She had an affair with him."

Hobart slapped her again, this time leaving fingermarks on her face. "Keep your voice down, you lying little bitch. What if someone heard you?"

She spoke in a raspy whisper, her fists clenched. "She did, she *did*! Every afternoon she pretended to nap in her cabin, but she was with *him,* in bed with *him*. At night she gave him the key, and after everyone had gone to their cabins, he went to hers. I heard them together! Ask Walford if you don't believe me! He was dazzled by her too, but it was Steven she wanted, my Steven. And she got him." Her whisper had become a tiny shriek, like the squeak of a bat.

"Be still," Hobart said, his face white with rage.

"So much for your paragon! She's nothing but a whore!"

He bent to pick up a pillow from the chair. "Be still or I'll smother you!"

She retreated before his vehemence, convinced he was capable of murder, of anything, even of having her locked up as he had threatened. Terror diluted her anger, then replaced it.

"Are you listening to me, Cynthia?" he demanded, and she nodded, her courage spent along with her venom.

"I'll send your maid to you now," he said. "You are to take some laudanum and go to bed at once! Tomorrow you will say you have a cold and stay in your room until I decide you are fit to come out. And you will marry Walford in Washington this coming June. If you rebel, you'll be taken to where you can do no harm for the rest of your life. Have I made myself clear?"

Disheveled, her face streaming with tears, she nodded again, not moving even after the door had closed behind him. She was still standing there when Baxter came in, carrying a glass and a spoon which she put down as soon as she saw Cynthia's face.

"Miss Cynthia!" Baxter ran to her side. "Holy Mother of God, what's happened?"

Cynthia burst into noisy tears and let Baxter comfort her with soothing sounds as she undressed Cynthia and got her into bed. She mixed the medicine with water, added sugar, and gave it to the girl. Cynthia drank it and lay back on the pillows, still crying. Baxter sat beside her, holding her hand until her sobs gradually slowed and finally vanished in sleep.

———— · ————

In her bedroom at some distance from Cynthia's, Miranda let Rooney brush her hair. She felt far too languid to do it herself as she usually did.

"You're lookin' pale, ma'am," her maid said, gathering her clothes. "And gettin' thinner every day."

Rooney was sure she knew why. It was she who burned the bloody cloths when her mistress had her monthlies—and there had been none for some weeks. Mrs. Paul was coming into her changes, and that accounted for her headaches and lack of appetite, even for the transformation of her personality: she was very quiet, unlike her usual spirited self. It took women differently, Rooney told herself, that time of life.

"You'll feel better when we're back at home," Rooney said.

Miranda only nodded and signaled that her hair had been brushed enough. Rooney helped her remove her dressing gown and get into the bed.

"It's much smoother," Miranda said, patting the mattress.

"I made them change it for a better one," Rooney said with an injured sniff. "Expecting a lady to sleep on a lumpy old thing like that. These people don't care as much about comfort as they do about show."

Miranda smiled. "Thank you, Rooney. You're very thoughtful."

Actually Miranda had been too sleepy lately to care about the lumpy mattress. She closed her eyes while Rooney pulled up the covers, lowered the lamp, and withdrew. Moments passed in silence, and then Paul knocked on the communicating door and came in.

He advanced to the bed and stood looking down at her. Her heart pounded but she steeled herself and opened her eyes, catching him with a look on his face that broke her heart. It was sweet, like the old Paul, and heavy with desire, like the new Paul. It was everything she wanted and all she needed.

"Tired?" he asked. Most nights he had no need to ask because her welcome was so warm.

"Paul, we must talk."

Anxiety replaced the longing. "What about?"

She understood his wariness; he feared she would talk about Steven. "Sit down," she said, patting the bed. When he did not, "Something unexpected has happened," she said in haste to say it before her courage failed. "I'm going to have a child."

His face twisted. "Is it his?"

"No!" She was horrified that he should think that.

"How can I be sure?"

"Because I tell you so! I swear it on this infant's head. I'm only about two months along. Oh, Paul, that you could think I was capable of lying about that."

"You've done it before."

"Never! I've tried to tell you everything. You didn't want to know."

He sat down on the bed abruptly then, as if his legs had turned to jelly, and looked at her wild-eyed. He was calculating rapidly and she could almost read the sequence of his calculations on his face.

He was remembering when her last period had kept him out of her bed. That had been just before their departure for Cairo. The child was not her lover's. It was his.

"Oh, my God," he said, covering his face with his hands, overwhelmed by relief until he considered another aspect of it. Miranda's child was his, but who had been in her heart when the child was conceived? It was almost impossible for him to look at her.

"I'm sorry, Paul."

"Why?" He was wary again.

"It's embarrassing, having a child at our time of life! What will people think?"

"That we're still in love with each other." He said it mockingly. "That you're mine."

"But I am!" she said quickly. "Paul—"

"Have I ever told you," he interrupted, "that for me the two most beautiful words in the language used to be 'my wife'? Have I ever told you that?"

He looked at her briefly, with anguish, and did not wait for an answer but, getting up, strode out of the room.

She lay back on the pillows, exhausted by remorse. How cleverly fate inflicted punishment: in varying degrees, in blows delivered at irregular intervals so that one was never inured to them. Her mind insisted that suspicion and bitterness were the price of betrayal, but her heart protested that the estrangement had gone on long enough.

She had hoped news of the coming child would open the way for them to put away one week of madness and go on, recapturing more than sex. She had been mistaken. She wondered if he would ever make love to her again.

Weary, but relieved that the telling was over, her body curved protectively around the child in her womb and she let sleep take her without giving another thought to how anyone else would react to her pregnancy, least of all Hobart Cunningham.

Forty

Miranda did not have long to wait after their return to London. That afternoon Paul had a meeting at the Archeological Society and Cynthia stayed in bed, still nursing her cold. Miranda, with Rooney in attendance, was walking in the nearby park, when Hobart appeared at her side. She barely acknowledged him, but she objected when he ordered Rooney back to the hotel.

"I want her with me," Miranda said.

His voice fell to a conspiratorial whisper. "I don't think you'll want her to hear what I have to say."

"Then she can follow at a little distance," Miranda insisted. He agreed, and after she spoke to Rooney he took her arm.

"I know all about you," he said.

She made no answer.

"How saintly you are!" he said, his demeanor changing abruptly. "But why only with me when you were so eager to lie down for Steven James!"

She stopped abruptly, appalled by him, searching his face as if

she could tear away his flesh and see through to his mind. "Cynthia!" she said at length.

"Yes!" he returned, his hand clamped on her arm. "Cynthia. You're no fit chaperone for a cat, let alone an innocent young girl."

"I forbid you to speak to me like that!"

"I intend to do much more than speak to *you*. I fully intend to tell Paul about you—unless you and I can find a friendlier solution. If I tell him, he'll divorce you. Wouldn't it be easier to give me what you gave the senator? Then the whole story could remain our little secret." Her shiver of distaste only made him angrier.

"I don't care what you do," she said, her voice and her face testimony to her hopelessness. "Or whom you tell. And Paul already knows."

"He knows? And he did nothing?" He snorted. "But what should I expect from that sorry excuse for a man?"

She was trying to hold on to herself, but her control was fast slipping away. Paul's reaction the night before had been devastating, but he had every right to behave as he did. Hobart's slimy accusations were about to break her.

"He's worth ten of you!" she told him.

"A lot of people wouldn't agree with you about that," he said.

"I don't care!" she said again, turning to him. He believed her now. He had never seen a woman as furious as she was. "Go ahead and tell everyone. Tell the tabloids too. Just remember that if you do, there will be no wedding. There'll be a transatlantic scandal instead that will make Charlotte's curse look like a tea party." She threw him a look of utter contempt and walked on.

He grabbed her arm again, his fingers pressing into her flesh like iron bands. "What possessed you?" he demanded. "You could have ruined us all, your sons too, not to mention your lover. If Paul wasn't enough for you, I was there. You'd have been safe with me."

She stopped walking and faced him again, her voice rising. "You revolt me, don't you know that? Can't you see it? I never wanted your attentions, I never sought them. I would rather die than have you touch me. Do as you like, only leave me alone!"

"Be quiet," he commanded, glancing around at the passersby and then back at the maid following them. "You're making a spectacle of yourself."

"Oh, no! You're the spectacle. You'd do anything to get what you want."

"So, apparently, would you. You're a lusty woman. I always knew there was a lot more to you than meets the eye."

"Stop it!" she almost shouted. "I won't listen to you for another moment." She covered her ears with her hands, then turned very white and seemed to lose her balance.

He supported her while he led her toward a low stone wall and made her sit on it. "Are you sick?" he asked. He signaled to Rooney.

"Oh, it's much better than that," Miranda said with a coldly triumphant smile. "I'm pregnant."

He drew his breath in sharply but said nothing more as Rooney rushed up. "Don't make a fuss," he ordered the anxious maid. "Just help her up and between us we'll get her to the hotel."

Miranda was forced to lean on both of them, repugnant as it was to touch him. Dizziness overcame her again in the lift and she barely made it to the bathroom commode. Rooney held her head while Hobart rang the desk and ordered that a specialist be sent for.

Miranda felt weaker than ever when the retching was over. Rooney helped her undress and get into bed while Hobart waited in the family-shared parlor until Mr. Leeds, a specialist in female complaints and *accouchements,* arrived.

With Rooney standing by, he spent fifteen minutes with Miranda. He looked grave when he emerged. "You are her husband?" he asked Hobart.

"Her brother-in-law. My brother should be back shortly. Is it serious?"

"Childbearing is always serious. At her age it is especially so."

"You mean she might miscarry?" Hobart asked, hope in his chest.

"That, of course, is a possibility, but older women can have other serious complications." The doctor was glancing at his large gold pocket watch when Paul came in and was told what had happened.

Hobart watched him closely, but there was no sign that Paul was surprised by the pregnancy, nor did he appear to harbor any doubts about the child's paternity. And yet Miranda had said he knew about her shipboard affair. To judge from Miranda's figure, she was not very far along. So it had happened too recently—probably in Egypt—for this to be her lover's pup.

What was the secret of Miranda's power over men: Paul, Steven James, himself, and God alone knew how many others. Hobart's fevered imagination conjured her up engaged in erotic techniques and ecstasies not for ordinary mortals.

"She must not travel," the specialist was saying to Paul. "Can't have her jostled about on trains and ships until the first three months are well past."

"Which means we must stay in London for how long?" Hobart demanded as if the doctor were deliberately annoying him.

"At least another six weeks," Mr. Leeds said.

"There is no need for you to stay," Paul reminded Hobart. "You must go back with Cynthia this week as planned."

The doctor had scribbled something on a pad. "Here are instructions for a tonic I shall send over. She should stay in bed for three days and then come to see me. Then we shall know where we are." Paul accompanied him to the door of the suite, looking worried.

Hobart was smoking a cigar when he returned. "A pretty mess," he said.

"It never occurred to me that there was any danger," Paul said, pouring a whisky with trembling hands. "And put that thing out." He pointed to the cigar. "It nauseates her."

"She's not in here."

"The odor penetrates. Put it out."

Hobart obliged him; Paul was not usually so forceful. "She's not going to die," Hobart said. "Don't make a drama of it. The woman's always been healthy."

"She shouldn't bear a child at her time of life."

"You should have thought of that before you planted it."

Paul ignored him. "I don't care how long it takes, I'll stay here with her until it's safe for her to travel."

"Then I'll leave as soon as I can arrange it."

"Take Cynthia with you."

"I'll see what Walford has to say about that."

"Walford has nothing to say! Cynthia can't stay here unchaperoned, and Miranda's not up to it. Take Cynthia with you. Now I'm going in to see my wife."

Paul let himself into Miranda's bedroom quietly while Hobart sat in stony silence and watched the door close. He had been outflanked and he knew it. He hated Miranda more for refusing him than for accepting another man—or men. How many had there been? Once a woman took a bad turn, there was no stopping her. That was why they were not meant to enjoy intercourse. It was like catnip to them.

But there was nothing he could do by way of punishment. He would have stopped Paul from taking serious action. The twin blights of adultery and illegitimacy were not to be risked. It would be embarrassing enough that a supposedly decent matron had conceived a child at a time in life when husbands, their families complete, took their carnal pleasure elsewhere. It put Miranda in an unsavory light as a seductress of her own husband. There was bound to be some talk.

He got up and went to find his daughter.

———— · ————

Cynthia's swollen eyes had returned to normal since the stormy scene at Inderby, but she was still in bed, reading listlessly. Hobart waved her maid out and sat down in an armchair.

"I've just left your aunt Miranda," he said.

She shrugged.

"She's expecting a child."

Cynthia flinched. "That's impossible. She's too old."

"Apparently not. But she almost collapsed this morning and the doctor who came confirmed her condition and said there might be complications."

"Good!" Cynthia threw her book across the room. "I hope she dies. It's what she deserves." She paused. "Does Uncle Paul know?"

"Yes. He's very worried, of course."

"Does he know about the other thing?" Cynthia's eyes darted nervously.

"Cynthia, you are never to say or to even imply that this child might not be a Cunningham. It would cost us a title, and I won't have that."

"Oh, all right!" she said crossly. "But how can you be sure?"

"It's a matter of dates," he said casually, "which the doctor verified." It was not the sort of thing a man discussed with any woman, much less his maiden daughter.

She seemed to accept the doctor's verdict and asked, "What happens now?"

"She is forbidden to travel for several weeks. Business forces me to return. I might take you with me. I'll discuss that with Walford."

"Why not discuss it with me?" she demanded, her temper rising. "I'm the one most directly concerned. I'd rather stay here and tend my dear aunt."

"You need a chaperone and your aunt is not up to it."

"But Uncle Paul will be here. And my maid! Really, Father, there's no reason for me to scuttle home as if I had something to be ashamed of."

"Especially when Steven James remains here."

She shook her head. "I want nothing further to do with him."

"That's sensible, since he obviously wants nothing to do with you."

Her head drooped in total defeat.

"Not a pleasant feeling," he conceded with something approaching sympathy now that she was thoroughly tamed.

"No," she agreed. It was another new experience to talk to her father on this level.

He had half expected another tantrum from her, and her compliance pleased him so, he might even let her stay. He got up to go, telling her she seemed well enough to stop pouting and come down to dinner that evening.

When he was gone she kicked her feet and muffled her howls of protest with a pillow, resenting the way he directed her life.

Cynthia tossed aside the pillow and lay there thinking furiously, uncertain despite the doctor's declaration that the child was Paul's. She knew little of the time factors involved in conception and gestation. Either way, though, it completely finished Steven and Miranda and that had been Cynthia's intention since the crossing.

There remained only Kitt McAllister. What would she think when Miranda's delicate condition became known?

Cynthia was determined that she would think the very worst of Steven. If Cynthia could not have him, neither should Kitt! She rang for Baxter to bring her writing portfolio and began to compose a note.

—— · ——

Steven took Claire to Hampton Court the day before she sailed and they explored the famous palace together.

"You used to tell me stories of this place and the doomed young queens," he said. He took her hand. "Lord, I'm going to miss you, Claire."

"I'm counting on it," she said. "Maybe loneliness will bring you to your senses more quickly."

He shrugged. "As if I had any sense to start with! But I won't come home until the new treaty is official here and on its way to Washington for debate and ratification by the senate."

"And how long will that be?"

"A few months, no more."

Claire nodded. "I said good-bye to Lady Burdon and Miss McAllister yesterday," she went on. "Her fiancé has not yet returned from France."

"Claire, stop matchmaking!"

"You said I could meddle if I stayed another week," she told him, unruffled by his objections. "Just think of it. Louisa McAllister, daughter of a successful American merchant and a *Mayflower* Kittredge, would be the perfect wife for a United States senator! Of course, she would have to be more circumspect in what she says and how she says it—at least until after the first election—but she has every other quality."

"Not another word about her," Steven said, hurrying his sister to the next gallery.

"But you like her! I know you do!"

"Claire!" he protested. "I said good-bye to the love of my life not too long ago."

"And it was final. But you're not dead yet, Steven. Open your eyes and live while you can!"

After she sailed, Steven kept hearing those words. He was far more desolate than he had anticipated. He had too much time to reflect. The mourning all around him seemed to be for himself and Miranda.

But the nature of his love for her had changed, as had hers for him. He didn't love her any less; he loved her differently. She was removed from him now, locked in a world apart with Paul and his child, a world in which he had no place. It was symbolic of their relationship: she had never been uniquely his.

As for Kitt, he was as flattered as the next man to hear that she was deeply in love with him, and he was curious to know if it was true, if the crisp Miss McAllister was likely to love anyone madly, much less the reprobate she believed Steven to be.

He sent a note inviting her to dinner and waited as impatiently as a wallflower for her reply. She refused, gently but firmly. He was truly surprised, therefore, to receive an invitation from Lady Burdon to dine in St. John's Wood.

He was the only guest.

He had half hoped that Kitt would be there, but he didn't ask about her and Lady Burdon volunteered nothing. She indicated the chair opposite hers at the fireside. In his several visits to the mansion, Steven had not seen this comfortable, welcoming room, a large version of Kitt's parlor.

It takes a woman's touch, he thought, and then reproached himself for such sentimental nonsense.

"So Mrs. Harden has left and you are all alone," Lady Burdon said.

"Yes, I am."

"She didn't accomplish her mission. She told me she'd come to take you home to America."

He was annoyed that Claire had discussed him with Lady Burdon, but he smiled pleasantly. "She used to come for me when I was little and hid in the barn. I suppose she likes to think of me as a small boy still."

"That is how most women think of men, to their ultimate sorrow." She offered him a drink and he took a whisky and sat sipping it, rising only to light her cigarette. She was magnificently turned out—he had never seen her otherwise—and with her white hair piled high upon her head she looked regal.

He had seen the paintings of her as a young woman; she had been a great beauty. He had an unexpected insight into what it must be like for a beautiful woman when her beauty fades.

"Any news of Miss Cunningham and the viscount?" he asked.

Lady Burdon's eyes twinkled. "The wedding date has been announced. It's to be late June of this year. In Washington, if you can credit it!"

"I thought it would be here in London and over a year away."

"Did Cynthia tell you that at the National Gallery?" He was taken aback, and she raised her brows in mock surprise. "London is really a village, Senator James."

"I'm no longer a senator. My leave of absence expired and I resigned my seat in Albany."

"Albany's loss is our gain. But we were talking of Cynthia."

"And I should not have gone to meet her," he agreed. "But there was no polite way to refuse."

Lady Burdon watched the smoke from her cigarette float away. "I'm sure you acted with the best of intentions. And it's my guess your meeting had nothing to do with their decision to move up the wedding date. The Cunninghams simply don't want to be totally eclipsed by royals, either the quick or the dead."

"The change was probably Hobart Cunningham's idea," he said.

"I gather you are not terribly fond of him."

He crossed his long legs. "Is anyone? Have you met him?"

"Only briefly. He is not a prepossessing man."

The butler came to announce dinner, and Steven helped her up.

"American men are so tall," she said, taking his arm. "And so healthy."

He thought of the count, saying virtually the same thing about American girls when he first saw Kitt, on the day they sailed. He had not even met her, but the count had been immediately smitten.

Once they were seated in the small dining room, Lady Burdon opened another gambit. "Jean-Baptiste is convinced it's the water in America that makes you grow like weeds, since it cannot be the food."

"I can tell that you disagree." He smiled.

"I always say it's breeding," she said. "It's healthy to mix blood-lines."

"Oh, they don't mix that much in America. New immigrants tend to stay with their own kind and people in small towns to marry among themselves."

"In that case you'll have a population of half-wits in two or three generations. Look at the Spanish Bourbons, all of them peculiar, most of them chinless, and a few positively insane."

"We'll escape that if our means of transportation continues to expand at its present rate."

"I hadn't thought of that, but you're quite right. Even before the railroad, all it took was a few renegades eager enough to jump over the fence and head for the next village to mate. That is why God created animal passions."

"A notoriously risky basis on which to choose a life compan-ion."

"Emotionally, perhaps," she said. "But it produces healthy off-spring."

He laughed, sure she was fishing for a way to talk about Kitt—or even Miranda. He was damned if he'd give it to her, much as he liked her. He changed the subject as they were served oxtail soup followed by Dover sole, roast duckling, steamed pearl onions in a cream sauce, and the inevitable brussels sprouts; they talked of the twentieth century and the changes it would bring.

"All those superstitious fools predicting the world would end at the stroke of 1900!" she said while the butler poured more wine for both of them. "Whose stroke? Yours or ours? As if human time has anything to do with the cosmic variety."

"There are more ways than one for a world to end," he said.

"Alas, yes," she said sympathetically. Then, "What of Kitt?" she asked.

"What do you mean?" She had caught him unprepared.

"You must know it's on her account that I invited you tonight," she said.

"I know nothing of the kind." He began to bristle.

"I thought Claire would have told you. Your sister thought Kitt would be the perfect wife for you."

He colored. "My sister told me. She is sometimes overzealous in my behalf."

"As I am in Kitt's. I've no doubt she'd be the perfect wife for you, but you are not the best husband for her. Jean-Baptiste is."

"I don't know him well enough to judge."

"I do. I've known him since he was sixteen. Have you heard she'll soon be engaged to him?"

"Claire told me. I'm happy for her. What else should I be?"

"Sorry you let her get away," she suggested. "Determined to get her back."

"I don't care to discuss this," he said sharply.

"Mr. James, may I be blunt?"

"Aren't you always?"

She smiled. "Only with people I like. I find myself on the horns of a dilemma. There is Kitt, of whom I am more than fond, who had some romantic notions about you—possibly still does. First loves are almost impossible to forget. Then there is Jean-Baptiste, who loves her deeply and with no reservations, as she deserves. And finally there is you, a man with enormous charm but no judgment about how he uses it."

His patience evaporated. "Lady Burdon, you go too far!"

"I know. It is because of my desperation."

"There is no need to despair."

"Isn't there, when just the other day you invited Kitt to dine with you? Why did you do that when you knew she was about to be engaged?"

"We're friends!" He stood, too angry to sit quietly in a chair while this imperious woman cross-examined him. "And her engagement has not been announced."

"It seems to me that whenever you find yourself at loose ends you turn to Kitt. Well, I persuaded her to refuse your invitation—and I'll persuade her again if you persist."

He bowed. "Thank you for inviting me, Lady Burdon."

"Will you persist?"

"Good night," he said, and, turning, left the room. She watched him go. He was a most compelling man, seductive in more than appearance. She could understand why three very different women had fallen in love with him.

But she was determined to save Kitt and she thought that to-night she had. "If this doesn't work, I'll find something else," she promised herself.

———— · ————

Steven was still angry the following day. He resented being sent to stand in a figurative corner like an infant. He resented being told where his affections belonged. Kitt must be warned that Lady Burdon was playing her like a marionette, but having been refused by Kitt already, he was reluctant to send another invitation, only to receive another refusal. He looked for a way to talk to her face-to-face.

Unexpectedly, it was Lord Harry who told him where he might find her the next time he was in Blenkinsop's office to discuss the new treaty. That topic exhausted, Lord Harry began to grumble.

"That McAllister woman," he said. "Not content with making monkeys out of us, she's gone after the Whitlaw Line."

"What does she want?"

"The same thing she wanted from us, what she calls status for women who work aboard liners. It's monstrous that a chit of a girl can raise such a fuss. She's forced Whitlaw to sign the same agreement we did. They're making it official this morning." He looked at his watch. "Right now, as it happens."

———— · ————

Kitt was delighted to find Steven waiting for her when she left the Whitlaw offices. Despite her firm resolve to stay away from him, her heart sang at the mere sight of him. She was flattered that he cared enough to come and find her even after she had refused to see him.

She couldn't resist his invitation to lunch, and they went to a nearby restaurant and ordered chicken pies and a bottle of wine.

"You're looking extremely well," he said, admiring her pearl-gray walking suit trimmed with white ermine. An ermine toque sat atop her hair, making her appear even taller than she was.

"And you," she said. "But I suppose you miss Claire."

"Very much more than I expected," he said ruefully.

"So do I. We had a lovely time together. I'm sure we'd have been good friends no matter when we met."

"She told me about your engagement."

Kitt felt her cheeks blaze. "It hasn't been announced yet."

"But it soon will be?"

She met his eyes steadily. "I'm not sure. I shall have to meet his family before it can be official."

"Is it a large family?"

"Both his parents are living, although elderly. He has five older sisters, all of them married and with children."

He smiled. "They'll make an awful rumpus. I know because of my nieces and nephews." He put down his knife and fork. "Will you be angry if I'm as blunt as Lady Burdon is?"

"I'll try not to be," she said, wanting to touch his face, take his hand.

"It's presumptuous of me, but I wish you'd consider the life of a French countess more carefully. It carries many privileges but it has limitations you might not like."

How could she compare her passion for him with the far safer but more tepid affection she felt for the count? She took refuge in banter. "To the best of my knowledge," she said brightly, "you have never been a French countess, so how could you know?"

"Kitt, please don't joke about it. It's just possible, isn't it, that Lady Burdon is influencing your decision?"

"Isn't that what you're trying to do?"

He nodded. "But I know you'll weigh anything I say—and you might not be as careful about her opinions."

"Why do you tell me all of this?"

The waiter poured more wine for both of them. "Lady Burdon invited me to dinner the other night and told me in no uncertain terms to stay away from you until you were well and truly married to someone worthier than I."

She could not hide her dismay. "I had no idea! She should not have done that. I'm quite capable of making my own decisions!"

"I agree. But I don't think Lady Burdon does."

Something between indignation and hope rose in her. "Steven, I can't imagine why my private life should concern you in the least or why you come like the village curate to preach to me about marriage."

"Because we're friends and I wouldn't want you to make as many mistakes as I have."

Curiosity made her stop berating him. "What mistakes?" she asked.

He told her briefly about his first marriage, about his long bout of depression when it ended, and about his new quandary: whether or not to stay on in London. Miranda's name was glaring by its omission.

"My mind was made up before Claire arrived and made me homesick, and now I'm as confused as ever," he said. "Do you miss America?"

She shook her head. "Perhaps it's because I live in a very small New England town. It isn't very stimulating."

"You've never lived in New York City. *That* is stimulating." He smiled. "And there are thousands of working women to be organized."

"Are you poking fun at me?"

"Not at all! And you should finish what you've started—but you can't do that if you're a countess."

"I'd rather talk about your canal," she said abruptly.

"You're angry, aren't you?"

"It's not the first time I've been angry with you."

"I'd like to make amends in some small way. Let me take you and Lady Burdon to dinner."

She shook her head. "That would be awkward."

"Then just the two of us?"

"That would be even more awkward." She glanced at her lapel watch. "It's late. I must go."

He was silent for a moment, as disappointed as a boy denied the Christmas gift he had been promised.

"May I call on you?" he asked through the open window when Kitt was in the hansom.

"Please don't," she said softly, her eyes glistening. "It will be better for both of us if you don't." She shook her head. "I've had enough heartache and so have you. I wish you well, Steven, but you don't know what you want and I can't tell you." She rapped on the ceiling of the cab with her umbrella, a signal to the driver to move on. In moments the cab turned a corner and she was out of sight.

———— · ————

He walked for several hours, feeling utterly miserable, aware that he had unwittingly caused her great unhappiness. Claire was mistaken: Kitt was not in love with him. Even if she were, Kitt would never give in to her heart. Kitt was wise enough and strong enough to turn away from a man she believed, from his past behavior, she could not completely trust.

He was beginning to see Kitt differently, to recall moments when his response to her had been more than friendly. He recalled her candor when she told him about the beleaguered stewardess she eventually took under her wing. When he closed his eyes he could see her pouring out tea in the little parlor in Dover Street, hear her laugh, remember how time flew when he was with her.

He could see her tear-stained face at the opera on that ill-omened evening, how lovely she had looked in her ivory satin gown. He thought of her among the spools of ribbon and trimmings the first time he'd heard her speak that evening on Oxford Street. He remembered her lovely face and her copper hair and how he had imagined her with that glorious mane loose and tumbling over the velvety skin of her shoulders.

"Do you suppose," she had asked him, *"that you are the only person on the planet capable of a love like that?"*

He knew she was capable of it, but if she had ever loved him, he had destroyed it. He had overlooked something very rare.

He walked on, suspecting now that he had lost much more than her good opinion of him, feeling miserable and remorseful. He was no stranger to those feelings, but he was reluctant to pursue either of them to its source.

"I can't stop her from marrying him," he muttered to himself. "But, Lord, I'm going to miss her."

Forty-one

"I've come to see how you are, Aunt Miranda," Cynthia said for Rooney's benefit, but her voice always slid to a higher pitch when she was dissembling.

"How kind of you," Miranda replied, not in the least misled. They waited until Rooney left the room.

"What do you really want?" Miranda asked her niece.

"To say that you were wrong about Walford," Cynthia said proudly. "I proved it that day at the Hall when we went walking in the snow. He was very eager."

"Despite the snow?"

Cynthia laughed. "No, he took me to one of those folly houses. It's a strange-looking place—and it has the most nauseating ceiling in the bedroom."

"The bedroom? What happened?"

"Only a kiss or two." Cynthia blushed. "He was rough, but that was my fault. I led him on a little." She thought back to the incident. "He seemed angry as well, and that bothered me until I realized he was jealous of Steven."

"Should he be?"

"Well, I *was* infatuated with him," Cynthia said somewhat smugly. "I told Walford that no man is jealous unless he's in love and he said I was right."

"I'm delighted to hear it," Miranda said too readily, as if humoring a child.

"You don't believe me!"

"What I believe usually makes no difference to you."

"Why are you so determined to make me miserable?"

Miranda sighed. "That isn't true, Cynthia. You're quite capable of doing that for yourself, as I am, as we all are."

"In what way?"

"By expecting too much of everyone. By expecting people to return all that we give to the same degree and in exactly the same way."

Cynthia sprang out of the chair. "I know exactly what to expect from Walford. I'm going to marry him and have a lovely life! Wait and see." She started out of the room, then spun around. "The wedding plans have been changed," she said. "It's to be in Washington, this coming June."

"Why?"

"Papa insists—and so does Walford. We'd have had to wait until after the mourning period to have a really big wedding and until after the coronation for anyone to take notice of it." She tossed her head. "I don't mind. The Washington Cathedral is every bit as impressive as the Abbey. And *everyone* we know can attend. Papa's ordering a special train to Washington and back for the New Yorkers." She hesitated as a thought struck her. "Will you be able to come?"

"No, I'll be too large to go out in public."

"I hadn't thought of that," Cynthia said, pouting in disappointment. Her own mother was rarely sober enough to appear in public, much less organize a huge wedding. Miranda was more than capable of overseeing the whole affair, and whatever her rancorous feelings for her aunt, Cynthia needed her.

"Aunt Miranda, will you help me if you don't have to leave the house to do it?" Cynthia asked in a small voice.

"Help you with what?"

"Choosing my trousseau and the bridesmaids' dresses and the flowers and the menu and the favors—things like that. You know my mother can't."

Miranda felt a sudden surge of sympathy for her. She was too young to know how cruel she had been. And the girl was so alone! Her unhappy mother was probably the only person who loved her unreservedly, but they rarely saw each other even though they lived in the same house. The infamous Hobart was not an affectionate father, and she was about to marry a man whose nature was callous, particularly when it came to women. Miranda wondered how "rough" Walford would be with his bride.

Cynthia would probably be alone, in the most fundamental sense, all of her life. Beautiful, pampered, envied—and alone.

"Of course I'll help," Miranda said, too weary of discord to hold on to it, too sorry for Cynthia to refuse her.

Cynthia stood in silence for a few moments. "Things never turn out in the way we expect, do they?" she said.

"Almost never."

"Did you know I'm staying on until you can travel?"

"Paul told me."

"I'll look after you, Aunt Miranda. I really will."

"Thank you, Cynthia."

Cynthia drew a deep breath and seemed about to speak again, but left the room instead. Miranda closed her eyes, refusing to yield to the black tide of depression that threatened to engulf her. The benevolent world she had always known had, through her own actions, turned hostile. She would be destroyed unless she continued to play a part.

Paul would keep up appearances because he could not deal with the truth in any other way. Hobart would do likewise because he risked too much unless he did. Cynthia would because it was the only way to get what she had always wanted, never mind that she would have preferred it in a different package. They had all danced to the music of deceit, and now it was time to pay the piper.

Miranda put her hand over the place where the baby nested, protecting the one thing that was, for the moment, indisputably hers and totally loved.

———— · ————

Kitt sat rigidly in the cab after she left Steven and was relieved, when she reached home, that Alton was out. It was impossible to hide anything from Alton, and Kitt could not have discussed her anguish. She alternated between the conviction that she had done the right thing and a longing for Steven that defied common sense.

She would have to refuse the count. She would have to tell him that he deserved more than she could give him.

On the other hand, how could she give up a man who truly loved her for a man who, even if he turned to her, would always want someone else? But surely she had enough love in her for both of them! And maybe, in time, he would change!

And maybe he would not! And there was Jean-Baptiste, wanting only her.

But she had to be honest, to go wherever the truth might lead her. No matter how much it cost her, she had to risk it.

Another hour had passed before she looked at her mail and found Cynthia's invitation. Curiosity got the better of her and she wrote a note, accepting, and sent Alton to the Bristol with it before supper.

———— · ————

Kitt arrived at the Bristol promptly at four o'clock, dressed in the ermine-trimmed gray ensemble that she knew was very becoming. Cynthia was waiting for her in the Cunninghams' parlor, looking like a schoolgirl in a white silk shirtwaist with a ruffled jabot and a black skirt.

"Look!" she said, touching a cameo of the Three Graces at the high neck of her shirtwaist. "A gift from Lady Caroline. It's an heirloom."

Kitt felt more of a spinster than ever—as usual when she was with Cynthia—until she thought of Jean-Baptiste and his proposal.

She clutched at his offer of marriage as if it were a lifeline she was about to abandon. At the same time she was ashamed of herself for yielding to the conventional wisdom that a woman without a man was not a whole person, while a man without a woman was a catch.

"How well you look," Cynthia said, fairly bubbling with good spirits. "I want to bring Walford to your next lecture, but I've seen no notice of it."

"I've been in temporary retirement while I was negotiating with the Whitlaw Line," Kitt said. "That wound up yesterday. I'll let you know when the next lecture is scheduled. That is, if you're still here."

"Our plans have changed," Cynthia said. "Father will be going home, but I shall stay on to look after Aunt Miranda."

For both of them, talking of Miranda was only a step from talking of Steven. Specks of tension, like dust motes, floated in the room.

"Is she ill?" Kitt asked.

"She's expecting," Cynthia said with a telling glance. Maiden ladies were not supposed to discuss pregnancy or its unmentionable cause.

Kitt sat absolutely still.

"I know it's embarrassing," Cynthia warbled on, "but there it is. The doctor says she must not travel until she's a bit further along. He says it's a risky business for a woman of Aunt Miranda's age to have a baby at all."

Tea was brought in and Cynthia poured, giving Kitt some time to collect herself. She thought of the medical tomes she had pored over as a schoolgirl, the strange pictures in them.

Did the shadow shape forming inside Miranda resemble Steven James or Paul Cunningham?

Cynthia was holding out a cup and saucer, with sugar lumps in an accompanying spoon. She looked questioningly at Kitt.

"Sorry, I just remembered something I forgot to do," Kitt said, stirring the sugar into her tea. "Is your uncle pleased?

"He's so worried about her, it's hard to say. I suppose he's embarrassed too."

"Why all this embarrassment?" Kitt scoffed. "It's perfectly natural for married people to have children, no matter what their ages."

"But it's so indecorous," Cynthia insisted.

Kitt had to change the subject. "And how is Lord Walford?"

"Delightful," Cynthia said with a warm smile. She went on talking about the preparations for her wedding. "I want so much for you to be there," she said.

"Thank you, Cynthia, but I don't expect to be in the United States at that time."

"What a pity. Walford will be so disappointed."

Walford won't give two hoots, Kitt told herself.

"But surely you'll visit America from time to time," Cynthia persisted. "And you can arrange to be there in June. If the count and the senator come, it will be a reunion of shipmates—except for Aunt Miranda, of course."

"Won't she come to your wedding?" Kitt asked, avoiding mention of Steven's name.

"She'll be in no condition by then to travel," Cynthia said ambiguously.

Did she mean that Miranda would be close to giving birth or that she would be recovering from a recent confinement? In this particular puzzle, timing was key.

The rest of the visit went by in a blur. When Kitt left the Bristol, doubt nibbled at the edges of her mind.

She did not want to believe Steven knew the child was his and had abandoned Miranda, but it would not be the first time, by his own admission, that he had acted selfishly. He had married a girl he didn't love at all!

She was expected in St. John's Wood for dinner with Lady Burdon, and for a while she thought that she could not go. Then she realized that such an accomplished gossip would be likely to have heard something. She went back to Dover Street to change.

"You don't look like a woman about to announce her engagement," Lady Burdon said to Kitt after dinner.

"That's what comes of negotiating with shipping lines," Kitt parried, reluctant to share her doubts and suspicions even with this trusted friend.

"But, my dear, I've had word. Jean-Baptiste will soon be back." She took an envelope from her pocket and waved it at Kitt. "The moment of truth is at hand."

"I think we must postpone the moment of truth," Kitt said.

"Why?"

"I haven't decided yet. The life of a French countess may be far too restricted for me."

"Nonsense!" Lady Burdon peered intently at Kitt, then nodded as if she had found the reason for this unwelcome news. "Have you been seeing Steven James?"

"Only once. Today, as a matter of fact. He was at Whitlaw's when I was leaving and we had luncheon together."

"That was unwise." Lady Burdon sounded far more composed than she felt at this threat to Kitt's future.

"I know it was. I told him it would be the last time."

"A man like that is accustomed to eventual surrender. He'll find a way."

I hope so, Kitt prayed fervently. "The trouble is," she said, "that I still care for him."

"Or think you do."

"No," Kitt said. "I love him."

"My child, we both know it's dangerous to love an unstable man! What you feel is entirely glandular."

Kitt finished her coffee and went to the drinks tray to pour a crème de menthe. "Cognac?" she asked Lady Burdon, who nodded, feeling in need of it. Neither woman spoke until Kitt was back in her chair. Lady Burdon picked up the ratty embroidery she described as her life's work: "I do it slowly when I do it at all," she explained, "and so I shall be dead before it is finished."

Despite her peaceful demeanor, Lady Burdon was appalled by the possibility that one of the two people she most treasured would not marry the other when, clearly, they were ideally suited. Then, too, France was not as far away as the colonies. She could go to France now and then and they could visit St. John's Wood often. She found them so much more compatible than her stuffy and humorless sons.

But none of that would happen unless she could discredit Steven in Kitt's eyes once and for all. She already knew how.

She let the embroidery drop to her lap and took another sip of cognac, feeling the warmth of it spread inside her to strengthen her resolve.

"I have some gossip to divert you," she said. "Mrs. Cunningham is expecting."

Kitt nodded. "Cynthia told me this afternoon, but how did you know?"

"Mr. Leeds, who attends gentlewomen, was called to the Bristol to see her."

"But that could have been for any number of reasons!" Kitt said, for the first time critical of Lady Burdon's love of gossip.

"No. On the same evening Mr. Leeds told his wife he had called on an American lady who should have been too old to conceive another child after so many years, much less bear one safely, no matter how young and beautiful she looks. This morning Olive Leeds told me."

"I trust the doctor mentioned no names!"

"Of course not. But how many beautiful, pregnant American ladies of a certain age are staying at the Bristol?"

"Not all that many," Kitt agreed. "Cynthia says they are staying on in London until it's safer for Mrs. Cunningham to travel—with the exception of the odious Hobart, who is disliked by everyone who meets him."

"Mrs. Cunningham must be well along, then," Lady Burdon said, again picking up her embroidery. She felt a pang for the lovely woman she had befriended on the *Sylvania*. Unfortunately, Miranda had gambled everything on a few moments of madness. It remained to be seen if she had lost everything.

"No, she can't be that far along," Kitt said after thinking it over.

"Why not?"

"You know why not! You'd have heard rumors of divorce if the child were too far along to be her husband's!"

Lady Burdon shook her head. "With Cynthia's wedding at stake, this is no time for a scandal. Hobart Cunningham is absolutely set on the marriage and so is Walford. Then there's that business they're all involved in, something to do with a canal and a new treaty. An uproar is the last thing any of them wants, and the sooner the knot is tied, the safer. Hobart Cunningham will have his titled daughter and Walford will have his fortune."

"You're right, that must be why they pushed the wedding forward," Kitt said, torn between anger and despair, wondering what would happen afterward.

"It would seem so," Lady Burdon said. It hurt her to see Kitt so deeply wounded, but she did not regret her misleading suggestion— Lady Burdon had not actually lied—that Miranda was pregnant with Steven's child and it was being hushed up. Lady Burdon would have told Kitt the end of the world was at hand if it would persuade her to marry Jean-Baptiste and forget that handsome rogue.

Age was a frightening bridge between this world and the next, far more frightening than death, far too frightening to cross alone.

She wanted people of her own sort with her toward the end. And Kitt deserved the kind of adoration that only an older man could offer.

The women had fallen into thoughtful silence until Kitt stirred and said it was past ten and she must go. Lady Burdon rang, and in minutes Alton, who had been visiting in the servants' hall, appeared, saying the carriage had been sent for.

"Come and see me tomorrow," Lady Burdon invited, and Kitt nodded, kissed her hostess, and went swiftly to the waiting carriage, Alton at her heels.

Morning had come before Kitt finally slept, but she knew what she must do.

——— · ———

Miranda greeted her pleasantly from a chair near the window, but the warmth that had sprung up between them on the crossing had vanished. It surprised Miranda that Kitt had come at all. It must be difficult for the lovestruck girl to look at Steven's mistress.

"Cynthia told me you were not well. I came to help you pass the time."

"I've discovered that time passes all too quickly, but thank you for the thought."

It was hard to judge Miranda's girth under the quilt. The windows were open to the mild February day that seemed to herald spring, and Miranda wore a shawl as well. She was as lovely as ever, but there was a new fragility about her.

"I hope you don't mind the windows being open," Miranda said formally, sorry she had agreed to this visit. There was a pause. "I was feeling so cooped up on a lovely day like this."

Kitt said she was very comfortable with the windows open, and there was another pause.

"What do you want, Miss McAllister?" Miranda finally demanded.

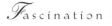

"Advice. I have no right to ask that of you, and it's difficult for me to find the words."

Miranda smiled thinly. "As I recall, you are never at a loss for words."

"I'm at a loss for more than that."

"Such as?"

"I don't know whether or not I should marry the Count d'Yveine."

"I'm hardly the one to advise you," Miranda said. "Ask Lady Burdon."

"I'm not deeply in love with him," Kitt went on. "I love someone else who might marry me because he's vulnerable and needs the kind of comfort marriage would provide. But that isn't the kind of love I want from him, as mine is not the kind the count has a right to expect from me. So I must tell the truth or go on pretending to both of them: to one that I love him and to the other that I don't."

"Pretense does not seem to me to be part of your nature."

"It never has been. But perhaps if I pretend long enough I can become what I'm pretending to be. Perhaps love will grow after marriage. I've never experienced either condition before."

"And you come to me for advice?"

"Because you've experienced both."

"I can only tell you that marriage is safer than passion. Passion is unruly. It drives people to do dangerous things when they shouldn't, to avoid taking risks when they should."

They sat in silence again. Kitt still could not bring herself to ask the insulting question she had come to ask.

"I came to talk about Steven James," she said abruptly.

Miranda nodded. "I thought so. He is the vulnerable object of your affections."

"I fell in love with him the moment I saw him," Kitt said. "But he was not free, although I didn't know that at first."

"And now he is?"

Kitt shook her head. "I don't think he ever will be, but I'm prepared to take him on any terms. I don't care what he's done. There is only one thing I couldn't overlook."

"And that is?"

Kitt took a deep breath, and her eyes lowered to Miranda's body and traveled back up to her face. "If he fathered a child and failed to acknowledge it."

Miranda reached for the bellpull and Rooney quickly appeared. "Miss McAllister is leaving," Miranda told her maid. "Please see her out."

"I'm sorry," Kitt said, getting up to go. "I simply had to know."

"And do you?" Miranda asked coldly.

"No," Kitt said, and, gathering her things, followed Rooney out.

Miranda covered her head with the quilt. She was shaken by the effrontery of the girl and bitterly content that she had given her the wrong impression.

Did people have nothing better to talk about than her child's paternity? Would it never stop? How long could Paul put up with vicious gossip?

She began to cry softly, remorse and loneliness mingling with fear. Paul mustn't know she was frightened about her coming confinement. She felt old and helpless, sure she was going to die. But she would not use fear to buy his pardon. That was something he had to give freely.

"Mrs. Paul?" It was Rooney's anxious voice. "Are you taken bad?"

Miranda's sobs were intensified by her maid's devotion. She desperately needed kindness even if she didn't deserve it. In addition to adultery, she had deliberately misled Kitt McAllister about this baby's real father.

Rooney ran to close the windows against the evening chill, then came to the chair. She knelt and patted Miranda's hand.

"There," she crooned, "there, there, Mrs. Paul, you're just feelin' blue. Let another few weeks go by and you'll bloom like a rose, just the way you did with Master Price and Master Miles. Remember? The mister used to say you was never more beautiful than when you was in the family way."

She helped Miranda out of the chair. "Come along, Mrs. Paul dear. It's back to bed for you. Don't cry anymore. Everything will be all right, you'll see, and when it's all over you'll have a lovely baby. Baxter thinks it'll be a girl and so do I. Won't it be lovely to have a daughter! They say a son's a son till he gets him a wife, but a daughter's a daughter for all of her life."

———— • ————

The Count d'Yveine stood near the fireplace in Kitt's parlor, the delighted smile gone from his face.

"I'm so sorry," Kitt said softly. "I wish it could be otherwise, for both our sakes."

"Why are you so much in love with him?"

"Is it possible to explain love?"

He sighed. "I suppose not. But how long can it last if it is not returned?"

"I don't know."

"I'm willing to wait until you find out."

"My dear friend, you must not. It might take forever."

He came back to his chair and sat down. On the table between them was a small velvet box containing the engagement ring he had brought her from his home near Paris. It sat there like a mute reproach to Kitt.

"What will you do with your life?" he asked.

"The same things I've been doing. Rocking the big ships. Supporting suffrage. Teaching Alton. We're going to Italy in the spring. It's where I was planning to go when I left New York." Kitt smiled ruefully. " 'There's a divinity that shapes our ends, rough-hew them as we will.' "

"Louisa, you were not born to be a spinster!"

He was very appealing, this man, but only days ago she had sat across a table from Steven and felt more love in her little finger than she did now in all of her body. If she could not feel that, she preferred to live alone.

"Perhaps I was born to love only once," she said. "We go stumbling through life like blind men with our arms outstretched, looking for a little corner of paradise, someone to hang our hopes on."

"Most of us never find that," he said. "But you believe you have and that is a dragon too powerful for me to fight."

He got up to go, and she took the small box and handed it to him. "I hope we can still be friends," she said.

"Of course."

But there was a gulf between them already as they walked to the front door. "How long will you be in London?" she asked him.

"I have no definite plans."

"My best to Lady Pat."

He nodded, bowed briefly over Kitt's hand, and left without another word. She went back to the parlor and stared at the fire until Alton came in.

"Miss Kitt, you didn't!"

"I had to, Mary Frances. Anything else would have been deceitful."

"My mum says almost everything in this life is half a lie."

"Almost everything," Kitt replied. "But not this."

Alton began to clear away the tea things. "Begging your pardon, Miss Kitt, you can't get by with telling the truth in a lying world. You'd have had such a good life with His Worship!"

"I don't have such a bad one. Oh, leave those things and come look at the travel folders. We're going to Italy."

A gleam of interest replaced Alton's grim expression. "Oh, that would be lovely, simply lovely."

"We'll stay until spring. Then we'll come back here and see what's to be done."

Together they pored over the maps and travel brochures.

There was nothing else I could do, Kitt was thinking. *And I can't sit here and wait for Steven, because he may never come.*

She felt she had come full circle, back to the conviction of her college days that she would never marry. There was no point in crying over that or over Steven. With a dead wife and child and Miranda in his heart, what room was left for Kitt?

But why had he married a young girl he didn't love?

For the same reason, no doubt, that Kitt might have married Jean-Baptiste: it suited the need of the moment. But marriage was for a lifetime!

She hoped Steven would return to the United States as Claire wanted him to, and be elected to the senate. She hoped he would be happy.

Forty-two

It was a perfect day for a wedding. Everyone said so, and these were the people who defined perfection. By ten o'clock that June morning a constant stream of broughams, light phaetons, and curricles deposited wedding guests near the steps of Washington Cathedral.

Lady Burdon and the Count d'Yveine were among the first to arrive and were ushered to their seats on the groom's side.

"Quite in order," Lady Burdon said. "I've known him much longer than I've known her, and I like him more."

"And why is that?"

"Because he's something of a scoundrel and one can always rely on his doing something interesting."

"I wonder why I'm here," the count said. "I barely know either of them."

"I told Walford I wouldn't come without you."

"I'm honored, Patricia. And you are dazzling, as always." He nodded appreciatively at her gown of mauve crêpe de chine flounced with lace-edged chiffon. The famous Burdon pearls adorned her from neck to bosom to waist.

They settled into their places to watch the parade of guests. The women's dresses, in ethereal pastels, were marvels of pleats and cascading ruffles, with the graceful but impractical short trains that had come in with the bustle and outstayed its welcome among the fashionable. Their hats, although somewhat smaller than in the nineties, were still large and lavishly trimmed.

"The guest list is a yard long and every American on it is a member of the Congress or richer than Croesus," Lady Burdon remarked, scanning one of the engraved vellum cards that had been placed on each seat. "This country positively shouts its wealth."

"Like the Romans in decline," the count said.

"Or France under Louis the Fifteenth," she added wickedly. "But I disagree about American decline. The country is still young and energetic. The people work hard at making money and fighting wars of expansion. If that ends and they need ever more violent spectacles as an escape for their killer instincts, as the Romans needed more and bloodier gladiatorial games, they will have arrived at decadence."

"Have no fear," the count said. "There will always be wars."

"And there'll always be an England." She nodded. "But I sometimes remember that the ancient Romans believed there would always be a Roman Empire."

Both of them watched the incoming guests for a while. The cathedral filled rapidly. It was considered lower class to be late for a wedding.

"Have you seen her?" Lady Burdon asked, not looking at him.

"No. Have you seen him?"

"No. I'll be amazed if either turns up," Lady Bowden said. "Do you think she'll ever forgive me?"

He shrugged. "Who can say? She has very strong principles."

"What principle doesn't permit a white lie to protect a friend?" She looked sad.

He took her hand. "That lie was hardly white, Patricia. You as much as told Louisa the child was not Paul Cunningham's. What else was she to think?"

"I did it as much for you as for her! And we didn't know whose it was!"

"We still don't. We must wait until it's born and perhaps grows up to resemble someone other than its parents. If that happens, Louisa might forgive you."

"Much good it will do me," Lady Burdon snapped. "By then I'll be dead."

They stopped talking when the wedding guests hushed in the way of a crowd sensing that the spectacle was about to begin. They turned to see.

A small flower girl appeared, wearing pale blue organdy and scattering rose petals from a filigree basket. At her side was a ring bearer, who was not much larger than she, in Gainsborough-blue velvet breeches and white silk shirt and hose.

Both were cousins of the groom, carefully drilled by their nannies on correct behavior during public appearances. "Little ladies and gentlemen," the nannies were fond of saying, "must not behave like savages, or they will be mistaken for Americans."

Eight bridesmaids emerged next, four American and four English girls, all beauties, wearing chiffon the color of Cynthia's eyes and carrying bouquets of violets and tiny pink roses. Each girl was escorted by a groomsman in a tailcoat and striped trousers, four of them Walford's friends, two of them Cynthia's brothers, two of them her cousins, Price and Miles Cunningham.

"As handsome as their father," Lady Burdon murmured appreciatively.

"But not as glorious as the groom."

"No man is as glorious as Walford," Lady Burdon said.

There was a rustle. The guests stood while Cynthia floated down the aisle in a gown of heavy ivory satin as exquisite as she was. It was decorous, although closely fitted to every line and curve of her torso. Its lace neckband was held in place by tiny stays, and the same lace, embroidered with seed pearls, covered her arms and shoulders. The skirt was tiered and looped with braids of satin, pearls, and diamonds. It was rumored to have cost a fortune, but money was no object to the man who was escorting his daughter down the aisle.

Looking from left to right, Hobart was gratified to see that the males on the bride's side were men of power and influence and those on the other side were titled or authoritative figures in England. Hobart was pleased with himself.

He had spent most of the last few months on Capitol Hill, bringing pressure to bear on the White House and the senate to accept the Hay-Pauncefote Treaty when it was finally submitted for ratification, giving control of the Panama Canal and its approaches to the United States. According to the latest word from Steven James, via Raymond Steele, that should be soon.

Hobart kept his distance from James and Haggerty. Haggerty was a crook, and, as for James, the Atlantic Ocean itself was not far enough away from that man to suit Hobart, no matter that the bastard got things done. The mere thought of Steven James provoked images in Hobart's imagination that infuriated as much as they aroused. How had the brute dared to seduce Miranda? Why had she yielded to him?

He was relieved that Miranda's pregnancy had kept her away today. It was difficult for him to look at her swollen body and almost impossible for him to speak to her without showing his contempt for what she had done. She had no right to imperil the family honor!

Paul, of course, had opted to stay in New York with her, like the tame house pet he was. Hobart disliked his brother, and now he had a far better apprentice in Walford. When the newlyweds returned to London, Walford and his father would lean on Lord Pauncefote to get the damned draft treaty approved by the British.

He looked toward the altar at the bridegroom. The viscount was almost as beautiful as Cynthia. He was every young girl's vision of Prince Charming.

"You're a lucky girl," he whispered to his daughter.

Her blue eyes flashed him an enigmatic look, but she was cold toward him in private. She had never forgiven him for striking her during her hysterical fit in England. Like all women, she fastened on a man's lapses, forgetting all his past kindness. But today she was as she should be, gentle and biddable and breathtaking. It was hard to believe that such beauty had been created by force and despite the tearful pleadings of his wife.

The last person Hobart looked for was his wife. His apprehension faded when he saw her, elegantly gowned and groomed, with a sweet smile on her ruined face, the same smile she'd had as a young girl when her innocence aroused him so much he had married her to ravish it.

Maybe, he thought now, he should have curbed himself, given her fewer children, demanded less of a girl who was not sensual by nature. But he had never been able to restrain himself with a woman, and she was his wife, by God! He had the right . . .

Hobart and Cynthia had arrived at the altar.

Kitt had been seated toward the back of the cathedral on the outside aisle at her specific request: she wasn't sure she could stay throughout the ceremony. The romantic haze of it might accentuate the harsher aspects of her life, might make her long for the impossible again. What woman, in the midst of flowers and white satin ribbons, of youth and love and loveliness, would not want to have it for herself?

Kitt sighed. If only she had dared to follow her instincts! They insisted that had it been Steven's child, he would never have let Miranda go. Miranda had confirmed it several days after that first painful encounter at the Bristol. She had never been as superb as she

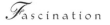

was that day, saying things few women could have said with such dignity.

"Why have you told me all this?" Kitt had asked when Miranda finished.

"Because you love him."

"And you no longer do, Mrs. Cunningham?"

Miranda had thought carefully before replying. "Some loves last a moment, some forever. One sort is no less profound than the other. I hope he'll have a lifetime with you. He deserves it—and so do you."

Kitt, usually skeptical about altruism, had no doubt that Miranda meant every word she said. The original sympathy between the two women had been almost completely restored by the time that second visit ended, and Kitt left, her heart singing.

But the song soon faded. She could hardly apologize to Steven for a wrong that existed only in her imagination! Nor could she simply tell him, out of the blue, that she was not engaged to Jean-Baptiste.

Kitt had quarreled bitterly with Lady Burdon for her meddling and had not seen her or the count since. Now three more people she treasured were gone from her life. She felt unutterably lonely and envious of Cynthia and had agreed to attend this wedding only in the feeble hope that Steven would be there.

A gentleman was standing in the aisle, waiting for Kitt to move over and let him have the end seat. She began to explain that she might have to leave early, when she saw that it was Steven. She moved.

They could not speak to each other. The guests were virtually silent now that the ceremony had begun. Kitt heard nothing of the solemn promises, the sacred oaths. She was aware only of Steven's nearness and her love for him.

I do love him. If I can't marry Steven, I will marry no one. I should have . . .

She could hear Sam's voice:

"The I-should-have window closes every day, Kitt. Don't let any golden moments go on by."

"But, Papa, how will I know which moments are golden?"

"You'll know."

This had to be one of those moments.

When Walford had kissed his wife lightly and discreetly, as befitted a public embrace, the couple started up the center aisle and Kitt and Steven turned to each other.

"I didn't expect to see you," Kitt said, flushed and happy.

"I didn't expect to be here, but at the last minute I had to come." His dark eyes studied her, searching for something he had once seen. Almost sure it was there, he was not confident enough to say so. "Lord Harry took pity on me," he went on, "and found me a cabin on one of his liners."

"How lovely of Lord Harry. I'm glad his disapproval of me didn't rub off on you."

"The tables have been turned. I've convinced him you're an exceptional person and it's a privilege to know you."

Even had she found something to say, she had no need to speak. The way she looked at him said it all. She knew a woman shouldn't look at a man with such open longing, but she was not an ordinary woman.

They both turned toward the center aisle. The newlyweds had reached their row and had stopped to smile at them. Cynthia's eyes flitted briefly over Kitt and lingered on Steven, while she clung to Walford's arm with the pride of ownership.

"May I take you to the reception?" Steven asked when people began to leave.

"Thank you, yes," Kitt said, forgetting that she had not accepted for the reception. "But let's stay here until the crowds clear off."

They sat down again. "I want to apologize for the last time we met," he said.

She was surprised. "I was about to say the same thing."

"Then let's consider that encounter canceled out, as if it had never happened."

She shook her head. "It happened. A lot of things have happened between us. I can't forget any of them."

His expression turned bleak. She wanted to put her arms around him.

"Not in a negative sense," she explained quickly. "I only mean they were important, although I might have expressed myself more gently."

"No, that isn't your way."

"But I hurt people," she said repentantly.

"People hurt *you*. I know I have."

"Do you believe that, or are you just being charitable?"

"We've already established that charity isn't one of my virtues." His expression was wistful: that lonely-man-lost look, the other side of his nature that had made her fall in love with him in the first place. "I've been wondering for months, Kitt, whether you could put up with me."

I hear you, Papa, Kitt said silently to Sam. She looked at Steven with a depth of affection she rarely showed. "You know I could."

He took her hand. "I don't know why I took so long to ask you that, Miss McAllister."

Her green eyes glowed with pleasure. "You saved me from asking you, Mr. James."

She knew that Steven would never be completely hers and that she could never ask him about Miranda. There were some things in life a wise woman did not ask and some wishes always left ungranted.

They sat there, both of them overcome by how simple words could say so much.

In time they left the cathedral, but they never got to the reception. They had too much to tell each other and too many plans to make. Only four people at the reception regretted their absence:

Lady Burdon, the Count d'Yveine, the new Lady Walford, and her groom.

Walford looked at himself in the mirror of his dressing room at the Willard Hotel. He was wearing blue silk pajamas piped in crimson. He had shaved again and his hair was tousled, but he decided not to comb it—this was not a moment for formality—and put on a blue brocaded robe. He waited until he heard Cynthia's maid depart.

" 'Once more unto the breach, dear friends,' " he told himself, and headed for the bridal suite's bedroom. Then he stopped, thinking about Steven James. Walford found it difficult to breathe when he thought of Steven, when he saw Steven. That had been far too seldom in London. The longer Alastair knew the American, the more he admired him, the more he wanted to be in his company.

The viscount shook off his disturbing thoughts and turned them to the defloration of his wife.

"My wife," he said aloud. The words had an unexpected impact on him. Up till that morning there had been Tri-Panalco and the wedding arrangements to preoccupy him, but now he was a husband and the girl waiting for him was his wife. He had given his word to protect her and cherish her and she had given hers to love and obey him.

He knocked on her door and her voice invited him in. She was sitting up in bed, wearing a high-necked nightdress of white silk that hinted at what it covered. She was reading a book. Who but Cynthia would be reading a book on her wedding night? He smiled as he approached her, wondering what it was.

"It went splendidly, didn't it!" she said.

"Absolute perfection," he agreed. "Not a hitch." He took off his robe and got into bed beside her. "What on earth are you reading?"

"Debrett's *Peerage,*" she said.

He laughed. "I thought you'd already committed all of England's peers to memory."

"I'm not sure about a few forms of address."

He took the book and put it on the bedside table. Then he leaned over and kissed her. "Are you nervous?" he asked her.

"Should I be? Are you planning to hurt me?"

"It might hurt a little the first time."

"How many wedding nights have you participated in?"

"Don't be a goose!"

"Then how do you know about a girl's first time?"

"Everyone knows that."

"I didn't."

He kissed her again. "Didn't your aunt Miranda tell you what to expect?" he asked, nuzzling her neck.

"More or less, but it was so mind-boggling, I can't recall if she said it would hurt."

"Cynthia, you are the limit! You must simply trust me."

"I do. I married you, even though Miranda tried to stop me."

He had always been expert at concealing his surprise. "Did she? What did she say?"

"Among other things, that you preferred men to women."

His laugh was convincingly hearty. "Depends upon what I'm doing."

"That's exactly what I told her!"

It was hard to control his face, and he reached up and put out the light. He remembered Miranda in the bazaar, threatening to tell Cynthia if she got nowhere by telling Hobart. Had she told him? Would Hobart be watching him?

Walford broke into a light sweat. Hobart seemed not to suspect anything, but Walford would have to be very careful! His performance tonight would have to be impeccable. He needed Cynthia to radiate newlywed bliss and, very soon, the expectation of an heir.

He turned to her. "Any more horror stories?"

"No," she said. She sounded tensely expectant, and he knew he must not delay. He had to consummate his marriage ardently but without frightening his bride. That would convince her that her aunt was a crazy woman capable of adultery and therefore of lying like a sailor.

He slipped one hand beneath her waist and with the other stroked her hair, her face, her neck with all the tenderness he could summon. After a while his kisses became deeper, hotter, but he had kissed her that way before and knew she liked it. She relaxed.

When he touched her pert little breasts through her gown he remembered that he had done that, too, that awful day in the folly. He must have been mad to attack her that way! But she had mistaken his anger for passion. Most women made that mistake.

His hand went under her gown and he pulled up the whisper-soft silk and bent to kiss her nipples. She gave a little sigh and seemed to respond to it, but she was shocked when his hand went between her thighs.

"What are you doing?" she demanded, pressing her knees together.

He pushed them apart. "You'll see." He slipped a finger into the soft cleft, found the little mound he was looking for, and flicked it gently. She moaned a little with pleasure and opened her thighs.

He was amazed at how wet she was, at how much she liked what he was doing. He kept on, wondering why his penis did not respond. He felt her tremble and peak. Her breathing was rapid. It was the moment to consummate, but he could not!

He was still soft as putty and getting frantic. He slid two fingers inside her, but Miranda would have told her what was supposed to happen! He had to consummate now! Right now!

She turned her head as if to speak and he stopped her mouth with his. He wanted no questions. Cynthia had been told how babies were conceived and knew it was not by digital penetration! She was responding to his caresses again and in his mind he replaced her

with Steven James, with Steven as he had been that morning just after the ceremony.

Steven's face, all planes and angles. His height. His manner. He was overwhelmingly male and he had an inner strength that matched his physique. Alastair admired the man more than anyone he had ever met.

The truth of it was he wanted him.

He did not deceive himself. Just to be in Steven's company was all Walford could hope for, but in his fantasies he had gone much farther than that.

He was hard now, and he had aroused Cynthia again so that she was not squeamish when he penetrated her, except to gasp when the membrane tore. Alastair, racing toward release now, no matter how or with whom he achieved it, moved as nature had designed him to move and climaxed soon after.

"Did I hurt you?" he asked moments later, more curious than concerned, since she had clearly experienced pleasure.

"Only a little," she said.

He pulled himself from her body and she reached under her pillow for the towel Miranda had told her to put there.

"Good idea," he said.

"There's one under your pillow," she told him.

"You're quite the thoughtful little wife," he said, pleased.

He cleaned up and put an arm around her and they talked for a few moments before he drifted off to sleep. He took Steven James with him into his dreams.

Cynthia would not sleep until she had mentally replayed her wedding day from start to finish. It *had* gone well. The women *had* been sincere when they marveled at her beauty and Walford's, and the girls were delightfully envious when they wished her well, envious of the name and rank she had married and of her handsome husband. She was Lady Walford! A viscountess! A wife!

Sex was not in the least horrible, just very messy. Walford had done to her only what she had been forbidden as a girl to do to herself—apart from the penetration part. It was really miraculous, how it got stiff enough to get inside her. She was glad Miranda had told her about that. What Cynthia had not been told was how it went in and out until it erupted, but she rather liked the feeling when it did, as if she commanded an otherwise completely male force. She wanted to see it in the light, both dormant—as logic told her it must be during the day—and distended.

She remembered again the allusions Miranda had made to sex between two men, but she could not imagine how it would be done and Miranda didn't know either. It was just talk, Cynthia decided, talk inspired by jealous resentment.

All in all, Cynthia was deliriously happy until memory intruded with an image of Steven that morning in the cathedral. A wave of something like grief shot through her. Steven had touched Miranda as Walford had just touched her! Steven had been inside Miranda, moving as Walford had just moved, in that primitive way that had nothing to do with mind, only body. She had heard them through the door, both of them rapturous!

She could still hear Miranda through that door, saying, "I love you, Steven, I love you!"

Would Steven do those things with Kitt now? Would he marry Kitt? The two had been deeply absorbed in each other until Cynthia and Walford stopped to greet them, far more than merely friendly. And, looking at Steven, Kitt had been exceptionally attractive today.

"Don't think about him," Cynthia whispered to herself. "You have what you've always wanted, so don't think about him."

But it was Steven she did think about, not the blond Adonis at her side. Just before sleep took her, she remembered that love had not been mentioned by either herself or her new husband, not once during this love-devoted day and night. She reminded herself that the English were not given to emotional demonstrations and, so comforted, she went to sleep.

———— • ————

"I feel as if I've been running like Atalanta in the myth," Miranda said to Paul late that evening.

She was lying on a chaise in what had been *their* bedroom before Paul moved into Price's room. It was for fear, he had said, of disturbing her rest. He came in every morning to see how she was and almost every evening to chat, but she wondered if he would move back after the baby came, if they would ever be friends again as well as the impassioned lovers they had been before her pregnancy put a stop to sex.

As usual, the doctors had advised against marital relations during pregnancy, and it had been difficult for them to share a bed and stay celibate. That meant he still wanted her.

It worried her that sex was her strongest hope of reconciliation. She longed for their old companionship as once she had longed for some mysterious fulfillment.

"I hope you didn't overdo because of the wedding preparations," he said, frowning.

"No," she said. "I've been very careful. I just hope Cynthia is well and duly married by now."

"She was well and duly married at noon." He glanced at her. "Oh," he said.

She nodded.

"Then you still have doubts about Walford?"

She recalled the day in the Cairo bazaar, Walford's vehement denial and his frightening threats. But what did her suspicions matter now? She had done all she could. All she wanted was to have her life back the way it was, and that could never be.

She shook her head. "No, I meant wedding nights in general."

"Did you explain the facts of life to her?"

"The basics. I hope I helped. It's so stupid to send girls into marriage totally ignorant of sex." She stopped and sipped the glass of milk Rooney had brought her, her stomach round and hard as a basketball under the light coverlet.

She took a deep breath. "Paul, I want to tell you something."

"No, Miranda! I don't want to hear it." He was wary again.

"Paul, what if something goes wrong? I'd never rest unless I'd told you what I want you to know."

"Don't talk like that!" he admonished her, his face white with dread. "Nothing will go wrong."

She went on as if he had not spoken. "I don't know why adultery is so much more terrible for a wife than it is for a husband."

He spoke as if he had thought long and hard about it. "It's the way nature designed it. We deposit. You receive."

"That's a specious argument. The mechanics don't matter. I know you've had affairs during your travels."

He colored. "That was different. They weren't important to me."

"Not even at the moment?"

"I suppose so, yes, but purely physically and not for a second afterward."

"It was the same for me." She lied because she owed him that half lie. At the very least, she owed him that.

"You never loved him?" He seemed both relieved and shocked. That she could have betrayed him without love was almost as bad as her having betrayed him at all.

"I have always loved *you,* Paul," she said. She would not tell him, either, that for a little while she had loved them both. What possible excuse could there be for lightening her own burden by adding weight to his? "I had one fleeting affair. I don't think you would call it love. But he's a good man, you recognized that when you met him. Still, it wasn't the man but where he took my senses that bewitched me."

"As I was bewitched by where you took mine." He sounded bitter.

"And so you pretended nothing had happened!"

He ran his fingers through his hair, distraught. "All right, Mi-

randa, since you insist. I thought talking about it would make it impossible for us to go on together and I didn't want it to stop. Almost more than I loved you, I loved making love with you. I'm ashamed of myself for that."

"Shame was at the heart of our one problem, wasn't it?"

He nodded.

"Don't you realize that you and I are alike!" she insisted. "We both yielded to a kind of sorcery, I with him and you with me."

"But, Miranda, you're my *wife!*" he said in confusion. "You belong to *me.*"

"And you're my husband, who swore to be faithful to me and had other women anyway, looking for something I couldn't give you because I didn't know how."

He looked at her, suddenly haggard. "What *you* were looking for, what I never gave *you.* You must have wanted it for a long time. Why did you suddenly choose that time and that man?"

"I don't know. Truly I don't." She wondered once more if he would ever touch her with something more than desire—even whether he would ever touch her at all. Apart from taking her arm when they walked together or kissing her cheek when he had to greet her with people present, it was weeks since he had.

He made no answer for a moment. Then he said, "Miranda, I decided to leave you after your confinement and go to Egypt, as everyone expects me to do. I hadn't planned on ever coming back."

"Oh, Paul," she said sadly, and felt the baby kick as if to join her protesting heart. They sat in agonizing silence for several moments.

Then he sighed. "But how can I leave you? I love you too much."

"I love you more," she said, her face luminous. "I'm sorry I hurt you so. I never intended any of it to happen. How could I? I didn't know what it was. It's what I wanted to tell you, what you must believe in case something should go wrong."

"Don't say that! I won't let anything go wrong!" He stood looking at her, and then, as if drawn by a force stronger than his injured pride, he went swiftly to her side. He knelt and put his arms around her, as if he could protect her from grim death itself.

She stroked his hair and brushed the tears from his face, ignoring her own. "Don't cry, my darling. Nothing can happen to me now."

Once, the thought that nothing more *could* happen had depressed her, had made her feel old and envious, even of poor Cynthia, had driven her to search for some unknown rapture buried deep inside her. But her years with Paul went beyond sexual desire and fulfillment.

Most men and all of the young mistook the implacable life force for something far deeper, but if a woman reached the age of reason, she knew there was more to love than fascination. There was an indescribable tenderness that was the sweetest thing in life. Not the only thing and perhaps not even the most essential but certainly the sweetest.

If only she could have that back—or something close to it! It would take time, but this was a start and she was willing to wait as long as it took.

"I think this one is a girl," she said. Her hands framed his face. There were new lines in it of sadness and worry. He was not the golden youth she had married, but he would always be the husband she loved. She kissed him. "Would you like that?"

He nodded.

She smoothed his hair and kissed him again. "I wonder if she'll be blond like you and Price or dark like Miles and me?"

He sat next to her on the chaise, an arm around her, and for a while they said nothing at all.

About the Author

LEONA BLAIR is the author of five previous novels, *A Woman's Place, With This Ring, Privilege, A World of Difference,* and *The Side of the Angels.* She has been published in ten languages. Educated in both the United States and Europe, she spent almost two decades living abroad, most of the time in Monte Carlo where she edited an English-language weekly. She currently lives in New York City and the Hamptons.